NON SANZ DROICT.

William Shakespeare

The Second Part of

[*KING*] *HENRY IV*

With New Dramatic Criticism
and an Updated Bibliography

EDITED BY NORMAN N. HOLLAND

The Signet Classic Shakespeare
GENERAL EDITOR: SYLVAN BARNET

C

A SIGNET CLASSIC

SIGNET CLASSIC
Published by the Penguin Group
Penguin Books USA Inc., 375 Hudson Street,
New York, New York 10014, U.S.A.
Penguin Books Ltd, 27 Wrights Lane,
London W8 5TZ, England
Penguin Books Australia Ltd, Ringwood,
Victoria, Australia
Penguin Books Canada Ltd, 10 Alcorn Avenue,
Toronto, Ontario, Canada M4V 3B2
Penguin Books (N.Z.) Ltd, 182–190 Wairau Road,
Auckland 10, New Zealand

Penguin Books Ltd, Registered Offices:
Harmondsworth, Middlesex, England

Published by Signet Classic, an imprint of Dutton Signet,
a division of Penguin Books USA Inc.

25 24 23 22 21 20 19 18 17 16

 REGISTERED TRADEMARK—MARCA REGISTRADA

Library of Congress Catalog Card Number: 86-62299

Printed in the United States of America

Contents

Shakespeare: Prefatory Remarks

Between the record of his baptism in Stratford on 26 April 1564 and the record of his burial in Stratford on 25 April 1616, some forty documents name Shakespeare, and many others name his parents, his children, and his grandchildren. More facts are known about William Shakespeare than about any other playwright of the period except Ben Jonson. The facts should, however, be distinguished from the legends. The latter, inevitably more engaging and better known, tell us that the Stratford boy killed a calf in high style, poached deer and rabbits, and was forced to flee to London, where he held horses outside a playhouse. These traditions are only traditions; they may be true, but no evidence supports them, and it is well to stick to the facts.

Mary Arden, the dramatist's mother, was the daughter of a substantial landowner; about 1557 she married John Shakespeare, who was a glove-maker and trader in various farm commodities. In 1557 John Shakespeare was a member of the Council (the governing body of Stratford), in 1558 a constable of the borough, in 1561 one of the two town chamberlains, in 1565 an alderman (entitling him to the appellation "Mr."), in 1568 high bailiff—the town's highest political office, equivalent to mayor. After 1577, for an unknown reason he drops out of local politics. The birthday of William Shakespeare, the eldest son of this locally prominent man, is unrecorded; but the Stratford parish register records that the infant was baptized on 26 April 1564. (It is quite possible that he was born on

23 April, but this date has probably been assigned by
tradition because it is the date on which, fifty-two years
later, he died.) The attendance records of the Stratford
grammar school of the period are not extant, but it is
reasonable to assume that the son of a local official attended the school and received substantial training in
Latin. The masters of the school from Shakespeare's
seventh to fifteenth years held Oxford degrees; the Elizabethan curriculum excluded mathematics and the natural
sciences but taught a good deal of Latin rhetoric, logic,
and literature. On 27 November 1582 a marriage license
was issued to Shakespeare and Anne Hathaway, eight
years his senior. The couple had a child in May, 1583.
Perhaps the marriage was necessary, but perhaps the
couple had earlier engaged in a formal "troth plight"
which would render their children legitimate even if no
further ceremony were performed. In 1585 Anne Hathaway bore Shakespeare twins.

That Shakespeare was born is excellent; that he married and had children is pleasant; but that we know
nothing about his departure from Stratford to London, or
about the beginning of his theatrical career, is lamentable
and must be admitted. We would gladly sacrifice details
about his children's baptism for details about his earliest
days on the stage. Perhaps the poaching episode is true
(but it is first reported almost a century after Shakespeare's death), or perhaps he first left Stratford to be
a schoolteacher, as another tradition holds; perhaps he
was moved by

> Such wind as scatters young men through the world,
> To seek their fortunes further than at home
> Where small experience grows.

In 1592, thanks to the cantankerousness of Robert
Greene, a rival playwright and a pamphleteer, we have
our first reference, a snarling one, to Shakespeare as an
actor and playwright. Greene warns those of his own
educated friends who wrote for the theater against an
actor who has presumed to turn playwright:

There is an upstart crow, beautified with our feathers, that with his *tiger's heart wrapped in a player's hide* supposes he is as well able to bombast out a blank verse as the best of you, and being an absolute Johannes-factotum is in his own conceit the only Shake-scene in a country.

The reference to the player, as well as the allusion to Aesop's crow (who strutted in borrowed plumage, as an actor struts in fine words not his own), makes it clear that by this date Shakespeare had both acted and written. That Shakespeare is meant is indicated not only by "Shake-scene" but by the parody of a line from one of Shakespeare's plays, *3 Henry VI:* "O, tiger's heart wrapped in a woman's hide." If Shakespeare in 1592 was prominent enough to be attacked by an envious dramatist, he probably had served an apprenticeship in the theater for at least a few years.

In any case, by 1592 Shakespeare had acted and written, and there are a number of subsequent references to him as an actor: documents indicate that in 1598 he is a "principal comedian," in 1603 a "principal tragedian," in 1608 he is one of the "men players." The profession of actor was not for a gentleman, and it occasionally drew the scorn of university men who resented writing speeches for persons less educated than themselves, but it was respectable enough: players, if prosperous, were in effect members of the bourgeoisie, and there is nothing to suggest that Stratford considered William Shakespeare less than a solid citizen. When, in 1596, the Shakespeares were granted a coat of arms, the grant was made to Shakespeare's father, but probably William Shakespeare (who the next year bought the second-largest house in town) had arranged the matter on his own behalf. In subsequent transactions he is occasionally styled a gentleman.

Although in 1593 and 1594 Shakespeare published two narrative poems dedicated to the Earl of Southampton, *Venus and Adonis* and *The Rape of Lucrece,* and may well have written most or all of his sonnets in the middle nineties, Shakespeare's literary activity seems to have been almost entirely devoted to the theater. (It may be significant that the two narrative poems were written in years when the plague closed the theaters for several months.) In 1594 he was a charter member of a theatrical company called the Chamberlain's Men (which in 1603 changed its name to the King's Men); until he retired to Stratford (about 1611, apparently), he was with this remarkably stable company. From 1599 the company acted primarily at the Globe Theatre, in which Shakespeare held a one-tenth interest. Other Elizabethan dramatists are known to have acted, but no other is known also to have been entitled to a share in the profits of the playhouse.

Shakespeare's first eight published plays did not have his name on them, but this is not remarkable; the most popular play of the sixteenth century, Thomas Kyd's *The Spanish Tragedy,* went through many editions without naming Kyd, and Kyd's authorship is known only because a book on the profession of acting happens to quote (and attribute to Kyd) some lines on the interest of Roman emperors in the drama. What is remarkable is that after 1598 Shakespeare's name commonly appears on printed plays—some of which are not his. Another indication of his popularity comes from Francis Meres, author of *Palladis Tamia: Wit's Treasury* (1598): in this anthology of snippets accompanied by an essay on literature, many playwrights are mentioned, but Shakespeare's name occurs more often than any other, and Shakespeare is the only playwright whose plays are listed.

From his acting, playwriting, and share in a theater, Shakespeare seems to have made considerable money. He put it to work, making substantial investments in Stratford real estate. When he made his will (less than a month before he died), he sought to leave his property intact to his descendants. Of small bequests to relatives and to friends (including three actors, Richard Burbage, John Heminges, and Henry Condell), that to his wife of the second-best bed has provoked the most comment; perhaps it was the bed the couple had slept in, the best being reserved for visitors. In any case, had Shakespeare not excepted it, the bed would have gone (with the rest of his household possessions) to his daughter and her husband. On 25 April 1616 he was buried within the chancel of the church at Stratford. An unattractive monument to his memory, placed on a wall near the grave, says he died on 23 April. Over the grave itself are the lines, perhaps by Shakespeare, that (more than his literary fame) have kept his bones undisturbed in the crowded burial ground where old bones were often dislodged to make way for new:

> Good friend, for Jesus' sake forbear
> To dig the dust enclosèd here.
> Blessed be the man that spares these stones
> And cursed be he that moves my bones.

Thirty-seven plays, as well as some nondramatic poems, are held to constitute the Shakespeare canon. The dates of composition of most of the works are highly uncertain, but there is often evidence of a *terminus a quo* (starting point) and/or a *terminus ad quem* (terminal point) that provides a framework for intelligent guessing. For example, *Richard II* cannot be earlier than 1595, the publication date of some material to which it is indebted; *The Merchant of Venice* cannot be later than 1598, the year Francis Meres mentioned it. Sometimes arguments for a date hang on an alleged topical allusion, such as the lines about the unseasonable weather in *A Midsummer Night's Dream*, II.i.81–117, but such an allusion (if indeed it is an allusion) can be variously interpreted, and in any case there is always the possibility that a topical allusion was inserted during a revision, years after the composition of a play. Dates are often attributed on the basis of style, and although conjectures about style usually rest on other conjectures, sooner or later one must relay on one's literary sense. There is no real proof, for example, that *Othello* is not as early as *Romeo and Juliet*, but one feels *Othello* is later, and because the first record of its performance is 1604, one is glad enough to set its composition at that date and not push it back into Shakespeare's early years. The following chronology, then, is as much indebted to informed guesswork and sensitivity as it is to fact. The dates, necessarily imprecise, indicate something like a scholarly consensus.

PLAYS

1588–93	*The Comedy of Errors*
1588–94	*Love's Labor's Lost*
1590–91	*2 Henry VI*
1590–91	*3 Henry VI*
1591–92	*1 Henry VI*
1592–93	*Richard III*
1592–94	*Titus Andronicus*
1593–94	*The Taming of the Shrew*
1593–95	*The Two Gentlemen of Verona*
1594–96	*Romeo and Juliet*
1595	*Richard II*
1594–96	*A Midsummer Night's Dream*
1596–97	*King John*
1596–97	*The Merchant of Venice*
1597	*1 Henry IV*
1597–98	*2 Henry IV*
1598–1600	*Much Ado About Nothing*
1598–99	*Henry V*
1599	*Julius Caesar*
1599–1600	*As You Like It*
1599–1600	*Twelfth Night*
1600–01	*Hamlet*
1597–1601	*The Merry Wives of Windsor*
1601–02	*Troilus and Cressida*
1602–04	*All's Well that Ends Well*
1603–04	*Othello*
1604	*Measure for Measure*
1605–06	*King Lear*
1605–06	*Macbeth*
1606–07	*Antony and Cleopatra*
1605–08	*Timon of Athens*
1607–09	*Coriolanus*
1608–09	*Pericles*

Shakespeare's Theater

In Shakespeare's infancy, Elizabethan actors performed wherever they could—in great halls, at court, in the courtyards of inns. The innyards must have made rather unsatisfactory theaters: on some days they were unavailable because carters bringing goods to London used them as depots; when available, they had to be rented from the innkeeper; perhaps most important, London inns were subject to the Common Council of London, which was not well disposed toward theatricals. In 1574 the Common Council required that plays and playing places in London be licensed. It asserted that

> sundry great disorders and inconveniences have been found to ensue to this city by the inordinate haunting of great multitudes of people, specially youth, to plays, interludes, and shows, namely occasion of frays and quarrels, evil practices of incontinency in great inns having chambers and secret places adjoining to their open stages and galleries,

and ordered that innkeepers who wished licenses to hold performances put up a bond and made contributions to the poor.

The requirement that plays and innyard theaters be

licensed, along with the other drawbacks of playing at
inns, probably drove James Burbage (a carpenter-turned-
actor) to rent in 1576 a plot of land northeast of the
city walls and to build here—on property outside the
jurisdiction of the city—England's first permanent construction designed for plays. He called it simply the
Theatre. About all that is known of its construction is
that it was wood. It soon had imitators, the most famous
being the Globe (1599), built across the Thames (again
outside the city's jurisdiction), out of timbers of the
Theatre, which had been dismantled when Burbage's
lease ran out.

There are three important sources of information about
the structure of Elizabethan playhouses—drawings, a
contract, and stage directions in plays. Of drawings, only
the so-called De Witt drawing (c. 1596) of the Swan—
really a friend's copy of De Witt's drawing—is of much
significance. It shows a building of three tiers, with a
stage jutting from a wall into the yard or center of the
building. The tiers are roofed, and part of the stage is
covered by a roof that projects from the rear and is sup-
ported at its front on two posts, but the groundlings, who
paid a penny to stand in front of the stage, were exposed
to the sky. (Performances in such a playhouse were held
only in the daytime; artificial illumination was not used.)
At the rear of the stage are two doors; above the stage
is a gallery. The second major source of information,
the contract for the Fortune, specifies that although the
Globe is to be the model, the Fortune is to be square,
eighty feet outside and fifty-five inside. The stage is to
be forty-three feet broad, and is to extend into the middle
of the yard (i.e., it is twenty-seven and a half feet deep).
For patrons willing to pay more than the general admission charged of the groundlings, there were to be three
galleries provided with seats. From the third chief source,
stage directions, one learns that entrance to the stage was
by doors, presumably spaced widely apart at the rear
("Enter one citizen at one door, and another at the
other"), and that in addition to the platform stage there
was occasionally some sort of curtained booth or alcove

allowing for "discovery" scenes, and some sort of playing space "aloft" or "above" to represent (for example)
the top of a city's walls or a room above the street. Doubtless each theater had its own peculiarities, but perhaps
we can talk about a "typical" Elizabethan theater if we
realize that no theater need exactly have fit the description, just as no father is the typical father with 3.7 children.
This hypothetical theater is wooden, round or polygonal
(in *Henry V* Shakespeare calls it a "wooden *O*"), capable
of holding some eight hundred spectators standing in the
yard around the projecting elevated stage and some fifteen
hundred additional spectators seated in the three roofed
galleries. The stage, protected by a "shadow" or "heavens"
or roof, is entered by two doors; behind the doors is the
"tiring house" (attiring house, i.e., dressing room), and
above the doors is some sort of gallery that may sometimes hold spectators but that can be used (for example)
as the bedroom from which Romeo—according to a stage
direction in one text—"goeth down." Some evidence suggests that a throne can be lowered onto the platform stage,
perhaps from the "shadow"; certainly characters can descend from the stage through a trap or traps into the cellar
or "hell." Sometimes this space beneath the platform
accommodates a sound-effects man or musician (in *Antony
and Cleopatra* "music of the hautboys is under the stage")
or an actor (in *Hamlet* the "Ghost cries under the stage").
Most characters simply walk on and off, but because there
is no curtain in front of the platform, corpses will have
to be carried off (Hamlet must lug Polonius' guts into
the neighbor room), or will have to fall at the rear, where
the curtain on the alcove or booth can be drawn to conceal them.

Such may have been the so-called "public theater."
Another kind of theater, called the "private theater" because its much greater admission charge limited its audience to the wealthy or the prodigal, must be briefly
mentioned. The private theater was basically a large room,
entirely roofed and therefore artificially illuminated, with
a stage at one end. In 1576 one such theater was established in Blackfriars, a Dominican priory in London that

had been suppressed in 1538 and confiscated by the Crown and thus was not under the city's jurisdiction. All the actors in the Blackfriars theater were boys about eight to thirteen years old (in the public theaters similar boys played female parts; a boy Lady Macbeth played to a man Macbeth). This private theater had a precarious existence, and ceased operations in 1584. In 1596 James Burbage, who had already made theatrical history by building the Theatre, began to construct a second Black-friars theater. He died in 1597, and for several years this second Blackfriars theater was used by a troupe of boys, but in 1608 two of Burbage's sons and five other actors (including Shakespeare) became joint operators of the theater, using it in the winter when the open-air Globe was unsuitable. Perhaps such a smaller theater, roofed, artificially illuminated, and with a tradition of a courtly audience, exerted an influence on Shakespeare's late plays.

Performances in the private theaters may well have had intermissions during which music was played, but in the public theaters the action was probably uninter-rupted, flowing from scene to scene almost without a break. Actors would enter, speak, exit, and others would immediately enter and establish (if necessary) the new locale by a few properties and by words and gestures. Here are some samples of Shakespeare's scene painting:

This is Illyria, lady.

Well, this is the Forest of Arden.

This castle hath a pleasant seat; the air
Nimbly and sweetly recommends itself
Unto our gentle senses.

On the other hand, it is a mistake to conceive of the Elizabethan stage as bare. Although Shakespeare's Chorus in *Henry V* calls the stage an "unworthy scaffold" and urges the spectators to "eke out our performance with your mind," there was considerable spectacle. The last act of *Macbeth,* for example, has five stage directions

calling for "drum and colors," and another sort of appeal
to the eye is indicated by the stage direction "Enter Mac-
duff, with Macbeth's head." Some scenery and properties
may have been substantial; doubtless a throne was used,
and in one play of the period we encounter this direction:
"Hector takes up a great piece of rock and casts at Ajax,
who tears up a young tree by the roots and assails Hector."
The matter is of some importance, and will be glanced
at again in the next section.

The Texts of Shakespeare

Though eighteen of his plays were published during
his lifetime, Shakespeare seems never to have supervised
their publication. There is nothing unusual here; when a
playwright sold a play to a theatrical company he sur-
rendered his ownership of it. Normally a company would
not publish the play, because to publish it meant to allow
competitors to acquire the piece. Some plays, however,
did get published: apparently treacherous actors sometimes pieced together a play for a publisher, sometimes
a company in need of money sold a play, and sometimes
a company allowed a play to be published that no longer
drew audiences. That Shakespeare did not concern himself with publication, then, is scarcely remarkable; of his
contemporaries only Ben Jonson carefully supervised the
publication of his own plays. In 1623, seven years after
Shakespeare's death, John Heminges and Henry Condell
(two senior members of Shakespeare's company, who had
performed with him for about twenty years) collected his
plays—published and unpublished—into a large volume,
commonly called the First Folio. (A folio is a volume
consisting of sheets that have been folded once, each sheet
thus making two leaves, or four pages. The eighteen plays
published during Shakespeare's lifetime had been issued
one play per volume in small books called quartos. Each
sheet in a quarto has been folded twice, making four
leaves, or eight pages.) The First Folio contains thirty-six
plays; a thirty-seventh, *Pericles,* though not in the Folio,

is regarded as canonical. Heminges and Condell suggest in an address "To the great variety of readers" that the republished plays are presented in better form than in the quartos: "Before you were abused with diverse stolen and surreptitious copies, maimed and deformed by the frauds and stealths of injurious impostors that exposed them; even those, are now offered to your view cured and perfect of their limbs, and all the rest absolute in their numbers, as he [i.e., Shakespeare] conceived them."

Whoever was assigned to prepare the texts for publication in the First Folio seems to have taken his job seriously and yet not to have performed it with uniform care. The sources of the texts seem to have been, in general, good unpublished copies or the best published copies. The first play in the collection, *The Tempest,* is divided into acts and scenes, has unusually full stage directions and descriptions of spectacle, and concludes with a list of the characters, but the editor was not able (or willing) to present all of the succeeding texts so fully dressed. Later texts occasionally show signs of carelessness: in one scene of *Much Ado About Nothing* the names of actors, instead of characters, appear as speech prefixes, as they had in the quarto, which the Folio reprints; proofreading throughout the Folio is spotty and apparently was done without reference to the printer's copy; the pagination of *Hamlet* jumps from 156 to 257.

A modern editor of Shakespeare must first select his copy; no problem if the play exists only in the Folio, but a considerable problem if the relationship between a quarto and the Folio—or an early quarto and a later one—is unclear. When an editor has chosen what seems to him to be the most authoritative text or texts for his copy, he has not done with making decisions. First of all, he must reckon with Elizabethan spelling. If he is not producing a facsimile, he probably modernizes it, but ought he to preserve the old form of words that apparently were pronounced quite unlike their modern forms—"lanthorn," "alablaster"? If he preserves these forms, is he really preserving Shakespeare's forms or perhaps those of a compositor in the printing house? What is one to do when one finds "lanthorn" and "lantern" in adjacent lines? (The editors of this series in general, but not invariably, assume that words should be spelled in their modern form.) Elizabethan punctuation, too, presents problems. For example in the First Folio, the only text for the play, Macbeth rejects his wife's idea that he can wash the blood from his hand:

> no: this my Hand will rather
> The multitudinous Seas incarnardine,
> Making the Greene one, Red.

Obviously an editor will remove the superfluous capitals, and he will probably alter the spelling to "incarnadine," but will he leave the comma before "red," letting Macbeth speak of the sea as "the green one," or will he (like most modern editors) remove the comma and thus have Macbeth say that his hand will make the ocean *uniformly* red?

An editor will sometimes have to change more than spelling or punctuation. Macbeth says to his wife:

> I dare do all that may become a man,
> Who dares no more, is none.

For two centuries editors have agreed that the second line is unsatisfactory, and have emended "no" to "do": "Who dares do more is none." But when in the same play Ross says that fearful persons

> floate vpon a wilde and violent Sea
> Each way, and moue,

need "move" be emended to "none," as it often is, on the hunch that the compositor misread the manuscript? The editors of the Signet Classic Shakespeare have restrained themselves from making abundant emendations. In their minds they hear Dr. Johnson on the dangers of emending: "I have adopted the Roman sentiment, that it is more honorable to save a citizen than to kill an enemy." Some departures (in addition to spelling, punctuation, and lineation) from the copy text have of course been made, but the original readings are listed in a note following the play, so that the reader can evaluate them for himself.

The editors of the Signet Classic Shakespeare, following tradition, have added line numbers and in many cases act and scene divisions as well as indications of locale at the beginning of scenes. The Folio divided most of the plays into acts and some into scenes. Early eighteenth-century editors increased the divisions. These divisions, which provide a convenient way of referring to passages in the plays, have been retained, but when not in the text chosen as the basis for the Signet Classic text they are enclosed in square brackets [ ] to indicate that they are editorial additions. Similarly, although no play of Shakespeare's published during his lifetime was equipped with indications of locale at the heads of scene divisions, locales have here been added in square brackets for the convenience of the reader, who lacks the information afforded to spectators by costumes, properties, and gestures. The spectator can tell at a glance he is in the throne room, but without an editorial indication the reader may be puzzled for a while. It should be mentioned, incidentally, that there are a few authentic stage directions —perhaps Shakespeare's, perhaps a prompter's—that suggest locales: for example, "Enter Brutus in his orchard," and "They go up into the Senate house." It is hoped that the bracketed additions provide the reader with the sort of help provided in these two authentic directions, but it is equally hoped that the reader will remember that the stage was not loaded with scenery.

No editor during the course of his work can fail to recollect some words Heminges and Condell prefixed to the Folio:

> It had been a thing, we confess, worthy to have been wished, that the author himself had lived to have set forth and overseen his own writings. But since it hath been ordained otherwise, and he by death departed from that right, we pray you do not envy his friends the office of their care and pain to have collected and published them.

Nor can an editor, after he has done his best, forget
Heminges and Condell's final words: "And so we leave
you to other of his friends, whom if you need can be
your guides. If you need them not, you can lead yourselves, and others. And such readers we wish him."

SYLVAN BARNET
Tufts University

Introduction

Betrayal, someone has said, is the quintessential Shakespearean theme. Certainly, it would seem to be in *Henry IV* [*Part Two*], for this play hinges on two betrayals. Prince John promises the rebels in a battlefield parley their "griefs shall be with speed redressed. Upon my soul, they shall." Then, once the rebels' troops are discharged, he tells them he will indeed redress their grievances "with a most Christian care"—but executes them as rebels. "God, and not we, hath safely fought today." (Some outraged critics have called the line blasphemous.) Then, at the end of the play, after the death of Henry IV, Falstaff expects to be "one of the greatest men in this realm" in something other than size. He cheers his newly crowned Hal only to be answered by one of the most magnificent and brutal lines in all literature: "I know thee not, old man. Fall to thy prayers." Dismissed, banished, he dies in *Henry V* because "The King has killed his heart."

The ethical rightness or wrongness of these actions[1] constitutes one of the two bones of contention this play has cast among critics. The other is the relation of this play to Part One: are Parts One and Two[2] separate plays

---

[1] Mr. Stanley McKenzie, in an unpublished paper, very skillfully analyzes the ethical problem of the two "betrayals" in terms of the structure and imagery of the play. I am indebted to him for a number of the ideas which follow.

[2] "Part Two" in the title of an Elizabethan history play simply means that the play deals with events later in the reign of the king named in the title than those the Part One play deals with. It does not imply that the play in question is an integral part of a series, like a chapter in a novel.

or one long ten-act play? The answers to both (like all questions we ask of Shakespeare) must come from a recognition of the significant wholeness of the work of art he has created, for these two seeming betrayals, morally ambiguous as they may appear, make only two among a host of other such incidents in the play.

For example, in an episode that Shakespeare carefully retained from his sources, the old king, believing a prophecy he is to die "in Jerusalem," expects to die on a Crusade. Instead, he finds himself dying, not in the city Jerusalem but in a room in Westminster called "Jerusalem." Once Henry IV is dead, the Lord Chief Justice (who had clapped Hal in prison) thinks himself a man doomed, but instead, the new king creates him Chief Justice anew, "a father to my youth," and puts him in charge of Falstaff. Bringing these and many other such reversals to a fullness and completion is, of course, the reformation of Hal himself from the madcap prince to what he will be in *Henry V*, "the mirror of all Christian kings." "Let the end try the man," he had warned earlier; and at the end he acts

> To mock the expectation of the world,
> To frustrate prophecies, and to raze out
> Rotten opinion, who hath writ me down
> After my seeming.

"Expectation mocked" is the key, a theme that pervades and informs the comic scenes as well as the serious ones. To the Lord Chief Justice's amused outrage, Falstaff, who illustrates "all the characters of age," has the gall to set down his name "in the scroll of youth" and —even—call the Justice old. He manages to elude the legal powers of the Lord Chief Justice (roughly equivalent to the Chief Justice of the U. S. Supreme Court), and then he has the effrontery to try to borrow a thousand pounds from him. Mistress Quickly believes Falstaff will marry her (perhaps the silliest of all expectations in a play of silly expectations), and thus Falstaff manages to turn her lawsuit into a cozy dinner party. Old Justice

Shallow, in one of the most exquisite moments of the play, turns away from that death that hovers over all the characters to a startling image of vitality and (in Elizabethan English) virility:

> *Shallow.* Jesu, Jesu, the mad days that I have spent! And to see how many of my old acquaintance are dead!
> *Silence.* We shall all follow, cousin.
> *Shallow.* Certain, 'tis certain, very sure, very sure. Death, as the Psalmist saith, is certain to all, all shall die. How [much for] a good yoke of bullocks at Stamford Fair?

Shallow, the classic portrait of the old grad, makes much of "the wildness of his youth," but we find that his talk is all an old man's lying. Young Shallow was thin, puny, "ever in the rearward of the fashion," and yet, notes Falstaff ruefully, "Now has he lands and beeves." Everywhere expectation is overturned. Falstaff picks (from Shallow's point of view) precisely the wrong men for his recruits. Yet even so, Francis Feeble of valorous name turns out to have that stoical acceptance of destiny that constitutes (as we shall see) the essential ethic the play puts forward.

The same sense of expectation mocked permeates the language and imagery of the play. What should give hope or security does not. Armor "worn in heat of day . . . scald'st with safety," while, conversely, "In poison there is physic." Hopes, like ships, "touch ground and dash themselves to pieces," while even houses are "giddy and unsure." The very buds,

> which to prove fruit,
> Hope gives not so much warrant as despair
> That frost will bite them.

Fathers who care for their sons, like bees that gather honey, "are murdered for [their] pains." Sleep, in the King's lovely apostrophe, comes to the least likely, the shipboy suffering a storm in the crows' nest:

> Canst thou, O partial sleep, give thy repose
> To the wet sea-son in an hour so rude,
> And in the calmest and most stillest night,
> With all appliances and means to boot,
> Deny it to a king? Then happy low, lie down!
> Uneasy lies the head that wears a crown.

The least fortunate are most fortunate—one cannot predict, for premonitions themselves run by opposites:

> Against ill chances men are ever merry,
> But heaviness foreruns the good event.

Even the mere dramaturgic context of *2 Henry IV* mocks expectation. The madcap prince of Part Two reverses the reformation we have already seen in Part One (see pp. 219–23). The odd epilogue treats the plays as the unsuccessful payment of a debt—an expectation—and goes on to contract a further debt: "Our humble author will continue the story, with Sir John in it." But Falstaff does not appear in *Henry V*, and further, he is not to be confused with the character you expected him to be; "Oldcastle died martyr, and this is not the man" (see p. 169n.).

Even odder than the epilogue is the induction with Rumor as the presenter. Shakespeare, as always, sets up the internal logic of his work from the very opening lines: Rumor, whatever else he may be, is the creator and defeater of expectations par excellence, bringer of "smooth comforts false, worse than true wrongs." Here, he announces falsely a rebel victory at Shrewsbury and the death of Prince Hal under the sword of Northumberland's son Hotspur. Then, almost the entire first scene of the play deals with expectations created and defeated (even down to the opening lines in which a porter says that Northumberland will be found in the orchard, but then the Earl himself unexpectedly appears). And, of course, no one expected the madcap prince to overcome "the never-daunted Percy." Learning of his son's death, Northumberland says,

these news,
Having been well, that would have made me sick,
Being sick, have in some measure made me well.

Much later in the play, another old man, King Henry IV,
will echo his paradox: "Wherefore should these good news
make me sick?" In either case, news—words—seem to
have an effect opposite to what one would expect.

The first scene shifts to the second, from one diseased
old man to another:

Falstaff. Sirrah . . . what says the doctor to my water
    [i.e., urine]?
Page. He said, sir, the water itself was a good healthy
    water; but, for the party that [owned] it, he might have
    [more] diseases than he knew. . . .

The Page's response, itself a mockery of what we might
expect from a doctor, continues from the previous scene
the tension between words and body.

As we might expect from Falstaff's "throng of words"
or, indeed, the figure of Rumor, "painted full of tongues,"
words—"prophecies," "seeming," "rotten opinion,"
"news"—all play a key role in *2 Henry IV* in creating
expectations that deeds and persons then defeat in fact, as

chances, mocks,
And changes fill the cup of alteration
With divers liquors.

Most notably, Prince John tricks the rebels with his
"princely word": "I give it you, and will maintain my
word"—though the letter, not the spirit. But there are
others whose words create false expectations: Mistress
Quickly's malapropisms and Pistol's ranting in garbled
quotations make us expect to hear one thing; then, when
we hear their blunder, our expectation is mocked. And
the rebels, too, create false hopes with words:

We fortify in paper and in figures,
Using the names of men instead of men,

> Like one that draws the model of an house
> Beyond his power to build.

As Lord Bardolph's words hint, this play uses (unusually often for Shakespeare) names that tag their bearers in a manner almost Dickensian: Pistol, Shallow, Shadow, and Moldy; Doll Tearsheet and Jane Nightwork of amorous name; the sheriff's men, Fang and Snare; Mistress Quickly, whose name, in Elizabethan pronunciation, conceals a ribald pun; Goodman Puff, fat as Falstaff, and hungry Francis Pickbone; Traverse, who, in the opening scene, denies ("traverses") Lord Bardolph's report. Yet, as one would expect in a play of expectations mocked, the actual, physical characters often belie their tags; Sampson Stockfish is a fruiterer, Bullcalf a coward, and Feeble brave.

We would be wrong, though, to conclude that words always build up false expectations, that *2 Henry IV* envisions no larger plan that one can trust—such a skepticism would be utterly foreign to Shakespeare and the Elizabethans' sense of cosmic order. There is, as the King says, a plan, though a bitter one, "the book of fate" that lists the defeats of our expectations:

> O, if this were seen,
> The happiest youth, viewing his progress through,
> What perils past, what crosses to ensue,
> Would shut the book, and sit him down and die.

And Warwick goes on to make an important statement of the Elizabethans' anecdotal or symbolistic view of history:

> There is a history in all men's lives,
> Figuring the nature of the times deceased,
> The which observed, a man may prophesy,
> With a near aim, of the main chance of things
> As yet not come to life.

There is, then, a larger order, and some of the characters find their place in it. Others, notably Falstaff and the rebels who are "betrayed," do not. What is the essential

difference between those who find a place and those who
are "betrayed"?

As so often in Shakespeare, a peripheral episode tells
us, a scene superfluous to the main plot but one which
Shakespeare spent some pains to improve from his sources
(see pp. 183–89). Hal, thinking his father dead, takes
his crown into another room. His father revives and accuses him of wishing parricide. It is, of course, one more
episode of expectations mocked, but the King's words tell
us more: he accuses Hal of being "hasty," unable to
"stay," of wishing his father's death: "What! Canst thou
not forbear me half an hour?" Slowly, Hal answers. He
did not "affect," that is, crave, desire, the crown. Rather,
he took it as an enemy: it "hath fed upon the body of
my father." Its gold is no medicine, but rather "hast eat
thy bearer up." The King is pleased with his son's "pleading so wisely." Wherein does the wisdom lie?

The King explains in his next speech, "the very latest
counsel that ever I shall breathe," presumably, therefore,
the most important. He recalls the way he took the crown
from Richard in *Richard II,*

> How troublesome it sat upon my head.
> To thee it shall descend with better quiet.

> It seemed in me
> But as an honor snatched with boisterous hand.

> And now my death
> Changes the mood, for what in me was purchased
> Falls upon thee in a more fairer sort,
> So thou the garland wear'st successively.

The word "purchased" is important: a legal term, it refers to the acquiring of land other than by inherited succession ("successively"). The word reflects, as the whole
play does, the feudal and Renaissance prejudice against
those who violate the natural order of things by taking
for themselves against the ordained patterns of birth and
inheritance. Henry sinned when he "snatched" the crown,

but Hal will wear it free of such sin, for he inherits it. The King's accusations tell us Hal's wrong in taking the crown from his sleeping father lay in his inability to "forbear," to "stay," in his "wish," his being "hasty."

> Thou hast stolen that which after some few hours
> Were thine without offense.

Hal's answer is wise in that he says he did not crave the crown, but rather recognized that the crown is an enemy that feeds on its bearer, eats its bearer up.

Appetite is both the sin and the danger, that appetite which, as the Prince had jokingly confessed earlier, "was not princely got." To be truly a prince, one must not crave and try to take, but rather forbear, wait, trust, put oneself in that larger order: God's, nature's, his father's. Appetite governs the common man, not the prince, and, indeed, it was the common people's appetite that let Henry take the crown from Richard, though, says the Archbishop,

> The commonwealth is sick of their own choice;
> Their overgreedy love hath surfeited.

> Thou, beastly feeder, art so full of [Henry]
> That thou provok'st thyself to cast him up.
> So, so, thou common dog, didst thou disgorge
> Thy glutton bosom of the royal Richard;
> And now thou wouldst eat thy dead vomit up,
> And howl'st to find it. What trust is in these times?

The wise monarch provides for his people's appetites. Henry's last counsel—for his expectation was again foiled, his statement of Hal's rightful title was not his "latest counsel"—Henry's last advice is to "busy giddy minds with foreign quarrels," to turn appetite elsewhere, for Henry knows all too well the rebel and vain spirit is one that seeks to take for itself rather than accept the natural order of monarchy.

That larger order is not wholly beneficent, for it includes, as Shallow reminds us, death. "Death, as the

Psalmist saith, is certain to all, all shall die," all: Northumberland, the King, Shallow, Silence, Falstaff, the Lord
Chief Justice—all the old men in this play of old men
are dying. Some try to put it aside, like Falstaff: "Peace,
good Doll! Do not speak like a death's head. Do not bid
me remember my end." But death cannot be put aside.
In Sir Thomas Browne's beautiful sentence, "This world
is not an inn but an hospital," not a place to feed but a
place to die in. One may consult the doctor as Falstaff
does; or, as the Archbishop's rebellion tries to do,

> diet rank minds sick of happiness
> And purge the obstructions which begin to stop
> Our very veins of life.

But purges and potions, be they the medicinable gold
that the crown so distinctly is not or the sherris-sack
whose virtues Falstaff so eloquently proclaims, are of no
real use, for death is certain. Though it may be unexpected, in a chamber named Jerusalem instead of the city,
death itself is certain.

The play's images of medicines represent one kind of
defense against the acceptance of a larger, cosmic order
that includes disease and death; words represent another.
Thus, the rebels project and plan, emitting words, "publish[ing] the occasion of our arms." They "fortify with
the names of men." The Archbishop, so "deep within the
books of God," turns himself into "an iron man talking."
In general, the rebels emit words and then take them for
things, as their predecessor Hotspur did,

> who lined himself with hope
> Eating the air and promise of supply.

They forget their physical selves and ask only for their
"articles," "this schedule," their "conditions" in a "true
substantial form." And verbal form is all John gives them.

Falstaff, too, emits a "throng of words" that wrench
the "true cause the false way." Contrasted with them,
taking language in,

> The Prince but studies his companions
> Like a strange tongue, wherein, to gain the language,
> 'Tis needful that the most immodest word
> Be looked upon and learned,

but once learned, he will no longer speak, emit, such words, but rather take them "as a pattern or a measure" with which to judge the lives of others.

In other words, the Prince will not thrust up a merely verbal reality against the larger order. Rather, he will make himself and his language a part of that larger order, as Prince John does: "God, and not we, hath safely fought today." Pathetically, the rebels themselves try to become part of some larger order: "We are time's subjects."

> We see which way the stream of time doth run,
> And are enforced from our most quiet there
> By the rough torrent of occasion.

But "occasion" is a transitory thing, a creature of time, and time itself is a great betrayer. The King's party fits into a firmer order: "Construe the times to their necessities." When Warwick states the Elizabethan view of history, he speaks of it as a "necessary form." When King Henry disclaims any intent on his part of seizing Richard's crown, he says,

> Necessity so bowed the state
> That I and greatness were compelled to kiss.

And he accepts the rebel threat—

> Are these things then necessities?
> Then let us meet them like necessities.

The rebels, however, are responding, not to "necessities," but their "most just and right desires," the "demands" they seek to "enjoy." Appetite is their failure, and John's strategy simply traps them as animals are baited and trapped by their appetites. They drink as token of their wishes granted, but the drink also symbolizes their failure and defeat through appetite. (Indeed, the Archbishop after drinking finds himself "passing light in spirit.")

The real drinker, though, the very essence of appetite, is, of course, Falstaff. "He hath eaten me out of house and home," Mistress Quickly complains. "The old boar" (earlier he had been a sow) doth "feed in the old frank," monetarily, emotionally, and gastrically. At Shallow's, "We shall do nothing but eat, and make good cheer." Falstaff feeds on Shallow, too, taking a thousand pounds from him, promising to turn him into verbal jokes just as he himself ("the cause that wit is in other men") turns himself to words. Hal's succession provokes him into a riot of appetite: "Let us take any man's horses; the laws of England are at my commandment."

Thus, it is supremely appropriate that Hal reject him ("the feeder of my riots") in terms of food, as, earlier, he had taken leave of a Falstaff richly symbolized as a withered apple. In the coronation scene, Falstaff calls out, "My King! My Jove!" (thus identifying himself with Saturn, the titan who devoured his own children). Hal replies:

> I know thee not, old man. Fall to thy prayers.
> How ill white hairs becomes a fool and jester!
> I have long dreamt of such a kind of man,
> So surfeit-swelled, so old, and so profane,
> But, being awaked, I do despise my dream.
> Make less thy body hence, and more thy grace.
> Leave gormandizing. Know the grave doth gape
> For thee thrice wider than for other men.
> Reply not to me with a fool-born jest.

Not only does Hal put aside appetite—he fends off Falstaff's wordmongering (even as he himself lapses into two jokes—though he immediately counters, "Presume not that I am the thing I was"). Saddest of all, most brutal but most necessary, he reminds Falstaff of his role as an old man and of the grave's mouth that gapes so widely for him.

The mouth, food and medicine going into it, words

coming out, these images dominating a play of appetites
and expectations mocked—Shakespeare here harks back
to a truth of infancy, to a time when life was a life of the
mouth. Psychologists such as Erik Erikson have been
stressing in recent years the crucial importance of that
time when we must discover our own identities; when we
learn, taught by our own appetites, that we must await,
trust, expect another to feed us. It is this ability to trust
in another that enables the infant to experience that other
as an existence separate from his own desires, to experience, therefore, his own separateness, his identity. The
paradox continues into later life: it is the ability to give
up one's own desires, to trust, even to merge and identify
with the "necessity" represented by others, even, in a
sense, to tolerate being engulfed by or devoured by it (as
King Henry's crown, emblem of the larger order, has
eaten its bearer up), that enables us to reemerge, as we
did in earliest infancy, into a new sense of identity, a new
role. In a paradox almost Biblical, we must lose ourselves
to find ourselves.

So with Falstaff: to grow into the new role he should
assume now that Hal is king, he must curb his appetites
("Leave gormandizing") and learn to depend on another
(the "competence of life" his new king allows him). He
must live with the certainty that the grave gapes for him,
that he will himself be devoured. As for the rebels, they
do not let themselves be merged into the larger necessity
represented by the monarch; instead, they try to create
roles for themselves out of their own words (or mouths).
Necessarily, they fail.

Prince Hal, too, must give up an identity based on his
own appetites, that of the madcap prince, and accept an
identity set out for him, that of the hero-king. As Ernst
Kris points out in a psychoanalytic study of this play,[3]
Hal, until his father's death, refuses to fall back into the
role his father has planned for him. Rather, he puts aside
his father, stained and imperfect as a curber of appetites

---

[3] The critics referred to in this Introduction are either reprinted in the
Commentaries section of this edition, pp. 190–233, or listed in the Suggested References, pp. 239–40.

because he himself "snatched" the crown "with boisterous hand," and he takes an identity from Falstaff, a father-substitute. Once his real father is dead, however, he can put aside Falstaff (ultimately rendering him as dead as his true father) and be taken into the role his father wished for him. Indeed, he can even accept a proper father-substitute in the person of the Lord Chief Justice.

Food is our earliest experience of trust; justice is a later one. Again, we must learn to wait rather than try to grab—we must trust in the larger necessity of law. *2 Henry IV* gives us a pair of justices: a true one in the Lord Chief Justice, a false one in Shallow, who succumbs to his servant's entreaty to "bear out a knave against an honest man." Shallow lets himself merge into a larger order, but one of his servants' making, so that, as Falstaff points out, they become like foolish justices, he a justice-like servingman. The Lord Chief Justice, however, speaks to Hal with "the person of your father"; "the image of his power lay then in me." He justifies his earlier action of imprisoning the Prince by reminding the new young king that he, now, has a new identity—"As you are a king, speak in your state." And Hal responds by assuming his kingly role, merging himself in his father's identity so that "I live to speak my father's words." To the Lord Chief Justice,

> You shall be as a father to my youth.
> My voice shall sound as you do prompt mine ear.
> And I will stoop and humble my intents
> To your well-practiced wise directions.
>
> My father is gone wild into his grave,
> For in his tomb lie my [appetites]
> And with his spirits sadly I survive
> To mock the expectation of the world. . . .

Thus, Hal merges into his father and contrasts with the Archbishop, who rebelled though he was "the imagined voice of God himself"; he did

> misuse the reverence of [his] place,

> Employ the countenance and grace of heaven,
> As a false favorite does his prince's name,
> In deeds dishonorable.

The right people of the play merge into a larger order; the wrong people resist or misuse that larger order. Shallow's very name tells us something about their failure: as Prince John says to the rebels,

> You are too shallow, Hastings, much too shallow,
> To sound the bottom of the after-times.

The image is of a river, and the Archbishop had earlier compared himself and the other rebels to a river in flood, saying that, if their demands are granted, "We come within our awful banks again." Henry IV, too, is linked to a flooding river: in a detail Shakespeare retained from his sources, Henry (who was himself a rebel) dies as the Thames thrice floods without ebb. As for Hal,

> The tide of blood in me
> Hath proudly flowed in vanity till now.
> Now doth it turn and ebb back to the sea,
> Where it shall mingle with the state of floods
> And flow henceforth in formal majesty.

He has put aside flooding and merged himself into the identity ordained for him by that larger order, vast as the sea. The play can end now, as it began, with a rumor. But now a true rumor, for a bird sings the music of true expectation, the King's will merged into the nation's destiny.

In short, the theme of betrayal permeates and informs the language, incidents, and characters of *2 Henry IV,* but it is betrayal in a special sense: "expectations mocked." That is, the play begins with a sense of hunger or appetite:

> Open your ears, for which of you will stop
> The vent of hearing when loud Rumor speaks?

Then, against selfish or foolish appetite, the play poises a larger, parental plan of justice or monarchy or necessity that threatens to swallow up the characters by danger, disease, or death. And yet this larger necessity offers the paradoxical and unexpected possibility of a new identity, a kind of rebirth into a new self for those who can merge themselves into it. True princeliness calls for this ability to trust in the larger order, to achieve identity by the very act of curbing the self and its appetites and being merged into the greater plan. True rebellion means—in its most primitive sense—feeding oneself, resisting trust in that larger order by substituting one's own medicines, words, appetite, food, plans: "eating the air." And thus, the play itself answers the critics who have been troubled by Prince John's trick on the political rebels and Prince Hal's rejection of the appetitive rebel, Falstaff. These two "betrayals" become necessary and inevitable if we take the play on its own emotional and intellectual terms: the original failure of trust was the rebels' own inability to merge (without wordy conditions) into the larger order of nature.

Again, if we take the play on its own terms, we can see the answer to the second critical issue: the relation of Part Two to Part One. The external evidence from Elizabethan stage-practice that the two plays must have been separate and self-sufficient entities is clear enough. The internal evidence is clear, too. Part One and Part Two are quite different in their essential dramatic ideas, but they make a matched pair.

We can see the difference in the Falstaffs of the two parts. Twinned in avoirdupois, soldiering, and appetites, they nevertheless differ in some important ways. In both parts, Falstaff is a creature who defeats expectation, not only in the action, but also in our response (as Freud notes). From the point of view of the literary historian, as Bernard Spivack has shown, this mocking of our expectations places him in the tradition of the deceptive Vice of the morality plays or the tricky Ambidexter of a *Cambises*. But in Part One, Falstaff seems more triumphant: the Chaplinesque clown who, by his ability to play many parts, triumphs even over death, as (in the final battle) he feigns a death-and-rebirth. In Part Two, Falstaff resists, but succumbs to, the preordained role pointed out by Philip Williams and C. L. Barber. He becomes the slain god, the Lord of Misrule who must be banished to restore health to the land. Hal is absorbed into the role of the hero-king, while Falstaff is engulfed by a mythic significance that demands his rejection and death.

Miss Caroline Spurgeon noted some years ago that the Falstaff of Part One uses many images from books and the Bible, while the Falstaff of Part Two speaks in grotesque, rough, coarse similes drawn from body functions and appetites. We can add that Falstaff One uses a very distinctive figure of speech, the enthymeme: "If I travel but four foot by the squire further afoot, I shall break my wind." "If the rascal have not given me medicines to make me love him, I'll be hanged." "And 'twere not as good a deed as drink to turn true man and to leave these rogues, I am the veriest varlet that ever chewed with a tooth." (These all occur within ten lines in Part One, suggesting the frequency of the figure.) Falstaff Two almost entirely lacks this figure of speech; instead, he has become something of a monologist. He takes in a character, then turns him into a satirical portrait: we see Falstaff Two do this with himself, his page, his tailor, Pistol, Prince Hal, Poins, Bardolph, Shallow, Prince John, and, of course, sherris-sack, in monologues quite different in style from his catechism of honor in Part One (which tests a role). Falstaff Two may be responding to the same taste that led Jonson to put such incidental character sketches into *Every Man Out of his Humor* and *Cynthia's Revels* or that accounts for the popularity of the character-books of Hall, Overbury, and others in the early seventeenth century, but, in any case, he has shifted from acting out different roles (often taken from books and the Bible) to a more passive taking in of what he sees, then spewing it out in words (the image of vomit occurs several times in *2 Henry IV*). Falstaff One's big comic scene is the play-within-the-play in the tavern, when he tries on the roles of King

Henry and Prince Hal. Falstaff Two's big comic scene is the recruiting, when he looks at the prospective draftees and coins them into a mint of witty remarks. In short, he becomes the walking embodiment of everything the play rejects: appetite, wordmongering, resistance to one's proper role. He becomes, like Iago in the tragedies, or Autolycus and Caliban in the last plays, Shakespeare's *homo repudiandus,* the character who focuses in himself everything to be rejected. This, then, is the essential difference between the Falstaffs of Part One and Part Two: the earlier Falstaff actively tries on different roles; the later and more passive Falstaff finds himself forced into a pattern laid down for him by his context.

And so does Hal. In Part One, he actively chooses the role of hero; in Part Two, he lapses into kingship. The rest of the characters show the same passivity. Part One gave us an active, scrappy group of rebels; Part Two represents rebellion by talkers and bargainers. Part One sharply opposed characters as good son—bad son; good father—bad father; hot spur and false staff; and Hal forged a role for himself between such extremes. Part Two makes only one such sharp pairing: the good justice, who merges into his master's voice, as against the bad justice, who merges into his servant's. Mostly, Part Two bunches fairly nondescript characters into the roles they must assume—and so the Folio text lists them, in bracketed groups as "Opposites against King Henrie the Fourth," "Of the Kings Partie," "Country Soldiers," "Irregular Humorists," and the women. In the same way, Part Two abounds in references to parts of the body, parts of a house, parts of a kingdom—the later play constantly stresses a sense of role within a larger plan.

These different ways of dealing with role are what make Parts One and Two quite separate but nevertheless a matched pair. In both, the problem is to bring Hal to the role laid down for him by his father, his King, his God. Part One offers the active solution; Part Two, the passive. In the first play, Hal takes from the takers, robs Hotspur and Falstaff of the honors or money they had robbed from others. In the second, Hal is the taker taken: he

learns to put down his cravings and appetites and be
taken up into the larger plan. Part One is the sunnier
version—my pun is intentional—for it looks at the problem of Hal's achieving at-oneness with his father from
the point of view of the son who actively battles the rebel
within and without. Part Two sees the theme with the
eyes of a dying father, in terms of passive expectation,
trust, and acceptance of necessity. It is this atmosphere
of passivity that keeps the magnificent fighter-Hal of Part
One out of the action—what action there is—in Part
Two. Finally, in *Henry V*, these active and passive solu-
tions fuse. Hal's active battling fulfills the role he must
passively accept. He brings the drives and appetites of
others and their roles as Scot, Irishman, Welshman, or
French princess into the service of his kingly function:

> Upon the King! Let us our lives, our souls,
> Our debts, our careful wives,
> Our children, and our sins, lay on the King!

The King must bear all—all but a few traitors and "irregular humorists" who insist on keeping separate. They must
die.

Betrayal is the quintessential Shakespearean theme—
provided we recognize the special tone that Shakespeare
gives it. All his works deal with the taming of shrewish-
ness: the masking over or mastery of hate by love. Betrayal, for Shakespeare, seems to mean a situation in
which one can expect love, but in which love falls away
and reveals an unsuspected or unmastered hate beneath.
Iago is the obvious example, but we can look at all the
tragedies as situations in which the love between a man
and a woman, love either new or preexisting or expectable,
fails to master hate. When love succeeds, the issue is
comic, as in *Measure for Measure* and *The Merchant of
Venice*, which temper hard justice with feminine mercy.
All's well that ends well—that ends in love as Henry V's
wars in France will.

So understood, *2 Henry IV*, written near the end of

1597 or early in 1598, occupies a pivotal point in the Shakespearean canon. In the early comedies, romantic love overcomes feuds and hatreds, while in the early histories and tragedies, family or romantic love fails to control political and social aggressions. In the plays of 1598–1601, Shakespeare seems to play with the thought that passivity best counters aggression or romantic assertiveness. Claudio in *Much Ado* lets his Prince do his wooing for him. In *Twelfth Night,* the woman takes the role of wooer, as she does in *As You Like It. 2 Henry IV* also looks forward to the tragedies, the uncurbed and parricidal drives of Brutus and Cassius, and even more, to that character who, more than any other in Shakespeare, resists the role his father had set up for him, putting up instead his own smokescreen of words—Hamlet. In many ways, but notably in the special, paternal way love controls rebellion and aggression, *2 Henry IV* seems closer to the tragedies and "problem plays" than to the earlier histories.

The passivity of *2 Henry IV* may also explain why it has become less popular than the other histories. It was apparently as popular as Part One in the eighteenth century, but, then, eighteenth-century audiences were still committed to a larger, hierarchical plan in society. The nineteenth and twentieth centuries prize precisely the acquisitive, assertive behavior that resists inherited patterns and plans, and this particular history play, which so sharply rejects such social individualism, has fallen in popularity. But *2 Henry IV* can look for better days with newer approaches to Shakespeare. Nineteenth-century audiences concentrated on the events represented by the plays rather than on the plays as themselves events and, therefore, they wanted to see in the histories one long epic glorifying England's history—to them, *2 Henry IV* marked a sordid low. Today, however, we recognize that Shakespeare's histories embody Elizabethan political views, not nineteenth-century Whiggery, and we are better at accepting Shakespeare's plays on their own terms, as things-in-themselves. When we do so accept *2 Henry IV,* we find it offers moments as fine as any in the Shakespearean canon: the brilliant and pathetic portrait of Shallow; the grotesquery of Pistol; the Prince's reconciliation with his father; the King's apostrophe to sleep; the rejection of Falstaff. More important, when we accept the play itself as an event, our experience of the play becomes our own act of trust.

NORMAN N. HOLLAND
Massachusetts Institute of Technology

The Second Part of
[King] Henry IV

The Actors' Names

Rumor, the Presenter
King Henry the Fourth
Prince Henry, afterwards crowned King Henry the Fifth
Prince John of Lancaster ⎫
Humphrey of Gloucester ⎬ sons to Henry IV and
Thomas of Clarence ⎭ brethren to Henry V

[Earl of] Northumberland ⎫
[Richard Scroop] the Arch- ⎪
  bishop of York ⎪
[Lord] Mowbray ⎪
[Lord] Hastings ⎬ opposites against
Lord Bardolph ⎪ King Henry IV
Travers ⎪
Morton ⎪
[Sir John] Coleville ⎭

[Earl of] Warwick ⎫　　　　　Poins ⎫
[Earl of] Westmoreland ⎪　　　[Sir John] ⎪
[Earl of] Surrey ⎪ of the　　　　Falstaff ⎪
[Sir John Blunt] ⎬ King's　　Bardolph ⎬ irregular
Gower ⎪ party　　　Pistol ⎪ humorists
Harcourt ⎪　　　　　Peto ⎪
Lord Chief Justice ⎭　　　　[Falstaff's] ⎪
　　　　　　　　　　　　　　　　Page ⎭

[Robert] Shallow ⎱ both coun-
Silence ⎰ try justices　　　Northumberland's
Davy, servant to Shallow　　　　Wife
Fang and Snare, two sergeants　Percy's Widow
[Ralph] Moldy ⎫　　　　　　　[Lady Percy]
[Simon] Shadow ⎪　　　Drawers　Hostess Quickly
[Thomas] Wart ⎬ country Beadles　Doll Tearsheet
[Francis] Feeble ⎪ soldiers Grooms [A Dancer as]
[Peter] Bullcalf ⎭　　　　　　　Epilogue

[Porter, Messenger, Soldiers, Lords, Attendants

Scene: England]

The Second Part of
[King] Henry IV

[INDUCTION]

Enter Rumor, painted full of tongues.

[*Rumor.*] Open your ears, for which of you will stop
  The vent of hearing when loud Rumor speaks?
  I, from the orient to the drooping west,
  Making the wind my post-horse, still unfold
  The acts commencèd on this ball of earth.   5
  Upon my tongues continual slanders ride,
  The which in every language I pronounce,
  Stuffing the ears of men with false reports.
  I speak of peace while covert enmity
  Under the smile of safety wounds the world.   10
  And who but Rumor, who but only I,
  Make fearful musters and prepared defense
  Whiles the big year, swoln with some other grief,
  Is thought with child by the stern tyrant, war,
  And no such matter? Rumor is a pipe°¹   15
  Blown by surmises, jealousies, conjectures,
  And of so easy and so plain a stop
  That the blunt° monster with uncounted heads,
  The still-discordant wav'ring multitude,
  Can play upon it. But what need I thus   20
  My well-known body to anatomize
  Among my household?° Why is Rumor here?

1 The degree sign (°) indicates a footnote, which is keyed to the text by line number. Text references are printed in **boldface** type; the annotation follows in roman type.
Ind.15 **pipe** wind instrument   18 **blunt** dull   22 **my household** i.e., the audience

I run before King Harry's victory,
Who in a bloody field by Shrewsbury
25 Hath beaten down young Hotspur° and his troops,
Quenching the flame of bold rebellion
Even with the rebels' blood. But what mean I
To speak so true at first? My office is
To noise abroad that Harry Monmouth° fell
30 Under the wrath of noble Hotspur's sword,
And that the King before the Douglas' rage
Stooped his anointed head as low as death.
This have I rumored through the peasant towns
Between that royal field of Shrewsbury
35 And this worm-eaten hole of ragged° stone,
Where Hotspur's father, old Northumberland,
Lies crafty-sick.° The posts come tiring° on,
And not a man of them brings other news
Than they have learned of me. From Rumor's tongues
They bring smooth comforts false, worse than true
40   wrongs.   *Exit Rumor.*

25 **Hotspur** Harry Percy, the Earl of Northumberland's son, a rebel
against King Henry IV, killed by the Prince of Wales   29 **Harry
Monmouth** the Prince of Wales, Prince Hal   35 **ragged** rough-edged
37 **crafty-sick** feigning sickness   37 **tiring** exhausting themselves

[ACT I

Scene I. *Northumberland's castle.*]

Enter the Lord Bardolph at one door.

Lord Bardolph. Who keeps the gate here, ho? Where
   is the Earl?

Porter. [*Within*] What shall I say you are?

Lord Bardolph.   Tell thou the Earl
   That the Lord Bardolph doth attend him here.

Porter. His lordship is walked forth into the orchard.
   Please it your honor, knock but at the gate,   5
   And he himself will answer.

Enter the Earl [of] Northumberland.

Lord Bardolph.   Here comes the Earl.

Northumberland. What news, Lord Bardolph? Every
   minute now
   Should be the father of some stratagem.
   The times are wild. Contention, like a horse
   Full of high feeding, madly hath broke loose   10
   And bears down all before him.

Lord Bardolph.   Noble Earl,
    I bring you certain news from Shrewsbury.

Northumberland. Good, and° God will!

Lord Bardolph.   As good as heart can wish.
    The King is almost wounded to the death;
13 And, in the fortune of my lord your son,
    Prince Harry slain outright; and both the Blunts
    Killed by the hand of Douglas; young Prince John
    And Westmoreland and Stafford fled the field;
    And Harry Monmouth's brawn,° the hulk Sir John,
20 Is prisoner to your son. O, such a day,
    So fought, so followed, and so fairly won,
    Came not till now to dignify the times
    Since Caesar's fortunes!

Northumberland.   How is this derived?
    Saw you the field? Came you from Shrewsbury?

Lord Bardolph. I spake with one, my lord, that came
25   from thence,

Enter Travers.

    A gentleman well bred and of good name,
    That freely rend'red me these news for true.

Northumberland. Here comes my servant Travers,°
        who I sent
    On Tuesday last to listen after news.

Lord Bardolph. My lord, I overrode° him on the
30   way,
    And he is furnished with no certainties
    More than he haply.° may retail from me.

Northumberland. Now, Travers, what good tidings
        comes with you?

Travers. My lord, Sir John Umfrevile turned me back
35 With joyful tidings, and, being better horsed,
    Outrode me. After him came spurring hard

I.i.13 **and** if   19 **brawn** fattened boar   28 **Travers** (to "traverse" **is**
to deny)   30 **overrode** outrode   32 **haply** perhaps

A gentleman, almost forspent° with speed,
That stopped by me to breathe his bloodied horse.
He asked the way to Chester, and of him
I did demand what news from Shrewsbury.   40
He told me that rebellion had bad luck,
And that young Harry Percy's spur was cold.
With that, he gave his able horse the head,
And bending forward struck his armèd heels
Against the panting sides of his poor jade°   45
Up to the rowel-head, and starting so
He seemed in running to devour the way,
Staying no longer question.

Northumberland.   Ha? Again.
Said he young Harry Percy's spur was cold?
Of Hotspur Coldspur? That rebellion   50
Had met ill luck?

Lord Bardolph.   My lord, I'll tell you what.
If my young lord your son have not the day,
Upon mine honor, for a silken point°
I'll give my barony. Never talk of it.

Northumberland. Why should that gentleman that
  rode by Travers   55
Give then such instances of loss?

Lord Bardolph.   Who, he?
He was some hilding° fellow that had stol'n
The horse he rode on, and, upon my life,
Spoke at a venture. Look, here comes more news.

Enter Morton.

Northumberland. Yea, this man's brow, like to a title-
  leaf,   60
Foretells the nature of a tragic volume.
So looks the strond° whereon the imperious flood
Hath left a witnessed° usurpation.
Say, Morton, didst thou come from Shrewsbury?

---

37 **forspent** totally used up   45 **jade** nag   53 **point** lace (used to tie
breeches up)   57 **hilding** base   62 **strond** shore   63 **witnessed** evidence of

65 *Morton.* I ran from Shrewsbury, my noble lord,
   Where hateful death put on his ugliest mask
   To fright our party.

   Northumberland.   How doth my son and brother?
   Thou tremblest, and the whiteness in thy cheek
   Is apter than thy tongue to tell thy errand.
70 Even such a man, so faint, so spiritless,
   So dull, so dead in look, so woebegone,
   Drew Priam's curtain in the dead of night,
   And would have told him half his Troy was burnt.
   But Priam found the fire ere he his tongue
75 And I my Percy's death ere thou report'st it.
   This thou wouldst say, "Your son did thus and
        thus;
   Your brother thus. So fought the noble Douglas,"
   Stopping my greedy ear with their bold deeds.
   But in the end, to stop my ear indeed,
80 Thou hast a sigh to blow away this praise,
   Ending with "Brother, son, and all are dead."

   Morton. Douglas is living, and your brother—yet;
   But, for my lord your son—

   Northumberland.   Why, he is dead!
   See what a ready tongue suspicion hath!
85 He that but fears the thing he would not know
   Hath by instinct knowledge from others' eyes
   That what he feared is chanced. Yet speak, Morton.
   Tell thou an earl his divination lies,
   And I will take it as a sweet disgrace
90 And make thee rich for doing me such wrong.

   Morton. You are too great to be by me gainsaid.
   Your spirit is too true, your fears too certain.

   Northumberland. Yet, for all this, say not that Percy's
        dead.
   I see a strange confession in thine eye.
95 Thou shak'st thy head and hold'st it fear, or sin,
   To speak a truth. If he be slain, say so.
   The tongue offends not that reports his death;

And he doth sin that doth belie the dead,
Not he which says the dead is not alive.
Yet the first bringer of unwelcome news   *100*
Hath but a losing office, and his tongue
Sounds ever after as a sullen bell,
Rememb'red tolling a departing friend.

Lord Bardolph. I cannot think, my lord, your son is
     dead.

Morton. I am sorry I should force you to believe   *105*
     That which I would to God I had not seen.
     But these mine eyes saw him in bloody state,
     Rend'ring faint quittance,° wearied and out-
          breathed,
     To Harry Monmouth, whose swift wrath beat down
     The never-daunted Percy to the earth,   *110*
     From whence with life he never more sprung up.
     In few,° his death, whose spirit lent a fire
     Even to the dullest peasant in his camp,
     Being bruited° once, took fire and heat away
     From the best-tempered courage in his troops.   *115*
     For from his mettle was his party steeled,
     Which once in him abated, all the rest
     Turned on themselves, like dull and heavy lead.
     And as the thing that's heavy in itself,
     Upon enforcement flies with greatest speed,   *120*
     So did our men, heavy in Hotspur's loss,
     Lend to this weight such lightness with their fear
     That arrows fled not swifter toward their aim
     Than did our soldiers, aiming at their safety,
     Fly from the field. Then was that noble Worcester   *125*
     So soon ta'en prisoner. And that furious Scot,
     The bloody Douglas, whose well-laboring sword
     Had three times slain th' appearance of the King,°
     'Gan vail his stomach° and did grace° the shame
     Of those that turned their backs, and in his flight,   *130*

---

108 **quittance** repaying (of blows)   112 **few** i.e., few words   114
bruited noised about   128 **th' appearance of the King** noblemen dis-
guised as the King   129 **'Gan vail his stomach** began to abate his
courage   129 **grace** favor

Stumbling in fear, was took. The sum of all
Is that the King hath won, and hath sent out
A speedy power to encounter you, my lord,
Under the conduct of young Lancaster
135   And Westmoreland. This is the news at full.

Northumberland. For this I shall have time enough to
      mourn.
In poison there is physic;° and these news,
Having been well, that° would have made me sick,
Being sick, have in some measure made me well.
140   And, as the wretch whose fever-weak'ned joints,
Like strengthless hinges, buckle under life,
Impatient of his fit, breaks like a fire
Out of his keeper's arms, even so my limbs,
Weak'ned with grief, being now enraged with
      grief,°
Are thrice themselves. Hence, therefore, thou nice°
145   crutch!
A scaly gauntlet now with joints of steel
Must glove this hand. And hence, thou sickly
      quoif!°
Thou art a guard too wanton° for the head
Which princes, fleshed with° conquest, aim to hit.
150   Now bind my brows with iron, and approach
The ragged'st° hour that time and spite dare bring
To frown upon th' enraged Northumberland!
Let heaven kiss earth! Now let not Nature's hand
Keep the wild flood confined! Let order die!
155   And let this world no longer be a stage
To feed contention in a ling'ring act!°
But let one spirit of the firstborn Cain
Reign in all bosoms, that, each heart being set
On bloody courses, the rude scene may end,
160   And darkness be the burier of the dead!

137 **physic** medicine   138 **Having been well, that** that, had they been
well   144 **grief . . . grief** sickness . . . sorrow   145 **nice** delicate
147 **quoif** nightcap   148 **wanton** light   149 **fleshed with** having sa-
vored   151 **ragged'st** roughest   156 **act** (1) deed (2) section of a
play

Lord Bardolph. This strainèd passion doth you wrong,
  my lord.

Morton. Sweet Earl, divorce not wisdom from your
  honor.
  The lives of all your loving complices
  Lean on your health, the which, if you give o'er
  To stormy passion, must perforce decay.   *165*
  You cast th' event° of war, my noble lord,
  And summed the account of chance, before you
    said,
  "Let us make head."° It was your presurmise
  That, in the dole° of blows, your son might drop.
  You knew he walked o'er perils, on an edge,   *170*
  More likely to fall in than to get o'er.
  You were advised his flesh was capable
  Of wounds and scars and that his forward spirit
  Would lift him where most trade of danger ranged.
  Yet did you say, "Go forth." And none of this,   *175*
  Though strongly apprehended, could restrain
  The stiff-borne° action. What hath then befall'n,
  Or what hath this bold enterprise brought forth,
  More than that being which was like to be?

Lord Bardolph. We all that are engagèd° to this loss   *180*
  Knew that we ventured on such dangerous seas
  That if we wrought out life 'twas ten to one.
  And yet we ventured, for the gain proposed
  Choked the respect° of likely peril feared.
  And since we are o'erset,° venture again.   *185*
  Come, we will all put forth,° body and goods.

Morton. 'Tis more than time. And, my most noble
    lord,
  I hear for certain, and dare speak the truth:
  The gentle Archbishop of York is up
  With well-appointed pow'rs.° He is a man   *190*

166 **cast th' event** estimated the outcome   168 **make head** raise an
army   169 **dole** dealing out   177 **stiff-borne** determinedly carried on
180 **engagèd** bound by contract   184 **respect** consideration   185
o'erset (1) upset, capsized (2) outwagered   186 **put forth** wager
190 **well-appointed pow'rs** well-equipped armies

Who with a double° surety binds his followers.
My lord your son had only but the corpse,
But shadows and the shows of men, to fight.
For that same word "rebellion" did divide
195 The action of their bodies from their souls,
And they did fight with queasiness, constrained,
As men drink potions, that their weapons only
Seemed on our side. But for their spirits and souls,
This word "rebellion," it had froze them up
200 As fish are in a pond. But now the Bishop
Turns insurrection to religion.
Supposed sincere and holy in his thoughts,
He's followed both with body and with mind,
And doth enlarge his rising with the blood
Of fair King Richard, scraped from Pomfret°
205 stones;
Derives from heaven his quarrel and his cause;
Tells them he doth bestride a bleeding land,
Gasping for life under great Bolingbroke;°
And more and less° do flock to follow him.

Northumberland. I knew of this before; but, to speak
210 truth,
This present grief had wiped it from my mind.
Go in with me, and counsel every man
The aptest way for safety and revenge.
Get° posts and letters, and make° friends with
speed.
213 Never so few, and never yet more need.   *Exeunt.*

---

191 **double** i.e., of body and soul   205 **Pomfret** Pomfret castle
(where Richard II was murdered)   208 **Bolingbroke** King Henry IV
209 **more and less** high and low   214 **Get** beget   214 **make** collect

[Scene II. *London*.]

Enter Sir John [Falstaff] alone, with his Page
bearing his sword and buckler.

Falstaff. Sirrah, you giant,° what says the doctor to
my water?°

Page. He said, sir, the water itself was a good healthy
water; but, for the party that owed° it, he might
have moe° diseases than he knew for.   5

Falstaff. Men of all sorts take a pride to gird° at me.
The brain of this foolish compounded clay, man°
is not able to invent anything that intends to
laughter more than I invent or is invented on me.
I am not only witty in myself, but the cause that   10
wit is in other men. I do here walk before thee like
a sow that hath overwhelmed all her litter but one.
If the Prince put thee into my service for any other
reason than to set me off, why then I have no judgment. Thou whoreson mandrake,° thou art fitter   15
to be worn in my cap than to wait at my heels. I
was never manned with an agate° till now, but
I will inset you neither in gold nor silver, but in
vile apparel, and send you back again to your
master, for a jewel—the juvenal,° the Prince your   20
master, whose chin is not yet fledge.° I will sooner
have a beard grow in the palm of my hand than
he shall get one off his cheek, and yet he will not

I.ii.1 **giant** (the page was played by an unusually small boy, who
probably mimicked Falstaff)   2 **water** urine   4 **owed** owned   5 **moe**
more   6 **gird** mock   7 **compounded clay, man** man, compounded of
clay   15 **mandrake** man-shaped root   17 **manned with an agate**
attended by a servingman small as a figure carved in a jewel   20
juvenal juvenile (echoing jewel)   21 **fledge** feathered

stick to say his face is a face-royal.° God may fin-
25 ish it when he will, 'tis not a hair amiss yet. He may
keep it still at a face-royal,° for a barber shall
never earn sixpence out of it; and yet he'll be crow-
ing as if he had writ° man ever since his father was
a bachelor. He may keep his own grace,° but he's
30 almost out of mine, I can assure him. What said
Master Dummelton about the satin for my short
cloak and my slops?°

Page. He said, sir, you should procure him better
assurance° than Bardolph. He would not take his
35 band° and yours; he liked not the security.

Falstaff. Let him be damned, like the glutton!° Pray
God his tongue be hotter! A whoreson Achitophel!°
A rascal, yea-forsooth knave!° To bear a gentleman in hand, and then stand upon security! The
40 whoreson smooth-pates° do now wear nothing but
high shoes,° and bunches of keys° at their girdles;
and if a man is through with them in honest taking
up, then they must stand upon security.° I had as
lief they would put ratsbane in my mouth as offer
45 to stop it with "security." I looked 'a° should have
sent me two-and-twenty yards of satin, as I am a
true knight, and he sends me "security." Well, he
may sleep in security, for he hath the horn° of
abundance, and the lightness° of his wife shines

24, 26 **face-royal** the King's face on a ten-shilling coin (the royal),
which presumably would not need the attention of a barber   28 **writ**
styled himself   29 **grace** (1) title, "your Grace," (2) favor   32 **slops**
wide breeches   34 **assurance** security (Bardolph is not Lord Bardolph, but one of Falstaff's cronies)   35 **band** bond   36 **glutton**
Dives (who in Luke 16:24 asked for water to cool his tongue)
37 **Achitophel** the counselor who betrayed Absalom (II Samuel
15–17)   38 **yea-forsooth knave** (one who swears sissy oaths like
"yea, forsooth")   40 **smooth-pates** tradesmen (who wore their hair
short, not like a nobleman's)   41 **high shoes** (sign of pride)   41 **keys**
(sign of possessions)   42–43 **if a man . . . security** after a man completes a bargain on credit with them, they suddenly demand security
45 **'a** he   48 **horn** (1) cornucopia (2) cuckold's horn   49 **lightness**
unchastity

through it. And yet cannot he see, though he have   30
his own lanthorn° to light him. Where's Bardolph?

Page. He's gone into Smithfield° to buy your worship
a horse.

Falstaff. I bought him in Paul's,° and he'll buy me a
horse in Smithfield. And I could get me but a wife   35
in the stews,° I were manned, horsed, and wived.°

Enter Lord Chief Justice [and Servant].

Page. Sir, here comes the nobleman that committed°
the Prince for striking him about Bardolph.

Falstaff. Wait close—I will not see him.

Chief Justice. What's he that goes there?   60

Servant. Falstaff, and't please your lordship.

Chief Justice. He that was in question° for the
robb'ry?

Servant. He, my lord. But he hath since done good
service at Shrewsbury, and, as I hear, is now going   65
with some charge° to the Lord John of Lancaster.

Chief Justice. What, to York? Call him back again.

Servant. Sir John Falstaff!

Falstaff. Boy, tell him I am deaf.

Page. You must speak louder; my master is deaf.   70

Chief Justice. I am sure he is—to the hearing of anything good. Go, pluck him by the elbow. I must
speak with him.

Servant. Sir John!

51 **lanthorn** lantern (in which a light shines through horn panels)
52 **Smithfield** the horse market   54 **Paul's** (unemployed men loitered
in St. Paul's cathedral seeking service)   56 **stews** brothels   56
manned, horsed, and wived (a proverb: "Who goes to Westminster
for a wife, to Paul's for a man, or to Smithfield for a horse, may
meet with a whore, a knave, and a jade")   57 **committed** i.e., to
prison (notice that the audience needed only this brief allusion to
the story about Hal striking the Lord Chief Justice)   62 **in question**
suspected   66 **charge** commission for soldiers

75 *Falstaff.* What! A young knave, and begging! Is there
    not wars? Is there not employment? Doth not the
    King lack subjects? Do not the rebels need soldiers?
    Though it be a shame to be on any side but one, it
    is worse shame to beg than to be on the worst side,
80 were it worse than the name of rebellion can tell
    how to make it.

Servant. You mistake me, sir.

Falstaff. Why, sir, did I say you were an honest man?
    Setting my knighthood and my soldiership aside,°
85 I had lied in my throat if I had said so.

Servant. I pray you, sir, then set your knighthood and
    your soldiership aside and give me leave to tell you
    you lie in your throat if you say I am any other
    than an honest man.

90 *Falstaff.* I give thee leave to tell me so! I lay aside
    that which grows to me! If thou get'st any leave of
    me, hang me. If thou tak'st leave, thou wert better
    be hanged. You hunt counter.° Hence! Avaunt!

Servant. Sir, my lord would speak with you.

95 *Chief Justice.* Sir John Falstaff, a word with you.

Falstaff. My good lord! God give your lordship good
    time of day. I am glad to see your lordship abroad.
    I heard say your lordship was sick. I hope your
    lordship goes abroad by advice.° Your lordship,
100 though not clean past your youth, hath yet some
    smack of an age° in you, some relish of the salt-
    ness of time in you; and I most humbly beseech
    your lordship to have a reverent care of your
    health.

105 *Chief Justice.* Sir John, I sent for you before your
    expedition to Shrewsbury.

Falstaff. And't please your lordship, I hear his Majesty

84 **Setting . . . aside** i.e., because knights and soldiers ought not to lie
93 **counter** in the wrong direction   99 **advice** i.e., a physician's
advice   101 **age** (pun on "ague"; cf. IV.i.34)

is returned with some discomfor: from Wales.

Chief Justice. I talk not of his Majesty. You would
not come when I sent for you.　　　　　　　　　*110*

Falstaff. And I hear, moreover, his Highness is fall'n
into this same whoreson apoplexy.

Chief Justice. Well, God mend him! I pray you, let
me speak with you.

Falstaff. This apoplexy, as I take it, is a kind of *115*
lethargy, and't please your lordship, a kind of
sleeping in the blood, a whoreson tingling.

Chief Justice. What, tell you me of it? Be it as it is.

Falstaff. It hath it original° from much grief, from
study and perturbation of the brain. I have read the *120*
cause of his effects in Galen.° It is a kind of deaf-
ness.

Chief Justice. I think you are fall'n into the disease,
for you hear not what I say to you.

Falstaff. Very well, my lord, very well. Rather, and't *125*
please you, it is the disease of not listening, the
malady of not marking, that I am troubled withal.

Chief Justice. To punish you by the heels° would
amend the attention of your ears, and I care not
if I do become your physician.　　　　　　　　*130*

Falstaff. I am as poor as Job, my lord, but not so
patient. Your lordship may minister the potion of
imprisonment to me in respect of poverty; but how
I should be your patient to follow your prescrip-
tions, the wise may make some dram° of a scruple,° *135*
or indeed a scruple itself.

Chief Justice. I sent for you, when there were matters
against you for your life, to come speak with me.

---

119 **it original** its origin.　121 **Galen** Greek physician (A.D. 129–199)
whose writings dominated Renaissance medical practice　128 **punish
you by the heels** put you in fetters or the stocks　135 **dram, scruple**
apothecaries' small weights

Falstaff. As I was then advised by my learned counsel
140   in the laws of this land-service,° I did not come.

Chief Justice. Well, the truth is, Sir John, you live in
great infamy.

Falstaff. He that buckles himself in my belt cannot
live in less.

145   *Chief Justice.* Your means are very slender and your
waste is great.

Falstaff. I would it were otherwise. I would my means
were greater and my waist slender.

Chief Justice. You have misled the youthful Prince.

150   *Falstaff.* The young Prince hath misled me. I am the
fellow with the great belly,° and he my dog.

Chief Justice. Well, I am loath to gall a new-healed
wound. Your day's service at Shrewsbury hath a
little gilded over your night's exploit° on Gad's
155   Hill. You may thank th' unquiet time for your quiet
o'erposting° that action.

Falstaff. My lord?

Chief Justice. But since all is well, keep it so. Wake
not a sleeping wolf.

160   *Falstaff.* To wake a wolf is as bad as smell a fox.°

Chief Justice. What! You are as a candle, the better
part burnt out.

Falstaff. A wassail candle,° my lord, all tallow. If I
did say of wax,° my growth would approve the
165   truth.

---

140 **land-service** (a play on military service—in which Falstaff's
sword would be his "learned counsel"—as against the service of a
legal summons)   151 **belly** i.e., so large he cannot see where he is
going and therefore needs a dog to lead him (?), a reference to some
well-known beggar (?)   154 **exploit** (the robbery in *1 Henry IV*,
II.ii and iv)   155–56 **quiet o'erposting** quietly getting past   160
smell a fox be suspicious   163 **wassail candle** large candle designed
to last a whole night, as at a feast   164 **wax** a play on (1) beeswax
(2) grow

Chief Justice. There is not a white hair in your face
but should have his effect of gravity.

Falstaff. His effect of gravy,° gravy, gravy.

Chief Justice. You follow the young Prince up and
down like his ill angel.   170

Falstaff. Not so, my lord. Your ill angel° is light,° but
I hope he that looks upon me will take me without
weighing. And yet, in some respects, I grant, I cannot go.° I cannot tell. Virtue is of so little regard
in these costermongers'° times that true valor is   175
turned berod.° Pregnancy° is made a tapster, and
hath his quick wit wasted in giving reckonings.° All
the other gifts appertinent to man, as the malice of
this age shapes them, are not worth a gooseberry.
You that are old consider not the capacities of us   180
that are young. You do measure the heat of our
livers with the bitterness of your galls. And we that
are in the vaward° of our youth, I must confess,
are wags too.

Chief Justice. Do you set down your name in the   185
scroll of youth, that are written down old with all
the characters of age? Have you not a moist eye,
a dry hand, a yellow cheek, a white beard, a de-
creasing leg, an increasing belly? Is not your voice
broken, your wind short, your chin double, your   190
wit single,° and every part about you blasted with
antiquity, and will you yet call yourself young? Fie,
fie, fie, Sir John!

Falstaff. My lord, I was born about three of the clock
in the afternoon, with a white head and something   195
a round belly. For my voice, I have lost it with
hallowing° and singing of anthems. To approve°

168 **gravy** with pun on the sense fatty sweat   171 **ill angel** clipped
coin   171 **light** (1) not due weight (2) wanton   174 **go** (1) pass for
currency (2) copulate (?)   175 **costermongers'** hucksters'   176 **berod**
bear-herd, one who leads tame bears   176 **Pregnancy** quickness of
wit   177 **reckonings** tavern bills   183 **vaward** vanguard   191 **single**
weak   197 **hallowing** (1) sanctifying (2) "halloing," shouting to
hounds   197 **approve** prove

my youth further, I will not. The truth is, I am
only old in judgment and understanding; and he
200   that will caper° with me for a thousand marks, let
him lend me the money, and have at him! For the
box of the ear that the Prince gave you, he gave it
like a rude prince, and you took it like a sensible
lord. I have checked° him for it, and the young
205   lion repents, marry, not in ashes and sackcloth, but
in new silk and old sack.°

Chief Justice. Well, God send the Prince a better
companion!

Falstaff. God send the companion a better prince! I
210   cannot rid my hands of him.

Chief Justice. Well, the King hath severed you and
Prince Harry. I hear you are going with Lord John
of Lancaster against the Archbishop and the Earl
of Northumberland.

215 *Falstaff.* Yea, I thank your pretty sweet wit for it. But
look you° pray, all you that kiss my lady Peace at
home, that our armies join not in a hot day, for, by
the Lord, I take but two shirts out with me, and
I mean not to sweat extraordinarily. If it be a hot
220   day, and I brandish anything but a bottle, I would
I might never spit white° again. There is not a
dangerous action can peep out his head but I am
thrust upon it. Well, I cannot last ever. But it was
alway yet the trick of our English nation, if they
225   have a good thing, to make it too common. If ye
will needs say I am an old man, you should give
me rest. I would to God my name were not so ter-
rible to the enemy as it is. I were better to be eaten
to death with a rust than to be scoured to nothing
230   with perpetual motion.

Chief Justice. Well, be honest, be honest, and God
bless your expedition!

200 **caper** compete at dancing   204 **checked** reproved   206 **sack**
sherry   216 **look you** make sure you   221 **spit white** (1) suffer a dry
mouth from carousing (2) emit semen (?)

Falstaff. Will your lordship lend me a thousand pound to furnish me forth?

Chief Justice. Not a penny, not a penny. You are too 235
impatient to bear crosses.° Fare you well. Commend me to my cousin Westmoreland.

         [Exeunt Chief Justice and Servant.]

Falstaff. If I do, fillip° me with a three-man beetle.°
A man can no more separate age and covetousness
than 'a can part young limbs and lechery. But the 240
gout galls the one and the pox pinches the other,
and so both the degrees° prevent° my curses. Boy!

Page. Sir?

Falstaff. What money is in my purse?

Page. Seven groats° and twopence. 245

Falstaff. I can get no remedy against this consumption of the purse. Borrowing only lingers and lingers it out, but the disease is incurable. Go bear this letter to my Lord of Lancaster, this to the Prince, this to the Earl of Westmoreland, and this to old 250
Mistress Ursula, whom I have weekly sworn to marry since I perceived the first white hair of my chin. About it. You know where to find me. *[Exit Page.]* A pox of this gout! Or a gout of this pox!
For the one or the other plays the rogue with my 255
great toe. 'Tis no matter if I do halt°—I have the
wars for my color,° and my pension shall seem the
more reasonable. A good wit will make use of anything. I will turn diseases to commodity.° *[Exit.]*

236 **crosses** (1) afflictions (2) coins marked with a cross   238 **fillip**
flip   238 **three-man beetle** a battering-ram carried by three men
(what it would take to "fillip" Falstaff)   242 **degrees** stations in life
242 **prevent** act before   245 **groats** fourpenny coins   256 **halt** limp
257 **color** (1) pretense (2) battle flag   259 **commodity** something to
sell

[Scene III. *The rebels' meeting-place.*]

*Enter th' Archbishop, Thomas Mowbray
(Earl Marshal), the Lord Hastings and
[Lord] Bardolph.*

Archbishop. Thus have you heard our cause and
    known our means;
And, my most noble friends, I pray you all,
Speak plainly your opinions of our hopes.
And first, Lord Marshal, what say you to it?

5   *Mowbray.* I well allow the occasion° of our arms,
But gladly would be better satisfied
How in our means we should advance ourselves
To look with forehead bold and big enough
Upon the power and puissance° of the King.

10 *Hastings.* Our present musters grow upon the file°
To five-and-twenty thousand men of choice;
And our supplies° live largely in the hope
Of great Northumberland, whose bosom burns
With an incensèd fire of injuries.

Lord Bardolph. The question then, Lord Hastings,
15   standeth thus:
Whether our present five-and-twenty thousand
May hold up head without Northumberland?

Hastings. With him, we may.

Lord Bardolph.   Yea, marry,° there's the point.
But if without him we be thought too feeble,
20   My judgment is, we should not step too far
Till we had his assistance by the hand.

I.iii.5 **allow the occasion** approve the cause 9 **puissance** strength
10 **file** catalog 12 **supplies** reinforcements 18 **marry** by the Virgin
Mary (a mild oath)

For in a theme so bloody-faced as this,
Conjecture, expectation, and surmise
Of aids incertain should not be admitted.

Archbishop. 'Tis very true, Lord Bardolph, for indeed   25
It was young Hotspur's case at Shrewsbury.

Lord Bardolph. It was, my lord, who lined° himself
with hope,
Eating the air and promise of supply,
Flatt'ring himself in project of a power
Much smaller than° the smallest of his thoughts,   30
And so, with great imagination
Proper to madmen, led his powers to death
And, winking,° leaped into destruction.

Hastings. But, by your leave, it never yet did hurt
To lay down likelihoods and forms of hope   35

Lord Bardolph. Yes, if this present quality of war.°
Indeed the instant action, a cause on foot,
Lives so in hope as in an early spring
We see th' appearing buds, which to prove fruit,
Hope gives not so much warrant as despair°   40
That frosts will bite them. When we mean to build,
We first survey the plot, then draw the model.°
And when we see the figure° of the house,
Then must we rate the cost of the erection,
Which if we find outweighs ability,   45
What do we then but draw anew the model
In fewer offices,° or at least° desist
To build at all? Much more, in this great work,
Which is almost to pluck a kingdom down
And set another up, should we survey   50
The plot of situation and the model,

27 **lined** reinforced (as in tailoring)   29–30 **in project . . . smaller than** in planning on the basis of an army that in fact was much smaller than   33 **winking** shutting his eyes   36 **Yes . . . war.** (a famous obscurity, perhaps saying: Yes, it does do hurt to plan if this planning present [i.e., represent, substitute for] quality [i.e., true substance, strength] of war)   40 **despair** (supply: "gives warrant")   42 **model** plan   43 **figure** design   47 **offices** rooms for service   47 **least** worst

Consent° upon a sure foundation,
Question surveyors, know our own estate,
How able such a work to undergo,
33 To weigh against his opposite.° Or else
We fortify in paper and in figures,
Using the names of men instead of men,
Like one that draws the model of an house
Beyond his power to build it, who, half through,
60 Gives o'er and leaves his part-created cost°
A naked subject to the weeping clouds
And waste for churlish winter's tyranny.

Hastings. Grant that our hopes, yet likely of fair birth,
Should be stillborn, and that we now possessed
65 The utmost man of expectation,
I think we are so, body strong enough
Even as we are, to equal with the King.

Lord Bardolph. What, is the King but five-and-twenty
thousand?

Hastings. To us no more, nay, not so much, Lord
Bardolph.
70 For his divisions, as the times do brawl,
Are in three heads: one power against the French,
And one against Glendower, perforce a third
Must take up us. So is the unfirm king
In three divided, and his coffers sound
75 With hollow poverty and emptiness.

Archbishop. That he should draw his several° strengths
together
And come against us in full puissance°
Need not to be dreaded.

Hastings.   If he should do so,
He leaves his back unarmed, the French and
Welsh
80 Baying him at the heels. Never fear that.

---

52 **Consent** agree 55 **his opposite** its opposition 60 **part-created
cost** half-realized expenditure 76 **several** separate 77 **puissance**
power

Lord Bardolph. Who is it like° should lead his forces
   hither?

Hastings. The Duke of Lancaster and Westmoreland.
   Against the Welsh, himself and Harry Monmouth.
   But who is substituted against the French,
   I have no certain notice.

Archbishop.   Let us on,   85
   And publish the occasion of our arms.
   The commonwealth is sick of their own choice;
   Their overgreedy love hath surfeited.
   An habitation giddy and unsure
   Hath he that buildeth on the vulgar heart.   90
   O thou fond many,° with what loud applause
   Didst thou beat° heaven with blessing Bolingbroke,
   Before he was what thou wouldst have him be!
   And being now trimmed° in thine own desires,
   Thou, beastly feeder, art so full of him   95
   That thou provok'st thyself to cast him up.
   So, so, thou common dog, didst thou disgorge
   Thy glutton bosom of the royal Richard;
   And now thou° wouldst eat thy dead vomit up,
   And howl'st to find it. What trust is in these times?   100
   They that when Richard lived would have him die
   Are now become enamored on his grave.
   Thou° that threw'st dust upon his goodly head
   When through proud London he came sighing on
   After th' admired heels of Bolingbroke   105
   Criest now, "O earth, yield us that king again,
   And take thou this!" O thoughts of men accursed!
   "Past and to come seems best, things present
      worst."°

Mowbray. Shall we go draw our numbers° and set on?

Hastings. We are time's subjects, and time bids be
   gone.   *Exeunt.*   110

81 **like** likely   91 **fond many** foolish multitude   92 **beat** assault
(with noise or prayer)   94 **trimmed** dressed   99 **thou** the multitude
(compared to a dog, as described in Proverbs 16:11)   103 **Thou** the
multitude   108 **Past . . . worst** (proverbial)   109 **draw our numbers**
assemble our troops

[ACT II

Scene I. *London.*]

*Enter Hostess of the Tavern and an Officer or
two [Fang and another, followed by Snare].*

Hostess. Master Fang, have you ent'red the action?°

Fang. It is ent'red.

Hostess. Where's your yeoman?° Is't a lusty yeoman?
Will 'a stand to't?°

5 *Fang.* Sirrah—where's Snare?°

Hostess. O Lord, ay! Good Master Snare!

Snare. Here, here.

Fang. Snare, we must arrest Sir John Falstaff.

Hostess. Yea, good Master Snare, I have ent'red him
10 and all.

Snare. It may chance cost some of us our lives, for he
will stab.

Hostess. Alas the day! Take heed of him. He stabbed
me in mine own house, and that most beastly. In
15 good faith, 'a cares not what mischief he does, if
his weapon be out. He will foin° like any devil; he
will spare neither man, woman, nor child.

II.i.1 **ent'red the action** filed the lawsuit (with a ribald second meaning) 3 **yeoman** assistant (i.e., constable) 4 **stand to't** not collapse in the face of danger (with a ribald second meaning) 5 **Snare** (evidently hanging back) 16 **foin** thrust (with, again, a second meaning)

68

Fang. If I can close with him, I care not for his thrust.

Hostess. No, nor I neither. I'll be at your elbow.

Fang. And I but fist him once, and 'a come but within   20
my vice°—

Hostess. I am undone by his going. I warrant you, he's
an infinitive° thing upon my score.° Good Master
Fang, hold him sure. Good Master Snare, let him
not 'scape. 'A comes continuantly° to Pie Corner°   25
—saving° your manhoods—to buy a saddle; and he
is indited° to dinner to the Lubber's Head° in Lum-
bert° Street, to Master Smooth's the silkman. I
pray you, since my exion° is ent'red and my case
so openly known to the world, let him be brought   30
in to his answer. A hundred mark is a long one for
a poor lone woman to bear, and I have borne,°
and borne, and borne, and have been fubbed off,°
and fubbed off, and fubbed off, from this day to
that day, that it is a shame to be thought on. There   35
is no honesty in such dealing, unless a woman
should be made an ass and a beast, to bear every
knave's wrong. Yonder he comes, and that arrant
malmsey-nose° knave, Bardolph, with him. Do your
offices, do your offices. Master Fang and Master   40
Snare, do me, do me, do me your offices.

Enter Sir John and Bardolph, and the Boy.

Falstaff. How now! Whose mare's dead?° What's the
matter?

Fang. Sir John, I arrest you at the suit of Mistress
Quickly.   45

21 **vice** grip   23 **infinitive** infinite   23 **score** account at the tavern
25 **continuantly** a mix-up of "continually" and "incontinently" (Mistress Quickly speaks in a stream of malapropisms, many with indecent second meanings)   25 **Pie Corner** the cooks' quarter (with
an indecent pun)   26 **saving** no offense meant to   27 **indited** i.e., in-
vited   27 **Lubber's Head** Libbard's (i.e., Leopard's) Head   27–28
Lumbert Lombard   29 **exion** i.e., action   32 **borne** endured (with a
second, ribald sense)   33 **fubbed off** put off   39 **malmsey-nose** nose
reddened from winebibbing   42 **Whose mare's dead?** what's all the
commotion?

Falstaff. Away, varlets! Draw, Bardolph! Cut me off⸱
the villain's head. Throw the quean° in the channel.°

Hostess. Throw me in the channel! I'll throw thee in
30   the channel. Wilt thou? Wilt thou? Thou bastardly°
rogue! Murder, murder! Ah, thou honeysuckle° villain! Wilt thou kill God's officers and the King's?
Ah, thou honeyseed° rogue! Thou art a honeyseed,
a man-queller,° and a woman-queller.

35 *Falstaff.* Keep them off, Bardolph.

Fang. A rescue!° A rescue!

Hostess. Good people, bring a rescue or two. Thou
wo't, wo't thou? Thou wo't, wo't ta? Do, do, thou
rogue! Do, thou hempseed!°

60 *Page.* Away, you scullion!° You rampallian!° You
fustilarian!° I'll tickle your catastrophe.°

Enter Lord Chief Justice and his Men.

Chief Justice. What is the matter? Keep the peace
here, ho!

Hostess. Good my lord, be good to me. I beseech
65   you, stand to me.°

Chief Justice. How now, Sir John! What are you
brawling here?
Doth this become your place, your time and business?
You should have been well on your way to York.
Stand from him, fellow. Wherefore hang'st thou
upon him?

---

47 **quean** scold   47–48 **channel** gutter   50 **bastardly** mixing "das-
tardly" and "bastard" (1) illegitimate (2) a sweetened wine   51 **hon-
eysuckle** i.e., homicidal   53 **honeyseed** i.e., homicide   54 **man-queller** i.e., man-killer   56 **rescue** forcible taking of persons out of legal
custody   59 **hempseed** a child destined for the gallows (but also
homicide, as in line 53—Mistress Quickly is referring to the Page)
60 **scullion** kitchen wench   60 **rampallian** rampant whore   61 **fustilarian** (derived from "fustilugs," a frowsy, fat woman)   61 **catastrophe** ending   65 **stand to me** be firm for me (with a second sense)

Hostess. O my most worshipful lord, and't please your   70
Grace, I am a poor widow of Eastcheap, and he is
arrested at my suit.

Chief Justice. For what sum?

Hostess. It is more than for some, my lord, it is for
all I have. He hath eaten me out of house and   75
home; he hath put all my substance into that fat
belly of his. But I will have some of it out again,
or I will ride thee o' nights like the mare.°

Falstaff. I think I am as like to ride the mare,° if I
have any vantage of ground° to get up.   80

Chief Justice. How comes this, Sir John? What man
of good temper would endure this tempest of exclamation? Are you not ashamed to enforce a poor
widow to so rough a course to come by her own?

Falstaff. What is the gross sum that I owe thee?   85

Hostess. Marry, if thou wert an honest man, thyself
and the money too. Thou didst swear to me upon a
parcel-gilt° goblet, sitting in my Dolphin° chamber,
at the round table, by a sea-coal fire, upon Wednesday in Wheeson° week, when the Prince broke   90
thy head for liking° his father to a singing-man of
Windsor, thou didst swear to me then, as I was
washing thy wound, to marry me and make me my
lady thy wife. Canst thou deny it? Did not good-
wife Keech, the butcher's wife, come in then and   95
call me gossip° Quickly? Coming in to borrow a
mess of vinegar, telling us she had a good dish of
prawns,° whereby thou didst desire to eat some,
whereby I told thee they were ill for a green°
wound? And didst thou not, when she was gone   100
downstairs, desire me to be no more so familiarity

78 **mare** nightmare   79 **mare** female (but also the "two-legged
mare," i.e., the gallows)   80 **vantage of ground** advantage of higher
ground   88 **parcel-gilt** partly gilded   88 **Dolphin** i.e., the sign marking the room   90 **Wheeson** Whitsun   91 **liking** likening   96 **gossip**
friend (a common form of address)   98 **prawns** shrimp   99 **green**
new

with such poor people, saying that ere long they
should call me "Madam"? And didst thou not kiss
me and bid me fetch thee thirty shillings? I put thee
105 now to thy book-oath. Deny it, if thou canst.

Falstaff. My lord, this is a poor mad soul, and she
says up and down the town that her eldest son is
like you. She hath been in good case,° and the
truth is, poverty hath distracted her.° But for these
110 foolish officers, I beseech you I may have redress
against them.

Chief Justice. Sir John, Sir John, I am well acquainted
with your manner of wrenching the true cause the
false way. It is not a confident brow, nor the throng
115 of words that come with such more than impudent
sauciness from you, can thrust me from a level°
consideration. You have, as it appears to me, practiced upon° the easy-yielding spirit of this woman,
and made her serve your uses both in purse and in
120 person.

Hostess. Yea, in truth, my lord.

Chief Justice. Pray thee, peace. Pay her the debt you
owe her and unpay the villainy you have done with
her. The one you may do with sterling money, and
125 the other with current° repentance.

Falstaff. My lord, I will not undergo this sneap° without reply. You call honorable boldness impudent
sauciness. If a man will make curtsy and say nothing, he is virtuous. No, my lord, my humble duty
130 remeb'red, I will not be your suitor. I say to you,
I do desire deliverance from these officers, being
upon hasty employment in the King's affairs.

Chief Justice. You speak as having power to do
wrong. But answer in th' effect of° your reputation,
135 and satisfy the poor woman.

108 case situation, i.e., well-to-do   109 distracted her driven her mad
116 level straight   117–18 practiced upon deceived   125 current
(1) progressive (2) opposite of counterfeit   126 sneap snub   134 in
th' effect of so as to fulfill

Falstaff. Come hither, hostess.

Enter a Messenger [Gower].

Chief Justice. Now, Master Gower, what news?

Gower. The King, my lord, and Harry Prince of Wales
Are near at hand. The rest the paper tells.
                                        [They draw aside.]

Falstaff. [*To Hostess*] As I am a gentleman!   140

Hostess. Faith, you said so before.

Falstaff. As I am a gentleman, come, no more words
of it.

Hostess. By this heavenly ground I tread on, I must
be fain° to pawn both my plate and the tapestry   145
of my dining chambers.

Falstaff. Glasses, glasses, is the only drinking.° And
for thy walls, a pretty slight drollery,° or the story
of the Prodigal, or the German hunting° in waterwork,° is worth a thousand of these bed-hangers°   150
and these fly-bitten tapestries. Let it be ten
pound, if thou canst. Come, and 'twere not for thy
humors,° there's not a better wench in England.
Go, wash thy face, and draw° the action. Come,
thou must not be in this humor with me. Dost not   155
know me? Come, come, I know thou wast set on to
this.

Hostess. Pray thee, Sir John, let it be but twenty nobles.° I' faith, I am loath to pawn my plate, so God
save me, la!
                                                    160

Falstaff. Let it alone; I'll make other shift. You'll be
a fool still.°

---

145 **fain** obliged   147 **glasses, is the only drinking** i.e., glasses are in
fashion now, not metal tankards   148 **drollery** comic picture   149
German hunting hunting the boar   149–50 **waterwork** imitation
tapestry   150 **bed-hangers** bed-curtains   153 **humors** (1) whims (2)
general character   154 **draw** withdraw   158–59 **nobles** coins worth
six shillings eight. pence   161–62 **be a fool still** always lose your
chance

Hostess. Well, you shall have it, though I pawn my
    gown. I hope you'll come to supper. You'll pay me
165 all together?

Falstaff. Will I live? [*To Bardolph*] Go, with her, with
    her. Hook on,° hook on!

Hostess. Will you have Doll Tearsheet meet you at
    supper?

170 *Falstaff.* No more words. Let's have her.
                            Exit Hostess and Sergeant
                            [*Fang, Bardolph and others*].

Chief Justice. [*To Gower*] I have heard better news.

Falstaff. What's the news, my lord?

Chief Justice. [*Ignoring Falstaff*] Where lay the King
    tonight?°

175 *Gower.* At Basingstoke, my lord.

Falstaff. I hope, my lord, all's well. What is the news,
    my lord?

Chief Justice. Come all his forces back?

Gower. No. Fifteen hundred foot, five hundred horse,
180 Are marched up to my Lord of Lancaster,
    Against Northumberland and the Archbishop.

Falstaff. Comes the King back from Wales, my noble
    lord?

Chief Justice. [*To his men*] You shall have letters of
    me presently.
185 Come, go along with me, good Master Gower.

Falstaff. My lord!

Chief Justice. What's the matter?

Falstaff. Master Gower, shall I entreat you with me to
    dinner?

167 **Hook on** stick to her   174 **tonight** last night

Gower. I must wait upon my good lord here, I thank   *190*
you, good Sir John.

Chief Justice. Sir John, you loiter here too long, being
you are to take soldiers up° in counties as you go.

Falstaff. Will you sup with me, Master Gower?

Chief Justice. What foolish master taught you these   *195*
manners, Sir John?

Falstaff. Master Gower, if they become me not, he was
a fool that taught them me. This is the right° fencing grace, my lord—tap for tap, and so part fair.

Chief Justice. Now the Lord lighten° thee! Thou art   *200*
a great fool.   [*Exeunt.*]

[Scene II. *The Prince's house.*]

Enter the Prince [*Henry*], *Poins, with others.*

Prince. Before God, I am exceeding weary.°

Poins. Is't come to that? I had thought weariness durst
not have attached° one of so high blood.

Prince. Faith, it does me, though it discolors the com-
plexion° of my greatness to acknowledge it. Doth   *5*
it not show vilely in me to desire small beer?

Poins. Why, a prince should not be so loosely studied°
as to remember so weak a composition.°

Prince. Belike, then, my appetite was not princely
got,° for, by my troth, I do now remember the   *10*

193 **take soldiers up** recruit men   198 **right** correct   200 **lighten**
(1) enlighten (2) make [you] weigh less   II.ii.1 **weary** (having just
ridden from Wales)   3 **attached** arrested   4–5 **discolors the com-**
plexion causes a blush   7 **loosely studied** carelessly or wantonly applied   8 **so weak a composition** so unstable and trivial a compound
(as small beer)   10 **got** begotten

poor creature, small beer. But indeed these humble
considerations make me out of love with my greatness. What a disgrace is it to me to remember thy
name!° Or to know thy face tomorrow! Or to take
15 note how many pair of silk stockings thou hast, viz.
these, and those that were thy peach-colored ones!
Or to bear the inventory of thy shirts, as: one for
superfluity and another for use! But that the tennis-
court-keeper knows better than I; for it is a low
20 ebb of linen with thee when thou keepest not racket
there,° as thou hast not done a great while, because
the rest of thy low countries° have made a shift° to
eat up thy holland.° And God knows whether those
that bawl out the ruins of thy linen shall inherit
25 His kingdom. But the midwives say the children are
not in the fault,° whereupon the world increases,
and kindreds° are mightily strengthened.

Poins. How ill it follows, after you have labored so
hard, you should talk so idly! Tell me, how many
30 good young princes would do so, their fathers being
so sick as yours at this time is?

Prince. Shall I tell thee one thing, Poins?

Poins. Yes, faith, and let it be an excellent good thing

Prince. It shall serve among wits of no higher breeding
35 than thine.

Poins. Go to. I stand the push° of your one thing that
you will tell.

Prince. Marry, I tell thee, it is not meet° that I should
be sad, now my father is sick. Albeit I could tell to
40 thee, as to one it pleases me, for fault of a better,

13–14 **disgrace . . . remember thy name** i.e., unlike "graceful"
courtiers who affect to forget the names of their inferiors 19–21 **it
is . . . racket there** i.e., if you have as many as two shirts, one to play
in, a second to change into, you frequent the tennis courts 22 **low
countries** Netherlands (with an obscene pun) 22 **shift** (1) con-
trivance (2) shirt 23 **holland** linen made in Holland 26 **in the fault**
share the sin (of their illegitimacy, with a pun on French, *foutre* =
to copulate) 27 **kindreds** clans 36 **push** thrust 38 **meet** fitting

to call my friend, I could be sad, and sad indeed, too.

Poins. Very hardly° upon such a subject.

Prince. By this hand, thou thinkest me as far in the devil's book as thou and Falstaff for obduracy and 45 persistency. Let the end° try the man. But I tell thee, my heart bleeds inwardly that my father is so sick. And keeping such vile company as thou art hath in reason taken from me all ostentation° of 50 sorrow.

Poins. The reason?

Prince. What wouldst thou think of me if I should weep?

Poins. I would think thee a most princely hypocrite.

Prince. It would be every man's thought, and thou art 55 a blessed fellow to think as every man thinks. Never a man's thought in the world keeps the roadway better than thine. Every man would think me an hypocrite indeed. And what accites° your most worshipful thought to think so? 60

Poins. Why, because you have been so lewd and so much engraffed° to Falstaff.

Prince. And to thee.

Poins. By this light, I am well spoke on; I can hear it with mine own ears. The worst that they can say 65 of me is that I am a second brother° and that I am a proper fellow of my hands,° and those two things I confess I cannot help. By the mass, here comes Bardolph.

Enter Bardolph and Boy [Page].

43 **Very hardly** with great difficulty   46 **end** outcome   49 **ostentation** show   59 **accites** summons (a judicial term)   62 **engraffed** grafted (like a plant)   66 **a second brother** i.e., one who inherits nothing   67 **proper fellow of my hands** skillful with my hands as a fighter (or as a thief?)

70   *Prince.* And the boy that I gave Falstaff. 'A had him
       from me Christian, and look if the fat villain have
       not transformed him ape.°

     Bardolph. God save your Grace.

     Prince. And yours, most noble Bardolph.

75   *Poins.* Come, you virtuous ass, you bashful fool, must
       you be blushing?° Wherefore blush you now? What
       a maidenly man-at-arms are you become! Is't such
       a matter to get a pottle-pot's° maidenhead?

     Page. 'A calls me e'en now, my lord, through a red
80   lattice,° and I could discern no part of his face
       from the window. At last I spied his eyes, and me-
       thought he had made two holes in the ale-wife's
       petticoat and so peeped through.

     Prince. Has not the boy profited?°

85   *Bardolph.* Away, you whoreson upright rabbit, away!

     Page. Away, you rascally Althaea's dream,° away!

     Prince. Instruct us, boy. What dream, boy?

     Page. Marry, my lord, Althaea dreamed she was de-
       livered of a firebrand, and therefore I call him her
90   dream.

     Prince. A crown's worth of good interpretation. There
       'tis, boy. [*Tips him.*]

     Poins. O, that this blossom could be kept from
       cankers!° Well, there is sixpence to preserve° thee.

95   *Bardolph.* And you do not make him hanged among
       you, the gallows shall have wrong.

---

72 **transformed him ape** dressed him fantastically   76 **blushing** red-
faced (from drinking)   78 **pottle-pot** two-quart tankard   79–80 **red
lattice** (such a window was the sign of an alehouse)   84 **profited** i.e.,
from his association with Falstaff   86 **Althaea's dream** (the dream
he describes in lines 88–90 was actually Hecuba's. The Fates told
Althaea her son would live only as long as a log on the fire remained
unconsumed. Perhaps the boy has not "profited" as much as the
Prince thought)   94 **cankers** plant-destroying worms   94 **preserve**
i.e., because Elizabethan coins bore crosses

Prince. And how doth thy master, Bardolph?

Bardolph. Well, my lord. He heard of your Grace's coming to town. There's a letter for you.

Poins. Delivered with good respect. And how doth the 100 martlemas,° your master?

Bardolph. In bodily health, sir.

Poins. Marry, the immortal part needs a physician, but that moves not him. Though that be sick, it dies not. 105

Prince. I do allow this wen° to be as familiar with me as my dog, and he holds his place, for look you how he writes.

Poins. [*Reads*] "John Falstaff, knight"——every man must know that, as oft as he has occasion to name 110 himself. Even like those that are kin to the King, for they never prick their finger but they say, "There's some of the King's blood spilt." "How comes that?" says he that takes upon him not to conceive. The answer is as ready as a borrowed cap,° "I am the 115 King's poor cousin, sir."

Prince. Nay, they will be kin to us, or they will fetch it from Japhet.° But the letter. [*Reads*] "Sir John Falstaff, knight, to the son of the King nearest his father, Harry Prince of Wales, greeting." 120

Poins. Why, this is a certificate.°

Prince. Peace! [*Reads*] "I will imitate the honorable Romans in brevity."

Poins. He sure means brevity in breath, short-winded.

[*Prince reads.*] "I commend me to thee, I commend 125 thee, and I leave thee. Be not too familiar with

101 **martlemas** i.e., a beef fattened for slaughter before winter on Martinmas Day (November 11); see pp. 208–09　106 **wen** swelling　115 **borrowed cap** (which the borrower promptly tips)　117–18 **fetch it from Japhet** i.e., fetch their ancestry from that one of Noah's sons whose offspring peopled Europe　121 **certificate** patent (in formal style)

Poins, for he misuses thy favors so much that he
swears thou art to marry his sister Nell. Repent at
idle times as thou mayst, and so farewell.

130   "Thine, by yea and no, which is as much as to
say, as thou usest him, JACK FALSTAFF with
my familiars, JOHN with my brothers and sisters, and SIR JOHN with all Europe."

Poins. My lord, I'll steep this letter in sack and make
135   him eat it.

Prince. That's to make him eat twenty of his words.
But do you use me thus, Ned? Must I marry your
sister?

Poins. God send the wench no worse fortune! But I
140   never said so.

Prince. Well, thus we play the fools with the time, and
the spirits of the wise sit in the clouds and mock
us. Is your master here in London?

Bardolph. Yea, my lord.

145 *Prince.* Where sups he? Doth the old boar feed in the
old frank?°

Bardolph. At the old place, my lord, in Eastcheap.

Prince. What company?

Page. Ephesians, my lord, of the old church.°

150 *Prince.* Sup any women with him?

Page. None, my lord, but old Mistress Quickly and
Mistress Doll Tearsheet.

Prince. What pagan° may that be?

Page. A proper gentlewoman, sir, and a kinswoman of
155   my master's.

---

146 **frank** sty (presumably a glance at the famous Boar's Head tavern)
149 **Ephesians . . . church** libertines (who had to be corrected by St.
Paul—Ephesians 5:3–8)   153 **pagan** prostitute (love-worshipper)

Prince. Even such kin as the parish heifers are to the
    town bull. Shall we steal upon them, Ned, at sup-
    per?

Poins. I am your shadow, my lord; I'll follow you.

Prince. Sirrah,° you boy, and Bardolph, no word to   160
    your master that I am yet come to town. There's
    for your silence. [*Tips them.*]

Bardolph. I have no tongue, sir.

Page. And for mine, sir, I will govern it.

Prince. Fare you well; go. [*Exeunt Bardolph and*   165
    Page.] This Doll Tearsheet should be some road.°

Poins. I warrant you, as common as the way between
    Saint Alban's and London.

Prince. How might we see Falstaff bestow himself to-
    night in his true colors, and not ourselves be seen?   170

Poins. Put on two leathern jerkins° and aprons, and
    wait upon him at his table as drawers.°

Prince. From a God to a bull? A heavy descension!
    It was Jove's case.° From a prince to a prentice?
    A low transformation! That shall be mine, for in   175
    everything the purpose must weigh with° the folly.
    Follow me, Ned.   *Exeunt.*

---

160 **Sirrah** (form of address to an inferior)   166 **road** prostitute (one
to be ridden, open to all)   171 **jerkins** jackets   172 **drawers** tavern
waiters   174 **Jove's case** (he transformed himself into a bull to
seduce Europa)   176 **weigh with** match

[Scene III. *Northumberland's castle.*]

*Enter Northumberland, his Wife [Lady Northumber-
land], and the Wife to Harry Percy [Lady Percy].*

Northumberland. I pray thee, loving wife, and gentle
    daughter,°
    Give even way° unto my rough affairs.
    Put not you on the visage of the times
    And be like them to Percy° troublesome.

Lady Northumberland. I have given over; I will speak
5   no more.
    Do what you will, your wisdom be your guide.

Northumberland. Alas, sweet wife, my honor is at
    pawn,
    And, but° my going, nothing can redeem it.

Lady Percy. O yet, for God's sake, go not to these
    wars!
10   The time was, father, that you broke your word,
    When you were more endeared to it than now,
    When your own Percy, when my heart's dear Harry,
    Threw many a northward look to see his father
    Bring up his powers, but he did long in vain.
15   Who then persuaded you to stay at home?
    There were two honors lost, yours and your son's.
    For yours, the God of heaven brighten it!
    For his, it stuck upon him as the sun
    In the gray vault of heaven, and by his light
20   Did all the chivalry of England move
    To do brave acts. He was indeed the glass°
    Wherein the noble youth did dress themselves.

II.iii.1 **daughter** daughter-in-law 2 **Give even way** allow free pas-
sage 4 **Percy** i.e., Northumberland, "the Percy" 8 **but** except for
21 **glass** looking glass

He° had no legs that practiced not his° gait;
And speaking thick,° which nature made his blem-
   ish,
Became the accents of the valiant,   25
For those that could speak low and tardily
Would turn their own perfection to abuse,
To seem like him. So that in speech, in gait,
In diet, in affections of delight,°
In military rules, humors of blood,°   30
He was the mark and glass, copy and book,
That fashioned others. And him! O wondrous! Him!
O miracle of men! Him did you leave,
Second to none, unseconded by you,
To look upon the hideous god of war   35
In disadvantage, to abide a field°
Where nothing but the sound of Hotspur's name
Did seem defensible. So you left him.
Never, O never, do his ghost the wrong
To hold your honor more precise and nice°   40
With others than with him! Let them alone.
The Marshal and the Archbishop are strong.
Had my sweet Harry had but half their numbers,
Today might I, hanging on Hotspur's neck,
Have talked of Monmouth's° grave.

Northumberland.   Beshrew° your heart,   45
Fair daughter, you do draw my spirits from me
With new lamenting ancient oversights.
But I must go and meet with danger there,
Or it will seek me in another place
And find me worse provided.

Lady Northumberland.   O, fly to Scotland,°   50
Till that the nobles and the armèd commons
Have of their puissance° made a little taste.

---

23 He i.e., any man   23 his i.e., Harry Percy's   24 thick fast
(crowding the words)   29 affections of delight preferences in pleasure   30 humors of blood disposition   36 abide a field endure on a
battlefield   40 nice punctilious   45 Monmouth's Prince Hal's   45
Beshrew cursed be   50 Scotland i.e., far from the battle   52 puissance strength

Lady Percy. If they get ground and vantage of the
    King,
    Then join you with them, like a rib of steel,
55   To make strength stronger. But, for all our loves,
    First let them try themselves. So did your son;
    He was so suff'red.° So came I a widow,
    And never shall have length of life enough
    To rain° upon remembrance with mine eyes,
60   That it may grow and sprout as high as heaven,
    For recordation° to my noble husband.

Northumberland. Come, come, go in with me. 'Tis
    with my mind
    As with the tide swelled up unto his height,
    That makes a still-stand, running neither way.
65   Fain would I go to meet the Archbishop,
    But many thousand reasons hold me back.
    I will resolve for Scotland. There am I,
    Till time and vantage° crave my company.

                   Exeunt.

[Scene IV. *Mistress Quickly's tavern.*]

Enter a Drawer or two [*Francis and another*].

Francis. What the devil hast thou brought there?
    Apple-johns?° Thou knowest Sir John cannot en-
    dure an apple-john.

Drawer. Mass, thou say'st true. The Prince once set
3   a dish of apple-johns before him, and told him
    there were five more Sir Johns, and, putting off his
    hat, said, "I will now take my leave of these six

57 **suff'red** allowed (to fight alone) 59 **rain** drop tears 61 **record-
ation** memorial 68 **vantage** profitable opportunity II.iv.2 **Apple-
johns** (apples ripened on St. John's Day, midsummer, but eaten two
years later when withered—perhaps they remind Sir John of age or
impotency)

dry, round, old, withered knights." It ang'red him
to the heart. But he hath forgot that.

Francis. Why, then, cover,° and set them down. And   10
see if thou canst find out Sneak's noise.° Mistress
Tearsheet would fain hear some music.

Enter Will [a third Drawer].

Will. Dispatch! The room where they supped is too
hot. They'll come in straight.

Francis. Sirrah, here will be the Prince and Master   15
Poins anon, and they will put on two of our jerkins
and aprons, and Sir John must not know of it.
Bardolph hath brought word.

Drawer. By the mass, here will be old Utis.° It will
be an excellent stratagem.   20

Francis. I'll see if I can find out Sneak.   *Exit.*

*Enter Mistress Quickly [the Hostess] and
Doll Tearsheet.*

Hostess. I' faith, sweetheart, methinks now you are in
an excellent good temperality.° Your pulsidge°
beats as extraordinarily as heart would desire, and
your color, I warrant you, is as red as any rose, in   25
good truth, la! But, i' faith, you have drunk too
much canaries,° and that's a marvelous searching
wine, and it perfumes the blood ere one can say,
"What's this?" How do you now?

Doll. Better than I was. Hem!   30

Hostess. Why, that's well said. A good heart's worth
gold. Lo, here comes Sir John.

Enter Sir John [Falstaff].

Falstaff. [Sings] "When Arthur first in court"°—

10 **cover** spread the tablecloth · 11 **noise** band of musicians   19 **old
Utis** grand festival (*utaves* was the eighth day or "octave" of a feast)
23 **temperality** i.e., temper or temperance   23 **pulsidge** i.e., pulse
27 **canaries** Canary wine   33 **When Arthur first in court** (first line of
a ballad)

Empty the jordan!°—"And was a worthy king."—
35 How now, Mistress Doll!

Hostess. Sick of a calm,° yea, good faith.

Falstaff. So is all her sect.° And they be once in a
calm, they are sick.

Doll. A pox damn you, you muddy° rascal, is that all
40 the comfort you give me?

Falstaff. You make fat rascals,° Mistress Doll.

Doll. I make them? Gluttony and diseases make, I
make them not.

Falstaff. If the cook help to make the gluttony, you
45 help to make the diseases, Doll. We catch of you,
Doll, we catch of you. Grant that, my poor virtue,
grant that.

Doll. Yea, joy, our chains and our jewels.

Falstaff. "Your brooches, pearls, and ouches."° For
50 to serve bravely is to come halting off, you know.
To come off the breach with his pike bent bravely,
and to surgery bravely; to venture upon the charged
chambers° bravely—

Doll. Hang yourself, you muddy conger,° hang your-
55 self!

Hostess. By my troth, this is the old fashion. You
two never meet but you fall to some discord. You
are both, i' good truth, as rheumatic° as two dry
toasts.° You cannot one bear with another's con-

---

34 **jordan** chamber pot   36 **calm** i.e., qualm   37 **sect** prostitutes
(love-worshippers)   39 **muddy** filthy   41 **You make fat rascals** (a
rascal was a lean deer—you say or cause the lean to fat, i.e., become
bloated or to sweat as a cure for the pox)   49 **Your brooches, pearls,
and ouches** (another scrap of ballad; "ouches" are both brooches
and scabs)   52–53 **charged chambers** loaded cannon (used, like
other words in this speech, with a bawdy second meaning)   54 **conger** eel   58 **rheumatic** (she means splenetic or choleric, the hot and
dry humor—like toast)   58–59 **dry toasts** (that would scratch one
another)

firmities.° What the goodyear!° One must bear,°   60
and that must be you [*to Doll*]. You are the weaker
vessel, as they say, the emptier vessel.

Doll. Can a weak empty vessel bear such a huge full
hogshead? There's a whole merchant's venture of
Bordeaux stuff° in him. You have not seen a hulk   65
better stuffed in the hold. Come, I'll be friends
with thee, Jack. Thou art going to the wars, and
whether I shall ever see thee again or no, there is
nobody cares.

Enter Drawer.

Drawer. Sir, Ancient° Pistol's below and would speak   70
with you.

Doll. Hang him, swaggering° rascal! Let him not
come hither. It is the foul-mouthed'st rogue in
England.

Hostess. If he swagger, let him not come here. No, by   75
my faith. I must live among my neighbors. I'll no
swaggerers. I am in good name and fame with the
very best. Shut the door, there comes no swaggerers
here. I have not lived all this while to have swaggering now. Shut the door, I pray you.   80

Falstaff. Dost thou hear, hostess?

Hostess. Pray ye, pacify yourself, Sir John. There
comes no swaggerers here.

Falstaff. Dost thou hear? It is mine Ancient.

Hostess. Tilly-fally, Sir John, ne'er tell me. And your   85
ancient swagg'rer comes not in my doors. I was
before Master Tisick,° the debuty, t' other day,
and, as he said to me, 'twas no longer ago than
Wednesday last, "I' good faith, neighbor Quickly,"

59–60 **confirmities** i.e., infirmities   60 **What the goodyear!** what the
plague!   60 **bear** (1) endure (2) support   64–65 **merchant's venture
of Bordeaux stuff** shipload of wine   70 **Ancient** ensign, standard-
bearer   72 **swaggering** blustering   87 **Tisick** phthisic, consumption
(?)

90 says he—Master Dumbe, our minister, was by then
    —"neighbor Quickly," says he, "receive those that
    are civil, for," said he, "you are in an ill name."
    Now 'a said so, I can tell whereupon. "For," says
    he, "you are an honest woman, and well thought
95 on; therefore take heed what guests you receive.
    Receive," says he, "no swaggering companions."°
    There comes none here. You would bless you to
    hear what he said. No, I'll no swagg'rers.

Falstaff. He's no swagg'rer, hostess, a tame cheater,°
100 i' faith. You may stroke him as gently as a puppy
    greyhound. He'll not swagger with a Barbary hen,°
    if her feathers turn back in any show of resistance.
    Call him up, drawer.   [*Exit Drawer.*]

Hostess. Cheater, call you him? I will bar no honest
105 man my house, nor no cheater. But I do not love
    swaggering, by my troth. I am the worse when one
    says "swagger." Feel, masters, how I shake, look
    you, I warrant you.

Doll. So you do, hostess.

110 *Hostess.* Do I? Yea, in very truth, do I, and 'twere
    an aspen leaf. I cannot abide swagg'rers.

    *Enter Ancient Pistol, [Bardolph], and Bardolph's
    Boy [Page].*

Pistol. God save you, Sir John!

Falstaff. Welcome, Ancient Pistol.° Here, Pistol, I
    charge° you with a cup of sack. Do you discharge°
115 upon mine hostess.

Pistol. I will discharge upon her, Sir John, with two
    bullets.°

---

96 **companions** fellows   99 **cheater** cardsharper's decoy   101 **Barbary hen** guinea hen (whose feathers are already ruffled; also, a prostitute)   113 **Pistol** (pronounced almost like "pizzle" [= penis] hence leading to this series of obscene puns)   114 **charge** (1) toast (2) load (a pistol)   114 **discharge** go off (i.e., sound a return toast, explode like a pistol—or sexually)   117 **bullets** (an indecency)

Falstaff. She is pistol-proof, sir; you shall not hardily°
offend her.

Hostess. Come, I'll drink no proofs nor no bullets. 120
I'll drink no more than will do me good, for no
man's pleasure, I.

Pistol. Then to you, Mistress Dorothy; I will charge
you.

Doll. Charge me! I scorn you, scurvy companion. 125
What! You poor, base, rascally, cheating, lack-
linen mate! Away, you moldy rogue, away! I am
meat° for your master.

Pistol. I know you, Mistress Dorothy.

Doll. Away, you cut-purse rascal! You filthy bung,° 130
away! By this wine, I'll thrust my knife in your
moldy chaps,° and you play the saucy cuttle° with
me. Away, you bottle-ale° rascal! You basket-hilt
stale juggler,° you! Since when, I pray you, sir?
God's light, with two points° on your shoulder? 135
Much!

Pistol. God let me not live but I will murder your
ruff° for this.

Falstaff. No more, Pistol; I would not have you go off
here. Discharge yourself of our company, Pistol. 140

Hostess. No, good Captain Pistol, not here, sweet
Captain.

Doll. Captain! Thou abominable damned cheater, art
thou not ashamed to be called Captain? And captains were of my mind, they would truncheon° you 145
out for taking their names upon you before you

---

118 not hardily by no means   **128 meat** flesh   **130 bung** pickpocket
132 chaps cheeks   **132 cuttle** (1) cutthroat (2) cuttlefish (that
spews out a fluid used for sauce)   **133 bottle-ale** cheap (?)   **133–34
basket-hilt stale juggler** doer of sword-tricks with an old-fashioned
sword with hilt shaped like a basket   **135 points** laces for tying on
armor   **137–38 murder your ruff** tear your collar   **145 truncheon**
cudgel

have earned them. You a captain! You slave, for
what? For tearing a poor whore's ruff in a bawdy
house? He a captain! Hang him, rogue! He lives
150 upon moldy stewed prunes° and dried cakes. A
captain! God's light, these villains will make the
word as odious as the word "occupy,"° which was
an excellent good word before it was ill sorted.°
Therefore captains° had need look to't.

155 *Bardolph.* Pray thee, go down, good Ancient.

Falstaff. Hark thee hither, Mistress Doll.

Pistol. Not I! I tell thee what, Corporal Bardolph, I
could tear her! I'll be revenged of her!

Page. Pray thee, go down.

160 *Pistol.* I'll see her damned first, to Pluto's damnèd
lake,° by this hand, to th' infernal deep, with
Erebus° and tortures vile also.° Hold hook and
line,° say I. Down, down, dogs! Down, faitors!°
Have we not Hiren° here?

165 *Hostess.* Good Captain Pizzle, be quiet. 'Tis very late,
i' faith. I beseek you now, aggravate° your choler.

Pistol. These be good humors, indeed! Shall pack-
horses
And hollow pampered jades° of Asia,
Which cannot go but thirty mile a day,
170 Compare with Caesars, and with Cannibals,°
And Trojan Greeks? Nay, rather damn them with

---

150 **stewed prunes** (put in the windows of brothels, "stews," as a sign)
152 **occupy** (had acquired the sense of "fornicate")   153 **ill sorted**
put in bad company   154 **captains** (Falstaff is a captain)   161 **lake**
(he means the river Styx)   162 **Erebus** passageway to Hades   162
and tortures vile also (Pistol begins to rave in his characteristic way,
spewing out garbled scraps from old declamatory plays—or, indeed,
any line that comes to his mind)   162–63 **Hold hook and line** (a
fisherman's cry)   163 **faitors** fates (?)   164 **Hiren** (Pistol applies
this name [Irene] from a play to his sword, punning on "iron")
166 **aggravate** (she means moderate)   168 **jades** nags   170 **Cannibals** (he means Hannibals)

King Cerberus,° and let the welkin° roar.
Shall we fall foul for toys?°

Hostess. By my troth, Captain, these are very bitter
words.   175

Bardolph. Be gone, good Ancient. This will grow to a
brawl anon.

Pistol. Die men like dogs! Give crowns like pins! Have
we not Hiren here?

Hostess. O' my word, Captain, there's none such here.   180
What the goodyear! Do you think I would deny
her?° For God's sake, be quiet.

Pistol. Then feed, and be fat, my fair Calipolis.
Come, give's some sack.
"Si fortune me tormente, sperato me contento."°   185
Fear we broadsides? No, let the fiend give fire.
Give me some sack. And, sweetheart, lie thou there.
                          [*Lays down his sword.*]
Come we to full points° here, and are etceteras°
no things?°

Falstaff. Pistol, I would be quiet.

Pistol. Sweet knight, I kiss thy neaf.° What! We have   190
seen the seven stars.°

Doll. For God's sake, thrust him downstairs. I cannot
endure such a fustian° rascal.

Pistol. Thrust him downstairs! Know we not Galloway nags?°
                                                               195

---

172 **Cerberus** three-headed dog that guarded Hades   172 **welkin** sky
173 **toys** trivia (like Doll)   181–82 **deny her** (the Hostess evidently
thinks Pistol is calling for a special girl)   185 **Si fortune ... contento**
(a garbled proverb—"If fortune torments me, hope contents me")
188 **full points** stops, periods (closed sentences)   188 **etceteras**
(open-ended statements—with an obscene sense)   188 **no things**
(with a second meaning: women who are "naught." The line as a
whole means: Aren't we going to do anything more here?)   190 **kiss
thy neaf** kiss thy fist (a chivalric gesture)   191 **seven stars** the
Pleiades (we have made a night of it)   193 **fustian** cheap cloth or
'alk   194–95 **Galloway nags** small Irish horses (bad to ride)

Falstaff. Quoit° him down, Bardolph, like a shove-
groat shilling.° Nay, and 'a do nothing but speak
nothing, 'a shall be nothing here.

Bardolph. Come, get you downstairs.

Pistol. What! Shall we have incision? Shall we im-
200   brue?°   [*Snatches up his sword.*]
Then death rock me asleep, abridge my doleful
days!
Why, then, let grievous, ghastly, gaping wounds
Untwined the Sisters Three!° Come, Atropos, I
say!

Hostess. Here's goodly stuff toward!

205 *Falstaff.* Give me my rapier, boy.

Doll. I pray thee, Jack, I pray thee, do not draw.

Falstaff. Get you downstairs!
                                    [*Draws, and threatens Pistol.*]

Hostess. Here's a goodly tumult! I'll forswear keeping
house afore I'll be in these tirrits° and frights. So,
210   murder, I warrant now. Alas, alas! Put up your
naked weapons, put up your naked weapons.
          [*Falstaff drives Pistol out, Bardolph following.*]

Doll. I pray thee, Jack, be quiet. The rascal's gone.
Ah, you whoreson little valiant villain, you!

Hostess. Are you not hurt i' th' groin? Methought 'a
215   made a shrewd thrust at your belly.

          [*Enter Bardolph.*]

Falstaff. Have you turned him out o' doors?

Bardolph. Yea, sir. The rascal's drunk. You have hurt
him, sir, i' th' shoulder.

Falstaff. A rascal! To brave° me!

196 **Quoit** pitch (with a pun on "quiet")   196–97 **shove-groat shilling**
coin used in a game like shuffleboard ("shove-ha'penny")   200 **im-
brue** shed blood   203 **Sisters Three** the Fates who spun the thread
of life, cut by the third, Atropos   209 **tirrits** (a blending of terrors
and fits?)   219 **brave** defy

Doll. Ah, you sweet little rogue, you! Alas, poor ape,   220
how thou sweat'st! Come, let me wipe thy face.
Come on, you whoreson chops.° Ah, rogue! I'
faith, I love thee. Thou art as valorous as Hector
of Troy, worth five of Agamemnon, and ten times
better than the Nine Worthies.° Ah, villain!   225

Falstaff. A rascally slave! I will toss the rogue in a
blanket.

Doll. Do, and thou dar'st for thy heart. And thou dost,
I'll canvas° thee between a pair of sheets.

[*Enter Musicians.*]

Page. The music is come, sir.   230

Falstaff. Let them play. Play, sirs. Sit on my knee,
Doll. A rascal bragging slave! The rogue fled from
me like quicksilver.

Doll. I' faith [*aside*] and thou followedst him like a
church. Thou whoreson little tidy Bartholomew   235
boar-pig,° when wilt thou leave fighting o' days and
foining° o' nights, and begin to patch up thine old
body for heaven?

Enter Prince and Poins [disguised].

Falstaff. Peace, good Doll! Do not speak like a
death's-head.° Do not bid me remember mine end.°   240

Doll. Sirrah, what humor's the Prince° of?

Falstaff. A good shallow young fellow. 'A would have
made a good pantler,° 'a would ha' chipped° bread
well.

Doll. They say Poins has a good wit.   245

222 **chops** fat-cheeked man   225 **Nine Worthies** Hector, Alexander,
Julius Caesar, Joshua, David, Judas Maccabaeus, King Arthur,
Charlemagne, Godfrey of Bouillon   229 **canvas** toss (as in a canvas)
235–36 **Bartholomew boar-pig** young male pig fattened as a special
delicacy for the Bartholomew Fair on August 24th at West Smithfield   237 **foining** thrusting (as a sword)   240 **death's-head** figure
of a skull used to remind one of mortality   240 **end** (double sense)
241 **Prince** (Doll may have spied Hal and Poins)   243 **pantler**
pantryworker   243 **chipped** chopped

Falstaff. He a good wit? Hang him, baboon! His wit's
as thick as Tewksbury mustard.° There's no more
conceit° in him than is in a mallet.°

Doll. Why does the Prince love him so, then?

250 *Falstaff.* Because their legs are both of a bigness, and
'a plays at quoits well, and eats conger and fennel,°
and drinks off candles' ends for flap-dragons,° and
rides the wild-mare° with the boys, and jumps upon
joined-stools,° and swears with a good grace, and
255 wears his boots very smooth, like unto the Sign of
the Leg,° and breeds no bate° with telling of dis-
creet stories; and such other gambol° faculties 'a
has, that show a weak mind and an able body, for
the which the Prince admits him. For the Prince
260 himself is such another; the weight of a hair will
turn scales between their avoirdupois.

Prince. Would not this nave° of a wheel have his ears
cut off?

Poins. Let's beat him before his whore.

265 *Prince.* Look, whe'r° the withered elder° hath not his
poll° clawed° like a parrot.

Poins. Is it not strange that desire should so many
years outlive performance?

Falstaff. Kiss me, Doll.

270 *Prince.* Saturn and Venus this year in conjunction!
What says th' almanac to that?

---

247 **Tewksbury mustard** (Tewksbury was famed for good mustard)
248 **conceit** conception   248 **mallet** i.e., a blockhead   251 **conger
and fennel** eel (the eating of which was thought to make one stupid)
dressed or flattered by fennel sauce   252 **flap-dragons** (flaming
raisins were floated on spirit and the players tried to snap them up;
or drink the liquor; here candle ends are used to fool Poins)   253
wild-mare seesaw   254 **joined-stools** carefully carpentered stools
255-56 **Sign of the Leg** sign over a bootmaker's   256 **bate** debate,
quarrel   257 **gambol** playful   262 **nave** (1) fat hub on a cart wheel
(2) pun on "knave"   265 **whe'r** whether   265 **elder** (1) old man (2)
sapless tree   266 **poll** hair   266 **clawed** i.e., by Doll

Poins. And look whether the fiery Trigon,° his man, be not lisping to his master's old tables,° his note-book, his counsel-keeper.

Falstaff. Thou dost give me flattering busses.°   *273*

Doll. By my troth, I kiss thee with a most constant heart.

Falstaff. I am old, I am old.

Doll. I love thee better than I love e'er a scurvy young boy of them all.   *280*

Falstaff. What stuff wilt have a kirtle° of? I shall receive money o' Thursday. Shalt have a cap tomorrow. A merry song, come. 'A grows late; we'll to bed. Thou'lt forget me when I am gone.

Doll. By my troth, thou'lt set me a-weeping, and thou   *285* say'st so. Prove that ever I dress myself handsome till thy return. Well, hearken o' th' end.°

Falstaff. Some sack, Francis.

Prince.
Poins. } Anon, anon, sir.

[*Coming forward.*]

Falstaff. Ha! A bastard son of the King's? And art not   *290* thou Poins his brother?

Prince. Why, thou globe of sinful continents,° what a life dost thou lead!

Falstaff. A better than thou. I am a gentleman, thou art a drawer.   *293*

Prince. Very true, sir, and I come to draw you out by the ears.

272 **fiery Trigon** the conjunction of the three fiery signs of the Zodiac: Aries, Leo, and Sagittarius (in Bardolph's face)   273 **tables** tablet or engagement book (i.e., bawd, Mistress Quickly)   275 **busses** kisses   281 **kirtle** skirt   287 **hearken o' th' end** i.e., see how it turns out   292 **continents** (1) vast land surfaces (2) contents (3) pun on "continence"

Hostess. O, the Lord preserve thy Grace! By my troth,
welcome to London. Now, the Lord bless that sweet
300 face of thine! O Jesu, are you come from Wales?

Falstaff. Thou whoreson mad compound° of majesty,
by this light° flesh and corrupt blood, thou art
welcome.

Doll. How, you fat fool! I scorn you.

305 *Poins.* My lord, he will drive you out of your revenge
and turn all to a merriment, if you take not the
heat.

Prince. You whoreson candle-mine° you, how vilely
did you speak of me now before this honest, virtu-
310 ous, civil gentlewoman!

Hostess. God's blessing of your good heart! And so
she is, by my troth.

Falstaff. Didst thou hear me?

Prince. Yea, and you knew me, as you did when you
315 ran away by Gad's Hill.° You knew I was at your
back, and spoke it on purpose to try my patience.

Falstaff. No, no, no, not so. I did not think thou wast
within hearing.

Prince. I shall drive you then to confess the willful
320 abuse, and then I know how to handle you.

Falstaff. No abuse, Hal, o' mine honor, no abuse.

Prince: Not to dispraise me and call me pantler and
bread-chipper and I know not what?

Falstaff. No abuse, Hal.

325 *Poins.* No abuse?

Falstaff. No abuse, Ned, i' th' world. Honest Ned,
none. I dispraised him before the wicked, that the

301 **compound** mixture   302 **light** unchaste (he is referring to Doll)
308 **candle-mine** reservoir of tallow   314–15 **as . . . Gad's Hill** (the
robbery of the robbers in *1 Henry IV*, II.ii and iv)

wicked might not fall in love with thee. In which
doing, I have done the part of a careful friend and
a true subject, and thy father is to give me thanks   *330*
for it. No abuse, Hal. None, Ned, none. No, faith,
boys, none.

Prince. See now, whether pure fear and entire cowardice doth not make thee wrong this virtuous
gentlewoman to close° with us. Is she of the   *335*
wicked? Is thine hostess here of the wicked? Or is
thy boy of the wicked? Or honest Bardolph, whose
zeal burns in his nose, of the wicked?

Poins. Answer, thou dead elm, answer.

Falstaff. The fiend hath pricked down° Bardolph irre-   *340*
coverable, and his face is Lucifer's privy-kitchen,
where he doth nothing but roast malt-worms.° For
the boy, there is a good angel about him, but the
devil blinds him too.

Prince. For the women?   *345*

Falstaff. For one of them, she's in hell already, and
burns° poor souls. For th' other, I owe her money,
and whether she be damned for that, I know not.

Hostess. No, I warrant you.

Falstaff. No, I think thou art not. I think thou art quit   *350*
for that.° Marry, there is another indictment upon
thee, for suffering flesh° to be eaten in thy house,
contrary to the law, for the which I think thou wilt
howl.

Hostess. All victuallers do so. What's a joint of mut-   *355*
ton° or two in a whole Lent?

Prince. You, gentlewoman—

Doll. What says your Grace?

335 **close** make peace   340 **pricked down** checked off   342 **malt-
worms** (1) weevils in beer (2) drunkards (3) the white material in
Bardolph's pimples   347 **burns** gives burning diseases to   350–51
quit for that paid off for that   352 **flesh** (1) meat (2) womanflesh
355–56 **mutton** (also meant a prostitute)

Falstaff. His Grace says that which his flesh rebels
360 against.°   *Peto knocks at door.*

Hostess. Who knocks so loud at door? Look to th'
door there, Francis.

[*Enter Peto.*]

Prince. Peto, how now! What news?

Peto. The King your father is at Westminster,
365   And there are twenty weak and wearied posts°
Come from the north. And as I came along
I met and overtook a dozen captains,
Bareheaded, sweating, knocking at the taverns,
And asking everyone for Sir John Falstaff.

370 *Prince.* By heaven, Poins, I feel me much to blame,
So idly to profane the precious time,
When tempest of commotion,° like the south°
Borne with black vapor,° doth begin to melt
And drop upon our bare unarmèd heads.
375   Give me my sword and cloak. Falstaff, good night.
Exeunt Prince and Poins, [Peto, and Bardolph].

Falstaff. Now comes in the sweetest morsel of the
night, and we must hence and leave it unpicked.
[*Sound of knocking.*] More knocking at the door?

[*Enter Bardolph.*]

How now! What's the matter?

380 *Bardolph.* You must away to court, sir, presently.°
A dozen captains stay at door for you.

Falstaff. [*To the Page*] Pay the musicians, sirrah. Farewell, hostess. Farewell, Doll. You see, my good
wenches, how men of merit are sought after. The
385   undeserver may sleep when the man of action is

359–60 **His Grace . . . against** i.e., nis Grace calls her a gentlewoman,
but his animal flesh rises up at the idea   365 **posts** messengers
372 **commotion** rebellion   372 **south** south wind   373 **Borne with
black vapor** laden with black clouds   380 **presently** at present, at
once

called on. Farewell, good wenches. If I be not sent
away post,° I will see you again ere I go.

Doll. I cannot speak. If my heart be not ready to
burst—well, sweet Jack, have a care of thyself.

Falstaff. Farewell, farewell.   *Exit* [*with Bardolph*].   390

Hostess. Well, fare thee well. I have known thee these
twenty-nine years, come peascod-time,° but an
honester and truer-hearted man—well, fare thee
well.

Bardolph. [*Within*] Mistress Tearsheet!   395

Hostess. What's the matter?

Bardolph. [*Within*] Bid Mistress Tearsheet come to
my master.

Hostess. O, run, Doll, run, run, good Doll. Come. [*To
Bardolph within*] She comes blubbered.° Yea, will   400
you come, Doll?   *Exeunt.*

---

387 post posthaste   392 **peascod-time** early summer (but there is
evidently a ribald sense, too)   400 **blubbered** disfigured with weeping

[ACT III

Scene I. *The Palace*.]

Enter the King in his nightgown,° alone.

King. [*To a Page, within*] Go, call the Earls of Surrey
and of Warwick.
But, ere they come, bid them o'erread these letters
And well consider of them. Make good speed!
How many thousand of my poorest subjects
5   Are at this hour asleep! O sleep, O gentle sleep,
Nature's soft nurse, how have I frighted thee,
That thou no more wilt weigh my eyelids down
And steep my senses in forgetfulness?
Why rather, sleep, liest thou in smoky cribs,°
10   Upon uneasy pallets° stretching thee
And hushed with buzzing night-flies° to thy
slumber,
Than in the perfumed° chambers of the great,
Under the canopies of costly state,°
And lulled with sound of sweetest melody?
15   O thou dull god, why li'st thou with the vile
In loathsome beds, and leavest the kingly couch
A watchcase° or a common 'larum-bell?°

III.i.s.d. **nightgown** dressing gown (the customary indoor garment)
9 **smoky cribs** chimneyless hovels   10 **uneasy pallets** comfortless
straw beds   11 **night-flies** nocturnal insects   12 **perfumed** (Elizabethans who could afford perfume tried to keep out fresh air)
13 **canopies of costly state** bed-curtains of those in a wealthy state
17 **watchcase** (1) sentry box (2) case of a constantly ticking watch
17 **'larum-bell** alarm-bell (hence, constantly watchful)

Wilt thou upon the high and giddy mast
Seal up the ship-boy's eyes, and rock his brains
In cradle of the rude imperious surge   20
And in the visitation of the winds,
Who take the ruffian billows by the top,
Curling their monstrous heads and hanging them
With deafing° clamor in the slippery clouds,
That, with the hurly,° death itself awakes?   25
Canst thou, O partial° sleep, give thy repose
To the wet sea-son in an hour so rude,
And in the calmest and most stillest night,
With all appliances and means to boot,°
Deny it to a king? Then happy low,° lie down!   30
Uneasy lies the head that wears a crown.

   Enter Warwick, Surrey, and Sir John Blunt.

Warwick. Many good morrows to your Majesty!

King. Is it good morrow, lords?

Warwick. 'Tis one o'clock, and past.

King. Why, then, good morrow to you all, my lords.   35
   Have you read o'er the letter that I sent you?

Warwick. We have, my liege.

King. Then you perceive the body of our kingdom
   How foul it is, what rank° diseases grow,
   And with what danger, near the heart of it.   40

Warwick. It is but as a body yet distempered,°
   Which to his former strength may be restored
   With good advice and little medicine.
   My Lord Northumberland will soon be cooled.

King. O God, that one might read the book of fate,   45
   And see the revolution of the times
   Make mountains level, and the continent,°
   Weary of solid firmness, melt itself

24 **deafing** deafening 25 **hurly** hurly-burly .26 **partial** not impartial
29 **means to boot** measures to further (sleep) 30 **low** lowborn
39 **rank** swelling 41 **yet distempered** as yet but sickened 47 **continent** land surface

Into the sea! And other times to see
50   The beachy girdle of the ocean
Too wide for Neptune's hips. How chances, mocks,
And changes fill the cup of alteration
With divers liquors! O, if this were seen,
The happiest youth, viewing his progress through,
55   What perils past, what crosses° to ensue,
Would shut the book, and sit him down and die.
'Tis not ten years gone
Since Richard and Northumberland, great friends,
Did feast together,° and in two years after
60   Were they at wars. It is but eight years since
This Percy was the man nearest my soul,
Who like a brother toiled in my affairs
And laid his love and life under my foot,°
Yea, for my sake, even to the eyes of Richard
65   Gave him defiance. But which of you was by—
[To Warwick] You, cousin Nevil,° as I may re-
      member—
When Richard, with his eye brimful of tears,
Then checked° and rated° by Northumberland,
Did speak these words, now proved a prophecy:
70   "Northumberland, thou ladder by the which
My cousin Bolingbroke ascends my throne"—
Though then, God knows, I had no such intent,
But that necessity so bowed the state
That I and greatness were compelled to kiss—
75   "The time shall come," thus did he follow it,
"The time will come that foul sin, gathering head,°
Shall break into corruption."° So went on,
Foretelling this same time's condition
And the division of our amity.

80   *Warwick.* There is a history in all men's lives,
Figuring° the nature of the times deceased,

55 crosses punishments   59 Did feast together (Shakespeare here
alters history for dramatic purposes; this appears neither in Holinshed nor his own *Richard II*)   63 under my foot in subservience to
me   66 Nevil (historical error for Beauchamps)   68 checked, rated
rebuked   76 gathering head (1) coming to a head (2) collecting an
army   70–77 Northumberland . . . corruption (paraphrased from
Richard II, V.i.55ff.)   81 Figuring symbolizing

The which observed, a man may prophesy,
With a near aim, of the main chance of things
As yet not come to life, who in their seeds
And weak beginning lie intreasurèd.　　*85*
Such things become the hatch and brood of time,
And by the necessary form of this°
King Richard might create a perfect guess
That great Northumberland, then false to him,
Would of that seed grow to a greater falseness,　　*90*
Which should not find a ground to root upon,
Unless on you.

King.　　　　　　Are these things then necessities?
Then let us meet them like necessities.
And that same word even now cries out on us.
They say the Bishop and Northumberland　　*95*
Are fifty thousand strong.

Warwick.　　　　　　It cannot be, my lord.
Rumor doth double, like the voice and echo,
The numbers of the feared. Please it your Grace
To go to bed. Upon my soul, my lord,
The powers that you already have sent forth　　*100*
Shall bring this prize in very easily.
To comfort you the more, I have received
A certain instance° that Glendower is dead.
Your Majesty hath been this fortnight ill,
And these unseasoned° hours perforce must add　　*105*
Unto your sickness.

King.　　　　　　I will take your counsel.
And were these inward° wars once out of hand,°
We would, dear lords, unto the Holy Land.
　　　　　　　　　　　　　　　Exeunt.

---

87 **necessary form of this** inevitable operation of this principle of
analogy　103 **instance** proof　105 **unseasoned** unusual　107 **inward**
internal　107 **out of hand** finished

[Scene II. *Outside Justice Shallow's house.*]

Enter Justice Shallow and Justice Silence [with Moldy, Shadow, Wart, Feeble, Bullcalf].

Shallow. Come on, come on, come on. Give me your hand, sir, give me your hand, sir; an early stirrer, by the rood!° And how doth my good cousin Silence?

Silence. Good morrow, good cousin Shallow.

5   *Shallow.* And how doth my cousin, your bedfellow? And your fairest daughter and mine, my goddaughter Ellen?

Silence. Alas, a black ousel,° cousin Shallow!

Shallow. By yea and no,° sir, I dare say my cousin
10   William is become a good scholar. He is at Oxford still, is he not?

Silence. Indeed, sir, to my cost.

Shallow. 'A must, then, to the Inns o' Court° shortly. I was once of Clement's Inn,° where I think they
15   will talk of mad Shallow yet.

Silence. You were called "lusty Shallow" then, cousin.

Shallow. By the mass, I was called anything. And I would have done anything indeed too, and roundly° too. There was I, and little John Doit of Stafford-
20   shire, and black George Barnes, and Francis Pickbone, and Will Squele,° a Cotswold° man; you had

III.ii.3 **rood** cross 8 **ousel** blackbird 9 **By yea and no** (a puritan's oath) 13 **Inns o' Court** law schools (which functioned as universities for the gentry) 14 **Clement's Inn** (one of the Inns of Chancery, admitting students unable to get into the Inns of Court) 18 **roundly** fully 19–21 **Doit . . . Barnes . . . Pickbone . . . Squele** (the names are suggestive of insignificance, a doit being a half-farthing; country wealth [barns]; stinginess; squealing cowardice) 21 **Cotswold** (a range of hills in Gloucestershire)

not four such swinge-bucklers° in all the Inns o'
Court again. And I may say to you we knew where
the bona-robas° were and had the best of them all
at commandment. Then was Jack Falstaff, now Sir   25
John, a boy, and page to Thomas Mowbray, Duke
of Norfolk.

Silence. This Sir John, cousin, that comes hither anon
 · about soldiers?

Shallow. The same Sir John, the very same. I see him   30
break Scoggin's° head at the court-gate, when 'a
was a crack° not thus high. And the very same day
did I fight with one Sampson Stockfish,° a fruiterer,
behind Gray's Inn.° Jesu, Jesu, the mad days that
I have spent! And to see how many of my old   35
acquaintance are dead!

Silence. We shall all follow, cousin.

Shallow. Certain, 'tis certain, very sure, very sure.
Death, as the Psalmist saith, is certain to all, all
shall die. How° a good yoke of bullocks at Stam-   40
ford Fair?

Silence. By my troth, I was not there.

Shallow. Death is certain. Is old Double° of your
town living yet?

Silence. Dead, sir.   45

Shallow. Jesu, Jesu, dead! 'A drew a good bow, and
dead! 'A shot a fine shoot. John a Gaunt° loved
him well and betted much money on his head.
Dead! 'A would have clapped i' th' clout at twelve
score, and carried you a forehand shaft a fourteen   50
and fourteen and a half,° that it would have done a

22 **swinge-bucklers** shield-beaters (i.e., blusterers)   24 **bona-robas**
high-class whores (Italian *buonaroba*, good material)   31 **Scoggin's**
(the name means a coarse joker)   32 **crack** perky boy   33 **Stockfish** a dried fish (suggestive of an impotent man)   34 **Gray's Inn**
another Inn of Court   40 **How** how much for   43 **Donble** (suggests
one doubled over with age)   47 **John a Gaunt** Henry IV's father
49–51 **clapped . . . and a half** hit the bull's-eye at 240 yards, and
shot a heavy arrow (for point-blank shooting) 280 or 290 yards

man's heart good to see. How a score of ewes now?

Silence. Thereafter as they be.° A score of good ewes
may be worth ten pounds.

35 *Shallow.* And is old Double dead?

Silence. Here come two of Sir John Falstaff's men, as
I think.

   Enter Bardolph and one with him.

Good morrow, honest gentlemen.

Bardolph. I beseech you, which is Justice Shallow?

60 *Shallow.* I am Robert Shallow, sir, a poor esquire° of
this county, and one of the King's justices of the
peace. What is your good pleasure with me?

Bardolph. My captain, sir, commends him to you, my
captain, Sir John Falstaff, a tall° gentleman, by
65 heaven, and a most gallant leader.

Shallow. He greets me well, sir. I knew him a good
backsword° man. How doth the good knight? May
I ask how my lady his wife doth?

Bardolph. Sir, pardon, a soldier is better accommo-
70 dated° than with a wife.

Shallow. It is well said, in faith, sir, and it is well said
indeed too. "Better accommodated"! It is good, yea,
indeed, is it. Good phrases are surely, and ever
were, very commendable. "Accommodated"! It
75 comes of *"accommodo."* Very good, a good phrase.

Bardolph. Pardon, sir. I have heard the word.
"Phrase" call you it? By this good day, I know not
the phrase, but I will maintain the word with my
sword to be a soldier-like word, and a word of ex-
80 ceeding good command, by heaven. "Accommodated," that is, when a man is, as they say, accom-

---

53 **Thereafter as they be** according to their condition   60 **esquire**
gentleman (ranking just below a knight)   64 **tall** brave   67 **back-
sword** stick with a hilt used by apprentices in fencing   69–70 **accommodated** provided (a "perfumed term," according to Ben Jonson)

modated; or when a man is, being, whereby 'a may
be thought to be accommodated, which is an excellent thing.

Enter Falstaff.

Shallow. It is very just.° Look, here comes good Sir   85
John. Give me your good hand, give me your worship's good hand. By my troth, you like° well and
bear your years very well. Welcome, good Sir John.

Falstaff. I am glad to see you well, good Master
Robert Shallow. Master Surecard,° as I think?   90

Shallow. No, Sir John, it is my cousin Silence, in com-
mission° with me.

Falstaff. Good Master Silence, it well befits you should
be of the peace.

Silence. Your good worship is welcome.   95

Falstaff. Fie! This is hot weather, gentlemen. Have
you provided me here half a dozen sufficient men?

Shallow. Marry, have we, sir. Will you sit?

Falstaff. Let me see them, I beseech you.

Shallow. Where's the roll? Where's the roll? Where's   100
the roll? Let me see, let me see, let me see. So, so,
so, so, so, so—so. Yea, marry, sir. Rafe Moldy!
Let them appear as I call, let them do so, let them
do so. Let me see, where is Moldy?

Moldy. Here, and't please you.   105

Shallow. What think you, Sir John? A good-limbed
fellow, young, strong, and of good friends.

Falstaff. Is thy name Moldy?

Moldy. Yea, and't please you.

Falstaff. 'Tis the more time thou wert used.   110

85 just exact   87 like get on   90 Surecard absolute winner (at cards)
91–92 in commission commissioned as justice of the peace

Shallow. Ha, ha, ha! Most excellent, i' faith! Things that are moldy lack use. Very singular good! In faith, well said, Sir John, very well said.

Falstaff. Prick him.°

115 *Moldy*. I was pricked° well enough before, and you could have let me alone. My old dame° will be undone now for one to do her husbandry and her drudgery. You need not to have pricked me. There are other men fitter to go out than I.

120 *Falstaff*. Go to. Peace, Moldy, you shall go. Moldy, it is time you were spent.

Moldy. Spent?

Shallow. Peace, fellow, peace. Stand aside. Know you where you are? For th' other, Sir John, let me see. 125 Simon Shadow!°

Falstaff. Yea, marry, let me have him to sit under. He's like to be a cold soldier.

Shallow. Where's Shadow?

Shadow. Here, sir.

130 *Falstaff*. Shadow, whose son art thou?

Shadow. My mother's son, sir.

Falstaff. Thy mother's son! Like enough, and thy father's shadow. So the son° of the female is the shadow of the male. It is often so, indeed, but 135 much° of the father's substance!

Shallow. Do you like him, Sir John?

Falstaff. Shadow will serve for summer. Prick him, for we have a number of shadows fill up the musterbook.

114 **Prick him** check him off   115 **pricked** (1) chosen (2) worried (and a ribald third meaning)   116 **dame** old wife (or mother) 125 **Shadow** (1) likeness (2) shade (3) fictitious name in the muster roll for which an officer collected pay (Falstaff jokes on all three meanings)   133 **son** (he is punning on "sun")   135 **much** little (sarcastic)

Shallow. Thomas Wart!

Falstaff. Where's he?

Wart. Here, sir.

Falstaff. Is thy name Wart?

Wart. Yea, sir.

Falstaff. Thou art a very ragged° wart.   *145*

Shallow. Shall I prick him, Sir John?

Falstaff. It were superfluous,° for his apparel is built upon his back and the whole frame stands upon pins. Prick him no more.

Shallow. Ha, ha, ha! You can do it,° sir! You can do *150* it! I commend you well. Francis Feeble!

Feeble. Here, sir.

Shallow. What trade art thou, Feeble?

Feeble. A woman's tailor, sir.

Shallow. Shall I prick him, sir?   *155*

Falstaff. You may. But if he had been a man's tailor, he'd a' pricked you. Wilt thou make as many holes in an enemy's battle° as thou hast done in a woman's petticoat?

Feeble. I will do my good will, sir. You can have no *160* more.

Falstaff. Well said, good woman's tailor! Well said, courageous Feeble! Thou wilt be as valiant as the wrathful dove or most magnanimous° mouse. Prick the woman's tailor well,° Master Shallow, deep,° *165* Master Shallow.

Feeble. I would Wart might have gone, sir.

145 **ragged** having rough projections (referring to his pinned-together clothes)   147 **superfluous** i.e., to "prick him," pin his clothes together   150 **you can do it** you know how to joke   158 **battle** battle line   164 **magnanimous** big-spirited   165 **well, deep** (quibbles on Shallow's name)

Falstaff. I would thou wert a man's tailor, that thou
mightst mend him and make him fit to go. I can-
170   not put him to° a private soldier that is the leader
of so many thousands.° Let that suffice, most forcible Feeble.

Feeble. It shall suffice, sir.

Falstaff. I am bound to thee, reverend Feeble. Who is
175   next?

Shallow. Peter Bullcalf o' th' green!

Falstaff. Yea, marry, let's see Bullcalf.

Bullcalf. Here, sir.

Falstaff. 'Fore God, a likely fellow! Come, prick°
180   Bullcalf till he roar again.

Bullcalf. O Lord, good my lord captain—

Falstaff. What, dost thou roar before thou art
pricked?

Bullcalf. O Lord, sir, I am a diseased man.

185 *Falstaff.* What disease hast thou?

Bullcalf. A whoreson cold, sir, a cough, sir, which I
caught with ringing in° the King's affairs upon his
coronation day, sir.

Falstaff. Come, thou shalt go to the wars in a gown.°
190   We will have away thy cold, and I will take such
order that thy friends shall ring for thee.° Is here
all?

Shallow. Here is two more called than your number.
You must have but four° here, sir. And so, I pray
195   you, go in with me to dinner.

---

170 put him to set him to the occupation of   **171 thousands** i.e., of
lice   **179 prick** (here the word refers to the sticking of a bull with a
goad in bullbaiting)   **187 ringing in** ringing the church bells to
celebrate   **189 gown** dressing gown   **191 ring for thee** i.e., toll your
funeral   **194 four** (he settles for three)

Falstaff. Come, I will go drink with you, but I cannot tarry dinner. I am glad to see you, by my troth, Master Shallow.

Shallow. O, Sir John, do you remember since we lay all night in the Windmill° in Saint George's Field? *200*

Falstaff. No more of that, Master Shallow.

Shallow. Ha! 'Twas a merry night. And is Jane Night-work alive?

Falstaff. She lives, Master Shallow.

Shallow. She never could away with° me. *205*

Falstaff. Never, never, she would always say she could not abide Master Shallow.

Shallow. By the mass, I could anger° her to th' heart. She was then a bona-roba. Doth she hold her own well? *210*

Falstaff. Old, old, Master Shallow.

Shallow. Nay, she must be old. She cannot choose but be old. Certain she's old, and had Robin Night-work by old Nightwork before I came to Clement's Inn. *215*

Silence. That's fifty-five year ago.

Shallow. Ha, cousin Silence, that thou hadst seen that that this knight and I have seen! Ha, Sir John, said I well?

Falstaff. We have heard the chimes at midnight, *220* Master Shallow.

Shallow. That we have, that we have, that we have, in faith, Sir John, we have. Our watchword was "Hem,° boys!" Come, let's to dinner, come, let's to dinner. Jesus, the days that we have seen! Come, *225* come.   *Exeunt [Falstaff and the Justices].*

---

200 **Windmill** (evidently a brothel)   205 **away with** put up with
208 **anger** inflame   224 **Hem** (the equivalent of "Bottoms up!")

Bullcalf. Good Master Corporate° Bardolph, stand my
　　friend, and here's four Harry ten shillings in French
　　crowns° for you. In very truth, sir, I had as lief be
230　　hanged, sir, as go. And yet for mine own part, sir,
　　I do not care, but rather, because I am unwilling,
　　and, for mine own part, have a desire to stay with
　　my friends. Else, sir, I did not care, for mine own
　　part, so much.

235　*Bardolph.* Go to, stand aside.

Moldy. And, good Master Corporal Captain, for my
　　dame's sake, stand my friend. She has nobody to
　　do anything about her when I am gone, and she is
　　old and cannot help herself. You shall have forty,°
240　　sir.

Bardolph. Go to, stand aside.

Feeble. By my troth, I care not. A man can die but
　　once. We owe God a death.° I'll ne'er bear a base
　　mind. And't be my destiny, so. And't be not, so.
245　　No man's too good to serve's Prince. And let it go
　　which way it will, he that dies this year is quit° for
　　the next.

Bardolph. Well said. Th' art a good fellow.

Feeble. Faith, I'll bear no base mind.

　　　　　Enter Falstaff and the Justices.

250　*Falstaff.* Come, sir, which men shall I have?

Shallow. Four of which you please.

Bardolph. Sir, a word with you. [*Aside*] I have three
　　pound to free Moldy and Bullcalf.

Falstaff. Go to, well.

227 **Corporate** (blunder for "corporal")　228–29 **four Harry . . .
crowns** (a country way of counting out £1: the amount of four
pieces, formerly of ten shillings' value but currently five, rendered in
five four-shilling pieces, "French crowns"; Bullcalf is offering around
$200 in today's values)　239 **forty** forty shillings (about $400 today)
243 **death** (pronounced like "debt," hence a pun)　246 **is quit** owes
nothing

Shallow. Come, Sir John, which four will you have? 255

Falstaff. Do you choose for me.

Shallow. Marry, then, Moldy, Bullcalf, Feeble, and
Shadow.

Falstaff. Moldy and Bullcalf. For you, Moldy, stay at
home till you are past service.° And for your part, 260
Bullcalf, grow till you come unto it. I will none of
you.

Shallow. Sir John, Sir John, do not yourself wrong.
They are your likeliest men, and I would have you
served with the best. 265

Falstaff. Will you tell me, Master Shallow, how to
choose a man? Care I for the limb, the thews,° the
stature, bulk, and big assemblance° of a man? Give
me the spirit, Master Shallow! Here's Wart. You
see what a ragged appearance it is. 'A shall charge 270
you and discharge you with the motion of a pewter-
er's hammer,° come off and on swifter than he that
gibbets on the brewer's bucket.° And this same
half-faced fellow, Shadow. Give me this man. He
presents no mark to the enemy: the foeman may 275
with as great aim level at the edge of a penknife.
And for a retreat, how swiftly will this Feeble the
woman's tailor run off! O, give me the spare men,
and spare me the great ones. Put me a caliver° into
Wart's hand, Bardolph. 280

Bardolph. Hold, Wart, traverse.° Thus, thus, thus.

Falstaff. Come, manage me your caliver. So. Very
well. Go to. Very good, exceeding good. O, give me
always a little, lean, old, chopped,° bald shot.°

---

260 **service** i.e., (1) military (2) domestic (3) bull's   267 **thews** bodily
forces   268 **assemblance** appearance   271–72 **motion of a pewter-
er's hammer** i.e., with a rapid tap-tap   273 **gibbets on the brewer's
bucket** hoists with the beam ("bucket") of a brewer's crane   279
caliver light musket   281 **traverse** cross over   284 **chopped** chapped
284 **shot** shooter (musketeers had to run nimbly behind the pikemen
or spearmen to reload)

285   Well said, i' faith, Wart. Th' art a good scab.°
      Hold, there's a tester° for thee.

Shallow. He is not his craft's master, he doth not do
      it right. I remember at Mile-End Green, when I
      lay at Clement's Inn—I was then Sir Dagonet in
290   Arthur's show°—there was a little quiver° fellow,
      and 'a would manage you his piece thus, and 'a
      would about and about, and come you in and come
      you in. "Rah, tah, tah," would 'a say, "Bounce,"
      would 'a say, and away again would 'a go, and
295   again would 'a come. I shall ne'er see such a fellow.

Falstaff. These fellows would do well, Master Shallow.
      God keep you, Master Silence. I will not use many
      words with you. Fare you well, gentlemen both.
      I thank you. I must a dozen mile tonight. Bardolph,
300   give the soldiers coats.

Shallow. Sir John, the Lord bless you! God prosper
      your affairs! God send us peace! At your return
      visit our house, let our old acquaintance be re-
      newed. Peradventure I will with ye to the court.

305 *Falstaff.* 'Fore God, would you would.

Shallow. Go to, I have spoke at a word.° God keep
      you.

Falstaff. Fare you well, gentle gentlemen. [*Exeunt
      Justices*]. On, Bardolph, lead the men away.
310   [*Exeunt all but Falstaff.*] As I return, I will fetch
      off° these justices. I do see the bottom of Justice
      Shallow. Lord, Lord, how subject we old men are
      to this vice of lying! This same starved justice hath
      done nothing but prate to me of the wildness of his
315   youth and the feats he hath done about Turnbull
      Street,° and every third word a lie, duer° paid to

---

285 **scab** i.e., wart   286 **tester** sixpence   290 **Arthur's show** (an an-
nual archery show at Mile-End Green in which the contestants took
the names of knights of the Round Table. Sir Dagonet was Arthur's
fool)   290 **quiver** nimble   306 **at a word** on an impulse   310–311 **fetch
off** trick   315–16 **Turnbull Street** (a red-light district)   316 **duer**
more duly, regularly

the hearer than the Turk's tribute.° I do remember
him at Clement's Inn like a man made after supper
of a cheese-paring. When 'a was naked, he was, for
all the world, like a forked radish, with a head   320
fantastically carved upon it with a knife. 'A was so
forlorn that his dimensions to any thick° sight were
invisible. 'A was the very genius° of famine, yet
lecherous as a monkey, and the whores called him
mandrake.° 'A came ever in the rearward of the   325
fashion, and sung those tunes to the overscutched
huswives° that he heard the carmen whistle, and
sware they were his fancies or his goodnights.° And
now is this Vice's dagger° become a squire, and
talks as familiarly of John a Gaunt as if he had   330
been sworn brother to him, and I'll be sworn 'a
ne'er saw him but once in the Tilt-yard, and then
he° burst his head for crowding among the marshal's men. I saw it, and told John a Gaunt he beat
his own name, for you might have thrust him and   335
all his apparel into an eel-skin—the case of a treble
hautboy° was a mansion for him, a court. And now
has he land and beeves. Well, I'll be acquainted
with him, if I return, and't shall go hard but I'll
make him a philosopher's two stones° to me. If the   340
young dace° be a bait for the old pike, I see no
reason in the law of nature but I may snap at him.
Let time shape, and there an end.   [*Exit.*]

---

317 than the Turk's tribute i.e., than tribute is paid to the Turk
322 thick imperfect   **323 genius** spirit   **325 mandrake** forked root,
shaped like the lower half of a man   **326–27 overscutched huswives**
often-whipped whores   **328 his fancies or his goodnights** musical
improvisations of his own or goodnight songs   **329 Vice's dagger**
thin wooden dagger carried by the Vice, clown in the old morality
plays   **333 he** i.e., John of Gaunt   **336–37 treble hautboy** smallest
oboe   **340 philosopher's two stones** (i.e., twice as profitable as one
philosopher's stone which would transmute base metals to gold—
and a ribald second sense)   **341 dace** thin, small fish

[ACT IV

Scene I. *With the rebel army.*]

*Enter the Archbishop [of York], Mowbray,
Hastings [and others], within the Forest of
Gaultree.*

Archbishop. What is this forest called?

Hastings. 'Tis Gaultree Forest, and't shall please your
Grace.

Archbishop. Here stand, my lords, and send discov-
erers° forth
To know the numbers of our enemies.

Hastings. We have sent forth already.

5   *Archbishop.*   'Tis well done.
My friends and brethren in these great affairs,
I must acquaint you that I have received
New-dated letters from Northumberland,
Their cold intent, tenor, and substance, thus:
10   Here doth he wish his person, with such powers°
As might hold sortance with his quality,°
The which he could not levy. Whereupon
He is retired, to ripe° his growing fortunes,
To Scotland, and concludes in hearty prayers
15   That your attempts may overlive° the hazard
And fearful meeting of° their opposite.

IV.i.3 **discoverers** spies   10 **powers** armies   11 **hold sortance with
his quality** accord with his rank   13 **ripe** ripen   15 **overlive** survive
15–16 **hazard/And fearful meeting of** the fearful risk of meeting

Mowbray. Thus do the hopes we have in him touch
ground°
And dash themselves to pieces.

Enter Messenger.

Hastings.   Now, what news?

Messenger. West of this forest, scarcely off a mile,
In goodly form comes on the enemy,   20
And, by the ground they hide, I judge their number
Upon or near the rate of thirty thousand.

Mowbray. The just proportion that we gave them
out.°
Let us sway° on and face them in the field.

Archbishop. What well-appointed° leader fronts° us
here?   25

Enter Westmoreland.

Mowbray. I think it is my Lord of Westmoreland.

Westmoreland. Health and fair greeting from our general,
The Prince, Lord John and Duke of Lancaster.

Archbishop. Say on, my Lord of Westmoreland, in
peace.
What doth concern your coming?

Westmoreland.   Then, my lord,   30
Unto your Grace do I in chief° address
The substance of my speech. If that rebellion
Came like itself, in base and abject routs,°
Led on by bloody youth, guarded with rage,°
And countenanced° by boys and beggary,°   35
I say, if damned commotion° so appeared,
In his true, native and most proper shape,

17 **touch ground** (like a ship)   23 **just proportion . . . out** exact
number we allowed for   24 **sway** move   25 **well-appointed** well-
furnished   25 **fronts** confronts   31 **in chief** chiefly   33 **routs** mobs
34 **guarded with rage** trimmed with false bluster (and pun on "rag")
35 **countenanced** faced out, added to   35 **beggary** beggars   36 **commotion** rebellion

You, reverend father, and these noble lords
Had not been here, to dress the ugly form
40 Of base and bloody insurrection
With your fair honors. You, Lord Archbishop,
Whose see° is by a civil peace maintained,
Whose beard the silver hand of peace hath touched,
Whose learning and good letters° peace hath tutored,
45 Whose white investments figure° innocence,
The dove and very blessèd spirit of peace,
Wherefore do you so ill translate° yourself
Out of the speech of peace that bears such grace,
Into the harsh and boisterous tongue of war,
50 Turning your books to graves, your ink to blood,
Your pens to lances, and your tongue divine
To a loud trumpet and a point of war?°

Archbishop. Wherefore do I this? So the question
    stands.
Briefly to this end: we are all diseased,
55 And with our surfeiting and wanton° hours
Have brought ourselves into a burning fever,
And we must bleed° for it. Of which disease
Our late king, Richard, being infected, died.
But, my most noble Lord of Westmoreland,
60 I take not on me here as a physician,°
Nor do I as an enemy to peace
Troop in the throngs of military men,
But rather show awhile like fearful war,
To diet rank° minds sick of happiness
65 And purge th' obstructions which begin to stop
Our very veins of life. Hear me more plainly.
I have in equal° balance justly weighed
What wrongs our arms may do, what wrongs we
    suffer,

---

42 **see** seat, throne, hence diocese   44 **good letters** humane scholarship   45 **investments figure** vestments symbolize   47 **translate** trans-
form (but note the extended metaphor of language in lines 48–52)
52 **point of war** bugle call   55 **wanton** self-indulgent   57 **bleed** be
bled (as a purgative)   60 **I take . . . physician** I do not presume to
act as the doctor (to do the bleeding; I will but "show"—line 63)
64 **rank** swollen   67 **equal** unbiased

And find our griefs° heavier than our offenses.
We see which way the stream of time doth run,   70
And are enforced from our most quiet there
By the rough torrent of occasion,
And have the summary of all our griefs,
When time shall serve, to show in articles;°
Which long ere this we offered to the King,   75
And might by no suit gain our audience.
When we are wronged and would unfold our griefs,
We are denied access unto his person
Even by those men that most have done us wrong.
The dangers of the days but newly gone,   80
Whose memory is written on the earth
With yet-appearing blood, and the examples
Of every minute's instance,° present now,
Hath put us in these ill-beseeming arms,
Not to break peace or any branch of it,   85
But to establish here a peace indeed,
Concurring both in name and quality.°

Westmoreland. When ever yet was your appeal de-
   nied?
Wherein have you been gallèd° by the King?
What peer hath been suborned to grate on° you,   90
That you should seal this lawless bloody book
Of forged rebellion with a seal divine?°

Archbishop. My brother general,° the commonwealth,
   I make my quarrel in particular.

Westmoreland. There is no need of any such redress,   95
   Or if there were, it not belongs to you.

Mowbray. Why not to him in part, and to us all
   That feel the bruises of the days before,
   And suffer the condition of these times

69 **griefs** grievances   74 **articles** formal listing   83 **Of every minute's instance** proof in every minute   87 **quality** substance   89 **gallèd**
irritated   90 **suborned to grate on** set on to vex   92 **divine** (see Textual Note, p. 173)   93 **brother general** (brother in a general sense as
opposed to my brother by birth; Henry IV had executed the Archbishop's brother—*1 Henry IV*, I.iii; see Textual Note, p. 173)

100   To lay a heavy and unequal° hand
    Upon our honors?

  Westmoreland.   O, my good Lord Mowbray,
    Construe the times to their necessities,°
    And you shall say indeed, it is the time,
    And not the King, that doth you injuries.
105 Yet for your part, it not appears to me
    Either from the King or in the present time
    That you should have an inch of any ground
    To build a grief on. Were you not restored
    To all the Duke of Norfolk's signories,°
110 Your noble and right well-rememb'red father's?

  Mowbray. What thing, in honor, had my father lost,
    That need to be revived and breathed in me?
    The King that loved him, as the state stood then,
    Was force perforce° compelled to banish him.
115 And then that Henry Bolingbroke and he,
    Being mounted and both rousèd in their seats,°
    Their neighing coursers daring of° the spur,
    Their armèd staves in charge, their beavers° down,
    Their eyes of fire sparkling through sights of steel,
120 And the loud trumpet blowing them together,
    Then, then, when there was nothing could have
      stayed
    My father from the breast of Bolingbroke—
    O, when the King did throw his warder° down
    His own life hung upon the staff he threw.
125 Then threw he down himself and all their lives
    That by indictment and by dint° of sword
    Have since miscarried° under Bolingbroke.

  Westmoreland. You speak, Lord Mowbray, now you
    know not what.

100 **unequal** not impartial   102 **Construe . . . necessities** interpret the present state of things according to the forces that inevitably make them the way they are   109 **signories** lands   114 **force perforce** willy-nilly (for the trial by battle described in lines 115–37, see *Richard II*, I.iii)   116 **seats** saddles   117 **daring of** ready for   118 **armèd staves . . . beavers** lances at the ready, their helmet-visors   123 **warder** ceremonial baton   126 **dint** force   127 **miscarried** perished

The Earl of Hereford was reputed then
In England the most valiant gentleman. *130*
Who knows on whom Fortune would then have
  smiled?
But if your father had been victor there,
He ne'er had borne it° out of Coventry.°
For all the country in a general voice
Cried hate upon him, and all their prayers and love *135*
Were set on Hereford, whom they doted on
And blessed and graced—and did more than° the
  King.
But this is mere digression from my purpose.
Here come I from our princely general
To know your griefs, to tell you from his Grace *140*
That he will give you audience, and wherein
It shall appear that your demands are just,
You shall enjoy them, everything set off°
That might so much as think you enemies.

Mowbray. But he hath forced us to compel this offer, *145*
And it proceeds from policy,° not love.

Westmoreland. Mowbray, you overween° to take it so.
This offer comes from mercy, not from fear.
For, lo, within a ken° our army lies,
Upon mine honor, all too confident *150*
To give admittance to a thought of fear.
Our battle° is more full of names° than yours,
Our men more perfect in the use of arms,
Our armor all as strong, our cause the best.
Then reason will° our hearts should be as good. *155*
Say you not then our offer is compelled.

Mowbray. Well, by my will we shall admit no parley.

Westmoreland. That argues but the shame of your
  offense.

---

133 **it** i.e., the prize   133 **Coventry** (the scene of this trial by battle)
137 **did more than** i.e., did so more than for   143 **set off** put aside,
ignored   146 **policy** statecraft   147 **overween** calculate too much
149 **ken** look   152 **battle** battle line   152 **names** men with warlike
reputations   155 **reason will** it will be reasonable that

A rotten° case abides no handling.

160 *Hastings.* Hath the Prince John a full commission,
In very ample virtue° of his father,
To hear and absolutely to determine
Of what conditions we shall stand upon?

Westmoreland. That is intended in the General's
name.°
165 I muse° you make so slight a question.

Archbishop. Then take, my Lord of Westmoreland,
this schedule,
For this contains our general grievances.
Each several article herein redressed,°
All members of our cause, both here and hence°
170 That are insinewed° to this action,
Acquitted by a true substantial form°
And present execution of our wills
To us and our purposes confined,°
We° come within our awful banks° again
175 And knit our powers to the arm of peace.

Westmoreland. This will I show the General. Please
you, lords,
In sight of both our battles we may meet,
And either end in peace—which God so frame—
Or to the place of diff'rence° call the swords
Which must decide it.

180 *Archbishop.* My lord, we will do so.
Exit Westmoreland.

Mowbray. There is a thing within my bosom tells me
That no conditions° of our peace can stand.

---

159 **rotten** fragile (proverbial statement) 161 **In very ample virtue**
with exactly the ample power 164 **intended in the General's name**
implicit in the King's making his son the general 165 **muse** am
puzzled 168 **Each . . . redressed** i.e., if each . . . is redressed, etc.
169 **hence** elsewhere 170 **insinewed** bound by strong sinews 171
substantial form firm formal agreement 172–173 **wills . . . confined**
demands restricted (in scope) to us and our grievances 174 **We**
i.e., then we 174 **banks** i.e., they will subside like a stream that had
been in flood 179 **diff'rence** conflict 182 **conditions** provisions in
the contract

Hastings. Fear you not that. If we can make our peace
　　Upon such large terms and so absolute
　　As our conditions shall consist upon,　　　　　*185*
　　Our peace shall stand as firm as rocky mountains.

Mowbray. Yea, but our valuation° shall be such
　　That every slight and false-derivèd cause,
　　Yea, every idle, nice, and wanton° reason
　　Shall to the King taste of this action,　　　　　*190*
　　That, were our royal faiths martyrs in love,°
　　We shall be winnowed with so rough a wind
　　That even our corn shall seem as light as chaff
　　And good from bad find no partition.°

Archbishop. No, no, my lord. Note this. The King is
　　weary　　　　　*195*
　　Of dainty° and such picking° grievances.
　　For he hath found to end one doubt by death
　　Revives two greater in the heirs of life,°
　　And therefore will he wipe his tables° clean
　　And keep no telltale to his memory　　　　　*200*
　　That may repeat and history his loss
　　To new remembrance. For full well he knows
　　He cannot so precisely° weed this land
　　As his misdoubts° present occasion.
　　His foes are so enrooted with his friends　　　　　*205*
　　That, plucking to unfix an enemy,
　　He doth unfasten so and shake a friend.
　　So that this land, like an offensive wife
　　That hath enraged him on to offer strokes,
　　As he is striking, holds his infant up　　　　　*210*
　　And hangs resolved correction° in the arm
　　That was upreared to execution.

Hastings. Besides, the King hath wasted all his rods

187 **valuation** i.e., in the King's eyes　189 **nice, and wanton** petty
and frivolous　191 **were . . . love** i.e., even if we were as faithful in
love to his royal self as martyrs　194 **partition** dividing　196 **dainty,
picking** finicky　197–98 **to end . . . life** i.e., to rid himself of one
doubtful subject by executing him creates two even more treacherous
foes in those who live on after the dead man　199 **tables** notebook
203 **precisely** thoroughly　204 **misdoubts** suspicions　211 **resolved
correction** a check on his resolution

On late offenders, that he now doth lack
215 The very instruments of chastisement.
So that his power, like to a fangless lion,
May offer,° but not hold.

Archbishop.   'Tis very true.
And therefore be assured, my good Lord Marshal,
If we do now make our atonement° well,
220 Our peace will, like a broken limb united,
Grow stronger for the breaking.

Mowbray.   Be it so.
Here is returned my Lord of Westmoreland.

Enter Westmoreland.

Westmoreland. The Prince is here at hand. Pleaseth
   your lordship
To meet his Grace just distance° 'tween our armies.

Enter Prince John [of Lancaster] and his army.

Mowbray. Your Grace of York, in God's name then,
225   set forward.

Archbishop. Before, and greet his Grace, my lord; we
   come.

[Scene II. *The same.*]°

Lancaster. You are well encount'red here, my cousin
   Mowbray.
Good day to you, gentle Lord Archbishop.
And so to you, Lord Hastings, and to all.
My Lord of York, it better showed with you
5 When that your flock, assembled by the bell,
Encircled you to hear with reverence

---

217 **offer** threaten   219 **atonement** becoming at one   224 **just dis-
tance** halfway   IV.ii.s.d. (notice there should be no scene division,
the action being continuous and the stage not having emptied)

Your exposition on the holy text
Than now to see you here an iron° man talking,
Cheering a rout of rebels with your drum,
Turning the word to sword and life to death.   10
That man that sits within a monarch's heart
And ripens in the sunshine of his favor,
Would he abuse the countenance of the King,
Alack, what mischiefs might he set abroach°
In shadow of such greatness! With you, Lord
    Bishop,   15
It is even so. Who hath not heard it spoken
How deep you were within the books of God?
To us the speaker in His parliament,
To us th' imagined voice of God himself,
The very opener and intelligencer°   20
Between the grace, the sanctities of heaven
And our dull workings.° O, who shall believe
But you misuse the reverence of your place,
Employ the countenance and grace of heaven,
As a false favorite doth his prince's name,   25
In deeds dishonorable? You have ta'en up,°
Under the counterfeited zeal° of God,
The subjects of His substitute,° my father,
And both against the peace of heaven and him
Have here upswarmed° them.

Archbishop.   Good my Lord of Lancaster,   30
I am not here against your father's peace,
But, as I told my Lord of Westmoreland,
The time misord'red doth, in common sense,°
Crowd us and crush us to this monstrous° form,
To hold our safety up. I sent your Grace   35
The parcels° and particulars of our grief,
The which hath been with scorn shoved from the
    court,

8 **iron** (1) armored (2) merciless 14 **abroach** open (like a cask)
20 **opener and intelligencer** interpreter and informant 22 **workings**
mental operations 26 **ta'en up** enlisted 27 **zeal** (with a pun on
"seal") 28 **substitute** deputy 30 **upswarmed** made (them) swarm
up 33 **in common sense** to anybody's senses 34 **monstrous** un-
natural 36 **parcels** small parts

Whereon this Hydra° son of war is born,
Whose dangerous eyes may well be charmed asleep
40 With grant of our most just and right desires,
And true obedience, of this madness cured,
Stoop tamely to the foot of majesty.

Mowbray. If not, we ready are to try our fortunes
To the last man.

Hastings.   And though we here fall down,
45 We have supplies to second° our attempt.
If they miscarry, theirs° shall second them,
And so success° of mischief shall be born
And heir from heir shall hold this quarrel up
Whiles England shall have generation.°

Lancaster. You are too shallow, Hastings, much too
50 shallow,
To sound° the bottom of the after-times.

Westmoreland. Pleaseth your Grace to answer them
directly
How far forth you do like their articles.

Lancaster. I like them all, and do allow them well,
55 And swear here, by the honor of my blood,
My father's purposes have been mistook,
And some about him have too lavishly°
Wrested° his meaning and authority.
My lord, these griefs shall be with speed redressed.
60 Upon my soul, they shall. If this may please you,
Discharge your powers unto their several counties,
As we will ours. And here between the armies
Let's drink together friendly and embrace,
That all their eyes may bear those tokens home
65 Of our restorèd love and amity.

Archbishop. I take your princely word for these re-
dresses.

---

38 **Hydra** many-headed monster   45 **supplies to second** reinforcements to back up   46 **theirs** i.e., their supplies   47 **success** succession   49 **generation** offspring   51 **sound** measure the depth of
57 **lavishly** loosely   58 **Wrested** twisted

Lancaster. I give it you, and will maintain my word.
　And thereupon I drink unto your Grace.
　　　　　　　　　　　　　　　　[He drinks.]

Hastings. Go, Captain, and deliver to the army
　This news of peace. Let them have pay, and part.°　*70*
　I know it will well please them. Hie thee, Captain.
　　　　　　　　　　　　　　　　[Exit Officer.]

Archbishop. To you, my noble Lord of Westmoreland.
　　　　　　　　　　　　　　　　[He drinks.]

Westmoreland. I pledge your Grace, and, if you knew
　　what pains
　I have bestowed to breed this present peace.
　You would drink freely. But my love to ye　　*75*
　Shall show itself more openly hereafter.

Archbishop. I do not doubt you.

Westmoreland.　　　　　　　I am glad of it.
　Health to my lord and gentle cousin, Mowbray.

Mowbray. You wish me health in very happy season,
　For I am, on the sudden, something° ill.　　*80*

Archbishop. Against° ill chances men are ever merry,
　But heaviness foreruns the good event.

Westmoreland. Therefore be merry, coz, since sudden
　　sorrow
　Serves to say thus, "Some good thing comes to-
　　morrow."

Archbishop. Believe me, I am passing° light in spirit.　*85*

Mowbray. So much the worse, if your own rule be
　　true.　　　　　　　　　　*Shout [within].*

Lancaster. The word of peace is rend'red. Hark, how
　they shout!

Mowbray. This had been cheerful after victory.

---

70 **part** depart　80 **something** somewhat　81 **Against** expecting　85
passing surpassingly

Archbishop. A peace is of the nature of a conquest,
90   For then both parties nobly are subdued,
        And neither party loser.

Lancaster.   Go, my lord,
        And let our army be dischargèd too.
                        [*Exit Westmoreland.*]
        And, good my lord, so please you, let our trains°
        March by us, that we may peruse the men
        We should have coped withal.°

95 *Archbishop.*   Go, good Lord Hastings,
        And, ere they be dismissed, let them march by.
                        [*Exit Hastings.*]

Lancaster. I trust, lords, we shall lie tonight together.

Enter Westmoreland.

Now cousin, wherefore stands our army still?

Westmoreland. The leaders, having charge from you
        to stand,
100   Will not go off until they hear you speak.

Lancaster. They know their duties.

Enter Hastings.

Hastings. My lord, our army is dispersed already.
        Like youthful steers unyoked, they take their
        courses
        East, west, north, south, or, like a school broke up,
105   Each hurries toward his home and sporting-place.°

Westmoreland. Good tidings, my Lord Hastings, for
        the which
        I do arrest thee, traitor, of high treason.
        And you, Lord Archbishop, and you, Lord Mow-
        bray,
        Of capital° treason I attach° you both.

93 **our trains** those who follow us   95 **coped withal** been matched
with   105 **sporting-place** playground   109 **capital** punishable by
death   109 **attach** arrest

Mowbray. Is this proceeding just and honorable?   110

Westmoreland. Is your assembly so?

Archbishop. [*To Prince John*] Will you thus break
    your faith?

Lancaster.   I pawned° thee none.
  I promised you redress of these same grievances
  Whereof you did complain, which, by mine honor,
  I will perform with a most Christian care.   115
  But for you, rebels, look to taste the due
  Meet for rebellion and such acts as yours.
  Most shallowly did you these arms commence,
  Fondly° brought here and foolishly sent hence.
  Strike up our drums, pursue the scatt'red stray.   120
  God, and not we, hath safely fought today.
  Some guard these traitors to the block of death,
  Treason's true bed and yielder up of breath.
                                        [*Exeunt.*]

[Scene III. *The same.*]°

Alarum. Enter Falstaff [and Coleville, meeting].
              Excursions.°

Falstaff. What's your name, sir? Of what condition°
    are you, and of what place?

Coleville. I am a knight, sir, and my name is Coleville
    of the Dale.°

Falstaff. Well, then, Coleville is your name, a knight   5
    is your degree, and your place the Dale. Coleville
    shall be still your name, a traitor your degree, and

---

112 **pawned** pledged   119 **Fondly** foolishly   IV.iii.s.d. (again, there
should be no scene division; see Textual Note, p. 174)   s.d. **Excur-**
sions brief combats   1 **condition** rank   4 **Dale** deep place

the dungeon your place, a place deep enough. So
shall you be still Coleville of the Dale.

10 *Coleville.* Are not you Sir John Falstaff?

Falstaff. As good a man as he, sir, whoe'er I am. Do
ye yield, sir, or shall I sweat for you? If I do sweat,
they are the drops of thy lovers,° and they weep for
thy death. Therefore rouse up fear and trembling,
15 and do observance to my mercy.

Coleville. I think you are Sir John Falstaff, and in
that thought yield me.

Falstaff. I have a whole school° of tongues in this
belly of mine, and not a tongue of them all speaks
20 any other word but my name. And I had but a belly
of any indifferency,° I were simply the most active
fellow in Europe. My womb,° my womb, my womb
undoes° me. Here comes our general.

*Enter [Prince] John [of Lancaster], Westmore-
land, [Blunt,] and the rest. Retreat [sounded].*

Lancaster. The heat° is past, follow no further now.
25 Call in the powers, good cousin Westmoreland.
                    [*Exit Westmoreland.*]
Now, Falstaff, where have you been all this while?
When everything is ended, then you come.
These tardy tricks of yours will, on my life,
One time or other break some gallows' back.

30 *Falstaff.* I would be sorry, my lord, but it should be
thus. I never knew yet but rebuke and check was
the reward of valor. Do you think me a swallow,
an arrow, or a bullet? Have I, in my poor and old
motion, the expedition of thought? I have speeded
35 hither with the very extremest inch of possibility.
I have found'red° nine score and odd posts,° and

---

13 drops of thy lovers teardrops of those who love you   **18 school**
multitude (he is saying "my belly proclaims my identity as loudly as
a multitude")   **21 indifferency** undistinguished quality   **22 womb**
belly   **23 undoes** unmans   **24 heat** hot fighting   **36 found'red**
lamed   **36 posts** post-horses (Falstaff is, after all, heavy)

here, travel-tainted as I am, have, in my pure and
immaculate valor, taken Sir John Coleville of the
Dale, a most furious knight and valorous enemy.
But what of that? He saw me, and yielded, that I   *40*
may justly say, with the hook-nosed fellow of
Rome, "There, cousin,° I came, saw, and over-
came."

Lancaster. It was more of his courtesy than your de-
serving.   *45*

Falstaff. I know not. Here he is, and here I yield him.
And I beseech your Grace, let it be booked with
the rest of this day's deeds, or, by the Lord, I will
have it in a particular ballad else,° with mine own
picture on the top on't, Coleville kissing my foot.   *50*
To the which course if I be enforced, if you do not
all show like gilt twopences° to° me, and I in the
clear sky of fame o'ershine you as much as the full
moon doth the cinders of the element,° which show
like pins' heads to her, believe not the word of the   *55*
noble. Therefore let me have right, and let desert
mount.

Lancaster. Thine's too heavy to mount.

Falstaff. Let it shine, then.

Lancaster. Thine's too thick to shine.   *60*

Falstaff. Let it do something, my good lord, that may
do me good, and call it what you will.

Lancaster. Is thy name Coleville?

Coleville. It is, my lord.

Lancaster. A famous rebel art thou, Coleville.   *65*

Falstaff. And a famous true subject took him.

Coleville. I am, my lord, but as my betters are

42 **There, cousin** (a gross familiarity to Prince John; the Folio reads
"their Caesar") 49 **particular ballad else** special broadside ballad
otherwise 52 **gilt twopences** (silver twopenny pieces, if gilded,
could pass for gold half crowns) 52 **to** in comparison to 54 **cinders of the element** stars

That led me hither. Had they been ruled by me,
You should have won them dearer than you have.

70 *Falstaff.* I know not how they sold themselves. But
thou, like a kind fellow, gavest thyself away gratis,
and I thank thee for thee.

Enter Westmoreland.

Lancaster. Now, have you left pursuit?

Westmoreland. Retreat is made° and execution
stayed.°

75 *Lancaster.* Send Coleville with his confederates
To York, to present° execution.
Blunt, lead him hence, and see you guard him sure.
     [*Exeunt Blunt and others with Coleville.*]
And now dispatch° we toward the court, my lords.
I hear the King my father is sore sick.
80 Our news shall go before us to his Majesty,
Which, cousin, you shall bear to comfort him,
And we with sober speed will follow you.

Falstaff. My lord, I beseech you give me leave to go
Through Gloucestershire. And when you come to
court,
85 Stand° my good lord in your good report.

Lancaster. Fare you well, Falstaff. I, in my condition,°
Shall better speak of you than you deserve.
     [*Exeunt all but Falstaff.*]

Falstaff. I would you had the wit. 'Twere better than
your dukedom. Good faith, this same young sober-
90 blooded boy doth not love me, nor a man cannot
make him laugh. But that's no marvel, he drinks
no wine. There's never none of these demure boys
come to any proof,° for thin drink doth so over-
cool their blood, and making many fish-meals, that

---

74 **Retreat is made** the order for retreat has been given   74 **stayed**
halted   76 **present** immediate   78 **dispatch** hurry   85 **Stand** act as
86 **condition** present state of mind (but Falstaff takes his meaning as
"rank")   93 **come to any proof** stand much testing

they fall into a kind of male green-sickness,° and   95
then, when they marry, they get° wenches. They
are generally fools and cowards, which some of us
should be too, but for inflammation.° A good
sherris-sack° hath a twofold operation in it. It
ascends me into the brain, dries me there all the   100
foolish and dull and cruddy° vapors which environ
it, makes it apprehensive,° quick, forgetive,° full
of nimble, fiery, and delectable shapes, which, delivered o'er to the voice, the tongue, which is the
birth, becomes excellent wit.° The second property   105
of your excellent sherris is the warming of the
blood, which, before cold and settled, left the liver°
white and pale, which is the badge of pusillanimity
and cowardice. But the sherris warms it and makes
it course from the inwards to the parts extremes. It   110
illumineth the face, which as a beacon gives warning to all the rest of this little kingdom, man, to
arm, and then the vital commoners and inland
petty spirits° muster me all to their captain, the
heart, who, great and puffed up with this retinue,   115
doth any deed of courage, and this valor comes of
sherris. So that skill in the weapon is nothing without sack, for that sets it a-work, and learning a
mere hoard of gold kept by a devil, till sack com-
mences it° and sets it in act and use. Hereof comes   120
it that Prince Harry is valiant, for the cold blood
he did naturally inherit of his father, he hath, like
lean, sterile, and bare land, manured,° husbanded,
and tilled with excellent endeavor of drinking good
and good store of fertile sherris, that he is become   125
very hot and valiant. If I had a thousand sons, the
first humane principle I would teach them should

---

95 **green-sickness** anemia common to young girls   96 **get** beget
98 **inflammation** i.e., of the spirits with liquor   99 **sherris-sack** sherry
(wine from the Jerez district in Spain; "sack" is from the French, *sec,*
dry)   101 **cruddy** curded   102 **apprehensive** quick to take in
102 **forgetive** begetting, procreative   105 **wit** intelligence   107 **liver**
(seat of the passions, including courage)   113–14 **vital . . . spirits**
(fluids within the body that give it life and motion)   119–20 **com-
mences it** gives it a university degree (licensing it to act)   123 **manured** tilled by hand

be to forswear thin potations and to addict themselves to sack.

Enter Bardolph.

130   How now, Bardolph?

Bardolph. The army is discharged all and gone.

Falstaff. Let them go. I'll through Gloucestershire,
and there will I visit Master Robert Shallow,
Esquire. I have him already temp'ring° between
135   my finger and my thumb, and shortly will I seal°
with him. Come away.   [*Exeunt.*]

[Scene IV. *Westminster.*]

*Enter the King, Warwick, Kent, Thomas Duke
of Clarence, Humphrey [Duke] of Gloucester,
[and others].*

King. Now, lords, if God doth give successful end
    To this debate that bleedeth at our doors,
    We will our youth lead on to higher fields
    And draw no swords but what are sanctified.°
5   Our navy is addressed,° our power° collected,
    Our substitutes in absence well invested,°
    And everything lies level° to our wish.
    Only, we want° a little personal strength
    And pause us, till these rebels, now afoot,
10   Come underneath the yoke of government.

Warwick. Both which we doubt not but your Majesty
    Shall soon enjoy.

---

134 **temp'ring** softening (like sealing wax)   135 **seal** (1) squeeze (2)
close the deal   IV.iv.4 **sanctified** i.e., in a Crusade   5 **addressed** at
the ready   5 **power** army   6 **invested** clothed (with authority)
7 **level** according   8 **want** lack

King.   Humphrey, my son of Gloucester,
  Where is the Prince your brother?

Gloucester. I think he's gone to hunt, my lord, at
  Windsor.

King. And how accompanied?

Gloucester.   I do not know, my lord.   *15*

King. Is not his brother, Thomas of Clarence, with
  him?

Gloucester. No, my good lord, he is in presence° here.

Clarence. What would my lord and father?

King. Nothing but well to thee, Thomas of Clarence.
  How chance thou art not with the Prince thy
      brother?   *20*
  He loves thee, and thou dost neglect him, Thomas;
  Thou hast a better place in his affection
  Than all thy brothers. Cherish it, my boy,
  And noble offices thou mayst effect
  Of mediation, after I am dead,   *25*
  Between his greatness and thy other brethren.
  Therefore omit him not, blunt not his love,
  Nor lose the good advantage of his grace
  By seeming cold or careless of his will.
  For he is gracious,° if he be observed.°   *30*
  He hath a tear for pity and a hand
  Open as day for meeting charity.
  Yet notwithstanding, being incensed, he's flint,
  As humorous° as winter and as sudden
  As flaws congealèd° in the spring of day.   *35*
  His temper, therefore, must be well observed.
  Chide him for faults, and do it reverently,
  When you perceive his blood inclined to mirth,
  But, being moody, give him time and scope,
  Till that his passions, like a whale on ground,   *40*

---

17 **presence** i.e., the royal presence   30 **gracious** full of royal grace
30 **observed** respected   34 **humorous** given to whims   35 **flaws congealèd** snowstorms turned to sleet

Confound° themselves with working.° Learn this,
  Thomas,
And thou shalt prove a shelter to thy friends,
A hoop of gold to bind thy brothers in,
That the united vessel of their blood,
45 Mingled with venom of suggestion°—
As, force perforce,° the age will pour it in—
Shall never leak, though it do work as strong
As aconitum° or rash gunpowder.

Clarence. I shall observe him with all care and love.

50 *King.* Why art thou not at Windsor with him, Thomas?

Clarence. He is not there today. He dines in London.

King. And how accompanied? Canst thou tell that?

Clarence. With Poins and other his continual followers.

King. Most subject is the fattest° soil to weeds,
55 And he, the noble image of my youth,
Is overspread with them. Therefore my grief
Stretches itself beyond the hour of death.
The blood weeps from my heart when I do shape
In forms imaginary th' unguided days
60 And rotten times that you shall look upon
When I am sleeping with my ancestors.
For when his headstrong riot hath no curb,
When rage° and hot blood are his counselors,
When means and lavish manners° meet together,
65 O, with what wings shall his affections° fly
Towards fronting° peril and opposed decay!

Warwick. My gracious lord, you look beyond° him
  quite.
The Prince but studies his companions

---

41 **Confound** defeat   41 **working** acting out   45 **suggestion** insinua-
tions   46 **force perforce** willy-nilly   48 **aconitum** wolfsbane (a poison)   54 **fattest** richest   63 **rage** passion   64 **lavish manners** loose
behavior   65 **affections** desires   66 **fronting** confronting   67 **look
beyond** misjudge, i.e., you look further into the future than the
evidence warrants

Like a strange tongue, wherein, to gain the lan-
    guage,
'Tis needful that the most immodest word   70
Be looked upon and learned, which once attained,
Your Highness knows, comes to no further use
But to be known and hated. So, like gross terms,
The Prince will in the perfectness of time
Cast off his followers, and their memory   75
Shall as a pattern or a measure live,
By which his Grace must mete° the lives of others,
Turning past evils to advantages.

King. 'Tis seldom when the bee doth leave her comb
In the dead carrion.° Who's here? Westmoreland?   80

Enter Westmoreland.

Westmoreland. Health to my sovereign, and new hap-
    piness
Added to that that I am to deliver.
Prince John your son doth kiss your Grace's hand.
Mowbray, the Bishop Scroop, Hastings and all
Are brought to the correction of your law.   85
There is not now a rebel's sword unsheathed,
But Peace puts forth her olive everywhere.
The manner how this action hath been borne
Here at more leisure may your Highness read,
With every course° in his particular.   90

King. O Westmoreland, thou art a summer bird,
Which ever in the haunch° of winter sings
The lifting up of day.

Enter Harcourt.

            Look, here's more news.

Harcourt. From enemies, heavens keep your Majesty,
And, when they stand against you, may they fall 95
As those that I am come to tell you of!
The Earl Northumberland and the Lord Bardolph,

---

77 mete measure, judge   79-80 'Tis seldom . . . carrion i.e., the bee
who has created sweetness in rottenness rarely abandons it 90
course occurrence 92 haunch back portion

With a great power of English and of Scots,
Are by the shrieve° of Yorkshire overthrown.
100 The manner and true order of the fight
This packet, please it you, contains at large.

King. And wherefore should these good news make
 me sick?
Will Fortune never come with both hands full,
But write her fair words still° in foulest letters?
105 She either gives a stomach° and no food—
Such are the poor, in health—or else a feast
And takes away the stomach—such are the rich
That have abundance and enjoy it not.
I should rejoice now at this happy news,
110 And now my sight fails, and my brain is giddy.
O me! Come near me. Now I am much ill.

Gloucester. Comfort, your Majesty!

Clarence.   O my royal father!

Westmoreland. My sovereign lord, cheer up yourself,
 look up.

Warwick. Be patient, Princes. You do know these fits
115 Are with his Highness very ordinary.
Stand from him, give him air, he'll straight° be well.

Clarence. No, no, he cannot long hold out these pangs.
Th' incessant care and labor of his mind
Hath wrought the mure° that should confine it in
120 So thin that life looks through and will break out.

Gloucester. The people fear me,° for they do observe
Unfathered° heirs and loathly° births off nature.
The seasons change their manners, as° the year
Had found some months asleep and leaped them
 over.

99 shrieve sheriff   104 still ever   105 stomach appetite   116 straight
straightway   119 wrought the mure worked the wall   121 fear me
make me fear   122 Unfathered supernaturally begotten   122 loathly
monstrous   123 as as if

Clarence. The river° hath thrice flowed,° no ebb be-
    tween,   125
  And the old folk, time's doting chronicles,
  Say it did so a little time before
  That our great-grandsire, Edward,° sicked and died.

Warwick. Speak lower, Princes, for the King recovers.

Gloucester. This apoplexy will certain be his end.   130

King. I pray you, take me up, and bear me hence
  Into some other chamber. Softly, pray.
                        [They bear him to another
                                part of the stage.]

[Scene V. *The same.*]°

[*King.*] Let there be no noise made, my gentle friends,
  Unless some dull and favorable° hand
  Will whisper music to my weary spirit.

Warwick. Call for the music in the other room.

King. Set me the crown upon my pillow here.   5

Clarence. His eye is hollow, and he changes° much.

Warwick. Less noise, less noise!

                Enter [Prince] Harry.

Prince.   Who saw the Duke of Clarence?

Clarence. I am here, brother, full of heaviness.

125 **river** Thames 125 **flowed** flooded 128 **Edward** Edward III
IV.v.s.d. (the stage is not emptied, the King being lifted onto a bed
and moved to the inner stage or another part of the outer stage, and
the Quarto and the Folio indicate no scene division; the conventional
nineteenth-century scene division is superfluous) 2 **dull and favor-
able** drowsy and kindly 6 **changes** i.e., changes color

Prince. How now! Rain° within doors, and none
      abroad!
10   How doth the King?

Gloucester. Exceeding ill.

Prince.   Heard he the good news yet?
      Tell it him.

Gloucester. He altered much upon the hearing it.

Prince. If he be sick with joy, he'll recover without
      physic.

Warwick. Not so much noise, my lords. Sweet Prince,
15   speak low.
      The King your father is disposed to sleep.

Clarence. Let us withdraw into the other room.

Warwick. Will't please your Grace to go along with
      us?

Prince. No, I will sit and watch here by the King.
                          [*Exeunt all but Prince Hal.*]
20   Why doth the crown lie there upon his pillow,
      Being so troublesome a bedfellow?
      O polished perturbation! Golden care!
      That keep'st the ports° of slumber open wide
      To many a watchful night! Sleep with it now!
25   Yet not so sound and half so deeply sweet
      As he whose brow with homely biggen° bound
      Snores out the watch of night. O majesty!
      When thou dost pinch thy bearer, thou dost sit
      Like a rich armor worn in heat of day,
30   That scald'st with safety.° By his gates of breath°
      There lies a downy feather which stirs not.
      Did he suspire,° that light and weightless down
      Perforce must move. My gracious lord, my father!
      This sleep is sound indeed. This is a sleep

---

9 **Rain** i.e., tears   23 **ports** city gates (as the eyes are to the mind)
26 **biggen** nightcap   30 **scald'st with safety** scorches while it protects
30 **gates of breath** i.e., lips   32 **suspire** breathe

That from this golden rigol° hath divorced   35
So many English kings. Thy due from me
Is tears and heavy sorrows of the blood,
Which nature, love, and filial tenderness
Shall, O dear father, pay thee plenteously.
My due from thee is this imperial crown,   40
Which, as immediate from° thy place and blood,
Derives° itself to me. [*Puts on the crown.*] Lo,
   where it sits,
Which God shall guard. And put the world's whole
   strength
Into one giant arm, it shall not force
This lineal° honor from me. This from thee   45
Will I to mine leave, as 'tis left to me.   *Exit.*

King. [*Waking*] Warwick! Gloucester! Clarence!

   Enter Warwick, Gloucester, Clarence.

Clarence. Doth the King call?

Warwick. What would your Majesty? How fares your
   Grace?

King. Why did you leave me here alone, my lords?   50

Clarence. We left the Prince my brother here, my
   liege,
Who undertook to sit and watch by you.

King. The Prince of Wales! Where is he? Let me see
   him.
He is not here.

Warwick. This door is open. He is gone this way.   55

Gloucester. He came not through the chamber where
   we stayed.

King. Where is the crown? Who took it from my pillow?

Warwick. When we withdrew, my liege, we left it here.

---

35 **rigol** circle   41 **as immediate from** i.e., as nothing is between me
and   42 **Derives** flows down   45 **lineal** inherited (as against taken)

    King. The Prince hath ta'en it hence. Go, seek him
        out.
60   Is he so hasty that he doth suppose
    My sleep my death?
    Find him, my Lord of Warwick, chide him hither.
                      [Exit Warwick.]
    This part° of his conjoins with my disease
    And helps to end me. See, sons, what things you
        are!
65   How quickly nature falls into revolt
    When gold becomes her object!
    For this the foolish overcareful fathers
    Have broke their sleep with thoughts,
    Their brains with care, their bones with industry.
70   For this they have engrossèd° and piled up
    The cank'red° heaps of strange-achievèd° gold;
    For this they have been thoughtful° to invest
    Their sons with arts° and martial exercises.
    When, like the bee, culling from every flower
75   The virtuous sweets, our thighs packed with wax,
    Our mouths with honey, we bring it to the hive,
    And, like the bees, are murdered for our pains.
    This bitter taste yields his engrossments°
    To the ending father.

                 Enter Warwick.

80   Now, where is he that will not stay so long
    Till his friend sickness hath determined° me?

    Warwick. My lord, I found the Prince in the next
        room,
    Washing with kindly° tears his gentle cheeks,
    With such a deep demeanor° in great sorrow
85   That tyranny, which never quaffed but blood,
    Would, by beholding him, have washed his knife
    With gentle eye-drops. He is coming hither.

---

63 **part** act   70 **engrossèd** bought up   71 **cank'red** (1) rusting (2)
malignant   71 **strange-achievèd** hard-won   72 **thoughtful** careful
73 **arts** i.e., liberal arts   78 **yields his engrossments** his accumulations
yield   81 **determined** ended   83 **kindly** natural   84 **deep demeanor**
intense manner

King. But wherefore did he take away the crown?

Enter [Prince] Harry.

Lo, where he comes. Come hither to me, Harry.
Depart the chamber, leave us here alone.   90
          Exeunt [Warwick and the others].

Prince. I never thought to hear you speak again.

King. Thy wish was father, Harry, to that thought.
I stay too long by thee,° I weary thee.
Dost thou so hunger for mine empty chair
That thou wilt needs invest thee with my honors   95
Before thy hour be ripe? O foolish youth!
Thou seek'st the greatness that will overwhelm thee.
Stay but a little, for my cloud of dignity
Is held from falling with so weak a wind°
That it will quickly drop. My day is dim.   100
Thou hast stol'n that which after some few hours
Were thine without offense, and at my death
Thou hast sealed up° my expectation.
Thy life did manifest thou lov'dst me not,
And thou wilt have me die assured of it.   105
Thou hid'st a thousand daggers in thy thoughts,
Which thou hast whetted on thy stony heart,
To stab at half an hour of my life.
What! Canst thou not forbear me half an hour?
Then get thee gone and dig my grave thyself,   110
And bid the merry bells ring to thine ear
That thou art crownèd, not that I am dead.
Let all the tears that should bedew my hearse
Be drops of balm° to sanctify thy head.
Only compound° me with forgotten dust.   115
Give that which gave thee life unto the worms.
Pluck down my officers, break my decrees,
For now a time is come to mock at form.°
Harry the Fifth is crowned. Up, vanity!
Down, royal state! All you sage counselors, hence! 120

---

93 **by thee** (1) with thee (2) in thy opinion   99 **wind** i.e., breath
103 **sealed up** confirmed   114 **balm** coronation oil   115 **Only compound** just mix   118 **form** order

And to the English court assemble now,
From every region, apes of idleness!
Now, neighbor confines,° purge you of your scum.
Have you a ruffian that will swear, drink, dance,
125 Revel the night, rob, murder, and commit
The oldest sins the newest kind of ways?
Be happy, he will trouble you no more.
England shall double gild his treble guilt,
England shall give him office, honor, might,
130 For the fifth Harry from curbed license plucks
The muzzle of restraint, and the wild dog
Shall flesh° his tooth on every innocent.
O my poor kingdom, sick with civil blows!
When that my care could not withhold thy riots,
135 What wilt thou do when riot is thy care?
O, thou wilt be a wilderness again,
Peopled with wolves, thy old inhabitants.

Prince. O, pardon me, my liege! But for my tears,
The moist impediments unto my speech,
140 I had forestalled this dear° and deep rebuke
Ere you with grief had spoke and I had heard
The course of it so far. There is your crown,
And He that wears the crown immortally
Long guard it yours. If I affect° it more
145 Than as your honor and as your renown,
Let me no more from this obedience° rise,
Which my most inward true and duteous spirit
Teacheth, this prostrate and exterior bending.
God witness with me, when I here came in,
And found no course° of breath within your
150   Majesty,
How cold it struck my heart. If I do feign,
O, let me in my present wildness die
And never live to show th' incredulous world
The noble change that I have purposèd.
155 Coming to look on you, thinking you dead,

123 **neighbor confines** nearby regions   132 **flesh** sink in flesh   140
dear heartfelt   144 **affect** desire   146 **obedience** low curtsy   150
course occurrence

And dead almost, my liege, to think you were,
I spake unto this crown as having sense,
And thus upbraided it: "The care on thee depend-
    ing
Hath fed upon the body of my father.
Therefore, thou best of gold art worst of gold.   160
Other, less fine in carat,° is more precious,
Preserving life in medicine potable,°
But thou, most fine, most honored, most renowned,
Hast eat thy bearer up." Thus, my most royal liege,
Accusing it, I put it on my head,   165
To try with it, as with an enemy
That had before my face murdered my father,
The quarrel of a true inheritor.
But if it did infect my blood with joy,
Or swell my thoughts to any strain° of pride,   170
If any rebel or vain spirit of mine
Did with the least affection of a welcome
Give entertainment to the might of it,
Let God forever keep it from my head
And make me as the poorest vassal is   175
That doth with awe and terror kneel to it.

King. O my son,
God put it in thy mind to take it hence,
That thou mightst win the more thy father's love,
Pleading so wisely in excuse of it!   180
Come hither, Harry, sit thou by my bed,
And hear, I think, the very latest° counsel
That ever I shall breathe. God knows, my son,
By what bypaths and indirect crooked ways
I met° this crown, and I myself know well   185
How troublesome it sat upon my head.
To thee it shall descend with better quiet,
Better opinion, better confirmation,
For all the soil° of the achievement goes
With me into the earth. It seemed in me   190

161 **carat** (with pun on "charact," character)   162 **medicine potable**
gold in solution (prescribed as medicine)   170 **strain** musical theme
(i.e., feeling)   182 **latest** last   185 **met** i.e., as one meets one's fate
189 **soil** dirt

But as an honor snatched with boisterous° hand,
And I had many living to upbraid
My gain of it by their assistances,
Which daily grew to quarrel and to bloodshed
195 Wounding supposèd peace. All these bold fears°
Thou seest with peril I have answered,
For all my reign hath been but as a scene
Acting that argument.° And now my death
Changes the mood,° for what in me was purchased°
200 Falls upon thee in a more fairer sort,
So thou the garland wear'st successively.°
Yet, though thou stand'st more sure than I could
      do,
Thou art not firm enough, since griefs are green.°
And all my friends, which thou must make thy
      friends,
205 Have but their stings and teeth newly ta'en out,
By whose fell° working I was first advanced
And by whose power I well might lodge a fear
To be again displaced. Which to avoid,
I cut them off, and had a purpose now
210 To lead out many to the Holy Land,
Lest rest and lying still might make them look
Too near° unto my state. Therefore, my Harry,
Be it thy course to busy giddy minds
With foreign quarrels, that action, hence borne
      out,°
215 May waste the memory of the former days.
More would I, but my lungs are wasted so
That strength of speech is utterly denied me.
How I came by the crown, O God forgive,
And grant it may with thee in true peace live!

220 *Prince.* My gracious liege,
      You won it, wore it, kept it, gave it me.

---

191 **boisterous** rough   195 **fears** things causing fear   198 **argument**
plot (in a play)   199 **mood** (punning on "mode")   199 **purchased** (a
legal term: acquired by deed rather than inheritance)   201 **successively** by hereditary succession   203 **green** fresh and growing   206
fell fierce   211–212 **look/Too near** (1) examine (2) aspire too closely
214 **hence borne out** carried on elsewhere

Then plain and right must my possession be,
Which I with more than with a common pain°
'Gainst all the world will rightfully maintain.

Enter [Prince John of] Lancaster [and Warwick].

King. Look, look, here comes my John of Lancaster.   225

Lancaster. Health, peace, and happiness to my royal
father!

King. Thou bring'st me happiness and peace, son
John,
But health, alack, with youthful wings is flown
From this bare, withered trunk. Upon thy sight
My worldly business makes a period.   230
Where is my Lord of Warwick?

Prince.   My Lord of Warwick!

King. Doth any name particular belong
Unto the lodging where I first did swoon?

Warwick. 'Tis called "Jerusalem,"° my noble lord.

King. Laud° be to God! Even there my life must end.   235
It hath been prophesied to me many years
I should not die but "in Jerusalem,"
Which vainly I supposed the Holy Land.
But bear me to that chamber; there I'll lie.
In that "Jerusalem" shall Harry die.   [*Exeunt.*]   240

---

223 **pain** effort (and note the formal rhymes)   234 **Jerusalem**
(Holinshed states correctly that the "Jerusalem chamber" is in Westminster Abbey, not Westminster Palace; Shakespeare leaves the
setting of IV.iv and v ambiguous until this line—see the stage direction at IV.iv.1)   235 **Laud** praise

[ACT V

Scene I. *Justice Shallow's home*.]

Enter Shallow, Falstaff, and Bardolph [and Page].

Shallow. By cock and pie,° sir, you shall not away
tonight. What, Davy, I say!

Falstaff. You must excuse me, Master Robert Shallow.

Shallow. I will not excuse you. You shall not be ex-
5   cused. Excuses shall not be admitted. There is no
excuse shall serve. You shall not be excused. Why,
Davy!

[*Enter Davy*.]

Davy. Here, sir.

Shallow. Davy, Davy, Davy, Davy, let me see, Davy.
10   Let me see, Davy, let me see. Yea, marry, William
cook, bid him come hither. Sir John, you shall not
be excused.

Davy. Marry, sir, thus, those precepts° cannot be
served. And, again, sir, shall we sow the headland°
15   with wheat?

Shallow. With red wheat,° Davy. But for William cook
—are there no young pigeons?

V.i.1 **By cock and pie** (a mild oath)   13 **precepts** orders   14 **head-
land** unploughed strip between two ploughed fields 16 **red wheat**
(sown in late August)

Davy. Yes, sir. Here is now the smith's note° for shoeing and plow-irons.

Shallow. Let it be cast° and paid. Sir John, you shall not be excused.   20

Davy. Now, sir, a new link to the bucket° must needs be had. And, sir, do you mean to stop any of William's wages, about the sack he lost the other day at Hinckley Fair?°   25

Shallow. 'A shall answer it. Some pigeons, Davy, a couple of short-legged hens, a joint of mutton, and any pretty little tiny kickshaws,° tell William cook.

Davy. Doth the man of war stay all night, sir?

Shallow. Yea, Davy. I will use him well. A friend i'   30
th' court is better than a penny in purse. Use his men well, Davy, for they are arrant knaves and will backbite.

Davy. No worse than they are backbitten,° sir, for they have marvelous foul linen.   35

Shallow. Well conceited,° Davy. About thy business, Davy.

Davy. I beseech you, sir, to countenance° William Visor of Woncot against Clement Perkes o' th' hill.

Shallow. There is many complaints, Davy, against that   40
Visor. That Visor is an arrant knave, on my knowledge.

Davy. I grant your worship that he is a knave, sir, but yet, God forbid, sir, but a knave should have some countenance at his friend's request. An honest   45
man, sir, is able to speak for himself, when a knave is not. I have served your worship truly, sir, this eight years—and I cannot once or twice in a quar-

18 **note** bill   20 **cast** checked   22 **link to the bucket** chain link for the yoke   25 **Hinckley Fair** (held August 26, thirty miles northeast of Stratford)   28 **kickshaws** fancy things (French, *quelquechoses*) 34 **backbitten** i.e., with lice   36 **conceited** conceived   38 **countenance** show favor to

ter bear out° a knave against an honest man, I have
50 but a very little credit with your worship. The knave
is mine honest friend, sir. Therefore, I beseech you,
let him be countenanced.

Shallow. Go to, I say he shall have no wrong. Look
about,° Davy! [*Exit Davy.*] Where are you, Sir
55 John? Come, come, come, off with your boots. Give
me your hand, Master Bardolph.

Bardolph. I am glad to see your worship.

Shallow. I thank thee with my heart, kind Master Bardolph. [*To the Page*] And welcome, my tall fellow.
60 Come, Sir John.

Falstaff. I'll follow you, good Master Robert Shallow.
[*Exit Shallow.*] Bardolph, look to our horses.
[*Exeunt Bardolph and Page.*] If I were sawed into
quantities,° I should make four dozen of such
65 bearded hermits' staves as Master Shallow. It is a
wonderful thing to see the semblable coherence° of
his men's spirits and his. They, by observing him,
do bear themselves like foolish justices. He, by
conversing with them, is turned into a justice-like
70 servingman. Their spirits are so married in conjunction with the participation of society° that they
flock together in consent,° like so many wild geese.
If I had a suit to Master Shallow, I would humor
his men with the imputation of being near their
75 master. If to his men, I would curry° with Master
Shallow that no man could better command his
servants. It is certain that either wise bearing° or
ignorant carriage is caught, as men take diseases,
one of another. Therefore let men take heed of
80 their company.° I will devise matter enough out of
this Shallow to keep Prince Harry in continual
laughter the wearing out of six fashions, which is

---

49 **bear out** help out   53–54 **Look about** look sharp!   64 **quantities**
lengths   66 **semblable coherence** visible similarity   71 **society** association   72 **in consent** unanimously   75 **curry** i.e., curry favor
77 **bearing** behavior   79–80 **take heed of their company** (ironical,
coming from Falstaff)

four terms,° or two actions,° and 'a shall laugh
without intervallums.° O, it is much that a lie with
a slight oath and a jest with a sad brow will do with   85
a fellow that never had the ache in his shoulders! O,
you shall see him laugh till his face be like a wet
cloak ill laid up!°

Shallow. [*Within*] Sir John!

Falstaff. I come, Master Shallow. I come, Master Shal-   90
low.   [*Exit.*]

[Scene II. *London.*]

*Enter the Earl of Warwick and the
Lord Chief Justice* [*meeting*].

Warwick. How now, my Lord Chief Justice! Whither
away?

Chief Justice. How doth the King?

Warwick. Exceeding well. His cares are now all ended.

Chief Justice. I hope, not dead.

Warwick.   He's walked the way of nature,
And to our° purposes he lives no more.   5

Chief Justice. I would his Majesty had called me with
him.
The service that I truly° did his life
Hath left me open to all injuries.

Warwick. Indeed I think the young king loves you not.

83 **terms** court sessions (four in the year)   83 **actions** lawsuits
84 **intervallums** intersessions   88 **ill laid up** put away wrinkled
V.ii.5 **our** i.e., living men's as contrasted to God's   7 **truly** faithfully

10 *Chief Justice.* I know he doth not, and do arm myself
    To welcome the condition of the time,
    Which cannot look more hideously upon me
    Than I have drawn it in my fantasy.

    Enter [Prince] John [of Lancaster], Thomas
    [of Clarence], and Humphrey [of Gloucester].

Warwick. Here come the heavy issue° of dead Harry.
15 O that the living Harry had the temper°
    Of he,° the worst of these three gentlemen!
    How many nobles then should hold their places
    That must strike° sail to spirits of vile sort!

Chief Justice. O God, I fear all will be overturned!

Lancaster. Good morrow, cousin Warwick, good mor-
20   row.

Gloucester. }
          } Good morrow, cousin.
Clarence. }

Lancaster. We meet like men that had forgot to speak.

Warwick. We do remember, but our argument°
    Is all too heavy to admit much talk.

Lancaster. Well, peace be with him that hath made us
25   heavy.

Chief Justice. Peace be with us, lest we be heavier.

Gloucester. O, good my lord, you have lost a friend
    indeed,
    And I dare swear you borrow not that face
    Of seeming sorrow—it is sure your own.

Lancaster. Though no man be assured what grace to
30   find,
    You stand in coldest expectation.
    I am the sorrier. Would 'twere otherwise.

---

14 **heavy issue** grieving sons 15 **temper** temperament 16 **he** i.e.,
whoever is 18 **strike** lower (i.e., submit to pirates) 23 **argument**
situation

Clarence. Well, you must now speak Sir John Falstaff
  fair,
  Which swims against your stream of quality.°

Chief Justice. Sweet Princes, what I did, I did in
  honor,   35
  Led by th' impartial conduct of my soul,
  And never shall you see that I will beg
  A ragged and forestalled remission.°
  If truth and upright innocency fail me,
  I'll to the King my master that is dead,   40
  And tell him who hath sent me after him.

Warwick. Here comes the Prince.

Enter the Prince [as King Henry the Fifth] and Blunt.

Chief Justice. Good morrow, and God save your
  Majesty!

King. This new and gorgeous garment, majesty,
  Sits not so easy on me as you think.   45
  Brothers, you mix your sadness with some fear.
  This is the English, not the Turkish court.
  Not Amurath° an Amurath succeeds,
  But Harry Harry. Yet be sad, good brothers,
  For, by my faith, it very well becomes you.   50
  Sorrow so royally in you appears°
  That I will deeply° put the fashion on
  And wear it in my heart. Why then, be sad,
  But entertain no more of it, good brothers,
  Than a joint burden laid upon us all.   55
  For me, by heaven, I bid you be assured,
  I'll be your father and your brother too.
  Let me but bear your love, I'll bear your cares.
  Yet weep that Harry's dead, and so will I,
  But Harry lives, that shall convert those tears   60
  By number into hours of happiness.

34 swims . . . quality goes against the current of your disposition
and rank   38 ragged and forestalled remission beggarly and already
prevented pardon   48 Amurath Amurath IV of Turkey strangled
his brothers on his accession in 1574   51 appears (they are wearing
black, he royal red)   52 deeply (1) solemnly (2) within

Brothers. We hope no otherwise from your Majesty.

King. You all look strangely on me. [*To the Chief
    Justice*] And you most.
        You are, I think, assured I love you not.

65 *Chief Justice.* I am assured, if I be measured rightly,
        Your Majesty hath no just cause to hate me.

King. No?
        How might a prince of my great hopes forget
        So great indignities you laid upon me?
70   What! Rate,° rebuke, and roughly send to prison
        Th' immediate heir of England! Was this easy?°
        May this be washed in Lethe,° and forgotten?

Chief Justice. I then did use the person° of your
        father.
        The image of his power lay then in me.
75   And, in th' administration of his law,
        Whiles I was busy for the commonwealth,
        Your Highness pleasèd to forget my place,
        The majesty and power of law and justice,·
        The image of the King whom I presented,
80   And struck me in my very seat of judgment.
        Whereon, as an offender to your father,
        I gave bold way to my authority
        And did commit° you. If the deed were ill,
        Be you contented, wearing now the garland,
85   To have a son set your decrees at nought?
        To pluck down justice from your awful° bench?
        To trip the course of law and blunt the sword
        That guards the peace and safety of your person?
        Nay, more, to spurn at your most royal image
90   And mock your workings in a second body?°
        Question your royal thoughts. Make the case yours.

---

70 **Rate** berate   71 **easy** unimportant (the legend was well known;
see above, note to I.ii.57–58, below, pp. 175 and 184, and the Signet
Classic edition of *1 Henry IV*, pp. 192–200)   72 **Lethe** the river
of forgetfulness in Hades   73 **use the person** act in the character
83 **commit** send to prison   86 **awful** causing awe   90 **in a second
body** (i.e., one who uses your person, line 73)

Be now the father and propose° a son:
Hear your own dignity so much profaned,
See your most dreadful laws so loosely slighted,
Behold yourself so by a son disdained,   *95*
And then imagine me taking your part
And in your power soft silencing your son.
After this cold consideration,° sentence me,
And, as you are a king, speak in your state°
What I have done that misbecame my place,   *100*
My person, or my liege's sovereignty.

King. You are right, Justice, and you weigh this well.
Therefore still bear the balance and the sword.
And I do wish your honors may increase,
Till you do live to see a son of mine   *105*
Offend you—and obey you—as I did.
So shall I live to speak my father's words:
"Happy am I, that have a man so bold
That dares do justice on my proper° son,
And not less happy, having such a son   *110*
That would deliver up his greatness so
Into the hands of justice." You did commit me.
For, which, I do commit into your hand
Th' unstainèd sword that you have used to bear,
With this remembrance,° that you use the same   *115*
With the like bold, just, and impartial spirit
As you have done 'gainst me. There is my hand.
You shall be as a father to my youth.
My voice shall sound as you do prompt mine ear,
And I will stoop and humble my intents   *120*
To your well-practiced wise directions.
And, Princes all, believe me, I beseech you,
My father is gone wild° into his grave,
For in his tomb lie my affections,°
And with his spirits° sadly I survive,   *125*
To mock the expectation of the world,
To frustrate prophecies, and to raze° out

92 propose put the case of (legal term)   **98 cold considerance** cool
consideration   **99 state** station   **109 proper** own   **115 remembrance**
entry in the records (legal term)   **123 wild** uncivilized   **124 affections** appetites   **125 spirits** character (based on his humors)
127 raze erase

Rotten opinion, who hath writ me down
After my seeming.° The tide of blood in me
130   Hath proudly flowed in vanity till now.
Now doth it turn and ebb back to the sea,
Where it shall mingle with the state of floods°
And flow henceforth in formal majesty.
Now call we our high court of parliament.
135   And let us choose such limbs of noble counsel
That the great body of our state may go
In equal rank with the best-governed nation;
That war, or peace, or both at once, may be
As things acquainted and familiar to us,
140   In which you, father, shall have foremost hand.
Our coronation done, we will accite,°
As I before rememb'red,° all our state.°
And, God consigning° to my good intents,
No prince nor peer shall have just cause to say,
145   God shorten Harry's happy life one day!

                              Exit [with the rest].

[Scene III. *Justice Shallow's home.*]

*Enter Sir John [Falstaff], Shallow, Silence, Davy,
Bardolph, Page.*

Shallow. Nay, you shall see my orchard, where, in an
     arbor, we will eat a last year's pippin° of mine own
     graffing,° with a dish of caraways,° and so forth.
     Come, cousin Silence. And then to bed.

---

129 **my seeming** the way I seem outwardly   132 **state of floods**
majesty of the ocean   141 **accite** summon   142 **rememb'red** noted
(cf. line 115)   142 **state** great men of the land   143 **consigning**
signing ratification (legal term; notice Hal's knowledge of different
"languages")   V.iii.2 **pippin** type of apple   3 **graffing** grafting
3 **caraways** caraway seeds

Falstaff. 'Fore God, you have here a goodly dwelling   *5*
and a rich.

Shallow. Barren, barren, barren. Beggars all, beggars
all, Sir John. Marry, good air. Spread, Davy,
spread, Davy. Well said, Davy.

Falstaff. This Davy serves you for good uses. He is   *10*
your servingman and your husband.°

Shallow. A good varlet,° a good varlet, a very good
varlet, Sir John. By the mass, I have drunk too
much sack at supper. A good varlet. Now sit down,
now sit down. Come, cousin.   *15*

Silence. Ah, sirrah, quoth-a,° we shall
    [*Sings*] Do nothing but eat, and make good cheer,
        And praise God for the merry year,
        When flesh° is cheap and females dear,
        And lusty lads roam here and there   *20*
            So merrily,
        And ever among so merrily.

Falstaff. There's a merry heart! Good Master Silence,
I'll give you a health for that anon.

Shallow. Give Master Bardolph some wine, Davy.   *25*

Davy. Sweet sir, sit, I'll be with you anon. Most sweet
sir, sit. Master page, good master page, sit. [*Makes
them sit down, at another table.*] Proface!° What
you want° in meat, we'll have in drink. But you
must bear,° the heart's all.   [*Exit.*]   *30*

Shallow. Be merry, Master Bardolph, and, my little
soldier there, be merry.

Silence. [*Sings*] Be merry, be merry, my wife has all,
           For women are shrews, both short
              and tall.
           'Tis merry in hall when beards wag
              all,   *35*

11 **husband** housemanager   12 **varlet** servant   16 **quoth-a** said he
19 **flesh** meat (with a ribald second sense)   28 **Proface!** (a dinner
welcome)   29 **want** lack   30 **bear** endure

And welcome merry Shrovetide.°
Be merry, be merry.

Falstaff. I did not think Master Silence had been a
man of this mettle.

40 *Silence.* Who, I? I have been merry° twice and once
ere now.

Enter Davy.

Davy. [*To Bardolph*] There's a dish of leather-coats°
for you.

Shallow. Davy!

45 *Davy.* Your worship! [*To Bardolph*] I'll be with you
straight.—A cup of wine, sir?

Silence. [*Sings*] A cup of wine that's brisk and fine,
And drink unto the leman° mine,
And a merry heart lives long-a.

50 *Falstaff.* Well said, Master Silence.

Silence. [*Sings*] And we shall be merry, now comes in
the sweet o' the night.

Falstaff. Health and long life to you, Master Silence.

Silence. [*Sings*] Fill the cup, and let it come,
I'll pledge you a mile° to th'
55   bottom.

Shallow. Honest Bardolph, welcome. If thou want'st
anything, and wilt not call, beshrew° thy heart. [*To
the Page*] Welcome, my little tiny thief, and welcome indeed too. I'll drink to Master Bardolph,
60 and to all the cabileros° about London.

Davy. I hope to see London once ere I die.

Bardolph. And I might see you there, Davy—

---

36 **Shrovetide** period of feasting just before Lent   40 **merry** tipsy
(?)   42 **leather-coats** russet apples   48 **leman** sweetheart   55 **pledge
you a mile** drink in one draught though it were a mile deep
57 **beshrew** cursed be   60 **cabileros** cavaliers

Shallow. By the mass, you'll crack° a quart together,
    ha! Will you not, Master Bardolph?

Bardolph. Yea, sir, in a pottle-pot.°   65

Shallow. By God's liggens,° I thank thee. The knave
    will stick by thee, I can assure thee that. 'A will not
    out,° 'a. 'Tis true bred.

Bardolph. And I'll stick by him, sir.
                                    One knocks at door.

Shallow. Why, there spoke a king. Lack nothing. Be   70
    merry. Look who's at door there, ho! Who knocks?
                                    [*Exit Davy.*]

Falstaff. [*To Silence, seeing him drinking*] Why, now
    you have done me right.°

Silence. [*Kneels, drinks and sings*] Do me right,
                            And dub me
                                knight.°   75
                            Samingo.°

    Is't not so?

Falstaff. 'Tis so.

Silence. Is't so? Why then, say an old man can do
    somewhat.   80

[*Enter Davy.*]

Davy. And't please your worship, there's one Pistol
    come from the court with news.

Falstaff. From the court! Let him come in.

Enter Pistol.

    How now, Pistol!

Pistol. Sir John, God save you!   85

---

63 **crack** split, share   65 **pottle-pot** two-quart tankard   66 **By God's
liggens** (an oath of unknown meaning, possibly because Shallow is
tipsy)   68 **out** pass out   73 **done me right** i.e., pledged to my
pledge   75 **knight** (drinking a deep draught while kneeling entitled
one to be called "knight")   76 **Samingo** Monsieur Mingo, the hero
of the song

Falstaff. What wind blew you hither, Pistol?

Pistol. Not the ill wind which blows no man to good.
Sweet knight, thou art now one of the greatest men
in this realm.

90 *Silence.* By'r lady, I think 'a be, but goodman Puff°
of Barson.

Pistol. Puff!°
Puff i' thy teeth, most recreant coward base!
Sir John, I am thy Pistol and thy friend,
95 And helter-skelter have I rode to thee,
And tidings do I bring and lucky joys
And golden times and happy news of price.

Falstaff. I pray thee now, deliver them like a man of
this world.°

100 *Pistol.* A foutra° for the world and worldlings base!
I speak of Africa° and golden joys.

Falstaff. O base Assyrian° knight, what is thy news?
Let King Cophetua° know the truth thereof.

Silence. [*Sings*] "And Robin Hood, Scarlet, and John."

105 *Pistol.* Shall dunghill curs confront the Helicons?°
And shall good news be baffled?°
Then, Pistol, lay thy head in Furies' lap.

Shallow. Honest gentleman, I know not your breeding.

110 *Pistol.* Why then, lament therefore.°

Shallow. Give me pardon, sir. If, sir, you come with
news from the court, I take it there's but two ways,
either to utter them, or conceal them. I am, sir,
under the King, in some authority.

90 **but goodman Puff** except for yeoman Puff (whose name suggests
a shape and size as "great" as Falstaff's)   92 **Puff** swaggerer
98-99 **man of this world** ordinary man   100 **foutra** (French, *foutre*
accompanied by an indecent gesture)   101 **Africa** (where the gold
comes from)   102 **Assyrian** pun on "ass" (?) (Falstaff adopts Pistol's
style in hopes of communicating with him)   103 **Cophetua** African
king in a famous ballad   105 **Helicons** poets (?)   106 **baffled** treated
shamefully   110 **therefore** for that

Pistol. Under which king, Besonian?° Speak, or die.   115

Shallow. Under King Harry.

Pistol.   Harry the Fourth, or Fifth?

Shallow. Harry the Fourth.

Pistol.   A foutra for thine office!°
Sir John, thy tender lambkin now is king.
Harry the Fifth's the man. I speak the truth.
When Pistol lies, do this,° and fig me, like   120
The bragging Spaniard.

Falstaff. What, is the old king dead?

Pistol. As nail in door. The things I speak are just.

Falstaff. Away, Bardolph! Saddle my horse. Master
Robert Shallow, choose what office thou wilt in the   12⁵
land, 'tis thine. Pistol, I will double-charge° thee
with dignities.

Bardolph. O joyful day!
I would not take a knighthood for my fortune.

Pistol. What! I do bring good news.°   130

Falstaff. Carry Master Silence to bed. Master Shallow,
my Lord Shallow—be what thou wilt, I am fortune's steward! Get on thy boots! We'll ride all
night! O sweet Pistol! Away, Bardolph! [*Exit
Bardolph.*] Come, Pistol, utter more to me, and   135
withal devise something to do thyself good. Boot,
boot, Master Shallow. I know the young king is
sick for me. Let us take any man's horses;° the
laws of England are at my commandment. Blessed
are they that have been my friends, and woe to my   140
Lord Chief Justice!

---

115 **Besonian** beggarly recruit   117 **thine office** (the King's death
terminated Shallow's appointment)   120 **do this** (make an insulting
gesture, the "fig," by putting the thumb between the index and third
fingers)   126 **double-charge** twice-load (a pistol)   130 **What! . . .
news** (a knighthood is evidently not enough for Pistol or perhaps he
is responding to Silence's sudden collapse)   138 **take any man's
horses** i.e., "press" them (for they are on the King's service)

Pistol. Let vultures vile seize on his lungs also!
  "Where is the life that late I led?"° say they.
  Why, here it is. Welcome these pleasant days!
                        Exit [*with the rest*].

[Scene IV. *London.*]

Enter Beadle° *and three or four Officers* [*with
  Hostess Quickly and Doll Tearsheet*].

Hostess. No, thou arrant knave, I would to God that
  I might die, that I might have thee hanged.° Thou
  hast drawn my shoulder out of joint.

Beadle. The constables have delivered her over to
5 me, and she shall have whipping-cheer,° I warrant
  her. There hath been a man or two killed about°
  her.

Doll. Nut-hook,° nut-hook, you lie. Come on, I'll tell
  thee what, thou damned tripe-visaged° rascal, and
10 the child I go with do miscarry, thou wert better
  thou hadst struck thy mother, thou paper-faced°
  villain.

Hostess. O the Lord, that Sir John were come! I
  would make this a bloody day to somebody. But
15 I pray God the fruit of her womb miscarry!°

Beadle. If it do, you shall have a dozen of cushions
  again. You have but eleven° now. Come, I charge

---

143 **Where . . . led** scrap of an old song V.iv.s.d. **Beadle** parish officer (who punished petty offenders) 2 **hanged** i.e., for murdering
me 5 **whipping-cheer** hospitality of the whip 6 **about** (1) because
of, or (2) in the presence of 8 **Nut-hook** (slang for the "catchpole"
carried by beadles) 9 **tripe-visaged** pock-marked 11 **paper-faced**
thin and pale 15 **miscarry** (she goes along with Doll's threat)
17 **eleven** (Doll having used one to simulate pregnancy)

you both go with me, for the man is dead that you
and Pistol beat amongst you.

Doll. I'll tell you what, you thin man in a censer,° I   20
will have you as soundly swinged° for this—you
blue-bottle° rogue, you filthy famished correctioner,
if you be not swinged, I'll forswear half-kirtles.°

Beadle. Come, come, you she-knight-errant, come.

Hostess. O God, that right should thus overcome   25
might!° Well, of sufferance° comes ease.

Doll. Come, you rogue, come. Bring me to a justice.

Hostess. Ay, come, you starved bloodhound.

Doll. Goodman death, goodman bones!

Hostess. Thou atomy,° thou!   30

Doll. Come, you thin thing! Come, you rascal!°

Beadle. Very well.   [*Exeunt.*]

[Scene V. *London.*]

Enter Strewers of rushes.

First Strewer. More rushes, more rushes!°

Second Strewer. The trumpets have sounded twice.

Third Strewer. 'Twill be two o'clock ere they come
from the coronation. Dispatch, dispatch. [*Exeunt.*]

---

20 **thin man in a censer** figure of a man stamped on the lid of a pan
for burning incense (?)   21 **swinged** beaten   22 **blue-bottle** (beadles,
like modern policemen, wore blue coats)   23 **half-kirtles** skirts
25–26 **O God . . . might!** (a typical Quickly blunder)   26 **of sufferance** out of suffering (but "sufferance" means tolerance)   30 **atomy**
atom (does she mean "anatomy," "cadaver"?)   31 **rascal** lean deer
V.v.1 **rushes** (the usual floor covering; here, strewn in the streets)

Trumpets sound, and the King and his Train pass
over the stage. After them enter Falstaff, Shallow,
Pistol, Bardolph, and the Boy.

5 *Falstaff.* Stand here by me, Master Shallow. I will
make the King do you grace.° I will leer° upon him
as 'a comes by, and do but mark the countenance
that he will give me.

Pistol. God bless thy lungs, good knight.

10 *Falstaff.* Come here, Pistol, stand behind me. [*To
Shallow*] O, if I had had time to have made new
liveries,° I would have bestowed the thousand
pound I borrowed of you. But 'tis no matter; this
poor show doth better. This doth infer° the zeal I
15 had to see him.

Pistol. It doth so.

Falstaff. It shows my earnestness of affection—

Pistol. It doth so.

Falstaff. My devotion—

20 *Pistol.* It doth, it doth, it doth.

Falstaff. As it were, to ride day and night, and not to
deliberate, not to remember, not to have patience
to shift me°—

Shallow. It is best, certain.

25 *Falstaff.* But to stand stained with travel, and sweating with desire to see him, thinking of nothing else,
putting all affairs else in oblivion, as if there were
nothing else to be done but to see him.

Pistol. 'Tis "*semper idem*,"° for "*obsque hoc nihil
30 est*."° 'Tis all in every part.°

6 **do you grace** show you favor   6 **leer** glance slyly (instead of
reverently bowing his head)   12 **liveries** servants' uniforms   14 **infer**
imply   23 **shift me** change my clothes   29 **semper idem** ever the
same   29–30 **obsque hoc nihil est** without this, nothing (both
phrases are mottoes, the second garbled)   30 **all in every part** absolute (another motto)

Shallow. 'Tis so, indeed.

Pistol. My knight, I will inflame thy noble liver,°
And make thee rage.
Thy Doll, and Helen of thy noble thoughts,
Is in base durance and contagious° prison,   35
Haled thither by most mechanical° and dirty hand.
Rouse up revenge from ebon° den with fell
    Alecto's° snake,
For Doll is in. Pistol speaks nought but truth.

Falstaff. I will deliver her.

Pistol. There roared the sea, and trumpet clangor
    sounds.   40

[*Trumpets sound.*] *Enter the King and his Train*
    [*including the Lord Chief Justice*].

Falstaff. God save thy Grace, King Hal, my royal Hal!

Pistol. The heavens thee guard and keep, most royal
imp° of fame!

Falstaff. God save thee, my sweet boy!

King. My Lord Chief Justice, speak to that vain man.   45

Chief Justice. Have you your wits? Know you what
    'tis you speak?

Falstaff. My king! My Jove! I speak to thee, my heart!

King. I know thee not,° old man. Fall to thy prayers.
How ill white hairs becomes a fool and jester!
I have long dreamt of such a kind of man,
So surfeit-swelled, so old, and so profane,   50
But, being awaked, I do despise my dream.
Make less thy body hence,° and more thy grace.
Leave gormandizing. Know the grave doth gape
For thee thrice wider than for other men.   55

32 **liver** seat of the passions (love as well as rage)   35 **contagious**
pestilential   36 **mechanical** working-class   37 **ebon** black   37 **Alecto**
one of the Furies   43 **imp** (1) scion (2) graft (in falconry or gardening—that which adds to)   48 **I know thee not** (see Matthew 25:10–
12)   53 **hence** henceforth

Reply not to me with a fool-born° jest.
Presume not that I am the thing I was,
For God doth know, so shall the world perceive,
That I have turned away my former self.
60 So will I those that kept me company.
When thou dost hear I am as I have been,
Approach me, and thou shalt be as thou wast,
The tutor and the feeder of my riots.
Till then, I banish thee, on pain of death,
65 As I have done the rest of my misleaders,
Not to come near our person by ten mile.
For competence of life° I will allow you,
That lack of means enforce you not to evils.
And, as we hear you do reform yourselves,
70 We will, according to your strengths and qualities,
Give you advancement. Be it your charge, my lord,
To see performed the tenor of my word.
Set on.   [*Exeunt the King and his Train.*]

Falstaff. Master Shallow, I owe you a thousand pound.

75 *Shallow*. Yea, marry, Sir John, which I beseech you
to let me have home with me.

Falstaff. That can hardly be, Master Shallow. Do not
you grieve at this. I shall be sent for in private to
him. Look you, he must seem thus to the world.
80 Fear not your advancements; I will be the man yet
that shall make you great.

Shallow. I cannot perceive how, unless you give me
your doublet and stuff me out with straw. I beseech
you, good Sir John, let me have five hundred of my
85 thousand.

Falstaff. Sir, I will be as good as my word. This that
you heard was but a color.°

Shallow. A color° that I fear you will die° in, Sir John.

---

56 **fool-born** (note the pun)   67 **competence of life** allowance for
necessaries   87 **color** pretense   88 **color** (punning on "choler," and
"collar," i.e., noose)   88 **die** (punning on "dye")

Falstaff. Fear no colors.° Go with me to dinner. Come,
   Lieutenant° Pistol. Come, Bardolph. I shall be sent   90
   for soon at night.°

   *Enter [Lord Chief] Justice and Prince John [of
             Lancaster, and Officers].*

Chief Justice. Go, carry Sir John Falstaff to the Fleet.°
   Take all his company along with him.

Falstaff. My lord, my lord—

Chief Justice. I cannot now speak. I will hear you
   soon.   95
   Take them away.

Pistol. "Si fortuna me tormenta, spero contenta."°

   Exeunt [all but Prince John and the Chief Justice].

Lancaster. I like this fair proceeding of the King's.
   He hath intent his wonted° followers
   Shall all be very well provided for,   100
   But all are banished till their conversations
   Appear more wise and modest to the world.

Chief Justice. And so they are.

Lancaster. The King hath called his parliament, my
   lord.

Chief Justice. He hath.   105

Lancaster. I will lay odds that, ere this year expire,
   We bear our civil swords° and native fire
   As far as France. I heard a bird so sing,
   Whose music, to my thinking, pleased the King.
   Come, will you hence?   [*Exeunt.*] 110

---

89 **colors** enemy flags (a proverb) 90 **Lieutenant** (note the promo-
tion) 91 **soon at night** at early evening 92 **Fleet** prison for distinguished prisoners temporarily detained for inquiry ("I will hear
you soon"—line 95) 97 **Si fortuna ... contenta** if fortune torments
me, hope contents me 99 **wonted** customary 107 **civil swords**
i.e., swords presently used in civil war

EPILOGUE°

[*Spoken by a Dancer*]

First my fear,° then my curtsy, last my speech. My
fear is your displeasure; my curtsy my duty; and my
speech to beg your pardons. If you look for a good
speech now, you undo° me, for what I have to say
5 is of mine own making, and what indeed I should say
will, I doubt,° prove mine own marring. But to the
purpose, and so to the venture. Be it known to you,
as it is very well, I was lately here in the end of a displeasing play,° to pray your patience for it and to
10 promise you a better. I meant indeed to pay you with
this, which, if like an ill venture° it come unluckily
home, I break,° and you, my gentle creditors, lose.
Here I promised you I would be and here I commit
my body to your mercies. Bate me some° and I will
15 pay you some and, as most debtors do, promise you
infinitely, and so I kneel down before you, but, indeed, to pray for the Queen.

If my tongue cannot entreat you to acquit me, will
you command me to use my legs? And yet that were
20 but light payment, to dance out of your debt. But a
good conscience will make any possible satisfaction,
and so would I. All the gentlewomen here have forgiven me.° If the gentlemen will not, then the gentlemen do not agree with the gentlewomen, which was
25 never seen in such an assembly.

One word more, I beseech you. If you be not too
much cloyed with fat meat, our humble author will

Epilogue (evidently, as in *Midsummer Night's Dream*, a mingling of
epilogues: the first paragraph is for one occasion, the second and
third for another, and epilogues for any occasion could be built up
out of separate parts)   1 **fear** stage fright (pretended)   4 **undo** ruin
6 **doubt** fear   8–9 **displeasing play** (unidentified)   11 **venture** i.e.,
business venture   12 **break** (1) break my promise (2) go bankrupt
14 **Bate me some** forgive part of my debt   22–23 **have forgiven me**
(perhaps the Epilogue was spoken by the Page)

continue the story, with Sir John in it,° and make you
merry with fair Katharine of France. Where, for anything I know, Falstaff shall die of a sweat, unless   30
already 'a be killed with your hard opinions, for Old-
castle° died martyr, and this is not the man. My
tongue is weary. When my legs are too, I will bid you
good night.

[*End with a dance.*]

FINIS

28 **Sir John in it** (but Falstaff does not appear in *Henry V*)
31–32 **Oldcastle** (Sir John Oldcastle was the name of the Prince's
boon companion in the source play, *The Famous Victories of Henry
V*, and, evidently, in Shakespeare's first versions of the *Henry IV*
plays. *Old.* appears as a speech tag at Quarto 2 *Henry IV* I.ii.125.
[See also the Signet Classic edition of *Part One*, I.ii.43–44 and
pp. 181–208.] In this Epilogue, Shakespeare is saying his Falstaff
is not the historical Oldcastle, executed in 1417 and honored by
Protestant chroniclers as a Lollard martyr [though Catholic chroniclers said he was a drunkard and a robber]. The name was probably
removed from Shakespeare's plays at the behest of Oldcastle's de-
scendant, Lord Cobham—who was promptly nicknamed by the
Essex faction Sir John Falstaff).

Textual Note

Henry IV [*Part Two*] comes to us in two—or really, three—texts: the Folio of 1623 and the Quarto of 1600; the Quarto, however, occurs in two forms, the second (Qb) a modification of the first, evidently to admit a scene (III.i) omitted in Qa. The researches of a number of scholars[1] have now converged to give us a history of these three texts.

Shakespeare wrote the play in late 1597 or early 1598, and from his manuscript (called "foul papers") the Chamberlain's Men had a transcript made to serve as the promptbook for performances. In 1600, possibly to forestall pirating, the company sold the publication rights to *Much Ado About Nothing* and *2 Henry IV*, which were then entered in the Stationers' Register on August 23. The foul papers were sent to the printshop of Valentine Simmes for publication in quarto form. While there, perhaps while the copy was being cast off into page-length units for the compositors, the sheets containing Act III, scene i were misplaced (perhaps mixed into the sheets of *Much Ado,* which were in the same handwriting). At this point, the deputy of the Bishop of London, whose task it was to censor the play, read the manuscript and ordered the deletion of eight short passages that might conceivably compare Elizabeth to Richard II or otherwise tend to rebellion. He did not, however, see and censor the longer and more important references to Richard in Act III,

1 Notably J. Dover Wilson, Matthias Shaaber, James McManaway, and John H. Smith.

scene i, for the sheets containing that scene had been mislaid. In due course, Simmes and his men finished and issued the first quarto version of *2 Henry IV*, Qa, and turned to work on *Much Ado*. But then someone discovered a scene was missing, and Simmes had to put aside *Much Ado* and, at some cost to himself, correct his error by resetting two leaves as four to accommodate the omitted scene. Simmes then issued this second version of the Quarto, Qb.

Shakespeare's acting company, meanwhile, was using a transcript of the foul papers for their prompt copy and altering it to indicate their stage-practices: removing profanity, omitting mute characters, revising stage business, and so on. There is, of course, no way to tell whether Shakespeare agreed to these changes or whether they simply accumulated over the years. Further, at some point, the prompt copy itself may have been recopied—perhaps for a collector of plays, perhaps preparatory to printing the Folio; if so, the copyist was probably someone used to working with play texts, who systematically took out colloquial and vulgar expressions, improved the punctuation, and rewrote the stage directions. The Folio text of the play was then set up either directly from the altered prompt copy or indirectly through a transcript of it.

Thus, Qa (supplemented by III.i from Qb) comes closest to Shakespeare's original words and imagined staging—though often in the form of "bunched" stage directions (simply an initial listing at the beginning of a scene of the characters who will appear in it). The Folio suggests alterations in staging that Shakespeare may (or may not) have participated in, and it supplies eight passages the censor removed, but for the most part the Folio is authoritative only to correct obvious blunders or otherwise help in deciphering the oddly punctuated quarto text. Accordingly, I have modernized spelling and punctuation, regularized the speech-tags and the printing of prose and verse, and supplied the Globe act and scene divisions used in standard reference books, but otherwise I have followed the quartos closely, with a few exceptions.

The eight passages I have supplied from the Folio that

do not appear in Qa or Qb are: I.i.166–79, *You cast . . . to be?* I.i.189–209, *The gentle . . . follow him.* I.iii.21–24, *Till we . . . admitted.* I.iii.36–55, *Yes, if . . . Or else.* I.iii.85–108, *Let us . . . worst.* II.iii.23–45, *He had . . . grave.* IV.i.55–79, *And with . . . wrong.* IV.i.101–37, *O, my . . . the King.* The Folio also includes many small expansions, some of a word or two, others of whole sentences or phrases. I have included the longer ones, but not those so short as likely to be mere compositors' expansions. Finally, the list of characters appearing at the end of the Folio text I have here reproduced at the beginning.

Occasionally I have adopted certain readings that do not appear in the quartos; these readings are listed in the following, with the accepted reading first in italics, the rejected reading second in roman. Since, in almost all these cases, I have used the Folio reading instead of the quartos', unless otherwise indicated, the accepted reading is from the Folio (F), the rejected from quarto Qa.

Induction 36 *Where* When 40s.d. *Rumor* [ed.] Rumours

I.i.96 *say so* [Q omits] 161 *Lord Bardolph* Vmfr[evile] 162 *Morton* Bard. [Mour. at line 163] 164 *Lean on your* Leaue on you 166–79 [Q omits; F, with editorial *brought* from "bring" at line 178] 189–209 [Q omits]

I.ii.40 *smooth* smoothy 51 *Where's Bardolph* [after "through it" in Q] 52 *into* in 100 *hath* haue 101 *an age* [ed.] an ague [Q] age [F] 179 *this age shapes them, are* his age shapes the one 211–12 *and Prince Harry* [Q omits]

I.iii.s.d. [Q includes a mute character, Fauconbridge] 21–24 [Q omits] 26 *case* [ed.] cause [F, Q] 36–55 [Q omits] 71 *Are* And 79 *He . . . Welsh* French and Welch he leaues his/back vnarmde, they 85–108 [Q omits] 109 *Mowbray* Bish.

II.i.14 *and that* [Q omits] 21 *vice* view 25 *continuantly* continually 44 *Sir John* [Q omits] 151 *tapestries* tapestrie 175 *Basingstoke* Billingsgate

II.ii.s.d. *Poins, with* [ed.] Poynes, sir Iohn Russel, with 15 *viz.* with 16 *ones* once 22 *thy* the 22 *made a shift to* [Q omits] 79 *e'en now* [ed.] enow [Q] euen now [F] 89 *rabbit* rabble 125–33 [Q and F give to Poins] 132 *familiars* family

II.iii.11 *endeared* endeere 23–44 [Q omits]

II.iv.12s.d. [occurs after line 18, Q; F omits] 13 Will Dra[wer] [Q; F omits] 178 *Die men* Men 226 *A* Ah 273 *master's* master 286 *so* to

III.i.26 *thy* them [Qb] 81 *nature of* natures or [Qb]

III.ii.1 *come on.* [Qa] come on sir [Qb] 114 *Falstaff. Prick him.* Iohn prickes him. [as stage direction, Q] 147 *his* [Q omits] 296 *would* [ed.] will [F] wooll [Q] 308 *Exeunt* [ed.] exit 309–43 [Q assigns this speech to Shallow] 323 *invisible* [ed.] inuincible [Q, F] 325 *ever* ouer

IV.i.s.d. *Mowbray, Hastings* Mowbray, Bardolfe, Hastings 12 *could* ["would" in some copies of Q] 30 *Then, my lord* [omitted in some copies of Q] 36 *appeared* [ed.] appeare 45 *figure* ["figures" in some copies of Q] 55–79 [Q omits] After line 92, line omitted: And consecrate commotions bitter edge. [appears in some copies of Q] After line 93, line omitted: To brother borne an houshold cruelty [appears in some copies of Q, but it seems probable that Shakespeare had marked on his ms. that both these lines were to be deleted] 101–37 [Q omits] 114 *force* [ed.] forc'd [F] 178 *And* [ed.] At [Q, F] 183 *not that. If* [ed.] not, that if [F, Q]

IV.ii.1 [notice that there should be no scene division, the action being continuous, and the stage not having emptied. The stage direction at IV.i.224 follows Q] 8 *Than* That 19 *imagined* [ed.] imagine [Q, F] 24 *Employ* Imply 48 *this* his 67–71 [as in F; Q assigns 67–68 to Bishop, 69–71 to Prince] 117 *and such acts as yours* [Q omits] 122 *these traitors* this traitour

IV.iii.1 [as at IV.ii.1, there should be no scene division]

IV.iv.33 *he's* he is 52 *Canst thou tell that?* [Q omits] 77 *others* other 104 *write* wet 104 *letters* termes 120 *and will break out* [Q omits] 132 *Softly, pray* [Q omits]

IV.v.1 [as at IV.ii.1, there should be no scene division] 13 *altered* vttred [Q, some copies] 49 *How fares your Grace?* [Q omits] 60–61 [one line in Q] 74 *culling* toling 75–79 [text follows F] Our thigh, packt with waxe our mouthes with hony,/We bring it to the hiue: and like the bees,/Are murdred for our paines, this bitter taste/Yeelds his engrossements to the ending father [Q] 79s.d. at line 81 in Q 81 *hath* hands 107 *Which* Whom 160 *worst of* worse then 161 *is* [Q omits] 177 *O my son* [Q omits] 178 *it* [Q omits] 204 *my* [ed.] *thy* [Q,F] 220 *My gracious liege* [Q omits]

V.i.24 *the other day* [Q omits] 25 *Hinckley* Hunkly 50 *but a very* [Q omits]

V.ii.s.d. *Enter the Earl of Warwick and the Lord Chief Justice.* Enter Warwike, duke Humphrey, L. chiefe Iustice, Thomas Clarence, Prince, Iohn Westmerland 46 *mix* mixt

V.iii.5–6 *a, a* [Q omits] 35 *wag* wags 129 *knighthood* Knight

V.iv.s.d. *Beadle* Sincklo [Q, and so in the Q speech-tags for this scene; Sincklo was a small-part actor in Shakespeare's company]

V.v.25 *Falstaff* [Q omits] 30 *all* [Q omits]

The Sources of *Henry IV, Part Two*

As was his custom in the histories, Shakespeare developed *Henry IV* [*Part Two*] from several sources. Chiefly, he used his favorite, Raphael Holinshed's *Chronicles of England, Scotland, and Ireland* (probably the 1587 edition), and an old, anonymous play, *The Famous Victories of Henry V* (performed before 1588, but the earliest extant printing is of 1598). Almost certainly, he drew a few details from Samuel Daniel's long narrative poem, *The First Four Books of the Civil Wars between the Two Houses of Lancaster and York* (1595). He may also have looked at Edward Hall's earlier chronicle, more moralistic than Holinshed's, *The Union of the Two Noble and Illustre Famelies of Lancastre and Yorke* (1548) or John Stow's *The Chronicles of England* (1580). The story of the Prince's giving the Lord Chief Justice a box on the ear and being sent to prison for it was first printed in Sir Thomas Elyot's *Boke Named the Governour* (1531), though the story was widely retold and much stressed in the *Famous Victories*.

Shakespeare took from the *Famous Victories* (reprinted in the Signet Classic edition of *1 Henry IV*) the broad outlines of the comic sections of Parts One and Two and the battles of *Henry V*. The old play was strong on Hal's roistering and his swaggering companions, and, though it has neither Pistol nor Mistress Quickly, it does offer a crude prototype of Falstaff in "Jockey" or "Sir John Oldcastle" (see p. 169), though he is no more than a tadpole compared to Shakespeare's full-blown conception. Holinshed,

Daniel, and the other sources were used for the portrait of
Henry IV as a king sick in body and soul and also for
facts about the various rebellions and battles.

Shakespeare saved from his chronicle sources even small
details if they fitted his theme, the failure to fit into a
larger order because of a selfish appetite for food, drink,
words, or power. Thus, he dutifully recounted from
Holinshed the drinking between the armies, the Archbishop's preoccupation with his articles, and the floods
that mark Henry IV's death. At the same time, he altered
large patterns of history where it suited his purpose. Of
these changes, one stands out particularly. Shakespeare
attributes the "betrayal" of the rebels to Prince John as
well as to Westmoreland, though Holinshed had painted
Westmoreland as the sole author of the strategy. Obviously, to understand the play fully, we must be able to
account for such a marked and faintly discrediting change.

It is interesting, too, to see how Shakespeare's style of
thought differs from his contemporaries'. One can see it
by examining three episodes from Shakespeare's play in
which he does follow his sources fairly closely. They are
rich moments in the Shakespearean world: the scene of
the King's death with Hal's precipitate taking of the
crown; the coronation scene with the rejection of Falstaff;
the forgiving of the Lord Chief Justice. Holinshed (pp.
182–84) sees the first with the eye of a political reporter,
interested in events and statecraft, while Daniel sees the
King's death in terms of the psychology of the noble
classes (pp. 185–89). The anonymous author of the
Famous Victories pleased his broader public with the
almost folkloric regeneration of a prodigal son (see Signet
Classic *1 Henry IV,* pp. 181–208). Reading *2 Henry IV,*
IV.v, V.v, and V.ii against these parts of the sources, one
experiences not only Shakespeare's fusing of popular and
courtly traditions but also that special transmuting touch
which was his alone.

RAPHAEL HOLINSHED

from *Chronicles of England, Scotland, and Ireland*

[A New Conspiracy Against Henry IV]

But at the same time, to his further disquieting, there
was a conspiracy put in practice against him at home by
the Earl of Northumberland, who had conspired with
Richard Scroop, Archbishop of York, Thomas Mowbray,
Earl Marshal, son to Thomas Duke of Norfolk, who for
the quarrel betwixt him and King Henry had been banished (as ye have heard), the Lords Hastings, Falconbridge, Bardolph, and divers others. It was appointed that
they should meet all together with their whole power upon
Yorkswold, at a day assigned, and that the Earl of Northumberland should be chieftain, promising to bring with
him a great number of Scots. The Archbishop, accompanied with the Earl Marshal, devised certain articles of
such matters, as it was supposed that not only the com-
monalty of the realm but also the nobility found themselves grieved with, which articles they showed first unto
such of their adherents as were near about them and after
sent them abroad to their friends further off, assuring them
that for redress of such oppressions they would shed the
last drop of blood in their bodies, if need were.

The Archbishop, not meaning to stay after he saw himself accompanied with a great number of men that came
flocking to York to take his part in this quarrel, forthwith
discovered his enterprise, causing the articles aforesaid to
be set up in the public streets of the city of York and

upon the gates of the monasteries, that each man might understand the cause that moved him to rise in arms against the King, the reforming whereof did not yet appertain unto him. Hereupon knights, esquires, gentlemen, yeomen, and other of the commons as well of the city, towns, and countries about, being allured either for desire of change or else for desire to see a reformation in such things as were mentioned in the articles, assembled together in great numbers. And the Archbishop, coming forth amongst them clad in armor, encouraged, exhorted and by all means he could pricked them forth to take the enterprise in hand and manfully to continue in their begun purpose, promising forgiveness of sins to all them whose hap it was to die in the quarrel. And thus not only all the citizens of York but all other in the countries about that were able to bear weapon came to the Archbishop and the Earl Marshal. Indeed, the respect that men had to the Archbishop caused them to like the better of the cause, since the gravity of his age, his integrity of life and incomparable learning with the reverent aspect of his amiable personage moved all men to have him in no small estimation.

The King, advertised of these matters, meaning to prevent them, left his journey into Wales and marched with all speed toward the north parts. Also, Ralph Neville, Earl of Westmoreland, that was not far off, together with the Lord John of Lancaster, the King's son, being informed of this rebellious attempt, assembled together such power as they might make, and together with those which were appointed to attend on the said Lord John to defend the borders against the Scots (as the Lord Henry Fitzhugh, the Lord Ralph Evers, the Lord Robert Umfreville, and others) made forward against the rebels, and coming into a plain within the forest of Gaultree, caused their standards to be pitched down in like sort as the Archbishop had pitched his, over against them, being far stronger in number of people than the other, for (as some write) there were of the rebels at the least twenty thousand men.

When the Earl of Westmoreland perceived the force of

the adversaries, and that they lay still and attempted not to come forward upon him, he subtly devised how to quell their purpose and forthwith dispatched messengers unto the Archbishop to understand the cause, as it were, of that great assembly, and for what cause (contrary to the King's peace) they came so in armor. The Archbishop answered that he took nothing in hand against the King's peace, but that whatsoever he did tended rather to advance the peace and quiet of the commonwealth than otherwise. And where he and his company were in arms, it was for fear of the King, to whom he could have no free access by reason of such a multitude of flatterers as were about him. And therefore he maintained that—his purpose—to be good and profitable, as well for the King himself as for the realm, if men were willing to understand a truth. And herewith he showed forth a scroll in which the articles were written whereof before ye have heard.

The messengers, returning to the Earl of Westmoreland, showed him what they had heard and brought from the Archbishop. When he had read the articles, he showed in word and countenance outwardly that he liked of the Archbishop's holy and virtuous intent and purpose, promising that he and his would prosecute the same in assisting the Archbishop, who, rejoicing hereat, gave credit to the Earl and persuaded the Earl Marshal (against his will, as it were) to go with him to a place appointed for them to commune together. Here, when they were met with like number on either part, the articles were read over, and, without any more ado, the Earl of Westmoreland and those that were with him agreed to do their best to see that a reformation might be had according to the same.

The Earl of Westmoreland, using more policy than the rest, "Well," said he, "then our travel is come to the wished end; and where our people have been long in armor, let them depart home to their wonted trades and occupations. In the meantime, let us drink together in sign of agreement that the people on both sides may see it and know that it is true that we be light at a point." They had no sooner shaken hands together but that a knight was

sent straightways from the Archbishop to bring word to
the people that there was peace concluded, commanding
each man to lay aside his arms and to resort home to
their houses. The people, beholding such tokens of peace
as shaking of hands and drinking together of the lords in
loving manner, they, being already wearied with the un-
accustomed travail of war, brake up their field and returned homewards. But, in the meantime, whilst the
people of the Archbishop's side withdrew away, the number of the contrary part increased, according to order
given by the Earl of Westmoreland. And yet the Archbishop perceived not that he was deceived until the Earl
of Westmoreland arrested both him and the Earl Marshal
with diverse other. Thus saith Walsingham.

But others write somewhat otherwise of this matter,
affirming that the Earl of Westmoreland, indeed, and the
Lord Ralph Evers procured the Archbishop and the Earl
Marshal to come to a communication with them upon a
ground just in the midway betwixt both the armies, where
the Earl of Westmoreland in talk declared to them how
perilous an enterprise they had taken in hand so to raise
the people and to move war against the King, advising
them therefore to submit themselves without further delay
unto the King's mercy and his son the Lord John, who was
present there in the field with banners spread, ready to
try the matter by dint of sword if they refused this counsel.
And therefore he willed them to remember themselves
well, and, if they would not yield and crave the King's
pardon, he bade them do their best to defend themselves.

Hereupon as well the Archbishop as the Earl Marshal
submitted themselves unto the King and to his son the
Lord John that was there present and returned not to their
army. Whereupon their troops scaled [i.e., came away in
small groups] and fled their ways, but, being pursued,
many were taken, many slain, and many spoiled of that
that they had about them and so permitted to go their
ways.

Howsoever the matter was handled, true it is that
the Archbishop and the Earl Marshal were brought to
Pomfret to the King, who in this meanwhile was advanced

thither with his power, and from thence he went to York,
whither the prisoners were also brought, and there beheaded the morrow after Whitsunday in a place without
the city, that is to understand, the Archbishop himself, the
Earl Marshal, Sir John Lampley, and Sir Robert Plump-
ton. Unto all which persons though indemnity were promised, yet was the same to none of them at any hand
performed. By the issue hereof, I mean the death of the
foresaid, but specially of the Archbishop, the prophecy of
a sickly canon of Bridlington in Yorkshire fell out to be
true, who darkly enough foretold this matter and the unfortunate event thereof in these words hereafter following,
saying:

Pacem tractabunt, sed fraudem subter arabunt,
   Pro nulla marca, salvabitur ille hierarcha.
[They will treat for peace but foster secret deceit; nor
shall that great priest be saved for all his distinction—
Holinshed's marginal translation]

The Archbishop suffered death very constantly, inso-
much as the common people took it he died a martyr,
affirming that certain miracles were wrought as well in the
field where he was executed as also in the place where he
was buried. And immediately upon such bruits, both men
and women began to worship his dead carcass, whom
they loved so much when he was alive, till they were for-
bidden by the King's friends, and for fear gave over to
visit the place of his sepulture. The Earl Marshal's body,
by the King's leave, was buried in the cathedral church,
many lamenting his destiny. But his head was set on a
pole aloft on the walls for a certain space, till by the
King's permission (after the same had suffered many a
hot, sunny day and many a wet shower of rain) it was
taken down and buried together with the body.
After the King, accordingly as seemed to him good,
had ransomed and punished by grievous fines the citizens
of York (which had borne armor on their Archbishop's
side against him), he departed from York with an army
of thirty and seven thousand fighting men furnished with

all provision necessary, marching northwards against the Earl of Northumberland. At his coming to Durham, the Lord Hastings, the Lord Falconbridge, Sir John Coleville of the Dale, and Sir John Griffith, being convicted of the conspiracy, were there beheaded.

[Just Before the Death of Henry IV]

In this year [1411] and upon the twelfth day of October, were there three floods in the Thames, the one following upon the other and no ebbing in between, which thing no man then living could remember the like to be seen.

[The Death of King Henry IV]

In this fourteenth and last year of King Henry's reign, a council was holden in the Whitefriars in London, at the which, among other things, order was taken for ships and galleys to be builded and made ready and all other things necessary to be provided for a voyage which he meant to make into the Holy Land, there to recover the city of Jerusalem from the infidels. For it grieved him to consider the great malice of Christian princes, that were bent upon a mischievous purpose to destroy one another, to the peril of their own souls, rather than to make war against the enemies of the Christian faith, as in conscience (it seemed to him) they were bound. He held his Christmas this year at Eltham, being sore vexed with sickness, so that it was thought sometime that he had been dead. Notwithstanding, it pleased God that he somewhat recovered his strength again, and so passed that Christmas with as much joy as he might.

The morrow after Candlemas day began a Parliament, which he had called at London, but he departed this life before the same Parliament was ended, for now that his provisions were ready and that he was furnished with sufficient treasure, soldiers, captains, victuals, munitions, tall ships, strong galleys, and all things necessary for such a royal journey as he pretended to take into the Holy Land, he was eftsoons taken with a sore sickness—which

was not a leprosy stricken by the hand of God (saith
Master Hall), as foolish friars imagined, but a very apoplexy of the which he languished till his appointed hour,
and had none other grief nor malady, so that what man
ordaineth, God altereth at his good will and pleasure, not
giving place more to the prince than to the poorest creature living, when He seeth His time to dispose of him this
way or that, as to His omnipotent power and Divine
Providence seemeth expedient.

During this last sickness, he caused his crown (as some
write) to be set on a pillow at his bed's head, and suddenly his pangs so sore troubled him that he lay as though
all his vital spirits had been from him departed. Such as
were about him, thinking verily that he had been departed,
covered his face with a linen cloth.

The Prince, his son, being hereof advertised, entered
into the chamber, took away the crown, and departed.
The father, being suddenly revived out of that trance,
quickly perceived the lack of his crown, and, having
knowledge that the Prince his son had taken it away,
caused him to come before his presence, requiring of him
what he meant, so to misuse himself. The Prince with a
good audacity answered, "Sir, to mine and all men's judg-
ments, you seemed dead in this world, wherefore I, as
your next heir apparent, took that as mine own and not
as yours."

"Well, fair son," said the King with a great sigh, "what
right I had to it, God knoweth." —

"Well," said the Prince, "if you die king, I will have
the garland and trust to keep it with the sword against all
mine enemies, as you have done."

"Then," said the King, "I commit all to God, and remember you to do well." With that he turned himself in
his bed and shortly after departed to God in a chamber
of the Abbot's of Westminster called "Jerusalem". . . . he
was so suddenly and grievously taken, that such as were
about him feared lest he would have died presently, wherefore to relieve him (if it were possible) they bare him into
a chamber that was next at hand, belonging to the Abbot
of Westminster, where they laid him on a pallet before the

fire and used all remedies to revive him. At length, recovering his speech and understanding, and perceiving himself in a strange place which he knew not, he willed to know if the chamber had any particular name, whereunto answer was made that it was called "Jerusalem." "Then," said the King, "lauds be given to the Father of Heaven, for now I know that I shall die here in this chamber, according to the prophecy of me declared, that I should depart this life in Jerusalem."

Whether this was true that so he spake, as one that gave too much credit to foolish prophecies and vain tales, or whether it was feigned, as in such cases it commonly happeneth, we leave it to the advised reader to judge.

[The Coronation of Henry V]

He was crowned the ninth of April, being Passion Sunday, which was a sore, ruggie, and tempestuous day, with wind, snow and sleet, that men greatly marveled thereat, making divers interpretations what the same might signify. But the King even at first appointing with himself to show that in his person princely honors should change public manners, he determined to put on him the shape of a new man. For whereas aforetime he had made himself a companion unto misruly mates of dissolute order and life, he now banished them all from his presence (but not unrewarded or else unpreferred), inhibiting them upon a great pain not once to approach, lodge, or sojourn within ten miles of his court or presence; and in their places he chose men of gravity, wit, and high policy, by whose wise counsel he might at all times rule to his honor and dignity, calling to mind how once, to high offense of the King his father, he had with his fist stricken the Chief Justice for sending one of his minions (upon desert) to prison, when the Justice stoutly commanded himself also straight to ward, and he (then Prince) obeyed. The King after expelled him out of his Privy Council, banished him the court, and made the Duke of Clarence (his younger brother) President of Council in his stead.

from *The First Four Books of the Civil Wars between the Two Houses of Lancaster and York*

The Third Book

115

But now the King retires him to his peace,
A peace much like a feeble sick man's sleep
(Wherein his waking pains do never cease
Though seeming rest his closed eyes doth keep),
For, O, no peace could ever so release
His intricate turmoils and sorrows deep,
But that his cares kept waking all his life
Continue on till death conclude the strife.

116

Whose herald sickness, being sent before
With full commission to denounce his end,
And pain, and grief, enforcing more and more,
Besieged the hold that could not long defend,
And so consumed all that emboldening store
Of hot gain-striving blood that did contend,
Wearing the wall so thin that now the mind
Might well look through, and his frailty find.

117

When, lo, as if the vapors vanished were,
Which heat of boiling blood and health did breed
(To cloud the sense that nothing might appear
Unto the thought, that which it was indeed),
The lightened soul began to see more clear
How much it was abused, and notes with heed
The plain discovered falsehood open laid
Of ill persuading flesh that so betrayed.

118

And lying on his last afflicted bed
Where death and conscience both before him stand,
The one holding out a book, wherein he read
In bloody lines the deeds of his own hand;
The other shows a glass, which figured
An ugly form of foul corrupted sand—
Both bringing horror in the highest degree
With what he was, and what he straight should be.

119

Which seeing, all confused, trembling with fear,
He lay awhile, as overthrown in spirit,
At last commands some that attending were
To fetch the crown and set it in his sight,
On which with fixed eye and heavy cheer
Casting a look, "O God," saith he, "what right
I had to thee my soul doth now conceive—
Thee, which with blood I got, with horror leave.

120

"Wert thou the cause my climbing care was such
To pass those bounds nature and law ordained?
Is this that good which promised so much,
And seemed so glorious ere it was attained?
Wherein was never joy but gave a touch
To check my soul to think how thou were gained,
And now, how do I leave thee unto mine,
Which it is dread to keep, death to resign?"

121

With this the soul, rapt wholly with the thought
Of such distress, did so attentive weigh
Her present horror, whilst, as if forgot,
The dull, consumed body senseless lay,
And now as breathless quite, quite dead is thought,
When, lo, his son comes in, and takes away
The fatal crown from thence, and out he goes
As if unwilling longer time to lose.

122

And whilst that sad confused soul doth cast
Those great accounts of terror and distress,
Upon this counsel it doth light at last
How she might make the charge of horror less,
And finding no way to acquit that's past,
But only this, to use some quick redress
Of acted wrong, with giving up again
The crown to whom it seemed to appertain.

123

Which found, lightened with some small joy she lies,
Rouses her servants that dead-sleeping lay
(The members of her house) to exercise
One feeble duty more during her stay;
And, opening those dark windows, he espies
The crown for which he looked was borne away,
And, all aggrieved with the unkind offense,
He caused him bring it back that took it thence.

124

To whom (excusing his presumptuous deed
By the supposing him departed quite)
He said, "O son, what needs thee make such speed
Unto that care, where fear exceeds thy right,
And where his sin whom thou shalt now succeed
Shall still upbraid thy inheritance of might,
And if thou canst live, and live great from woe
Without this careful travail—let it go."

125

"Nay, father, since your fortune did attain
So high a stand, I mean not to descend,"
Replies the Prince, "as if what you did gain
I were of spirit unable to defend.
Time will appease them well that now complain,
And ratify our interest in the end.
What wrong hath not continuance quite outworn?
Years make that right which never was so born."

126

"If so, God work his pleasure," said the King,
"And, O, do thou contend with all thy might
Such evidence of virtuous deeds to bring,
That well may prove our wrong to be our right,
And let the goodness of the managing
Rase out the blot of foul attaining quite,
That discontent may all advantage miss
To wish it otherwise than now it is.

127

"And since my death my purpose doth prevent
Touching this sacred war I took in hand
(An action wherewithal my soul had meant
T'appease my God and reconcile my land)
To thee is left to finish my intent,
Who, to be safe, must never idly stand,
But some great actions entertain thou still
To hold their minds who else will practice ill.

128

"Thou hast not that advantage by my reign
To riot it (as they whom long descent
Hath purchased love by custom), but with pain
Thou must contend to buy the world's content.
What their birth gave them, thou hast yet to gain
By thine own virtues and good government,

And that unless thy worth confirm the thing
Thou canst not be the father to a king.

129

"Nor art thou born in those calm days, where rest
Hath brought a sleepy, sluggish security,
But in tumultuous times, where minds addressed
To factions are inured to mutiny,
A mischief not by force to be suppressed
Where rigor still begets more enmity.
Hatred must be beguiled with some new course
Where states are strong, and princes doubt their force."

130

This and much more, affliction would have said
Out of the experience of a troublous reign,
For which his high desires had dearly paid
The interest of an ever-toiling pain,
But that this all-subduing power here stayed
His faltering tongue and pain r'inforced again
And cut off all the passages of breath
To bring him quite under the state of death.

Commentaries

Critical essays on *2 Henry IV* tend to focus on three topics: the rightness or wrongness of Prince John's trick on the rebels; the character of Falstaff and Hal's rejection of him; the relation of Part Two to Part One. Since two of these topics concern Part One as well as Part Two, they are frequently discussed in essays on Part One. The reader should consult the Commentaries in the Signet Classic edition of *1 Henry IV* as well as those reprinted here.

Of these, Hazlitt gives the traditional view of the rejection of Falstaff, a view which A. C. Bradley greatly expanded in *Oxford Lectures on Poetry*. Freud and Philip Williams present two modern approaches to Falstaff. Freud's is psychological, an analysis of our response to Falstaff, while Williams considers Falstaff a mythic figure, a Lord of Misrule who must be banished to cleanse the land (a view developed at greater length in C. L. Barber's excellent and readily available book, *Shakespeare's Festive Comedy*). Harold Jenkins wittily summarizes the view of those who consider Parts One and Two a single ten-act play and presents cogent arguments to the contrary.

WILLIAM HAZLITT

from *Characters of Shakespear's Plays*

Henry IV in Two Parts

If Shakespear's fondness for the ludicrous sometimes led to faults in his tragedies (which was not often the case) he has made us amends by the character of Falstaff. This is perhaps the most substantial comic character that ever was invented. Sir John carries a most portly presence in the mind's eye; and in him, not to speak it profanely, "we behold the fullness of the spirit of wit and humor bodily." We are as well acquainted with his person as his mind, and his jokes come upon us with double force and relish from the quantity of flesh through which they make their way, as he shakes his fat sides with laughter, or "lards the lean earth as he walks along." Other comic characters seem, if we approach and handle them, to resolve themselves into air, "into thin air"; but this is embodied and palpable to the grossest apprehension: it lies "three fingers deep upon the ribs," it plays about the lungs and the diaphragm with all the force of animal enjoyment. His body is like a good estate to his mind, from which he receives rents and revenues of profit and pleasure in kind, according to its extent, and the richness of the soil. Wit is often a meager substitute for pleasurable sensation; an effusion of spleen and petty spite at the comforts of others, from feeling none in itself. Falstaff's wit is an emanation of a fine constitution; an exuberance of good humor and good nature; an overflowing of his love of

From *Characters of Shakespear's Plays*, by William Hazlitt. 2nd ed. London: Taylor & Hessey, 1818. One long quotation in the essay has been replaced by a citation.

laughter and good-fellowship; a giving vent to his heart's ease, and overcontentment with himself and others. He would not be in character if he were not so fat as he is; for there is the greatest keeping in the boundless luxury of his imagination and the pampered self-indulgence of his physical appetites. He manures and nourishes his mind with jests, as he does his body with sack and sugar. He carves out his jokes, as he would a capon or a haunch of venison, where there is *cut and come again;* and pours out upon them the oil of gladness. His tongue drops fatness, and in the chambers of his brain "it snows of meat and drink." He keeps up perpetual holiday and open house, and we live with him in a round of invitations to a rump and dozen. —Yet we are not to suppose that he was a mere sensualist. All this is as much in imagination as in reality. His sensuality does not engross and stupefy his other faculties, but "ascends me into the brain, clears away all the dull, crude vapors that environ it, and makes it full of nimble, fiery, and delectable shapes." His imagination keeps up the ball after his senses have done with it. He seems to have even a greater enjoyment of the freedom from restraint, of good cheer, of his ease, of his vanity, in the ideal exaggerated description which he gives of them, than in fact. He never fails to enrich his discourse with allusions to eating and drinking, but we never see him at table. He carries his own larder about with him, and he is himself "a tun of man." His pulling out the bottle in the field of battle is a joke to show his contempt for glory accompanied with danger, his systematic adherence to his Epicurean philosophy in the most trying circumstances. Again, such is his deliberate exaggeration of his own vices, that it does not seem quite certain whether the account of his hostess's bill, found in his pocket, with such an out-of-the-way charge for capons and sack with only one half-penny-worth of bread, was not put there by himself as a trick to humor the jest upon his favorite propensities, and as a conscious caricature of himself. He is represented as a liar, a braggart, a coward, a glutton, etc., and yet we are not offended but delighted with him; for he is all these as much to amuse others as to gratify himself. He openly assumes all these characters to show the humorous part of them. The unrestrained indulgence of his own ease, appetites, and convenience, has neither malice nor hypocrisy in it. In a word, he is an actor in himself almost as much as upon the stage, and we no more object to the character of Falstaff in a moral point of view than we should think of bringing an excellent comedian, who should represent him to the life, before one of the police offices. We only consider the number of pleasant lights in which he puts certain foibles (the more pleasant as they are opposed to the received rules and necessary restraints of society) and do not trouble ourselves about the consequences resulting from them, for no mischievous consequences do result. Sir John is old as well as fat, which gives a melancholy retrospective tinge to the character; and by the disparity between his inclinations and his capacity for enjoyment, makes it still more ludicrous and fantastical.

The secret of Falstaff's wit is for the most part a masterly presence of mind, an absolute self-possession, which nothing can disturb. His repartees are involuntary suggestions of his self-love; instinctive evasions of everything that threatens to interrupt the career of his triumphant jollity and self-complacency. His very size floats him out of all his difficulties in a sea of rich conceits; and he turns round on the pivot of his convenience with every occasion and at a moment's warning. His natural repugnance to every unpleasant thought or circumstance, of itself makes light of objections, and provokes the most extravagant and licentious answers in his own justification. His indifference to truth puts no check upon his invention, and the more improbable and unexpected his contrivances are, the more happily does he seem to be delivered of them, the anticipation of their effect acting as a stimulus to the gaiety of his fancy. The success of one adventurous sally gives him spirits to undertake another: he deals always in round numbers, and his exaggerations and excuses are "open, palpable, monstrous as the father that begets them." His dissolute carelessness of what he says discovers itself in the first dialogue with the Prince.

"*Falstaff*. By the lord, thou say'st true, lad; and is not mine hostess of the tavern a most sweet wench?

P. Henry. As the honey of Hibla, my old lad of the castle, and is not a buff-jerkin a most sweet robe of durance?

Falstaff. How now, how now, mad wag, what in thy quips and thy quiddities? what a plague have I to do with a buff-jerkin?

P. Henry. Why, what a pox have I to do with mine hostess of the tavern?"

In the same scene he afterwards affects melancholy, from pure satisfaction of heart, and professes reform, because it is the farthest thing in the world from his thoughts. He has no qualms of conscience, and therefore would as soon talk of them as of anything else when the humor takes him.

"*Falstaff*. But Hal, I pr'ythee trouble me no more with vanity. I would to God thou and I knew where a commodity of good names were to be bought: an old lord of council rated me the other day in the street about you, sir; but I mark'd him not, and yet he talked very wisely, and in the street too.

P. Henry. Thou didst well, for wisdom cries out in the street, and no man regards it.

Falstaff. O, thou hast damnable iteration, and art indeed able to corrupt a saint. Thou hast done much harm unto me, Hal; God forgive thee for it. Before I knew thee, Hal, I knew nothing, and now I am, if a man should speak truly, little better than one of the wicked. I must give over this life, and I will give it over, by the lord; an I do not, I am a villain. I'll be damn'd for never a king's son in Christendom.

P. Henry. Where shall we take a purse tomorrow, Jack?

Falstaff. Where thou wilt, lad, I'll make one; an I do not, call me villain, and baffle me.

P. Henry. I see good amendment of life in thee, from praying to purse-taking.

Falstaff. Why, Hal, 'tis my vocation, Hal. 'Tis no sin for a man to labor in his vocation."

Of the other prominent passages, his account of his pretended resistance to the robbers, "who grew from four men in buckram into eleven" as the imagination of his own valor increased with his relating it, his getting off when the truth is discovered by pretending he knew the Prince, the scene in which in the person of the old king he lectures the prince and gives himself a good character, the soliloquy on honor, and description of his new-raised recruits, his meeting with the chief justice, his abuse of the Prince and Poins, who overhear him, to Doll Tearsheet, his reconciliation with Mrs. Quickly who has arrested him for an old debt, and whom he persuades to pawn her plate to lend him ten pounds more, and the scenes with Shallow and Silence, are all inimitable. Of all of them, the scene in which Falstaff plays the part, first, of the King, and then of Prince Henry, is the one that has been the most often quoted. We must quote it once more in illustration of our remarks. [And Hazlitt quotes *1 Henry IV*, II.iv.380–461—ed.]

One of the most characteristic descriptions of Sir John is that which Mrs. Quickly gives of him when he asks her "What is the gross sum that I owe thee?"

> "*Hostess.* Marry, if thou wert an honest man, thyself, and the money too. Thou didst swear to me upon a parcel-gilt goblet, sitting in my Dolphin-chamber, at the round table, by a sea-coal fire on Wednesday in Whitsunweek, when the Prince broke thy head for likening his father to a singing man of Windsor; thou didst swear to me then, as I was washing thy wound, to marry me, and make me my lady thy wife. Canst thou deny it? Did not goodwife Keech, the butcher's wife, come in then, and call me gossip Quickly? coming in to borrow a mess of vinegar; telling us, she had a good dish of prawns; whereby thou didst desire to eat some; whereby I told thee, they were ill for a green wound? And didst thou not, when she was gone down stairs, desire me to be no more so familiarity with such poor people; saying, that ere long they should call me madam? And didst thou not kiss me, and bid me fetch

thee thirty shillings? I put thee now to thy book-oath;
deny it, if thou canst."

This scene is to us the most convincing proof of
Falstaff's power of gaining over the good will of those
he was familiar with, except indeed Bardolph's somewhat
profane exclamation on hearing the account of his death,
"Would I were with him, wheresoe'er he is, whether in
heaven or hell."

One of the topics of exulting superiority over others
most common in Sir John's mouth is his corpulence and
the exterior marks of good living which he carries about
him, thus "turning his vices into commodity." He accounts
for the friendship between the Prince and Poins, from
"their legs being both of a bigness"; and compares Justice
Shallow to "a man made after supper of a cheese-paring."
There cannot be a more striking gradation of character
than that between Falstaff and Shallow, and Shallow and
Silence. It seems difficult at first to fall lower than the
squire; but this fool, great as he is, finds an admirer and
humble foil in his cousin Silence. Vain of his acquaintance
with Sir John, who makes a butt of him, he exclaims,
"Would, cousin Silence, that thou had'st seen that which
this knight and I have seen!"—"Aye, Master Shallow, we
have heard the chimes at midnight," says Sir John. To
Falstaff's observation "I did not think Master Silence had
been a man of this mettle," Silence answers, "Who, I? I
have been merry twice and once ere now." What an idea
is here conveyed of a prodigality of living? What good
husbandry and economical self-denial in his pleasures?
What a stock of lively recollections? It is curious that
Shakespear has ridiculed in Justice Shallow, who was "in
some authority under the King," that disposition to un-
meaning tautology which is the regal infirmity of
later times, and which, it may be supposed, he acquired
from talking to his cousin Silence, and receiving no answers.

"*Falstaff.* You have here a goodly dwelling, and a rich.
Shallow. Barren, barren, barren; beggars all, beggars all;

Sir John: marry, good air. Spread Davy, spread Davy.
Well said, Davy.
Falstaff. This Davy serves you for good uses.
Shallow. A good varlet, a good varlet, a very good varlet.
By the mass, I have drank too much sack at supper.
A good varlet. Now sit down, now sit down. Come,
cousin."

The true spirit of humanity, the thorough knowledge of
the stuff we are made of, the practical wisdom with the
seeming fooleries in the whole of the garden scene at
Shallow's countryseat, and just before in the exquisite
dialogue between him and Silence on the death of old
Double, have no parallel anywhere else. In one point of
view, they are laughable in the extreme; in another they
are equally affecting, if it is affecting to show *what a little
thing is human life,* what a poor forked creature man is!

The heroic and serious part of these two plays founded
on the story of Henry IV is not inferior to the comic and
farcical. The characters of Hotspur and Prince Henry are
two of the most beautiful and dramatic, both in themselves
and from contrast, that ever were drawn. They are the
essence of chivalry. We like Hotspur the best upon the
whole, perhaps because he was unfortunate. —The characters of their fathers, Henry IV and old Northumberland,
are kept up equally well. Henry naturally succeeds by his
prudence and caution in keeping what he has got; Northumberland fails in his enterprise from an excess of the
same quality, and is caught in the web of his own cold,
dilatory policy. Owen Glendower is a masterly character.
It is as bold and original as it is intelligible and thoroughly
natural. The disputes between him and Hotspur are managed with infinite address and insight into nature. We
cannot help pointing out here some very beautiful lines,
where Hotspur describes the fight between Glendower and
Mortimer.

—"When on the gentle Severn's sedgy bank,
In single opposition hand to hand,
He did confound the best part of an hour

In changing hardiment with great Glendower:
Three times they breath'd, and three times did they drink,
Upon agreement, of swift Severn's flood;
Who then affrighted with their bloody looks,
Ran fearfully among the trembling reeds,
And hid his crisp head in the hollow bank,
Blood-stained with these valiant combatants."

The peculiarity and the excellence of Shakespear's poetry is, that it seems as if he made his imagination the handmaid of nature and nature the plaything of his imagination. He appears to have been all the characters and in all the situations he describes. It is as if either he had had all their feelings or had lent them all his genius to express themselves. There cannot be stronger instances of this than Hotspur's rage when Henry IV forbids him to speak of Mortimer, his insensibility to all that his father and uncle urge to calm him, and his fine abstracted apostrophe to honor, "By heaven methinks it were an easy leap to pluck bright honor from the moon," etc. After all, notwithstanding the gallantry, generosity, good temper, and idle freaks of the madcap Prince of Wales, we should not have been sorry, if Northumberland's force had come up in time to decide the fate of the battle at Shrewsbury; at least, we always heartily sympathize with Lady Percy's grief, when she exclaims,

"Had my sweet Harry had but half their numbers,
Today might I (hanging on Hotspur's neck)
Have talked of Monmouth's grave."

The truth is, that we never could forgive the Prince's treatment of Falstaff; though perhaps Shakespear knew what was best, according to the history, the nature of the times, and of the man. We speak only as dramatic critics. Whatever terror the French in those days might have of Henry V, yet, to the readers of poetry at present, Falstaff is the better man of the two. We think of him and quote him oftener.   [1817]

SIGMUND FREUD

from *Jokes and Their Relation to the Unconscious*

[Freud is pursuing the distinctions between wit, the comic, and humor, suggesting that the pleasure of humor comes from suddenly discovering we do not have to make an expenditure in emotion that we had expected to make. His view of Falstaff contrasts interestingly with Dr. Johnson's, quoted in the Signet Classic *1 Henry IV*.]

The grandiose humorous effect of a figure like that of the fat knight Sir John Falstaff rests on an economy in contempt and indignation. We recognize him as an undeserving gormandizer and swindler, but our condemnation is disarmed by a whole number of factors. We can see that he knows himself as well as we do; he impresses us by his wit, and, besides this, his physical misproportion has the effect of encouraging us to take a comic view of him instead of a serious one, as though the demands of morality and honor must rebound from so fat a stomach. His doings are on the whole harmless, and are almost excused by the comic baseness of the people he cheats. We admit that the poor fellow has a right to try to live and enjoy himself like anyone else, and we almost pity him because in the chief situations we find him a plaything in the hands of someone far his superior. So we cannot feel angry with him and we add all that we economize in indignation with him to the comic pleasure which he affords us apart from this. Sir John's own humor arises in fact from the superiority of an ego which neither his physical nor his moral defects can rob of its cheerfulness and assurance. [1905]

PHILIP WILLIAMS

The Birth and Death of Falstaff Reconsidered

In "Falstaff No Martyr," a paper read at a recent meeting of the South Atlantic Modern Language Association, Prof. Allan Gilbert said:

> Perhaps the most striking lack of the critics for many years and to no small extent at present is failure to consider the question: What are the proper limits of literary interpretation? Art is universal, we are told. But that hardly means that anything can be brought into the exposition of a speech or character. The middle ages . . . had a formula for exegesis. . . . Ridiculous enough, in our eyes, are some of their interpretations. But we may admire their clarity. A medieval preacher must have realized when he went over from the literal Samson to the allegorical Christ. But for a modern going from Falstaff, a fat man trying to run, to Falstaff the spirit of humanity, there is no post to mark the boundary. Do we have deduction straight from the play, or do we have the critic's fancy? Or, the boundaries of interpretation can be differently considered. Academics as we are here, we lay some importance on detailed study, even of the single word. How far can we go in allowing critics the very utmost from every word, from insisting on its absolute connection with every other word in the play? Or if they take the play just as something to be put on the stage, played so rapidly that a hearer cannot stop to reflect but

From *Shakespeare Quarterly*, VIII (1957), pp. 359–65. Reprinted by permission of *Shakespeare Quarterly*, The Shakespeare Association of America, Inc.

must rely on a hurried impression, a total rather than a detailed effect, how far can we trust such an impression as adequate?

These are difficult questions, and I profess no answers. But a recent book on Shakespeare by the distinguished Lecturer in English at Christ Church, Oxford, and the review of that book by an even more distinguished American scholar, afford a convenient case on which to speculate. I refer to Mr. J. I. M. Stewart's *Character and Motive in Shakespeare,* and "A Freudian Detective's Shakespeare," the long review of it by Prof. E. E. Stoll. The subject for consideration here can conveniently be limited to Stewart's final chapter, "The Birth and Death of Falstaff."

In this chapter, Stewart first discusses the inadequacies of the familiar critical approaches, and then, by drawing freely on the formulations of psychology and anthropology, offers what seems to him a more satisfactory interpretation. The objections to his predecessors are tightly argued and cogently expressed; but the book is a thin one, and there is room for little documentation of the author's own critical insights. Having canvassed the interpretations of Falstaff from Morgann to Dover Wilson, Mr. Stewart presents his own contribution:

> I suggest that Hal, by a displacement common enough in the evolution of ritual, kills Falstaff instead of killing the king, his father. In a sense Falstaff *is* his father; certainly a father-substitute in the psychologist's word; and this makes the theory of a vicarious sacrifice the more colorable.

For Prof. Stoll, this is arrant nonsense. He writes:

> And Falstaff. Whether in the hands of [Mr. Stewart] he or Leontes is the more astounding the reader shall now judge for himself. After repeating many of the vagaries of Maurice Morgann and his followers on the subject, Mr. Stewart ends up by making him symbolical, the victim of a fertility ritual, as in *The Golden Bough.* (After Freud Frazer, but Sir James, I trust, would of this have none; and again we can determine what Shake-

speare's conception was *not*.) There is something "atavic" about the final rejection of him on the stage (to many of us now unacceptable) as there is, the critic thinks, also about the blinding of Gloucester, which reminds him (as possibly nobody else in the world) of Uranus castrated by his son Cronus (so long before Oedipus!) with the scythe. Similarly, the rejection is thought to be like the primeval religious rite of killing the king, and thus is made more acceptable. . . . But why, even if Shakespeare and the audience thus "instinctively" anticipated Freud and Frazer, Hal, the hero of Agincourt-to-be, should engage in a "vicarious sacrifice" of his real father, whose death he has mourned, does not satisfactorily appear. Nor does any reason why that should have reconciled the Elizabethan (however it may be with us) to the comic fat man's ignominious, though not unmerited end.

And all this at Oxford, the Oxford of Arnold, Raleigh, the late illustrious Bradley, Ker, and Mackail!

It must be emphasized that Mr. Stewart does not claim uniqueness for his interpretation. "I hope it will be clear," he writes, "that what I am . . . concerned with is the *multiple* significance of the Falstaff story. To assert that Falstaff is the sacrificial object in a fertility ritual is not in the least to deny that he is (a good deal less remotely indeed) the Riot of a Morality [as Dover Wilson would have it]." Nor does Mr. Stewart deny that Falstaff "is" Prof. Stoll's braggart soldier, or Prof. Draper's down-and-out military man. His primary concern is why we, in the theater if not in the study, accept the rejection and death as inevitable and right.

If we turn to the plays themselves, do we find that what Shakespeare wrote can possibly permit Mr. Stewart's startling interpretation, which proposes that instead of killing his real father, Hal kills Falstaff, a father-substitute; and that this killing is necessary before a diseased land can regain its health under a virile young king? Is this "deduction straight from the play," or is it "the critic's fancy"?

The antagonism between Prince Hal and his king-father is an important, and obvious, theme in these plays, from

the forward-looking scene near the end of *Richard II* in
which King Henry asks for news about his "unthrifty" son
and adds, "If any plague hang over us 'tis he," to the
deathbed scene near the end of *Henry IV, Part Two,* in
which the King sums up the antagonism between father
and son with the charge, "Thy life did manifest thou
lovedst me not." Embedded in this antagonism are latent
parricidal impulses, and King Henry IV is haunted by the
vision of being slain by the son he has publicly rejected
and whom he at times hates. For him, Hal is his "nearest
and dearest enemy." When, at the battle of Shrewsbury,
Hal rescues the king from Douglas, Henry is almost
surprised:

> Thou has redeem'd thy lost opinion,
> And show'd thou makest some tender of my life.

Hal's reply is curious, suggesting as it does that thoughts
of his father's death had indeed not been absent from his
mind:

> O God, they did me too much injury
> That ever said I hearkened for your death.
> If it were so, I might have let alone
> The insulting hand of Douglas over you
> Which would have been as speedy in your end
> As all the poisonous potions in the world,
> And saved the treacherous labor of your son.

When on his deathbed, Henry awakes to find the crown
gone, taken by his son, the theme of parricide receives
long and detailed statement:

> This part of his conjoins with my disease
> And helps to end me. See, sons, what things you are!
> How quickly nature falls into revolt
> When gold becomes her object!
> For this the foolish overcareful fathers
> Have broke their sleep with thoughts, their brains with care,
> Their bones with industry;
> For this they have engrossed and piled up

The cankered heaps of strange-achieved gold;
For this they have been thoughtful to invest
Their sons with arts and martial exercises:
When like the bee, culling from every flower
The virtuous sweets,
Our thighs packed with wax, our mouths with honey,
We bring it to the hive, and, like the bees,
Are murdered for our pains.

Hal then reenters, saying that he never thought to hear the King speak again. "Thy wish was father, Harry, to that thought," says the King, who then continues the parricide theme:

> Thou hid'st a thousand daggers in thy thoughts
> Which thou hast whetted on thy stony heart
> To stab at half an hour of my life.

In Hal's reply to these charges, he shifts the parricidal impulse from himself to the crown: It is not I but the crown who kills my father:

> I spake unto this crown as having sense,
> And thus unbraided it: "The care on thee depending
> Hath fed upon the body of my father. . . .
> [And] eat thy bearer up." Thus most royal liege
> Accusing it, I put it on my head,
> To try with it, as with an enemy
> That had before my face murdered my father.

In the corresponding scene in *The Famous Victories of Henry V,* based on hints found in the chronicles, Hal appears before the sick king with a drawn dagger. Shakespeare subtilizes his crude source, putting the daggers in Hal's mind rather than in his hand, but the overtones in both scenes are the same: parricide.

As a result of this antagonism between father and son, it is to be expected, the psychologist would say, that the son seeks a father-substitute. Given the character of the real father—sin-ridden, punctilious, lean, and cold—he would go further and predict what the father image would

be: it would be, of course, a Falstaff, the opposite of the
real father in all those qualities that the Prince resents,
and yet like enough the real father to make the identification possible. Falstaff, without a son of his own, has found
that son in Hal; and Hal, rejecting and rejected by his
real father, has found Falstaff. It is right, the psychologist
would add, that the ambivalent feeling of love-hate toward
the real father be transferred to the father image, and this
psychological insight may, in part at least, explain Hal's
paradoxical attitude toward Falstaff. ·

Falstaff's role as father to Hal is unobtrusively developed throughout the plays, but in certain scenes the father-
son relationship receives explicit statement. Falstaff's
possessive paternalism is fully revealed in the rejection
scene. "God save thy Grace, King Hal, my royal Hal!/God
save thee, my sweet boy!" are the words with which the
old knight greets the newly crowned king. This overt
statement has been carefully prepared for.

Perhaps most important because of its initial position
is the great tavern scene in Part One where, in the play
impromptu, Falstaff becomes Hal's father. Hal commands him to "stand for my father," and the father ruffian
complies willingly. Is it romanticizing this scene to sense
with what satisfaction Sir John says, "That thou art my
son" (and so on)? I think not. Then comes the ominous
word "depose." Hal becomes king, replacing Falstaff on
the joint-stool throne. Comic, yes; but we have here acted
out the major theme of the *Henry IV* plays. "When thou
art king," introduced by Falstaff in his second speech in
Part One, and echoed again and again by King Henry,
runs like a refrain through the plays. The image of
Falstaff as king-father being deposed by his prince-son is
printed indelibly on our minds, and we are prepared for
the rejection scene where the symbolic act of the play
impromptu is literally enacted. In making the play impromptu deal with the father-son relationship, Shakespeare
has again significantly deviated from his source, for in
The Famous Victories the subject is Hal's encounter with
the Chief Justice.

To emphasize the dual father roles of Falstaff and

Henry IV, Shakespeare makes them parallel characters. Both Falstaff and Henry are mistaken for dead by Hal, who then reveals a curious mixture of grief and satisfaction over the supposedly dead bodies. Hal "robs" both Falstaff and Henry while they sleep: Falstaff of a tavern reckoning, Henry IV of the crown. The deaths of both Falstaff and Henry are surrounded by the aura of folklore and superstition: Falstaff passing to Arthur's bosom "just between twelve and one, even at the turning of the tide"; Henry IV dying in the Jerusalem Chamber after the river had "thrice flowed, no ebb between." In Part Two, the King's apostrophe to sleep is structurally balanced by Falstaff's apostrophe to sack. The cumulative effect of these and other parallels is to define the equivalency of their twin roles of father to the young prince.

But the most striking parallel between Falstaff and King Henry leads to the second part of Stewart's thesis. Much has been written about what happens to Falstaff in Part Two. It has been suggested that he is degraded, that his wit fails, that Shakespeare grows tired of him, that he becomes, somehow, an unsympathetic character. But the truth is, I think, that like Henry IV he grows old. In Part One, although his age and white hairs are not neglected, it is Falstaff's size that receives the greatest emphasis. In Part Two, although his girth has not decreased (in spite of Falstaff's claim to the contrary), the emphasis shifts to his age and infirmities. And Falstaff's growing old, his physical decay, parallels what happens to King Henry IV, who, in Part Two, also grows suddenly old and sick. In most of the historical scenes, and in many of the comic scenes, the infirmities of the King are stressed. The garden imagery of *Richard II* has been superseded by the imagery of disease, and Richard's prediction (that Henry quotes)

> The time will come that foul sin, gathering head,
> Shall break into corruption

becomes literally true. Under the guilt-ridden, infirm, old king, England itself has become diseased.

> The body of our kingdom,
> How foul it is, what rank diseases grow
> And with what danger, near the heart of it,

says the King, who is acutely aware that his own infirmities are reflected in the land he rules. Nor is he alone in making this primitive connection.

Do we not find here, surprising as it may at first appear, a classic example of a situation that anthropologists—and poets—have so thoroughly investigated—the wasteland? Under the rule of an infirm and guilty king, England has become diseased, and before regeneration can come—as it so obviously does under King Henry V—sacrificial rites must be performed. The penitential pilgrimage to the Holy Land, by which Henry hoped to expiate his guilt in Richard's murder, was never undertaken. On his deathbed, Henry is fully aware that his death is necessary to remove that stain from the succession. "And now my death," he says to Hal, "changes the mode." Hal too senses that the death of the king-father expiates past sins, but when he says

> My father has gone wild into his grave,
> For in his tomb lie my affections [that is, my sins]

he is speaking only half the truth. Into Henry's grave went the guilt of Richard's murder, but another grave, a more momentous sacrifice, is needed to bring regeneration to a wasted land.

In more ways than one, Falstaff is the only sufficient object for the sacrifice. Not only his person (and all that person symbolizes) but also his relationship to Hal marks him as the inevitable choice.

Dover Wilson long ago detected the sacrificial and symbolic quality in Falstaff. Commenting on the epithet "Martlemas" that Poins once employs, Wilson explains:

> Martlemas, or the feast of St. Martin, on 11 November, was in those days of scarce fodder the season at which most of the beasts had to be killed off and salted

for the winter, and therefore the season for great ban-
quets of fresh meat. Thus it had been for centuries, long
before the coming of Christianity. In calling him a "Martlemas" Poins is at once likening Falstaff's enormous pro-
portions to the prodigality of fresh-killed meat which the
feast brought, and acclaiming his identity with Riot and
Festivity in general.

To this, Mr. Stewart would add:

But such festivals commemorate more than the need
to reduce stock against a winter season. They commemorate a whole mythology of the cycle of the year, and of
the sacrifices offered to secure a new fertility on the earth.
. . . Perhaps we glimpse here a further reason why the rejection of Falstaff is inevitable—not merely traditionally
and moralistically inevitable but symbolically inevitable
as well. And this may be why, when in the theater, we do
not really rebel against the rejection; why we find a fit-
ness too in its being sudden and catastrophic. . . . For the
killing carries something of the ritual suggestion, the obscure *pathos*, of death in tragedy. . . . And Falstaff is in
the end the dethroned and sacrificed king, the scapegoat
as well as the sweet beef. For Falstaff . . . so fit a sacrifice
. . . to lard the lean, the barren earth, is of that primitive
and magical world upon which all art, even with a pro-
found unconsciousness, draws.

If Falstaff is ritually slain by Hal, if his death is necessary for the regeneration of a diseased land, we should
expect to find further corroboration in the structure and
imagery of the plays. One example from each category will
have here to suffice. It is significant, in terms of the structure of *Henry V,* that Hal does not "assume the port of
Mars," does not become the hero-king, until *after* the
death of Falstaff. He is uncomfortable in his new role of
king in the last scenes of *Henry IV, Part Two,* and in the
early scenes of *Henry V* there is much talk of his miracu-
lous transformation, but it is only talk. Then, in Act II,
scene 3, comes Falstaff's death, and Henry V's next words
are:

> Once more unto the breach, dear friends, once more;
> Or close the wall up with our English dead!
> . . . On, on, you noblest English,
> Whose blood is fet from fathers of war proof!
> Fathers that, like so many Alexanders,
> Have in these parts from morn to even fought,
> And sheathed their swords for lack of argument.

For the first time, Henry V becomes in word and deed the national hero, the mirror of all Christian kings.

With a single image drawn from the rich storehouse of classic myth, Shakespeare sometimes found that he could present the essence of his play, a statement of its theme in miniature. In the first play of this tetralogy, *Richard II,* he accomplished this, for the whole play is contained in Richard's lines,

> Down, down I come like glistering Phaeton,
> Wanting the manage of unruly steeds.

And he may, I think, have accomplished the same thing in the rejection scene with Falstaff's climactic line,

> My King, my Jove, I speak to thee my heart!

For Hal is Falstaff's Jove, the son who deposes his king-father, old Saturn. It is only at this appropriate moment that Falstaff calls Hal Jove. He has never done so before, but Hal himself has made the identification. "It was Jove's case," he says as he dons the leather jerkin disguise to spy on Falstaff and Doll—Saturn and Venus as he calls them.

And for a final bit of evidence, not from the plays and yet not without significance: It is reassuring to note how often the critics have slipped unconsciously into the metaphor of making Falstaff a king and his rejection a de-thronement or sacrifice. A. C. Bradley, who wrote, "[Shakespeare] created so extraordinary a being, and fixed him so firmly on his intellectual throne, that when he sought to dethrone him he could not," is only one of many whose intuitive understanding of the situation is revealed in the metaphors they chose to describe it. Even Stoll himself has written: "The King casts [Falstaff] off, but morally, officially, it is to his credit. The poet's hand here is a bit heavy, but he would simply convey to the audience that as King of England, Henry has broken with the past." Is it Shakespeare's hand that is heavy, or the hand of Hal as he runs bad humors on the knight and kills his heart?

In the final analysis, Stoll's own approach to Falstaff and Stewart's are curiously similar: both attempt to explain Falstaff by discovering his ancestors. Stoll found them in the *milites gloriosi* of Latin comedy; Stewart finds them in those ritually slain kings whose diverse histories and lingering traditions are so copiously recorded in *The Golden Bough.* Fortunately, literary paternity, unlike biological, does not preclude the possibility of more than one father, and Falstaff's family tree has many branches. If to those branches already traced by Stoll and the other literary genealogists, Stewart would add yet another, must we reject it because, for Stoll at least, it means an "instinctive anticipation" of Freud and Frazer?

I would suggest that Sigmund Freud did not endow only twentieth-century man with a subconscious mind. Nor did Sir James Frazer trace the survivals—in England long after Shakespeare's day—of the magical connection between old kings and the lands they ruled, of rites and rituals by which fertility was assured, merely to plague the historical critics of Shakespeare. It is not, however, Freudian psychology (so objectionable to Stoll) but Carl Jung's concept of the collective unconscious of the race which offers a possible further explanation of why, as Stewart claims, the rejection and death of Falstaff are felt to be inevitable and just. Archetypal images of king-fathers and sacrificial rites are our inescapable heritage no less than they were Shakespeare's. We should be neither surprised nor alarmed that Shakespeare, in his greatest moments, penetrates this mysterious, rich, and largely unexplored region of the human psyche.

HAROLD JENKINS

The Structural Problem in Shakespeare's
Henry the Fourth

In having the honor to inaugurate a chair of English in
this college, I have thought it appropriate to devote my
inaugural lecture to the preeminent writer in English. A
professor of English who gives to Shakespeare such pri-
ority of his attention needs, I hope, no defense. But if
defense were necessary, I could of course plead the authority of that distinguished body which has honored me
this afternoon by the attendance of so many of its members, the Board of Studies in English, whose collective
wisdom has ensured that the syllabus studied in our London school of English gives to Shakespeare a greater
prominence than to any other author, not even excepting
the author of *Beowulf*. To confine myself to two—or is it
indeed only one?—of Shakespeare's masterpieces may be
less obviously justifiable. But it cannot be the task of an
hour to survey Shakespeare whole, much less Shakespear-
ian criticism. By accepting a restricted scope I must, I am
aware, forgo what Dr. Johnson called "the grandeur of
generality." But whatever may be the poet's business, the
scholar and the critic, in their humbler field, before they
can come at the grandeur of generality, must be willing
to "number the streaks of the tulip." Though they may
properly avoid the esoteric, they cannot ignore the particular. The qualm that I am left with is lest the particular
two-headed bloom I have picked for this occasion should
not seem the most suitable to present to a women's college. For I am told by one of the most remarkable women

Delivered in 1955 as an inaugural address at Westfield College, Uni-
versity of London, Mr. Jenkins' essay was published in book form by
Methuen & Co., Ltd., 1956. Reprinted by permission of Methuen & Co.,
Ltd.

in the history of the British theater that *Henry IV* "is a play which . . . most women dislike." According to Mrs. Inchbald, "many revolting expressions in the comic parts, much boisterous courage in the graver scenes, together with Falstaff's unwieldy person, offend every female auditor; and whilst a facetious Prince of Wales is employed taking purses on the highway, a lady would rather see him stealing hearts at a ball."[1] That, however, was before the emancipation. It would be small compliment to Westfield College if I failed to recognize the great change that has come about since Mrs. Inchbald's day. I take this opportunity of paying my respect to the part that Westfield College has taken in the education of women and in the consequent enlargement of women's freedom, which has been so conspicuous a feature of recent social history. A subsidiary aspect of this social change, though one that Constance Maynard can hardly at first have envisaged, is that battlefields and even taverns are now less closed to women than they were. So it is without apology that I cheerfully commend to my students the "infinite entertainment and instruction" that Mrs. Inchbald herself admitted might "be obtained from this drama even by the most delicate readers."

The first problem that confronts one in approaching *Henry IV,* and the one about which I propose to be particular, has inevitably introduced itself already. Is it one play or two? Some of you will dismiss this as an academic question, the sort of thing that only people like professors bother their heads about. Some of you will look askance at it as a metaphysical question, which in a sense it is. But it is also, surely, a practical question: how satisfactorily can either the first part or the second be shown in the theater without the other? What is gained, or indeed lost, by presenting the two parts, as the Old Vic are doing at the moment, on successive evenings? And thus of course the question becomes a problem of literary criticism. Until it has been answered, how can the dramatic quality of *Henry IV* be fully appreciated, or even defined? Yet the numerous literary critics who have attempted an answer

[1] Quoted in *1 Henry IV*, New Variorum, ed. Hemingway, p. 395.

to the question have reached surprisingly opposite con-
clusions.[2]

Answers began more than two hundred years ago in
the *Critical Observations on Shakespeare* by John Upton,
a man who deserves our regard for trying to scotch the
notion so strangely current in the eighteenth century that
"Shakespeare had no learning." Far from accepting that
Shakespeare's plays were the happy, or the not so happy,
products of untutored nature, Upton maintained that they
were constructed according to some principles of art; and
his examination of *Henry IV* suggested to him that each
of its two parts had, what Aristotle of course demanded,
its own beginning, middle, and end. Upton held it to be
an injury to Shakespeare even to speak of a first and
second *part* and thus conceal the fact that there were here
two quite independent plays.[3] To this Dr. Johnson retorted
that these two plays, so far from being independent, are
"two only because they are too long to be one." They
could appear as separate plays, he thought, only to those
who looked at them with the "ambition of critical discoveries." In these tart words Johnson shrewdly defined
what if not one of the deadly sins, is still a vice and one to
which universities are prone. The "ambition of critical
discoveries," a natural human vanity unnaturally nourished in our day by the requirements of the Ph.D. thesis
and the demand for "publications," has been responsible
for many interpretations of Shakespeare whose merit is in
their being new rather than their being true. Yet one must
not always accept the accepted. Dr. Johnson's contemporaries did not all find it as plain as he did that *Henry IV*
was just one continuous composition. It seemed probable
to Malone that Part Two was not even "conceived"[4] until
Part One had been a roaring success. Capell, on the other
hand, thought that both parts were "planned at the same
time, and with great judgment."[5]

[2] For particulars of the most important, see the appended Note, which
will usually obviate the necessity of further reference in the footnotes to
the works listed in it.

[3] *Op. cit.*, 1746. See especially pp. 11, 41–2, 70–1.

[4] *Shakespeare*, Johnson-Steevens Variorum, 2nd ed., 1778, vol. i. p. 300.

[5] *Notes and Various Readings to Shakespeare* [1775], p. 164.

Among present-day scholars Professor Dover Wilson is on Johnson's side. He insists that the two parts of *Henry IV* are "a single structure" with the "normal dramatic curve" stretched over ten acts instead of five. Professor R. A. Law, however, declares that *Henry IV* is "not a single ten-act play," but two organic units "written with different purposes in view." On the contrary, says Dr. Tillyard, "The two parts of the play are a single organism." Part One by itself is "patently incomplete." "Each part is a drama complete in itself," says Kittredge flatly.[6] In short, some two centuries after Upton and Johnson, scholars are still about equally divided as to whether *Henry IV* was "planned" as "one long drama" or whether the second part was, as they put it, an "unpremeditated sequel." A new professor, his ambition already dwindling at Johnson's warning, might well lapse into melancholy, or even modesty. Modest or not, he can hardly escape the conclusion, reached by another eighteenth-century dignitary in a somewhat different situation, that "much might be said on both sides." Like Sir Roger de Coverley, he "would not give his judgment rashly," yet like the late R. W. Chambers, whose pupil I am proud to have been, he may think that the modesty which forbears to make a judgment is disastrous.[7]

Words like "planned" and "unpremeditated" figure largely in this controversy; and of course they imply intention or the lack of it, and will therefore be suspect in those circles which denounce what is called "the intentional fallacy."[8] I am far from belonging to that school of criticism which holds that an author's own intention is irrelevant to our reading of his work; yet, as Lascelles Abercrombie says, aesthetic criticism must ultimately judge by results: a man's work is evidence of what he did, but you can never be sure what he intended.[9] This

6 *1 Henry IV*, ed. Kittredge, 1940, p. viii.

7 See *Beowulf, an Introduction to the Study of the Poem*, 2nd ed., 1932, p. 390.

8 This is actually the title of an article by W. K. Wimsatt and M. C. Beardsley in the *Sewanee Review*, LIV (1946), 468 ff., reprinted in Wimsatt's *The Verbal Icon*, 1954.

9 *A Plea for the Liberty of Interpreting*, British Academy Shakespeare Lecture, 1930, p. 6.

position, with the coming of the Freudian psychology, is finally inescapable, but in its extreme form it seems to me unnecessarily defeatist. When I find *Much Ado About Nothing* beginning with talk of a battle in which those killed are "few of any sort, and none of name," I may infer that Shakespeare intended to write a comedy and not a realistic one at that. But if I wish to play for safety, I may use a phrase of Lascelles Abercrombie's own and speak—not of what Shakespeare intended, but of what he "warned his audience to expect."[10] If we leave aside for the present all question of Shakespeare's intention, what does *Henry IV* itself, as it begins and proceeds along its course, warn us to expect?

The short first scene, filled with reports of wars—wars this time in which multitudes are "butchered"—makes an apt beginning for a history play. But its dialogue announces no main action. Yet certain topics, brought in with apparent casualness, naturally engage our interest. There is talk of two young men who do not yet appear, both called "young Harry," yet apparently unlike. The first of them, Hotspur, is introduced as "gallant," an epithet which is very soon repeated when he is said to have won "a gallant prize." The prisoners he has taken are, we are told, "a conquest for a prince to boast of." Already, before Prince Hal is even named, a contrast is being begun between a man who behaves like a prince though he is not one and another who is in fact a prince but does not act the part. The King makes this explicit. Hotspur, who has gained "an honorable spoil," is "a son who is the theme of honor's tongue," while the King's own son is stained with "riot and dishonor." In the second and third scenes the two Harrys in turn appear. First, the Prince, already associated with dishonor, instead of, like Hotspur, taking prisoners in battle, plans to engage in highway robbery. Then, when he has arranged to sup next night in a tavern, he is followed on the stage by Hotspur telling how, when he took his prisoners, he was "dry with rage and extreme toil." This practice of juxtaposing characters who exhibit opposite codes of conduct

10 *Ibid.*, p. 22.

is a common one in Shakespeare's drama. After the "un-savory similes" that Hal swaps with Falstaff, in which a squalling cat and a stinking ditch are prominent, there is Hotspur's hyperbole about plucking "bright honor from the pale-faced moon." It may not be a classical construc-tion, but there is enough suggestion here of arrangement to justify Upton's claim for Shakespeare's art. We expect that central to the play will be the antithesis between these two young men and the lives they lead. And we shall find that this antithesis precipitates a moral contest which is an important aspect of the historical action of the drama.

The historical action presents Hotspur's rebellion. It is an action which develops with a fine structural proportion throughout Part One. The act divisions, although they are not Shakespeare's of course, being first found in the Folio, may serve nevertheless as a convenient register of the way the action is disposed. In the first act the rebel plot is hatched, in the second Hotspur prepares to leave home, in the third he joins forces with the other rebel leaders, in the fourth the rebel army is encamped ready to give battle, in the fifth it is defeated and Hotspur is killed. Meantime, along with the military contest between Hotspur and the King, the moral contest between the Prince and Hotspur proceeds with an equally perfect balance. The opposition of honor and riot established in the first act is intensified in the second, where a scene of Hotspur at home prepar-ing for war is set against one of Hal reveling in the tavern. The revelry even includes a little skit by Hal on Hotspur's conversation with his wife, which serves not only to ad-just our view of Hotspur's honor by subjecting it to ridi-cule, but also to emphasize that the Prince is—with gleeful understatement—"not yet of Percy's mind." That he is not of Percy's mind leads the King in the third act to resume his opening plaint: it is not the Prince but Percy, with his "never-dying honor," who is fit to be a king's son. At this point the Prince vows to outshine his rival. He will meet "this gallant Hotspur"—the words echo the opening scene—this "child of honor," and overcome him. And so, when the rebels see the Prince in Act IV, he is "gallantly arm'd"—Hotspur's word is now applied to him—and he

vaults upon his horse "as if an angel dropp'd down from
the clouds"—with a glory, that is, already beyond Hotspur. All that then remains is that the Prince shall demonstrate his new chivalry in action, which of course he does
in the fifth act, first saving his father's life and finally
slaying Hotspur in single combat. Opposed to one another
throughout the play, constantly spoken of together, these
two are nevertheless kept apart till the fifth act, when
their first and last encounter completes in the expected
manner the pattern of their rivalry that began in the opening words. The two have exchanged places. Supremacy in
honor has passed from Hotspur to the Prince, and the
wayward hero of the opening ends by exhibiting his true
princely nature.

What then is one to make of the view of Professor
Dover Wilson that the Battle of Shrewsbury, in which the
Prince kills Hotspur, is not an adequate conclusion but
merely the "nodal point we expect in a third act"? If we
do expect a "nodal point" in a third act, then *Henry IV
Part One* will not disappoint us. For there *is* a nodal point,
and—I am tempted to say this categorically—it is in the
third act of Part One that it occurs. In this third act, when
the King rebukes his son, the Prince replies, "I will redeem all this . . ."; in the fifth act he fulfils this vow at
Shrewsbury, as is signalized by the King's admission that
the Prince has "redeem'd" his "lost opinion." Again, in
the third act, the Prince swears that he will take from
Hotspur "every honor sitting on his helm"; in the fifth act
Hotspur is brought to confess that the Prince has won
"proud titles" from him.[11] More significantly still, the
third act ends with the Prince saying,

> Percy stands on high;
> And either we or they must lower lie;

and then the fifth act shows us the spectacle of the hero
looking down upon his rival's prostrate form. The curve
of the plot could hardly be more firmly or more sym-
metrically drawn. It does not seem easy to agree with

[11] The connection here is reinforced by the Prince's use of his earlier
image: "all the budding honors on thy crest I'll crop."

Dr. Johnson and Professor Dover Wilson that *Henry IV Part One* is only the first half of a play.

If this were all there were to *Henry IV Part One*, the matter would be simple. But the Prince's conquest of honor is only one aspect of his progress; the other is his break with the companions of his riots. Interwoven with the story of the Prince and Hotspur are the Prince's relations with Falstaff, and these, from Falstaff's first appearance in the second scene of the play, are presented in a way which leads us to expect a similar reversal. The essential thing about Hal is that, scapegrace that he is, he is the future king—the "true prince," the "sweet young prince," the "king's son," the "heir apparent," as Falstaff variously calls him, with whatever degree of mockery, in their first dialogue together. More than that, this dialogue is constantly pointing forward to the moment when he will come to the throne. "When thou art king"—Falstaff uses these words four times in the first seventy lines and yet again before the scene is over. "Shall there be gallows standing in England when thou art king?" "Do not thou, when thou art king, hang a thief." And so on. With these words ringing in our ears, then, we are continually being reminded of what is to come. The words seem, however, to refer to some vague time in the distant future. The Prince's reign will inescapably become reality, but it is at present apprehended as a dream. Falstaff's irrepressible fancy blows up a vast gaily-colored bubble, and as Bradley recognized,[12] it is because this bubble encloses the dreams of all of us that we feel for Falstaff so much affection. In our dreams we all do exactly as we like, and the date of their realization is to be when Hal is king. Then, everything will be changed—except of course ourselves. *We* shall go on as before, our friend Falstaff will continue his nocturnal depredations, but highwaymen will not be regarded as thieves and punishments will be abolished. Unfortunately, in the real world outside the bubble, it is not the law but we ourselves that should change, as Falstaff recognizes when he says, "I must give over this life, and

I will give it over . . . I'll be damned for never a king's son in Christendom." The joke of this is that we know that Falstaff will never give over, nor means to; but the joke does not quite conceal the seriousness of the alternatives—give over or be damned; and the idea of damnation continues to dance before us, now and later, in further jests about Falstaff's selling his soul to the devil, wishing to repent, and having to "give the devil his due." What Falstaff's eventual doom is to be could be discerned more than dimly by a mind that came to this play unfurnished by literature or folklore. And none of us is quite as innocent as that. We cannot help being aware of an archetypal situation in which a man dallies with a diabolical tempter whom he either renounces or is destroyed by; and to the first audience of *Henry IV* this situation was already familiar in a long line of Christian plays, in some of which man's succumbing to temptation was symbolized in his selling his soul to the devil and being carried off to Hell. It is because it is so familiar that it is readily accepted as matter for jesting, while the jests give a hint of Falstaff's role in the play. I merely pick out one or two threads in the very complex fabric of the dialogue: you will be good enough, I trust, to believe that, in spite of some dubious precedents in the recent criticism of other plays, I am not seeking to interpret *Henry IV* as an allegory of sin and damnation. Falstaff is not a type-figure, though within his vast person several types are contained. And one of them is a sinner and provokes many piquant allusions to the typical fate of sinners, whether on the earthly gallows or in the infernal fire. There is also an ambiguity, to use the modern jargon, which permits Falstaff to be not only the sinner but the tempter as well. The jokes of a later scene will call him indeed a devil who haunts the Prince, a "reverend vice," an "old whitebearded Satan." What I think the play makes clear from the beginning is that neither as sinner nor as tempter will Falstaff come to triumph. Even as we share his dream of what will happen when Hal is king, we confidently await the bursting of his bubble.

To strengthen our expectation even further is what we

know of history, or at least of that traditional world where the territories of history and legend have no clear boundaries. The peculiarity of the history play is that while pursuing its dramatic ends, it must also obey history and steer a course reasonably close to an already known pattern of events. The story of Prince Hal was perfectly familiar to the Elizabethan audience before the play began, and it was the story of a prince who had a madcap youth, including at least one escapade of highway robbery, and then, on succeeding to the throne, banished his riotous companions from court and became the most valorous king England had ever had. Not only was this story vouched for in the chronicles, but it had already found its way on to the stage, as an extant play, *The Famous Victories of Henry the Fifth*, bears witness, in however garbled a text. It is hardly open to *our* play, then, to depart from the accepted pattern, in which the banishment of the tavern friends is an essential feature. Moreover, that they are to be banished the Prince himself assures us at the end of his first scene with Poins and Falstaff in that soliloquy which generations of critics have made notorious.

> I know you all, and will awhile uphold
> The unyoked humor of your idleness.

The word "awhile" plants its threat of a different time to come when a "humor" now "unyoked" will be brought under restraint. The soliloquy tells us as plain as any prologue what the end of the play is to be.

Yet although *Henry IV Part One* thus from its first act directs our interest to the time when Hal will be king, it is not of course until the last act of Part Two that Pistol comes to announce, "Sir John, thy tender lambkin now is king." It is not until the last act of Part Two that the Prince is able to institute the new régime which makes mock of Falstaff's dream-world. And it is not of course till the final scene of all that the newly crowned king makes his ceremonial entrance and pronounces the words that have threatened since he and Falstaff first were shown together. "I banish thee." To all that has been said about the rejection of Falstaff I propose to add very little. The chief of those who objected to it, Bradley himself, recognized the necessity of it while complaining of how it was done. Granted that the new king had to drop his former friend, might he not have spared him the sermon and parted from him in private?[13] Yet Professor Dover Wilson is surely right to maintain that the public utterance is the essential thing.[14] From the first, as I have shown, interest is concentrated on the Prince as the future sovereign and Falstaff builds hopes on the nature of his rule. Their separation, when it comes, is not then a reluctant parting between friends, but a royal decree promulgated with due solemnity. This is also the perfect moment for it, when the crown that has hovered over the hero from the beginning is seen, a striking symbol in the theater, fixed firmly on his head. The first words of the rejection speech elevate him still further—"I know thee not"—for the scriptural overtones here[15] make the speaker more than a king. The situation presents many aspects, but one of them shows the tempter vanquished and another the sinner cast into outer darkness. In either case the devil, we may say, gets his due.

The last act of Part Two thus works out a design which is begun in the first act of Part One. How then can we agree with Kittredge that each part is a complete play? Such a pronouncement fits the text no better than the opposite view of Johnson and Dover Wilson that Part One, though it ends in Hotspur's death and the Prince's glory, is yet only the first half of a play. If it were a question of what Shakespeare intended in the matter, the evidence provided by what he wrote would not suggest either that the two parts were planned as a single drama or that Part Two was an "unpremeditated sequel."

An escape from this dilemma has sometimes been sought in a theory, expounded especially by Professor Dover Wilson and Dr. Tillyard, that what *Henry IV* shows is one action with two phases. While the whole drama

13 *Ibid.*, p. 253.
14 *The Fortunes of Falstaff*, pp. 120–21.
15 *Cf.* Luke xiii. 25–7.

shows the transformation of the madcap youth into the virtuous ruler, the first part, we are told, deals with the chivalric virtues, the second with the civil. In the first part the hero acquires honor, in the second he establishes justice. But I see no solution of the structural problem here. For though it is left to Part Two to embody the idea of justice in the upright judge, the interest in justice and law is present from the start. On Falstaff's first appearance in Part One he jibes at the law as "old father antic." And he goes further. Included within his bubble is a vision of his future self not simply as a man freed from "the rusty curb" of the law but as a man who actually administers the law himself. "By the Lord, I'll be a brave judge," he says, making a mistake about his destined office which provokes Hal's retort, "Thou judgest false already." It is in the last act of Part Two that we have the completion of this motif. Its climax comes when on Hal's accession Falstaff brags, "The laws of England are at my commandment," and its resolution when the true judge sends the false judge off to prison. But it begins, we see, in the first act of Part One. The Prince's achievement in justice cannot, then, be regarded simply as the second phase of his progress. Certainly he has two contests: in one he outstrips Hotspur, in the other he puts down Falstaff. But these contests are not distributed at the rate of one per part. The plain fact is that in *Henry IV* two actions, each with the Prince as hero, begin together in the first act of Part One, though one of them ends with the death of Hotspur at the end of Part One, the other with the banishment of Falstaff at the end of Part Two.

Now, since the Falstaff plot is to take twice as long to complete its course, it might well be expected to develop from the beginning more slowly than the other. Certainly if it is to keep symmetry, it must come later to its turning-point. But is this in fact what we find? Frankly it is not. On the contrary, through the first half of Part One the Hotspur plot and the Falstaff plot show every sign of moving towards their crisis together.

Both plots, for example, are presented, though I think both are not usually observed, in the Prince's soliloquy in the first act which I have already quoted as foretelling the banishment of his tavern companions. It is unfortunate that this speech has usually been studied for its bearing on Falstaff's rejection; its emphasis is really elsewhere. It is only the first two lines, with the reference to the "un-yoked humor" of the Prince's companions, that allude specifically to them, and what is primarily in question is not what is to happen to the companions but what is to happen to the Prince. In the splendid image which follows of the sun breaking through the clouds we recognize a royal emblem and behold the promise of a radiant king who is to come forth from the "ugly mists" which at present obscure the Prince's real self. Since Falstaff has just been rejoicing at the thought that they "go by the moon . . . and not by Phœbus," it is apparent that his fortunes will decline when the prince emerges like Phœbus himself. It is equally apparent, or should be, that the brilliant Hotspur will be outshone.[16] There is certainly no clue at this stage that the catastrophes of Hotspur and Falstaff will not be simultaneous.

Our expectation that they will be is indeed encouraged as the two actions now move forward. While Hotspur in pursuit of honor is preparing war, Falstaff displays his cowardice (I use the word advisedly) at Gadshill. While Hotspur rides forth from home on the journey that will take him to his downfall, the exposure of Falstaff's make-believe in the matter of the men in buckram is the foreshadowing of his. The news of Hotspur's rebellion brings the Falstaffian revels to a climax at the same time as it summons the Prince to that interview with his father which will prove, as we have seen, the crisis of his career and the "nodal point" of the drama. That this interview is to be dramatically momentous is clear enough in advance: before we come to it, it is twice prefigured by the Prince and Falstaff in burlesque. But not only do the two mock-interviews excite our interest in the real one to come; the mock-interviews are in the story of the Prince and Falstaff

16 *i.e.,* This first-act soliloquy looks forward not only to the rejection of Falstaff but also to Vernon's vision of the Prince and his company before Shrewsbury, "gorgeous as the sun at midsummer."

what the real interview is in the story of the Prince and Hotspur. First, Falstaff, whose dream it is that he may one day govern England, basks in the make-believe that he is king; and then Hal, who, as we have so often been reminded, is presently to be king, performs in masquerade his future part. The question they discuss is central to the play: "Shall the son of England prove a thief and take purses?" Shall he in fact continue to associate with Falstaff? One should notice that although the two actors exchange roles, they do not really change sides in this debate. Whether he acts the part of king or prince, Falstaff takes the opportunity of pleading for himself. When he is king he instructs the Prince to "keep with" Falstaff; as prince he begs, "Banish not him thy Harry's company, banish not him thy Harry's company: banish plump Jack, and banish all the world." Falstaff's relations to the future king, a theme of speculation since the opening of the play, now come to a focus in this repeated word "banish." And when the Prince replies, "I do, I will," he anticipates in jest the sentence he is later to pronounce in earnest. If it were never to be pronounced in earnest, that would rob the masquerade of the dramatic irony from which comes its bouquet: those who accept Part One as a play complete in itself wrongly surrender their legitimate expectations. In this mock-interview the Prince declares his intentions towards Falstaff just as surely as in his real interview with his father he declares his intentions towards Hotspur. One declaration is a solemn vow, the other a glorious piece of fun, but they are equally prophetic and structurally their function is the same. We now approach the turning point not of one, but of both dramatic actions. Indeed we miss the core of the play if we do not perceive that the two actions are really the same. The moment at the end of the third act when the Prince goes off to challenge Hotspur is also the moment when he leaves Falstaff's favorite tavern for what we well might think would be evermore. It is at the exit from the tavern that the road to Shrewsbury begins; and all the signposts I see indicate one-way traffic only. There should be no return.

The various dooms of Hotspur and Falstaff are now in

sight; and we reasonably expect both dooms to be arrived
at in Act V. What we are not at all prepared for is that one
of the two will be deferred till five acts later than the other.
The symmetry so beautifully preserved in the story of
Hotspur is in Falstaff's case abandoned. Statistics are
known to be misleading, and nowhere more so than in
literary criticism; but it is not without significance that in
Henry IV Part One Falstaff's speeches in the first two acts
number ninety-six and in the last two acts only twenty-five.
As for Falstaff's satellites, with the exception of a single
perfunctory appearance on the part of Bardolph, the whole
galaxy vanishes altogether in the last two acts, only to
reappear with some changes in personnel in Part Two.
Falstaff, admittedly, goes on without a break, if broken
in wind; and his diminished role does show some trace of
the expected pattern of development. His going to war on
foot while Hal is on horseback marks a separation of these
erstwhile companions and a decline in Falstaff's status
which was anticipated in jest when his horse was taken
from him at Gadshill. When he nevertheless appears at
one council of war his sole attempt at a characteristic joke
is cut short by the Prince with "Peace, chewet, peace!" A
fine touch, this, which contributes to the picture of the
Prince's transformation: the boon companion whose jests
he has delighted in is now silenced in a word. There is
even the shadow of a rejection of Falstaff; over his supposed corpse the Prince speaks words that, for all their
affectionate regret, remind us that he has turned his back
on "vanity." But these things, however significant, are
details, no more than shorthand notes for the degradation
of Falstaff that we have so confidently looked for. What
it comes to is that after the middle of Part One *Henry IV*
changes its shape. And that, it seems to me, is the root
and cause of the structural problem.

Now that this change of shape has been, I hope I may
say, demonstrated from within the play itself, it may at
this stage be permissible to venture an opinion about the
author's plan. I do not of course mean to imply that
Henry IV, or indeed any other of Shakespeare's plays,
ever had a plan precisely laid down for it in advance. But

it has to be supposed that when Shakespeare began a play he had some idea of the general direction it would take, however ready he may have been to modify his idea as art or expediency might suggest. Though this is where I shall be told I pass the bounds of literary criticism into the province of biography or worse, I hold it reasonable to infer from the analysis I have given that in the course of writing *Henry IV* Shakespeare changed his mind. I am compelled to believe that the author himself foresaw, I will even say intended, that pattern which evolves through the early acts of Part One and which demands for its completion that the hero's rise to an eminence of valor shall be accompanied, or at least swiftly followed, by the banishment of the riotous friends who hope to profit from his reign. In other words, hard upon the Battle of Shrewsbury there was to come the coronation of the hero as king. This inference from the play is not without support from other evidence. The Prince's penitence in the interview with his father in the middle of Part One corresponds to an episode which, both in Holinshed and in the play of *The Famous Victories of Henry the Fifth,* is placed only shortly before the old king's death. And still more remarkable is the sequence of events in a poem which has been shown to be one of Shakespeare's sources.[17] At the historical Battle of Shrewsbury the Prince was only sixteen years old, whereas Hotspur was thirty-nine. But in Samuel Daniel's poem, *The Civil Wars,* Hotspur is made "young" and "rash" and encounters a prince of equal age who emerges like a "new-appearing glorious star."[18] It is Daniel, that is to say, who sets in opposition these two splendid youths and so provides the germ from which grows the rivalry of the Prince and Hotspur which is structural to Shakespeare's play. And in view of this resemblance between Daniel and Shakespeare, it is significant that Daniel ignores the ten years that in history elapsed between the death of Hotspur and the Prince's accession. Whereas in Holinshed the events of those ten years fill nearly twenty pages,

17 See F. W. Moorman, "Shakespeare's History Plays and Daniel's *Civile Wars," Shakespeare Jahrbuch,* XL (1904), pp. 77–83.
18 Book III, stanzas 97, 109–10.

Daniel goes straight from Shrewsbury to the old king's deathbed. This telescoping of events, which confronts the Prince with his kingly responsibilities directly after the slaying of Hotspur, adumbrates the pattern that Shakespeare, as I see it, must have had it in mind to follow out. The progress of a prince was to be presented not in two phases but in a single play of normal length which would show the hero wayward in its first half, pledging reform in the middle, and then in the second half climbing at Shrewsbury the ladder of honor by which, appropriately, he would ascend to the throne.

The exact point at which a new pattern supervenes I should not care to define. But I think the new pattern can be seen emerging during the fourth act. At a corresponding stage the history play of *Richard II* shows the deposition of its king, *Henry V* the victory at Agincourt, even *Henry IV Part Two* the quelling of its rebellion in Gaultree Forest. By contrast *Henry IV Part One,* postponing any such decisive action, is content with preparation. While the rebels gather, the Prince is arming and Falstaff recruiting to meet them. Until well into the fifth act ambassadors are going back and forth between the rival camps, and we may even hear a message twice over, once when it is despatched and once when it is delivered. True, this is not undramatic: these scenes achieve a fine animation and suspense as well as the lowlier feat of verisimilitude. But the technique is obviously not one of compression. Any thought of crowding into the two-hour traffic of one play the death of the old king and the coronation of the new has by now been relinquished, and instead the Battle of Shrewsbury is being built up into a grand finale in its own right. In our eagerness to come to this battle and our gratification at the exciting climax it provides, we easily lose sight of our previous expectations. Most of us, I suspect, go from the theater well satisfied with the improvised conclusion. It is not, of course, that we cease to care about the fate of individuals. On the contrary, the battle succeeds so well because amid the crowded tumult of the fighting it keeps the key figures in due prominence. Clearly showing who is killed, who is rescued, and who

shams dead, who slays a valiant foe and who only pre-
tends to, it brings each man to a destiny that we perceive
to be appropriate. We merely fail to notice that the destiny
is not in every case exactly what was promised. There is
no room now in Part One to banish Falstaff. A superb
comic tact permits him instead the fate of reformation, in
fact the alternative of giving over instead of being damned.
It is a melancholy fate enough, for it means giving over
being Falstaff: we leave him saying that if he is rewarded,
he will "leave sack, and live cleanly as a nobleman should
do." But since this resolution is conditional and need in
any case be believed no more than Falstaff has already
taught us to believe him, it has the advantage that it leaves
the issue open, which, to judge from the outcry there has
always been over the ending of Part Two, is how most
people would prefer to have it left. Shakespeare's brilliant
improvisation thus provides a dénouement to Part One
which has proved perfectly acceptable, while it still leaves
opportunity for what I hope I may call the original ending, if the dramatist should choose to add a second part.
I refrain, however, from assuming that a second part was
necessarily planned before Part One was acted.

Part Two itself does not require extended treatment.
For whenever it was "planned," it is a consequence of
Part One. Its freedom is limited by the need to present
what Part One so plainly prepared for and then left out.
Falstaff cannot be allowed to escape a second time. His
opposition to the law, being now the dominant interest,
accordingly shapes the plot; and the law, now bodied
forth in the half-legendary figure of the Lord Chief Justice, becomes a formidable person in the drama. The opening encounter between these two, in which Falstaff makes
believe not to see or hear his reprover, is symbolic of
Falstaff's whole attitude to law—he ignores its existence
as long as he can. But the voice which he at first refuses
to hear is the voice which will pronounce his final sentence. The theme of the individual versus the law proves so
fertile that it readily gives rise to subplots. Justice Shallow,
of course, claims his place in the play by virtue of the life
that is in him, exuberant in the capers of senility itself. He

functions all the same as the Lord Chief Justice's antithesis: he is the foolish justice with whom Falstaff has his
way and from whom he wrings the thousand pounds that
the wise justice has denied him. Even Shallow's servant
Davy has his relation to the law; and his view of law is
that though a man may be a knave, if he is my friend and
I am the justice's servant, it is hard if the knave cannot
win. In this humane sentiment Davy takes on full vitality
as a person; but he simultaneously brings us back to confront at a different angle the main moral issue of the play.
Is he to control the law or the law him? In fact, shall
Falstaff flourish or shall a thief be hanged?

It has sometimes been objected that Falstaff runs away
with Part Two. In truth he has to shoulder the burden of
it because a dead man and a converted one can give him
small assistance. Part Two has less opportunity for the in-
tegrated double action of Part One. To be sure, it attempts a double action, and has often been observed to be
in some respects a close replica of Part One—"almost a
carbon copy," Professor Shaaber says. At exactly the
same point in each part, for example, is a little domestic
scene where a rebel leader contemplates leaving home,
and in each part this is directly followed by the big tavern
scene in which revelry rises to a climax. And so on. An
article in a recent number of *The Review of English
Studies* has even called *Henry IV* a diptych, finding the
"parallel presentation of incidents" in the two parts the
primary formal feature. I do not wish to deny the aesthetic
satisfaction to be got from a recognition of this rhythmic
repetition; yet it is only the more superficial pattern that
can be thus repeated. With history and Holinshed oblig-
ing, rebellion can break out as before; yet the rebellion of Part Two, though it occupies our attention, has no
significance, nor can have, for the principal characters of
the play. The story of the Prince and Hotspur is over,
and the King has only to die.

The one thing about history is that it does not repeat itself. Hotspur, unlike Sherlock Holmes, cannot come back
to life. But there are degrees in all things; conversion has
not quite the same finality as death. And besides, there

is a type of hero whose adventures always can recur. Robin Hood has no sooner plundered one rich man than another comes along. It is the nature of Brer Fox, and indeed of Dr. Watson, to be incapable of learning from experience. In folklore, that is to say, though not in history, you can be at the same point twice. And it seems as if Prince Hal may be sufficient of a folklore hero to be permitted to go again through the cycle of riot and reform. In Part Two as in Part One the King laments his son's unprincely life. Yet this folklore hero is also a historical, and what is more to the point, a dramatic personage, and it is not tolerable that the victor of Shrewsbury should do as critics sometimes say he does, relapse into his former wildness and then reform again. The Prince cannot come into Part Two unreclaimed without destroying the dramatic effect of Part One. Yet if Part Two is not to forgo its own dramatic effect, and especially its splendid last-act peripeteia, it requires a prince who is unreclaimed. This is Part Two's dilemma, and the way that it takes out of it is a bold one. When the King on his deathbed exclaims against the Prince's "headstrong riot," he has not forgotten that at Shrewsbury he congratulated the Prince on his redemption. He has not forgotten it for the simple reason that it has never taken place. The only man at court who believes in the Prince's reformation, the Earl of Warwick, believes that it will happen, not that it has happened already. Even as we watch the hero repeating his folklore cycle, we are positively instructed that he has not been here before:

> The tide of blood in me
> Hath proudly flow'd in vanity till now.

In the two parts of *Henry IV* there are not two princely reformations but two versions of a single reformation. And they are mutually exclusive.[19] Though Part Two

[19] All this is very well exhibited by H. E. Cain (see appended Note). But his conclusion that the two parts therefore have no continuity is invalidated because, like many others, he is content to isolate particular elements in the problem and does not examine it whole. Except when the views of others are being quoted or discussed, the word "Falstaff" does not occur in his article.

frequently recalls and sometimes depends on what has happened in Part One, it also denies that Part One exists. Accordingly the ideal spectator of either part must not cry with Shakespeare's Lucio, "I know what I know." He must sometimes remember what he knows and sometimes be content to forget it. This, however, is a requirement made in some degree by any work of fiction, or as they used to call it, feigning. And the feat is not a difficult one for those accustomed to grant the poet's demand for "that willing suspension of disbelief . . . which constitutes poetic faith."

Henry IV, then, is both one play and two. Part One begins an action which it finds it has not scope for but which Part Two rounds off. But with one half of the action already concluded in Part One, there is danger of a gap in Part Two. To stop the gap Part Two expands the unfinished story of Falstaff and reduplicates what is already finished in the story of the Prince. The two parts are complementary, they are also independent and even incompatible. What they are, with their various formal anomalies, I suppose them to have become through what Johnson termed "the necessity of exhibition." Though it would be dangerous to dispute Coleridge's view that a work of art must "contain in itself the reason why it is so," that its form must proceed from within,[20] yet even works of art, like other of man's productions, must submit to the bondage of the finite. Even the unwieldy novels of the Victorians, as recent criticism has been showing, obey the demands of their allotted three volumes of space; and the dramatic masterpieces of any age, no less than inaugural lectures, must acknowledge the dimensions of time. The inaugural lecture has, however, this unique advantage: as its occasion is single, the one thing that can never be required of it is to make good its own deficiencies in a second part.

[20] This is a synthesis of several passages in Coleridge. The words in quotation marks are said of whatever can give permanent pleasure; but the context shows Coleridge to be thinking of literary composition. See *Biographia Literaria*, ed. Shawcross, vol. ii. p. 9. Also relevant are "On Poesy or Art," *ibid.*, vol. ii. p. 262; and *Coleridge's Shakespearean Criticism*, ed. T. M. Raysor, vol. i. pp. 223–24.

NOTE

Of the numerous critical writings on *Henry IV*, I have read most and learnt from many. So although my main thesis about its structure has not, as far as I am aware, been previously put forward, it necessarily incorporates some arguments which have. To my predecessors I gladly acknowledge my indebtedness. It is not least to some of those with whom I disagree—Professor Dover Wilson and Dr. Tillyard; from their work on *Henry IV* I have derived much insight and stimulus. The most important discussions of the particular problem are, I think, the following:

Johnson, *Shakespeare*, 1765, vol. iv. pp. 235, 355; C. H. Herford, *Shakespeare*, Eversley edition, 1899, vol. vi. pp. 253–54; C. F. Tucker Brooke, *The Tudor Drama*, 1912, pp. 333–35; R. A. Law, "Structural Unity in the Two Parts of *Henry the Fourth*," *Studies in Philology*, XXIV (1927), pp. 223ff.; J. Dover Wilson, *The Fortunes of Falstaff*, 1943, p. 4 and *passim*; E. M. W. Tillyard, *Shakespeare's History Plays*, 1944, pp. 264ff.; Dover Wilson, *1 Henry IV*, New Cambridge Shakespeare, 1946, pp. vii–xiii; M. A. Shaaber, "The Unity of *Henry IV*," *Joseph Quincy Adams Memorial Studies*, 1948, pp. 217ff.; H. E. Cain, "Further Light on the Relation of *1* and *2 Henry IV*," *Shakespeare Quarterly*, III (1952), pp. 21ff.; Law, "Links between Shakespeare's History Plays," *Studies in Philology*, L (1953), pp. 175–82; Tillyard, "Shakespeare's Historical Cycle: Organism or Compilation?" and Law, "Shakespeare's Historical Cycle: Rejoinder," *ibid.*, LI (1954), pp. 37–41; G. K. Hunter, *"Henry IV* and the Elizabethan Two-Part Play," *Review of English Studies*, n.s., V (1954), pp. 236ff.

For further references, see *2 Henry IV*, New Variorum, edited Shaaber, pp. 558–63.

JAMES L. CALDERWOOD

from *Metadrama in Shakespeare's Henriad*

From Shrewsbury Field to Gaultree Forest, from Hotspur to Pistol, from the tavern scene of Part One (II.iv) to its parallel in Part Two (II.iv)—what a falling off was there! Hal's comments on his own "case" (fall), his tactic of playing the princely *eiron*, sums up the movement from Part One to Part Two as well:

> From a God to a bull? A heavy descension! It was Jove's case. From a prince to a prentice? A low transformation! It shall be mine; for in everything the purpose must weigh with the folly.
>
> (2 *Hen. IV*, II.ii.173–77)

What is the purpose that weighs with such folly? Hal's purpose for his low transformation, as he told us in his "I know you all" soliloquy, is to astound and please his English audience with an unexpected high transformation when he becomes king. But Hal's weary, half-disgusted tones here and earlier in this scene hardly reflect the optimistic self-assurance of his "I know you all" soliloquy of Part 1. But, after all, why should they?—Hal has small

From *Metadrama in Shakespeare's Henriad* by James L. Calderwood. Berkeley: University of California Press, 1979, pp. 120–33.

reason to rejoice. Having risen to heroic distinction at Shrewsbury, he has been cheated of or at least obliged to share his battlefield honors, and now instead of receiving the crown he has sweated to earn he must defer his kingship for another play and go back to playing straight man to Falstaff again. It's enough to make a prince abandon the stage. In fact, that is precisely what he does for most of the play.

And what is the "purpose" that weighs with Shakespeare's "folly"? For the moment his purpose—to spend a play fooling with Falstaff for the entertainment of his audience—seems not to justify but to constitute his folly. As the existence of the play depends on lies—Hal's, Falstaff's, Shakespeare's at the end of 1 *Henry IV*—so its mode of existence *is* the lie. This is a play whose major action is the preparation for action, for a violence that never comes. The principal violence in 2 *Henry IV* is that which is done to words as they are torn free from facts and truth. Henry the Fourth, usurper of the name of king, is on the throne—or at least in the royal sickbed. Falstaff, usurper of Hal's honors at Shrewsbury, is "Sir John with all Europe." Prince John, official spokesman, lies to the rebels at Gaultree. Henry's pilgrimage to the Holy Land dwindles into a mortal pun in the Jerusalem Chamber. And prefacing all is Rumor, the harlequin figure of the Induction, "painted full of tongues," who asks "Why is Rumor here?" The answer is gross as a mountain, open, palpable: because expectations, lies, misconstructions, and bad faith govern not only the England of 2 *Henry IV* but 2 *Henry IV* also.

Political and social order within the state is inconceivable unless there is some assurance that expectations will be met, that words, promises, vows, oaths, contracts, treaties, laws, and so on will be honored. In 1 *Henry IV* the honoring of vows and the underwriting of truth were symbolized in Hotspur the "king of honor." It is fitting therefore that Northumberland, learning of Hotspur's death after hearing rumors of his victory, voices the consequences to a nation of Rumor's rule:

> Let order die!
> And let this world no longer be a *stage*
> To feed contention in a ling'ring *act*.
> But let one spirit of the first-born Cain
> Reign in all bosoms, that, each heart being set
> On bloody courses, the rude *scene* may end,
> And darkness be the burier of the dead!
> (I.i.154–160, my italics)

Hotspur dies, his conqueror Hal by and large disappears from the stage. Rumor ascends the throne, and order collapses. With the defeat of his own expectations, Northumberland raises expectations in us; we are promised a drama of civil butchery. But though he can say that his "honor is at pawn / And, but [his] going, nothing can redeem it," Northumberland, he who lay "crafty-sick" while Hotspur honored his commitment at Shrewsbury, goes not to Gaultree Forest but unredeemed to Scotland (II.iii.7–8).

Northumberland's speech, proclaiming the death of order by means of dramatic metaphors, comments not merely on the rebel cause but also on 2 *Henry IV* and the disorder that attends unfulfilled expectations in drama. In the next scene in which the rebels appear we find an un- usual stress on plotting, on the raising of hopes, on pru- dent forecasting. All of this concerns plotting a rebellion, of course, but since the rebellion is the primary historical action in 2 *Henry IV* it also concerns plotting a play. "It never yet did hurt," Hastings says, "To lay down likelihoods and forms of hope" (I.iii.34–35). Bardolph replies with one of those long, unrealistic speeches which often indicate that Shakespeare is backing away from the immediate drama into metadramatic reflections *on* the drama. It is dangerous to plan a

> great work,
> Which is almost to pluck a kingdom down
> And set another up

without being quite sure that your confederates will pay their debt of men on the day of battle (I.iii.48–50). Otherwise you will be "like one that draws the model of a house / Beyond his power to build it" (I.iii.58–59). Prudent planning geared to one's ability to pay, that's the thing.

We can hardly read this without being reminded of what happens at Gaultree Forest later on. The rebels have apparently planned well enough; their promised men show up. It is Shakespeare who has drawn the model of a house beyond his power or desire to build it. In all scenes focusing on the rebels, in the tavern scene in which Hal and Falstaff are called forth to the wars, in the court scenes where the king frets sleeplessly about the state, in the Gloucestershire scenes where Falstaff impresses soldiers to put down rebellion—in most of the play, that is, Shakespeare lays us down likelihoods and forms of hope that the plot of 2 *Henry IV*, like that of 1 *Henry IV*, is advancing toward a great battle that will resolve all issues. Yet these formal promises of combat, which constitute the playwright's word, degenerate at Gaultree into another kind of word, Prince John's lies—just as the potential combat between Falstaff and Colville of the Dale collapses into a surrender prompted by Falstaff's lying reputation. At Gaultree, Prince John, who speaks for England and claims divine inspiration, becomes humorlessly, without the excusing inspiration of sherris-sack, the official state version of Falstaff—the Falstaff who is master of the disavowed word and the disclaimed debt, who, with his belly full of tongues pronouncing his own name, has become the embodiment within the play of the prologue Rumor ("painted full of tongues").

Why? Why should Shakespeare spend an entire play preparing, and announcing his preparations, for an action that never materializes? Of course Shakespeare is bound to history, and Gaultree Forest did turn out roughly in this fashion. But he was not bound to incorporate the battle into his play (a messenger could have reported it, for example), nor to give to Prince John the role histor-

ically played by Westmoreland, nor to marshal all his dramatic resources and direct them toward this abortive end.
Having, like Rumor, stuffed our ears with false reports,
has Shakespeare become infected with Falstaff's and
Prince John's cynicism? Is he willing, with Northumberland, to let dramatic order die?

For the characters within the play one major expectation remains. It is voiced somewhat hysterically by the
dying King Henry, who thinks he has had earnest of its
fulfillment when Hal "steals" his crown:

> Pluck down my officers, break my decrees,
> For now a time is come to mock at form.
> Harry the Fifth is crowned! Up, vanity!
> Down, royal state!
>
> (IV.v.117–120)

Henry goes on at some length, calling up images of an
England given over to license and riot, and (as always, it
seems when Shakespeare describes the abandonment of
order) maligning wolves: "O thou wilt be a wilderness
again / Peopled with wolves, thy old inhabitants!"
(IV.v.136–137). Henry's fears that "a time is come to
mock at form" echo Northumberland's anarchic "Let
order die"—at a point, after Gaultree, when civil disorder
has just been quelled at the apparent expense of dramatic
form and order. If Henry's fears proved true at the end of
2 *Henry IV*, then a time would indeed have come to mock
at form. For the notion of Henry the Fifth as king of
vanity, plunging arm-in-arm with Falstaff from Westminster to Eastcheap—or, worse, to Agincourt—is the one
expectation we have been told not to entertain. Shakespeare has repeatedly put his dramatic honor in pawn by
pledging to us that Hal's long-proposed reversal of character and rejection of Falstaff will in fact come to pass.
We have it on Shakespeare's word that form will not be
mocked.

Henry's reign, lingered out in Part Two, is construed by Henry himself as a mere marking of historical time, a putting down of the rebellious consequences of his usurpation of the crown:

> For all my reign hath been but as a scene
> Acting that argument. And now my death
> Changes the mode; for what in me was purchased
> Falls upon thee in a more fairer sort,
> So thou the garland wear'st successively.
>
> (IV.v.197–201)

Henry, as he and Hal both recognize, is merely the political bridge that Henry the Fifth must burn behind him, a sacrificial figure who takes the "soil of the achievement" into the grave with him so that Hal can look to the future (to Agincourt, for instance) instead of back over his shoulder as he tries to trammel up the consequences of usurpation.

Like Henry's reign, 2 *Henry IV* represents a marking of time until Shakespeare can "change the mode" and reinstitute his own dramatic succession. Its "argument" too has been the suppression of rebellion, the maintenance of order. Part Two is necessarily a holding action. *Henry IV* can no more succeed *Henry IV* than Bolingbroke can succeed Bolingbroke. It can only linger out the life that was in the earlier play while repeating its formal structure, its dramatic order. Shakespeare is engaged not in an advance but in a doubling back, not in creation but in re-creation.

Gaultree Forest seems to present a Shakespearean judgment on the form of 2 *Henry IV* much as the destructive entrance of Mercade does on the form of *Love's Labor's Lost*. The negotiations there reveal that the structure but not the substance of 1 *Henry IV* is all that survives in 2 *Henry IV*, that we have been witness to "a low transformation." Prince John's role at Gaultree, as he evidently

sees it, is to preserve at any cost the political order of
Henry IV. Shakespeare's role in writing 2 *Henry IV* is
analogous—to preserve the dramatic order of *Henry IV*
(Part One) by maintaining a parallel presentation of incidents, a carbon copy of form. Prince John accomplishes
his task by crafting the substance of a lie into the affable
form of a truth, by extending to the rebels the letter of
accord masking the spirit of vengeance. Shakespeare, as
literally true to his word as Prince John is, brings his play
to a point that corresponds to the battle of Shrewsbury in
Part One. And, as at Shrewsbury, Henry's order is upheld.

But at what price? Surely the fact of a low transformation is well advertised. Instead of Hal's proposal of single
combat before the lines with Hotspur, instead of his later
defeat of Douglas and saving of Henry's life, we now have
Prince John's

> My lord, these griefs shall be with speed redressed.
> Upon my soul, they shall. If this may please you,
> Discharge your powers unto their several counties,
> As we will ours; and here between the armies
> Let's drink together friendly and embrace.
>
> (IV.ii.59–63)

Instead of Hal's liberality with defeated enemies (not to
mention triumphant friends!), his

> Go to the Douglas and deliver him
> Up to his pleasure, ransomless and free
>
> (V.v.27–28)

—we have Prince John's "Strike up our drums, pursue the
scattered stray" (IV.ii.120). And, by contrast, Prince
John's piously generous "God, and not we, hath safely
fought today" (line 121).

The cost of Shakespeare's retracing the pattern of
1 *Henry IV*, he seems to announce here, is nothing less than
dramatic form. The old order survives, but emptily, and
preserving it is seen to be at odds with the formal obliga-

tions imposed on the dramatist by the sequential nature of his art. He has put his audience, its expectations quite defeated, in a mood to ask of him, as Mowbray asks of John, "Is this proceeding just and honorable?" (IV.ii.110) and, with the Archbishop, "Will you thus break your faith?" (line 112). If he has not broken his faith with us, he has kept it only in the Prince John fashion, or in the way that Henry, arriving at "Jerusalem," keeps his vow to make a pilgrimage to the Holy Land.

The metadramatic implications of Gaultree Forest become comparatively explicit in IV.v when Henry and Hal acknowledge the interim nature of Henry's kingship and the saving virtues of the succession. 2 *Henry IV*, also an interim and to some extent opportunistic venture, has a kind of inauthentic legitimacy like Henry's reign. It has the name but not the substance and vitality of its predecessor, not the formal integrity that comes when a work finds its way to an order of its own shaping. Having parasitically fed on a dramatic order already largely used up, it has called order itself in question. Northumberland's remedy is anarchic, "Let order die!" Falstaff's is predatory, "I see no reason in the law of nature but I may snap at him." Prince John's is cynically casuistic. Hal's response has been to withdraw from the general contamination and wait. He and his father now recognize that the present order must be transcended or gone beyond. *Henry IV* must be succeeded by *Henry V*, whose splendors will give a retroactive sanction to the cloudy dramatic interim, much as the glories of Henry the Fifth will retroactively sanction (or at least meliorate) the indirect crooked ways by which Bolingbroke met the crown:

> for what in me was purchased
> Falls upon thee in a more fairer sort.
> So thou the garland wear'st successively.
>
> (IV.v.199–201)

Succession is all. What Shakespeare now appears to be banking on is the restoration of sequence. It is the nature of a lineal work that it may repeat itself, as 2 *Henry IV* has so weakly done; that its form is dependent on generating and fulfilling expectations in its audience, as 2 *Henry IV* has not done; and that its form is not fully established until the last word is delivered, as 2 *Henry IV* is preparing to do.

As Falstaff rides toward Westminster we know that expectations are bound to fail, but we are not precisely sure how. On the one hand, acting on the principle of the disclaimed debt and the broken word—the principle that dominates the play by means of Rumor, Falstaff, and Prince John—Shakespeare may renege on his structural promise as he did at Gaultree Forest and somehow accept Falstaff into Hal's graces. The ending of 1 *Henry IV* may come to mind; Falstaff reprieved, resurrected, rebelling, and finally enticed back into the play. On the other hand, Shakespeare may "falsify men's hopes" in the Prince Hal fashion. By having Hal reject Falstaff at Westminster he will demonstrate that we playgoers have misjudged *him* much as Hal's audience of disapproving Englishmen have misjudged their greatest king. Thus Hal and Shakespeare will redeem their loose behavior simultaneously, Hal redeeming time and Shakespeare redeeming his play when men think least they will.

We know of course which way Shakespeare chooses—has chosen from the beginning. "Let the end try the man," Hal told Poins (II.ii.46), and Shakespeare apparently says to us, "Let the end also try the play." In a play so shot through with irredeemable words, acts, and characters we may hesitate to endorse last-minute redemptions. Reinstituting the succession does not quite make up for "all the soil of the achievement." Nor, knowing what comes after, are we entirely reconciled to going on. We can spare Bolingbroke well enough, but losing Hal, Hotspur, and Falstaff to gain Henry the Fifth or *Henry V* is an expensive trade, no matter how vigorously we unfurl reminders of national destiny.

Still, Shakespeare's keeping a promise, his making even one word stand up, is something of an achievement in 2 *Henry IV*. The point is pressed on us when the payment of Shakespeare's and Hal's verbal and formal debt causes the rebuffed Falstaff to do what he seemed constitutionally incapable of doing: acknowledge a debt ("Master Shallow, I owe you a thousand pound" [V.v.74]) and maintain his word ("Sir, I will be as good as my word" [V.v.86]). In the Epilogue Shakespeare continues to play on the theme of the debt incurred, disregarded, and paid:

Be it known to you, as it is very well, I was lately here in the end of a displeasing play, to pray your patience for it and to promise you a better. I meant indeed to pay you with this, which if like an ill venture it come unluckily home, I break, and you, my gentle creditors, lose. Here I promised you I would be, and here I commit my body to your mercies. Bate me some and I will pay you some and, as most debtors do, promise you infinitely: and so I kneel down before you—but indeed to pray for the Queen.[1]

In 2 *Henry IV* Shakespeare has, as he says, done what most debtors do, promise us infinitely—become, like Falstaff with Mrs. Quickly, an infinitive thing upon our score. Still, when the debt fell due at the end, he paid—and so earns his right to the humor of the Epilogue—though he missed some payments elsewhere, at Gaultree for instance.

[1] I depart from the Folio text to present the first paragraph of the Epilogue here as it appeared in the Quarto. The Folio prints the clause after the colon—"and so I kneel down before you—but indeed to pray for the Queen"—at the end of the third paragraph of the Epilogue. I agree with the New Arden editor, A. R. Humphreys, when he says "The original form of the Epilogue was presumably the first paragraph only of the existing three" ("Introduction," xv [London, 1966]). Which means that at that time Shakespeare had no intention of continuing the story "with Sir John in it," as the later addition to the Epilogue states. Evidently Falstaff's box office appeal continued in force, however, and Shakespeare was persuaded at least temporarily to write him into *Henry V*, later changing his mind, revising him out of it, but leaving a few unobliterated traces of his former presence—some lard upon the plain.

Perhaps we must bate him some—take Gaultree off his score—and he will, as with Falstaff here, pay us some. The rejection of Falstaff cannot redeem all the debts racked up by 2 *Henry IV,* even if we let the end try the play. But Shakespeare indicates in the final lines of the play proper that he has not finished paying, there is more to come:

> *Lan.* I will lay odds that ere this year expire
>   We bear our civil swords and native fire
>   As far as France. I heard a bird so sing,
>   Whose music, to my thinking, pleased the King
>   (V.v.106–09)

It is through the succession, what is dramatically to come, that Shakespeare will be released from his debt—not by repeating past successes but by succeeding them with new forms, new orders. As experienced creditors, we may take leave to doubt that he can pay us in full with *Henry V.* But the dramatic succession from there on—which passes by lineal descent not to *Henry VI* but to *Julius Caesar,* who is succeeded by *Hamlet,* who is succeeded by *Othello,* and so on—that succession will warrant an infinite extension of credit to this most promising but sometimes late-paying playwright.

COPPÉLIA KAHN

from *Man's Estate:*
Masculine Identity in Shakespeare

[The Shrewsbury scene in the last act of Part One]
mainly restores [the] public images [of Hal and Henry] as
loyal prince and lawful king, while their private feelings
toward each other remain to be worked out and transformed. Henry's "buried fear" rises again in the form of
further rebellions · nourished by lingering resentments
against him as the usurper of Richard. It also takes the
form of the disease, aging, and death that pervade Part
Two. The king is sick and dying; his sins are still upon his
head, and spreading throughout his body and the kingdom's. At the same time, Hal hasn't quite given up Falstaff
and the still-attractive world he represents. The shadow of
Hal's misbehavior falls on his father's throne, casting its
legitimacy further in doubt, and the shadow of his father's
suffering falls on Hal's revels. Succession as Hal's full
acceptance of the crown his father has to give, and as the
public legitimation of his father's reign by virtue of that
acceptance, has yet to take place.

In the deathbed scenes of Part Two, succession comes
about in the completion of a mythic pattern that has given
form to the father-son relationship all along: the motif of
the Prodigal Son. Several specific references to the parable

From *Man's Estate: Masculine Identity in Shakespeare*, by Coppélia
Kahn. Berkeley: University of California Press, 1981, pp. 74–77.

of the Prodigal Son crop up in the Henry plays, but more prominently, the legend of the Wild Prince, one of Shakespear's sources for the plays, parallels the story of the young man who flouts expectations, sows his wild oats, and then reforms himself. In the parable, it is the younger son who demands his inheritance from his father, squanders it, and returns home contritely to receive not only his father's forgiveness but a royal welcome with dancing, rejoicing, and the fatted calf, while the dutiful elder son receives only his due. Hal is the first-born and heir-apparent, but he has scorned his status and acted like the prodigal second son who gets less wealth from his father.

Hal's prodigal behavior seems more strongly motivated, though, by a need to differentiate himself violently from his father, concealing and denying his likeness to and sympathy with him. It is as though he must first create the impression that he is not his father's son, that he is of a different nature altogether, before he can admit his family resemblance and accept his paternal inheritance. In fact, Hal never even intends his father to know that he is his son in the spirit as well as in the letter. Had Hal not been tricked by the appearance of his father's death and taken the crown as his "lineal honor," his father would never have accused him of seizing it unlawfully and wishing his death, and Hal would never have made his moving confession of love and loyalty. In effect, Hal reverses John Talbot's pattern of initial submission to the father and subsequent break away from him [in 1 *Henry IV*]; he breaks away first, by loitering in Eastcheap. But like the prodigal son, he breaks away only to make his eventual submission the more genuine.

In Hal's first scene in Part Two (II.ii), he confesses, "My heart bleeds inwardly that my father is so sick" (47), but it requires the mistaken belief that his father is actually dead for Hal to reveal just how much he shares with him. As in Part One, dramatic irony is the means of this revelation, through parallels between the soliloquies of father and son: Henry's meditation on sleep (III.i) and Hal's apostrophe to the crown (IV.iv). Both elaborate the same pair of comparisons between kingly luxury, "the perfum'd chambers of the great" and the polished gold of the crown, and humble poverty, with its "homely biggen" and "smoky crib"; between the king's sleepless "perturbation" and "care," and the lowly subject's slumber.

When Hal takes the crown from his father's bedside, he takes it in exactly the spirit Henry expects will legitimate his shadowed reign. His words stress the blood tie between father and son, and the son's restoration of the principle of succession the father denied when he took the crown:

> My due from thee is this imperial crown,
> Which, as immediate from thy place and blood,
> Derives itself to me. [*Putting it on his head*] Lo where it sits,
> Which God shall guard; and put the world's whole strength
> Into one giant arm, it shall not force
> This lineal honor from me. This from thee
> Will I to mine leave, as 'tis left to me.
>
> (IV.v.40–46)

Only when the king realizes that his son accepts the crown not as a license to riot but as the legacy due him as "a true inheritor" can he admit the "crook'd ways" by which he got it, and feel himself and his kingship redeemed by the succession:

> And now my death
> Changes the mood, for what in me was purchas'd
> Falls on thee in a more fairer sort;
> So thou the garland wear'st successively.
>
> (IV.v.198–201)

Hal does wear the garland successively, his title clear, his power assured. But he also succeeds to his father's guilt, which takes the form of a persistent private anxiety, and which actually inspires his French campaign—a stratagem suggested by his father's dying advice to "busy giddy minds with foreign quarrels . . . to waste the memory of former days" (IV.v.213–215). In the scene that takes place on the eve of Agincourt [*Henry V*, IV.i], Shakespeare is at pains to compare Henry and Hal as kings, showing how Hal has infused his new role with qualities he could only have gained through his regression and rebellion in Eastcheap, while at the same time revealing what of the father lives on in the son.

SIDNEY HOMAN

Henry IV, Part Two on Stage and Screen

Whatever its relation to *Henry IV, Part One*—by name certainly, by intention whether original or late-blooming on Shakespeare's part—*Henry IV, Part Two* is not, *cannot* be fully like its companion piece. For actors, directors, audiences—and for scholars—this fact has presented both problems and, in certain notable productions since the play's premiere in 1597 or 1598, some genuine challenges.

The play's popularity has been sporadic. It was regularly performed during the first seventy-five years of the eighteenth century, with James Quin or John Henderson as Falstaff. There were numerous stagings at Drury Lane and Covent Garden: Colley Cibber was a memorable Justice Shallow at the Drury Lane revival in 1720, and the great Garrick played the King there in 1758—twelve years earlier he had been Hotspur in *1 Henry IV*. The "Coronation Scene" (V.v) was used to complement the real-life coronation of George III, and so *2 Henry IV* played for an extended twenty-one days at Covent Garden in 1761. Sixty years later William Charles Macready would also use a coronation, this time that of William IV, to build an audience. Still, in the nineteenth century the play fell into disfavor. Nor was it popular in the United States: while there were almost thirty revivals of *1 Henry IV* on the American stage in the eighteenth century, there were no notable productions of its sequel. As we will see, directors began to rethink the work in the nineteenth and, especially, twentieth centuries. Yet objections were made early on about almost every aspect of *2 Henry IV*, with the majority of them centering—again—on the contention that it was not like, not as good as, the earlier *Henry* play.

For one thing, the character of Falstaff seems to represent a falling-off from the enormous comic genius, that Life Force, the embodiment of "merry old England" in the *1 Henry IV*. In the mid-eighteenth century *The Illustrated London News* condemned his wit for being "exhibited in its grossest form." In her introduction to the play (1808), the normally censorious Elizabeth Inchbald, while acknowledging that Hal's rejection of Falstaff was proper on historical and even moral grounds, still claimed that it "does not come with entire welcome to the breast of every spectator." Others would insist that here Falstaff seems to float free of the play itself, to have no real relation to Hal, that only in the often-maligned final scene is his presence justified by the plot. The tavern scene (II.iv) brought out a special chorus of detractors. John Oxenford, writing on Samuel Phelps's revival at Sadler's Wells, branded Doll Tearsheet "a *traviata* [i.e. fallen woman] of the most repulsive kind." In fact, in the second half of the eighteenth century her role was most often eliminated, thereby leaving the Hostess alone to contend with Pistol. Samuel Phelps compromised by having Falstaff invite Doll to sit beside him, rather than on his knees. In its May 4, 1894 edition, *The Stratford-upon-Avon Herald* similarly called upon directors to delete her character, this in a play where actresses have been quick to point out that there are no significant female roles. In the 1890s a schoolgirl informed Lady Benson that, having seen her onstage as Doll, she could never again bear to watch her as Juliet.

Then, too, there are other problems. The Gaultree Forest scene (IV.ii), showing Westmoreland's arrest of the rebels after they supposedly have been pardoned, seemed to violate everyone's sense of fair play. Further, money-conscious producers noted that the play requires more actors than does its predecessor. Besides, not having seen Part One, would audiences want to watch something called "Part Two"?

Given all this, it is little wonder that directors have been inclined to fiddle—more than normally—with Shakespeare's text. Predictably, parts have been doubled: Poins, for instance, may also play Feeble, Gloucester, Davy, or Justice Shallow. And since she has only one scene, Lady Percy has been frequently cut; in fact, II.iii was not really part of major productions until the 1920s. Scenes have been rearranged. In the 1721 production at Sadler's Wells, for instance, the opening scene was deleted so that the play began with Falstaff's banter with the Page in Scene ii. (Garrick's version in 1758, fairly faithful to Shakespeare's arrangement, was an exception.) In the nineteenth century, Charles Kemble ran the first and third scenes of Act V together, then Scene ii, while eliminating Scene iv. Falstaff's role was given more prominence. In our own time, in a 1984 studio reading at Santa Cruz, the parts of Falstaff, Hal, and Henry survived a text otherwise cut by two-thirds. Here also Falstaff's "sherris-sack" scene (IV.iii) was juxtaposed with the "Crown Scene" (IV.v).

A production at San Diego's Old Globe Theater (1963) illustrates the changes, for better or worse, that were dictated by this belief that in *2 Henry IV* Shakespeare's dramatic skills had somehow weakened. As an aid to the audience, the performance opened with the final two scenes of *1 Henry IV*. Lady Percy's scene was spliced into the opening scene where news is brought of Hotspur's death. In II.ii Hal and Poins met not in London but on the battlefield. Hal himself was introduced earlier.

If Hal, Falstaff, and Henry paled beside their counterparts in *1 Henry IV*, then the director of a 1980 production at the Colorado Shakespeare Festival opted for morality figures rather than fully realized characters. If the scenes involving the rebels' war council (I.i and I.iii) seemed too abstract, they too felt the knife. Since the play lacked the bucolic mood of its predecssor, Benson's production of 1894 reintroduced the countryside in the Justice Shallow scenes (III.ii and V.i), with sheep and pigeons brought onstage; a production in 1901 even showed a farmer upstage working at his chores. Because

2 Henry IV was thought to "need" its predecessor, a 1983–84 production at the Indiana Repertory Theater (retitled *Falstaff*) showed the events of the earlier play in silhouette by means of a dumb show enacted behind a thin curtain. The same practice was adopted by Joseph Anthony at the 1966 American Shakespeare Festival. In her production of *1 Henry IV* in 1945 Margaret Webster reversed this practice by interpolating the mustering scene (III.ii) from the later play. Especially in our century, putting the play within the context of a tetralogy— *Richard II, 1 Henry IV, 2 Henry IV, Henry V*—has been popular, as at Stratford-upon-Avon in 1951 and 1964. In 1975 the Royal Shakespeare Company offered a "new" tetralogy, dropping *Richard II* and adding *The Merry Wives of Windsor*. If female parts were scant, then actresses would take on Hal's role, as Julia Marlow did in 1895.

Yet however subject to complaints and the attendant cuts and rearrangements, still, in ways both small and large, *2 Henry IV* also seems to encourage—perhaps for these very same reasons—creative, often-productive rethinking on the part of actors and their directors. Inventive, albeit isolated decisions on characterization or blocking frequently color the entire production. Bridges-Adams's promptbook (1932) reveals a wonderful bit of stage business with the three letters Falstaff dispatches in I.ii. After his first two letters are passed to the Page, the promptbook notes: "Gives 3RD letter tied with ribbon, Robin laughs, Falstaff quickly changes them." As Arthur Colby Sprague notes, the action calls attention to "this unfortunate Mistress Ursula,'" whoever she may be, and thereby sets up II.i, where the Hostess attempts to have Falstaff arrested. If later (II.ii) Poins reads at least one-half the letter Falstaff has sent to Hal, then the audience is set up to watch Poins's face sour as he encounters the fat knight's slight on his character. Casting a diminutive Page adds to the humor when Falstaff tries to hide behind him when the Chief Justice enters.

Even the horror of the Gaultree Forest scene can be

used to advantage. In Douglas Searle's 1955 production
at the Old Vic, Mowbray gave a cynical laugh as he was
being led away, thereby undercutting Prince John's "God,
and not we, hath safely fought today" (IV.ii.121). In fact
that scene, much disliked in earlier centuries, holds a
special fascination for modern directors. At the Indiana
Repertory Theater in 1983–84 it was done in gangland
style, the rebels killed one by one. At the Barbican
Theater in 1982, as Prince John sentenced Colville, Falstaff looked away in horror: the audience thereby sympa-
thized with the otherwise cowardly knight in his distaste
for the amorality, however inevitable, of modern warfare.

Individual parts have offered rich opportunities for actors. Tom Davies remembers the wonderful range of
Cibber's Shallow, that "expression of such solemn insignificance" as the old man moves without a hitch from the
price of cattle to maxims on morality. Doubling the roles
of Henry and Shallow in 1865, Samuel Phelps thus suggested a graphic parallel between two old men long past
their prime. Indeed, for actors the play provides options
galore. If Feeble is little more than a dunce, then what
does one do with his beautiful line "A man can die but
once. We owe God a death" (III.ii.242–43)? In a performance at Oxford in 1926 the same character was portrayed as something of a yuppie—and a lusty one at that.
In his second meeting with Falstaff (II.ii), does the Chief
Justice simply anticipate Falstaff's end with his closing
line, "Now the Lord lighten thee! Thou are a great fool"?
Or is he being humane here, showing affection for Falstaff
in spite of himself?

If *1 Henry IV* seems lighter, or robust, more "Elizabethan," while its sequel appears more somber, even
"black," then in our time, after two horrendous world
wars and the cynicism attending them, the later history
play may strike us as strangely modern, as "relevant." Its
tone, thus perceived, has led to some radical, often-
compelling directorial "concepts"—that all-purpose theatrical term used to describe the mood, the atmosphere, the
larger statement established by a production. In this light,

set designers have found the play particularly fruitful. In the 1975 Royal Shakespeare Company production, the designer Farrah, with lighting by Stewart Leviton, offered a stage that, to one observer, resembled the bleak flight deck of an aircraft carrier, a stark, gaunt world, underscored by white wintry branches upstage, the floor scattered with dead leaves, to one side an unused cannon, with jagged pieces of paper beneath its mouth, like spent cannon balls recalling the confused words of which Rumor speaks in the prologue. Likewise, in 1964, at the RSC's production at Stratford-upon-Avon, the stage was defined by twin rotating walls, made of blackened, charred wood, symbolizing a lost world. At the Barbican Theater in 1982 four tall wooden structures were covered by extras going about their work, but, even-thus populated, the stage seemed curiously barren, cold; David Hersey's lighting was alternately harsh and glaring, or dim to the level of being depressing. The 1979 production for the Stratford Festival in Canada qualified its comic emphasis with an equal one on decay. Again, in the Barbican production the tone was that of malaise, a universal sickness infecting royalty and lowlife equally: Bardolph, in particular, appeared horribly rheumatic, with sores prominent over his body. In his excellent account of four recent productions, T. F. Wharton describes Mikel Lambert's Doll in the RSC's 1964 production as "voluptuously diseased."

The problems presented by the play, and the fact that it is "different" from *1 Henry IV*, are thus—more properly —challenges. And if it lacks the Hotspur of the earlier play, that role most actors prefer to Hal's, nevertheless, *2 Henry IV* offers a similar challenge, or rather continues the challenge of its predecessor, in that trinity wherein two fathers, Henry and Falstaff, compete for one son. In turn, an actor who plays any of the three roles influences and is influenced by the two others.

The variety of Hals equals, at the very least, those in productions of *1 Henry IV*. Ian Holm's (RSC, 1964) was fairly cold-blooded, a small, tidy man, always under control, and very self-centered. When Holm recreated the role in 1966—he was the sole survivor from the earlier production—he took Hal one step further, making him a man who almost seemed to relish inflicting pain, quite the opposite of Roy Dotrice's warm, engaging kilted Hotspur. James Horton at the 1982 Utah Festival split the character between a Machiavellian upstart and an attractive, very social fellow, while the Hal at the Shakespeare Festival in Illinois, held that same year, was something of a patient contriver, waiting, in one's viewer's account, for events to play themselves out so that he could assume the throne. Against such "cold" Hals one might contrast the "warm" ones, such as Gerald Murphy's impulsive Prince at the Barbican Theater. David Gwillin's Hal, in the 1979 BBC television broadcast, was more complex: fun-loving, affectionate (he gently kissed Falstaff on the cheek in the tavern scene), he could also be scoffing, cynical and, at times, even shallow, a man with no certain, clear identity.

In our time there has been an even greater range to the various Henrys. One of the most notable was Emrys James's at the 1975 Stratford production an aggressive king, full of life until illness suddenly strikes him down, given to ranting and raving, jumping on chairs, ramming the crown on Hal's head, for instance, in their famous confrontation. Eric Porter's more divided King, a dignified, graceful man relentlessly haunted by his past, was reflected in John Bury's set for the 1964 Stratford production: the stern, metal-plated walls were offset by a narrow stained-glass window upstage. Beset by illness, physical and mental, Porter still managed to remain aloof from his son, and, as has been observed, the son remained no less distant from the father. Before declaring his loyalty, Ian Holm first closed the door as if any confession of respect, let alone love, had to remain a secret between the two men. Patrick Stewart's Henry at the Barbican has been rightly described as a nobody, so controlled (with characteristic gestures such as taking a prudent sip of cordial) that he seemed incapable of any human friendship, so terribly isolated from others that he alone realized the irony of his dying in the Jerusalem Room. Jon Finch's

Henry in the BBC production was similarly stylized; here, by virtue of the close-up, the crown alone, rather than any human feelings, linked father and son. In particular, the degree of Henry's illness seems the most manifest clue to his character: Eric Porter was weak from the start, whereas Emrys James's affliction seemed to arrive late. Jon Finch's scarlet face, on the other hand, was grotesque, blatantly marked by a yellow crust about the eyes.

In his history of productions of *1 Henry IV* for the Signet edition, Sylvan Barnet distinguishes two basic kinds of Falstaffs: "the convivial boozer, the lovable reprobate" or "the shrewd—even depraved—contriver." In large measure, this distinction holds, I think, for the various Falstaffs of *2 Henry IV*, yet it is qualified by two factors. One is the sequel's shift in tone, variously described as less romantically heroic (especially with Hotspur's absence) or not as carefree, since Falstaff himself seems a far less potent force in Hal's "education." The other factor, a more specific one, is the final scene, "Falstaff's Rejection," which, however anticipated in both *Henry* plays, is also the point from which actors must work in developing their Falstaff. Whether inevitable or abrupt, this ending demands that an earlier psychological "logic" in the character lead to it.

Hugh Griffith's Falstaff (RSC, 1964) was the lovable type, a comedian, even a buffoon, yet capable of real pathos—as when he begs Doll not to speak like a "death's-head" (II.iv.239–40)—someone with an inordinate appetite for life and an equal dread of losing it. There have been even "lighter" Falstaffs: the Falstaff at the 1982 Utah Shakespeare Festival was a physically slight, even slender man, so charming that one wondered why Hal would ever think of rejecting him; at the 1962 Oregon Shakespeare Festival the Falstaff, in the words of one reviewer, seemed a creature of "innocuous rascality." Jerome Kilty's Falstaff, at the 1966 American Shakespeare Festival, was guilty of little more than "simpering coquetry." If Brewster Mason's Falstaff in the 1975 production of *1 Henry IV* lacked wickedness, this seemed to matter even less in the sequel. Here, indeed, was a gentlemanly Falstaff, pleasant but lacking any spiritual dimension, at once contrasting with and yet strangely complementing Emrys James's Henry, a self-made man, more solid in character perhaps, yet no more appealing.

In the BBC production Anthony Quayle portrayed Falstaff's darker side. A self-conscious entertainer, existing from one performance to the next, he was the leering betrayer of others, sharply clapping his jaws, for example, as he contemplated duping Justice Shallow (V.i), and in general taking an almost cruel delight in sharpening his wits on others. In the RSC's Barbican production Joss Ackland went even further. In Part One he was angry, envious, ostentatious, inspiring a nervous fear in those about him. In Part Two, however, among the Gloucestershire yokels, he seemed more relaxed, even—in the words of one observer—"torpid," his passions spent.

For many spectators as well as readers the one element that makes *2 Henry IV* unique in light of its predecessor, indeed the element that at times threatens to draw a disproportionate attention from the rest of the play, is Hal's dismissal of Falstaff at the coronation. To the old knight's tender, if self-interested, "My king! My Jove! I speak to thee, my heart!" Hal, now Henry V, replies simply (or properly or cruelly or crudely or even humanely), "I know thee not, old man" (V.v.48–49). How the actor plays this moment is determined, or should be determined, by the director's concept for the play as a whole. Hal's subsequent vow that in turning from Falstaff he has "turned away from [his] former self" (1. 59) needs to sound "probable," as Aristotle uses that term in defining plot. Yet as *King Lear* demonstrates, the pain of a child's being rejected by a father is at least equaled by that of a father's being rejected by a child, even if the latter pain is self-inflicted, or nothing more than a matter of perception, even foolish or clouded perception.

Reflecting on his film called *Chimes at Midnight* (retitled *Falstaff* for its 1966 American release), Orson Welles observed that he "directed everything and planned

everything with a view of preparing for the last scene,"
that Hal's turning from his former companion had itself
been foreshadowed four times in the two *Henry* plays. In
Welles's version Hal spoke his "I know thee not" through
a row of pikes, symbol of his newfound power and re-
sponsibility. Once rebuked, Falstaff slowly diminished in
size on the screen, and the Welles film ended with
Margaret Rutherford blubbering Quickly's speech on Falstaff's death from *Henry V*.

In a memorable production in our century Balliol
Holloway stood "thunderstruck," his back to the audience,
as Hal delivered his lines rejecting Falstaff. Holloway told
an actor friend that, as Falstaff, he "did try to put a good
face on [his] being rebuked," but that "Hal killed [his]
heart." Actors playing Hal, as well as those playing Falstaff, often try—understandably—to evoke the audience's
sympathy at this moment. Gerald Murphy (RSC, 1982)
left the line of nobles and gave his verdict to Falstaff with
a reluctant smile, even choking off sobs, after which Poins
appeared in the background, Hal's scholarly friend, in
effect, surviving where Falstaff did not. David Gwillim
(BBC, 1979) affected pity for Falstaff, but remained
shallow in his emotions.

There have also been less sympathetic versions. Emrys
James's cold Hal, a "machine" as a caption describes him
in a still from Terry Hands's RSC production (1975),
seemed far less majestic than Brewster Mason's courtly
Falstaff, or "man" in the words of the same caption. For
this scene, Farrah's otherwise stark set suddenly changed.
As T. F. Wharton describes it, stagehands ran from upstage to down-, drawing behind them a huge white cloth
on which gold marsh plants were strewn. The lighting
brightened as the King's assembly formed a line stage-
right, opposite Falstaff and friends, a ragged company in
contrast, stage-left:

> On the one side, there were the quaint cut-off smocks
> and wrinkled leggings of the rustics, the thonged-leather
> ballad-singer-like costume of Pistol, the curious Sinbad-

like clothes of Bardolph. On the other were the pure
white cloaks and scarlet St George's crosses of the
crowned nobility, and the scarlet robe and golden chain
of the Lord Chief Justice. The contrast was very con-
siderably to the disadvantage of the first group.

Hal's decision was a harsh one, but right, inevitable, the
prerequisite for *Henry V*.

In the production at San Diego's Old Globe Theater in
1963, as Hal knelt to receive the sword, orb, scepter, and
crown, all this to a non-Shakespearean speech by the
Archbishop, Falstaff suddenly elbowed his way past Warwick, who was about to bow before the new king. One
observer notes that the onstage court seemed no less
shocked than the offstage audience. After the rejection,
Hal ascended the stairs and then froze as Falstaff and a
dubious Shallow talked. With his back to the audience,
Falstaff faintly echoed a salute to the new monarch before
Hal and company unfroze and the scene moved to its end.
At the Indiana Shakespeare Festival Falstaff's bravado
could not disguise the fact that he knew he had been rejected. At the Illinois Shakespeare Festival he broke up
the ceremonies but gave no sign that he understood what
Hal then said to him.

In his introduction to the present edition, Norman
Holland notes that nineteenth-century audiences "concentrated on the events represented by the [history] plays
rather than on the plays as themselves events." Forced,
therefore, to take its place in the tetralogy, to come *after*
that splendid *1 Henry IV*, its sequel invariably came off
second best. Holland suggests, however, that with newer
approaches to Shakespeare, *2 Henry IV* "can look for
better days," that "when we accept the play itself as an
event, our experience . . . becomes our own act of trust."
Indeed, the experiences of audiences with the Falstaff of
Joss Ackland or Anthony Quayle, Emrys James's Henry
or Ian Holm's Hal, the directorial concept of Terry
Hands, or Farrah's set—to name just some recent examples—suggest that such trust is not misplaced.

Bibliographic note: A list of all the sources used in preparing this essay would almost equal the length of the essay, but readers who wish to study the stage history of *2 Henry IV* further may want some suggestions. Obviously newspapers and weekly news magazines are good sources for recent productions; *Shakespeare Quarterly* covers productions throughout the world, and *Shakespeare Survey* includes an annual essay on some English productions. Biographies of actors and directors are also obvious places to start.

For a concise survey of performances of *2 Henry IV* up to the 1930s consult the *New Variorum Edition of Henry the Fourth, Part II,* ed. M. A. Shaaber (1941). Also, see Samuel B. Hemingway's discussion of older productions in the Yale Shakespeare edition (1921). Especially useful is Arthur Colby Sprague's *Shakespeare's Histories: Plays for the Stage,* an insightful account of stagings over several centuries that includes practical observations about the play's own theatrical dimension. Also, see the plates in J. Dover Wilson and T. C. Worsley, *Shakespeare's Histories at Stratford, 1951.* Particularly valuable are the detailed accounts of three fairly recent Royal Shakespeare Company productions (1964, 1975, and 1982), along with the 1979 BBC television version, in T. F. Wharton, *Henry the Fourth, Parts 1 and 2: Text and Performance.* Samuel Crowl provides a helpful critique of Welles's film *Falstaff* (or *Chimes at Midnight*) in "The Long Goodbye: Welles and Falstaff," *Shakespeare Quaterrly* 31 (1980), 369–80. To follow a director as he readies the play's text for performance see Tom Markus, "Preparing the Text: *The History of Henry the Fourth, Part Two,*" *On Stage Studies* 4 (1980), 53–67. Also of value are: Richard David, *Shakespeare in the Theater*; Richard Foulkes, *Shakespeare and the Victorian Stage*; Martin Holmes, *Shakespeare and Burbage*; Philip Kolin, ed., *Shakespeare in the South: Essays on Performance*;

and Charles H. Shattuck, *Shakespeare on the American Stage: From the Hallams to Edwin Booth.* For a careful attempt to date the first production see *The Arden Edition of The Second Part of King Henry IV,* ed. A. R. Humphreys.

Suggested References

The number of possible references is vast and grows alarmingly. (The *Shakespeare Quarterly* devotes one issue each year to a list of the previous year's work, and *Shakespeare Survey* —an annual publication—includes a substantial review of recent scholarship, as well as an occasional essay surveying a few decades of scholarship on a chosen topic.) Though no works are indispensable, those listed below have been found especially helpful.

1. Shakespeare's Times

Byrne, M. St. Clare. *Elizabethan Life in Town and Country*. Rev. ed. New York: Barnes & Noble, 1961. Chapters on manners, beliefs, education, etc., with illustrations.

Joseph, B. L. *Shakespeare's Eden: The Commonwealth of England, 1558–1629*. New York: Barnes & Noble, 1971. An account of the social, political, economic, and cultural life of England.

Schoenbaum, S. *Shakespeare: The Globe and the World*. New York: Oxford University Press, 1979. A readable, handsomely illustrated book on the world of the Elizabethans.

Shakespeare's England. 2 vols. London: Oxford University Press, 1916. A large collection of scholarly essays on a wide variety of topics (e.g. astrology, costume, gardening, horsemanship), with special attention to Shakespeare's references to these topics.

Stone, Lawrence. *The Crisis of the Aristocracy, 1558–1641*, abridged edition. London: Oxford University Press, 1967.

2. Shakespeare

Barnet, Sylvan. *A Short Guide to Shakespeare*. New York: Harcourt Brace Jovanovich, 1974. An introduction to all of the works and to the dramatic traditions behind them.

Bentley, Gerald E. *Shakespeare: A Biographical Handbook*. New Haven, Conn.: Yale University Press, 1961. The facts about Shakespeare, with virtually no conjecture intermingled.

Bush, Geoffrey. *Shakespeare and the Natural Condition*. Cambridge, Mass.: Harvard University Press, 1956. A short, sensitive account of Shakespeare's view of "Nature," touching most of the works.

Chambers, E. K. *William Shakespeare: A Study of Facts and Problems*. 2 vols. London: Oxford University Press, 1930. An invaluable, detailed reference work; not for the casual reader.

Chute, Marchette. *Shakespeare of London*. New York: Dutton, 1949. A readable biography fused with portraits of Stratford and London life.

Clemen, Wolfgang H. *The Development of Shakespeare's Imagery*. Cambridge, Mass.: Harvard University Press, 1951. (Originally published in German, 1936.) A temperate account of a subject often abused.

Granville-Barker, Harley. *Prefaces to Shakespeare*. 2 vols. Princeton, N.J.: Princeton University Press, 1946–47. Essays on ten plays by a scholarly man of the theater.

Harbage, Alfred. *As They Liked It*. New York: Macmillan, 1947. A long, sensitive essay on Shakespeare, morality, and the audience's expectations.

Kernan, Alvin B., ed. *Modern Shakespearean Criticism: Essays on Style, Dramaturgy, and the Major Plays*. New York: Harcourt Brace Jovanovich, 1970. A collection of major formalist criticism.

————. "The Plays and the Playwrights." In *The Revels History of Drama in English*, general editors Clifford Leech and T. W. Craik. Vol. III. London: Methuen, 1975. A book-length essay surveying Elizabethan drama with substantial discussions of Shakespeare's plays.

Schoenbaum, S. *Shakespeare's Lives*. Oxford: Clarendon Press, 1970. A review of the evidence, and an examination of many biographies, including those by Baconians and other heretics.

————. *William Shakespeare: A Compact Documentary Life*. New York: Oxford University Press, 1977. A readable presentation of all that the documents tell us about Shakespeare.

Traversi, D. A. *An Approach to Shakespeare*. 3rd rev. ed. 2 vols. New York: Doubleday, 1968–69. An analysis of the plays beginning with words, images, and themes, rather than with characters.

Van Doren, Mark. *Shakespeare*. New York: Holt, 1939. Brief, perceptive readings of all of the plays.

3. Shakespeare's Theater

Beckerman, Bernard. *Shakespeare at the Globe, 1599–1609*. New York: Macmillan, 1962. On the playhouse and on Elizabethan dramaturgy, acting, and staging.

Chambers, E. K. *The Elizabethan Stage*. 4 vols. New York: Oxford University Press, 1945. A major reference work on theaters, theatrical companies, and staging at court.

Cook, Ann Jennalie. *The Privileged Playgoers of Shakespeare's London, 1576–1642*. Princeton, N.J.: Princeton University Press, 1981. Sees Shakespeare's audience as more middle-class and more intellectual than Harbage (below) does.

Gurr, Andrew. *The Shakespearean Stage: 1579–1642*. 2d edition. Cambridge: Cambridge University Press, 1980. On the acting companies, the actors, the playhouses, the stages, and the audiences.

Harbage, Alfred. *Shakespeare's Audience*. New York: Columbia University Press, 1941. A study of the size and nature of the theatrical public, emphasizing its representativeness.

Hodges, C. Walter. *The Globe Restored*. London: Ernest Benn, 1953; New York: Coward-McCann, Inc., 1954. A well-illustrated and readable attempt to reconstruct the Globe Theatre.

Hosley, Richard. "The Playhouses." In *The Revels History of Drama in English*, general editors Clifford Leech and T. W. Craik. Vol. III. London: Methuen, 1975. An essay of one hundred pages on the physical aspects of the playhouses.

Kernodle, George R. *From Art to Theatre: Form and Convention in the Renaissance*. Chicago: University of Chicago Press, 1944. Pioneering and stimulating work on the symbolic and cultural meanings of theater construction.

Nagler, A. M. *Shakespeare's Stage*. Tr. by Ralph Manheim. New Haven, Conn.: Yale University Press, 1958. A very brief introduction to the physical aspect of the playhouse.

Slater, Ann Pasternak. *Shakespeare the Director*. Totowa,

N.J.: Barnes & Noble, 1982. An analysis of theatrical effects (e.g., kissing, kneeling) in stage directions and dialogue.

Thomson, Peter. *Shakespeare's Theatre*. London: Routledge & Kegan Paul, 1983. A discussion of how plays were staged in Shakespeare's time.

4. Miscellaneous Reference Works

Abbott, E. A. *A Shakespearean Grammar*. New Edition. New York: Macmillan, 1877. An examination of differences between Elizabethan and modern grammar.

Bevington, David. *Shakespeare*. Arlington Heights, Ill.: A. H. M. Publishing, 1978. A short guide to hundreds of important writings on the works.

Bullough, Geoffrey. *Narrative and Dramatic Sources of Shakespeare*. 8 vols. New York: Columbia University Press, 1957–75. A collection of many of the books Shakespeare drew upon, with judicious comments.

Campbell, Oscar James, and Edward G. Quinn. *The Reader's Encyclopedia of Shakespeare*. New York: Crowell, 1966. More than 2,600 entries, from a few sentences to a few pages, on everything related to Shakespeare.

Greg, W. W. *The Shakespeare First Folio*. New York: Oxford University Press, 1955. A detailed yet readable history of the first collection (1623) of Shakespeare's plays.

Kökeritz, Helge. *Shakespeare's Names*. New Haven, Conn.: Yale University Press, 1959. A guide to the pronunciation of some 1,800 names appearing in Shakespeare.

———. *Shakespeare's Pronunciation*. New Haven, Conn.: Yale University Press, 1953. Contains much information about puns and rhymes.

Muir, Kenneth. *The Sources of Shakespeare's Plays*. New Haven, Conn.: Yale University Press, 1978. An account of Shakespeare's use of his reading.

The Norton Facsimile: The First Folio of Shakespeare. Prepared by Charlton Hinman. New York: Norton, 1968. A handsome and accurate facsimile of the first collection (1623) of Shakespeare's plays.

Onions, C. T. *A Shakespeare Glossary*. 2d ed., rev., with enlarged addenda. London: Oxford University Press, 1953. Definitions of words (or senses of words) now obsolete.

Partridge, Eric. *Shakespeare's Bawdy*. Rev. ed. New York:

Dutton; London: Routledge & Kegan Paul, 1955. A glossary of bawdy words and phrases.

Shakespeare Quarterly. See headnote to Suggested References.

Shakespeare Survey. See headnote to Suggested References.

Shakespeare's Plays in Quarto. A Facsimile Edition. Ed. Michael J. B. Allen and Kenneth Muir. Berkeley, Calif.: University of California Press, 1981. A book of nine hundred pages, containing facsimiles of twenty-two of the quarto editions of Shakespeare's plays. An invaluable complement to *The Norton Facsimile: The First Folio of Shakespeare* (see above).

Smith, Gordon Ross. *A Classified Shakespeare Bibliography 1936–1958*. University Park, Pa.: Pennsylvania State University Press, 1963. A list of some twenty thousand items on Shakespeare.

Spevack, Marvin. *The Harvard Concordance to Shakespeare*. Cambridge, Mass.: Harvard University Press, 1973. An index to Shakespeare's words.

Wells, Stanley, ed. *Shakespeare: Select Bibliographies*. London: Oxford University Press, 1973. Seventeen essays surveying scholarship and criticism of Shakespeare's life, work, and theater.

5. *Henry IV, Part Two*

Barber, C. L. "Rule and Misrule in Henry IV" in *Shakespeare's Festive Comedy*. Princeton, N.J.: Princeton University Press; London: Oxford University Press, 1959.

Berry, Edward I. "The Rejection Scene in *2 Henry IV*," *Studies in English Literature*, 17 (1971), 201–18.

Bradley, Andrew Cecil. "The Rejection of Falstaff" in *Oxford Lectures on Poetry*. New York: Macmillan, 1909.

Calderwood, James L. *Metadrama in Shakespeare's Henriad: Richard II to Henry V*. Berkeley, Los Angeles, and London: University of California Press, 1979. A selection from this book is reprinted in the present edition.

Hawkins, Sherman. *"Henry IV: The* Structural Problem Revisited," *Shakespeare Quarterly*, 33 (1982), 279–301.

Jenkins, Harold. "Shakespeare's History Plays: 1900–1951," *Shakespeare Survey*, 6 (1953), 1–15.

Kahn, Coppélia. *Man's Estate: Masculine Identity in Shakespeare*. Berkeley, Los Angeles, and London: University of

California Press, 1981. A selection from this book is reprinted in the present edition.

Knights, L. C. "Time's Subjects: The Sonnets and *King Henry IV, Part II*" in *Some Shakespearean Themes*. London: Chatto and Windus, 1959; Stanford, Calif.: Stanford University Press, 1960.

Kris, Ernst. "Prince Hal's Conflict." *Psychoanalytic Quarterly*, 17 (1948), 487–505; reprinted in *Psychoanalytic Explorations in Art*. New York: International Universities Press, 1952.

Leech, Clifford. "The Unity of *2 Henry IV*," *Shakespeare Survey*, 6, (1953), 16–24.

Ornstein, Robert. *A Kingdom for a Stage: The Achievement of Shakespeare's History Plays*. Cambridge, Mass.: Harvard University Press, 1972.

Porter, Joseph A. *The Drama of Speech Acts: Shakespeare's Lancastrian Tetralogy*. Berkeley, Los Angeles, and London: University of California Press, 1979.

Prior, Moody E. "Comic Theory and the Rejection of Falstaff," *Shakespeare Studies*, 9 (1979), 159–71.

Reese, M. M. *The Cease of Majesty: A Study of Shakespeare's History Plays*. New York: St. Martin's Press, 1961.

Shaaber, M. A. "The Unity of *Henry IV*" in *Joseph Quincy Adams Memorial Studies*, ed. James G. McManaway. Washington: The Folger Shakespeare Library, 1948.

Spivack Bernard. "Falstaff and the Psychomachia," *Shakespeare Quarterly*, 8 (1957), 449–59.

Tillyard, E. M. W. *"Henry IV"* in *Shakespeare's History Plays*. London: Chatto and Windus, 1944; New York: Macmillan, 1946.

Traversi, Derek. *"Henry the Fourth, Part II"* in *Shakespeare from Richard II to Henry V*. Stanford, Calif.: Stanford University Press, 1957; London: Hollis and Carter, Ltd., 1958.

Wilson, John Dover. *The Fortunes of Falstaff*. London: Cambridge University Press, 1943; New York: Macmillan, 1944. A selection from this book is reprinted in the Signet Classic edition of *Henry IV Part One*.

BRITISH CLASSICS

☐ **LORD JIM by Joseph Conrad.** (522346—$2.50)

☐ **HEART OF DARKNESS and THE SECRET SHARER by Joseph Conrad.**
Introduction by Albert J. Guerard. (523210—$2.95)

☐ **FAR FROM THE MADDING CROWD by Thomas Hardy.** Afterword by
James Wright Macalester. (523601—$3.95)

☐ **JUDE THE OBSCURE by Thomas Hardy. Foreword by A. Alvarez.**
(523709—$3.95)

☐ **THE MAYOR OF CASTERBRIDGE by Thomas Hardy.** Afterword by Walter
Allen. (525191—$2.95)

☐ **THE RETURN OF THE NATIVE by Thomas Hardy.** (524713—$3.50)

☐ **KIM by Rudyard Kipling. Afterword by Raymond Carney.**
(525493—$2.50)

☐ **CAPTAINS COURAGEOUS by Rudyard Kipling.** Afterword by C.A. Bodelsen.
(523814—$2.50)

☐ **THE JUNGLE BOOKS by Rudyard Kipling.** Afterword by Marcus Cunliffe.
(523407—$3.95)

☐ **JUST SO STORIES by Rudyard Kipling.** (524330—$3.50)

Prices slightly higher in Canada.

There's an epidemic with 27 million victims. And no visible symptoms.

It's an epidemic of people who can't read.

Believe it or not, 27 million Americans are functionally illiterate, about one adult in five.

The solution to this problem is you... when you join the fight against illiteracy. So call the Coalition for Literacy at toll-free **1-800-228-8813** and volunteer.

Volunteer Against Illiteracy. The only degree you need is a degree of caring.